GIFTED

GIFTED

A NOVEL BY

PATRICK EVANS

VICTORIA UNIVERSITY PRESS

TE WHARE WĀNANGA O TE ŪPOKO O TE IKA A MĀUI

VICTORIA
UNIVERSITY OF WELLINGTON

VICTORIA UNIVERSITY PRESS
Victoria University of Wellington
PO Box 600 Wellington
victoria.ac.nz/vup

National Library of New Zealand Cataloguing-in-Publication Data

Evans, Patrick, 1944-
Gifted / Patrick Evans.
ISBN 978-0-86473-637-6
I. Title.
NZ823.2—dc 22

Printed by Printlink, Wellington

For
Kate De Goldi
Simon Garrett
Paul Millar
&
John Newton

Gifted is a work of fiction.

CHAPTER 1

Sometimes I think I've made her up. I think she's a ghost from one of my earlier novels come back to haunt me, or a character from something I haven't got around to writing yet. And sometimes she seems like a ghost of her own, a phantasm called into being from her strange disturbing imaginary world. At other times, though, she's like one of those animated cartoon figures being drawn onscreen as you watch, moving and speaking while she's taking shape and the artist's hand works inside the frame, adding details or rubbing them out, a leg appearing here, a hand vanishing there.

And whenever I think that, I wonder if there's a way to rub her out myself, a way to make her disappear so there's no sign she ever turned up on the other side of my front hedge in the back seat of a pea-green Morris Minor one Saturday afternoon late in the summer of 1955, no sign that she ever came back a few days later and moved into the army hut in my back garden to my surprise and dismay, no sign that she lived and wrote there for the sixteen most extraordinary months of my life.

If I could do that, if I could rub her out like that—then the house would be mine again and free of the memory of her, it'd be no more than it was built for a few years before she came into my life, a place for me to live and work, somewhere to conduct my friendships and my other passions and to live my imaginary life in solitude. If I could rub her out I'd be able to go through my back door and across my tiny square of lawn to the hut, and open it to nothing more than the bed and the bench and the bare coat rack across the corner. And I'd have the garden back too, often neglected during her time with me but ready to be reclaimed and cared for as it used to be, ready to renew me, the loquat tree tapping its loaded branches at my windows to remind me it is still there, it is always there, the peach tree down the back showing its bright spring confetti once again, the apple trees and the nectarine behind them, and everywhere the bud upon the vine. Yet another summer: and myself untouched by her, not marked, not changed, not graced—

It seems always to have been in my life, this beachside section of land I live on, taken for granted like my tongue or my toes. When I was a child, our family home was ten miles away on the far, southern, side of the harbour, in a leafy suburb of bungalows east of the city. From the veranda of this wooden villa my father went at a half-trot to the tramcar at the bottom of the street every morning, and hence to *the city* as he used to call it, to wedge his ample posterior into the carver chair behind his solicitor's desk. From the same veranda my mother went each day to the shops up the road (butcher fruiterer draper and general store), or west to the church in whose rear hall she and other worthy middle-class trouts schemed charitable harassments of the poor. As for my tiny older brother and me, each weekday morning we trailed off to the east, creeping like snail unwillingly to school. And then, every Sunday, that endless ritual that would look so ridiculous if observed in a tribe of Hottentots: down on the knees and then up to sit, then down once more and up again, again and then yet again, until the harsh, indifferent Jehovah of my parents was placated wherever He hung his not inconsiderable Hat. Methodists, my parents, of a subsect now melted away but given then amongst other things to forcing grooves into the knees of its young: my brother and I used to compare our wounds as we stumbled back from the church to the Sunday mutton.

And yet all this predictability could be relieved any Friday summer evening when *oh joy* we would suddenly find ourselves being packed off in the tram to town, towards jetty ferry and wine-dark sea: *epi oinopa ponton*—well, just the harbour, in fact, but exciting enough in itself with the promise of its north-eastern corner, on the far shore, where another jetty and a brisk walk always brought us to the tangled half-acre my father had purchased as a rural investment, and to the little wooden dwelling he had built upon it: *the family cottage*, as my parents insisted on calling it, for all its modesty.

In front of this my father would stand, fumbling the hunter from his heaving paunch and the key ring out of a pocket:

Twenty-five minutes, he'd say, snapping the watchcase shut and dabbing at his red, glistening nape.

Then he'd fumble importantly with a padlock the size of a pensioner's reticule, until its jaws were parted and the door was opened and the little place was ours once more with its bosky, halitoxic puff of dry-rot and rat-droppings. Our *beachside cottage*—

Well, that is how my parents used to describe it to their friends: although, once the place had actually been sighted, the term tended to fall a little from use. Members of their church group, encouraged to take the fifteen-minute ferry trip across the harbour on a sunny summer Saturday afternoon and a further thirty-five in the bracing ozone of their slow, bovine stroll from the Bayswater jetty, paled, once delighted greetings had been exchanged, at the sight of the horrid little hutch that made our home-away-from-home. This was a jest, surely, surely the real beach cottage was somewhere nearby?—alas, no: tiny, primitive, even crude, this was it. Each time my recollections become too flattering, I rummage up the three or four snapshots that survive and remind myself how significantly different our holiday home was from the scoured, scrubbed domain in which, on the far side of the harbour, we lived our daily lives. A single room built up on shallow totara piles, the beachside cottage had a sort of porch at one end and a window in the side, a roof clad in corrugated iron and walls sheathed in weatherboards we tamed each year with yet another coat of Stockholm tar. For cooking, the driftwood-fired stove inside the porch, through whose roof it poked its metal chimney: for washing up, a system of buckets fed by the rainwater tank on the stand behind the hut: for evacuations, a noisome one-holer up against the farthest hedge, as near to being off the property as my parents could manage it. And, for all-over bodily hygiene: the snotgreen scrotumtightening sea, no more than a few furlongs distant.

This little wooden box I put to the torch several years ago, in a Viking funeral I knew was burning half my life away. For, as it was to turn out, I lived my first twenty adult years in it, mostly on my own but not (if I am to tell the truth the whole truth and nothing but the truth) entirely so. I started there a refugee, and have ended up somewhat better: richer, admittedly, in those things that cannot be seen weighed or counted than in those that can, but able, although with considerable difficulty, to scrape together the means of replacing, in due course, a mode of living that could still shock the more conventional of my friends who happened to drop by. Then, after eighteen years of living in my inherited and decaying little *beachside cottage* on the smell of a dry oil-rag, and with more conniving scheming and patience than I have ever managed in my life and not a little elbow grease of my own, I managed to shoo the last of the builder's gang off my property and take possession of the brand-new home they'd built for me—the house in which I sit now writing these very words, a dwelling modest enough, I must admit, and barely worthy of the name at merely twenty feet in one direction and the same mere twenty in the other, and but one each of bedroom outside door and fireplace: but, compared to the tiny, abandoned hovel whose exterior I was free to inspect (when once I'd shifted into my new cottage) through the clean, unflawed post-war glass of my brand-new linseed-smelling window, a veritable paradise on earth—earth which, to tell the truth, I'd been forced to sacrifice from my precious vegetable garden.

A flush toilet, a wireless radio built into the bookcase, running water, electric light bulbs—after twenty years of living in that terrible little family dogbox come rain come hail I had capitulated at last to Progress. It wasn't an easy decision, making the leap from the nineteenth century to the twentieth like that. And that is what I'd done. There was a New Zealand we've all forgotten and I felt that I was one of the last people who knew about it and cared about it: and I felt I'd left it behind, deserted and betrayed it, that night I abandoned the old hut and moved into the new place twenty feet away with its linseed-and-putty smell and a floor that thumped like a drum whenever I walked across it. Electric streetlights, even they had reached the beachside by then, they'd put one the other side of the macrocarpa hedge, and as I lay abed in my new house for the first time looking at its glow reflecting in strange places, on the half-filled bookshelf and bouncing up to the slope of the ceiling, it all felt so utterly wrong that I couldn't get to sleep. At two in the morning I half thought to go back outside to the old hut again. But I knew better, I understood that in carrying my few bits and pieces across the lawn from the old place to the new I was crossing a temporal Rubicon, that the hand of history had got hold of me and I could never go back.

And so it was that when one of my friends happened to

13

mention he was trying to get rid of an army hut a few months later, it felt like that historical hand knocking on my door once again. What he referred to was the little sheds the army sold off to the public as surplus now the Hitler war was over. You could see them all over town and country, in suburban backyards schools camping grounds and what have you, perhaps twelve foot long and a Biblical seven in width, with a door at one end a window at the other and nothing much else in between. You could bed four to six men in each: a pleasant and diverting thought that kept me going as a friend and his boy helped me carry the disassembled sides of the new hut from his trailer through the gap in the hedge and onto the property. Then, once we were done, the two men abandoned me to my funerary rites, knowing me well enough to understand that that is what they would be.

And so I waited alone till dusk and its moths, passing the time by hosing down the hedges and the shrubs and the ground nearby: and then, as darkness closed in, I tossed a lit rag through the little building's door. There was a soft *crump* as the petrol ignited that I'd splashed about inside, and within ten seconds the place was lighting up like Guy Fawkes Night and I was backing off with heat on my face and arms. As I played the garden hose against the macrocarpa hedge and the little burning flakes floated up I tried to settle the emotion that I felt, to identify it and make it shapely. Fed by the aeons of Stockholm stored in the wood the fire spread, climbed, making a soft insistent roar as if some animal were being consumed. I tried to remember that day I landed there a refugee, and my father turning up to find me the following morning as he did, and my first night there six years later with my dear friend Harry, whom eventually you will meet. And I tried to remember the time before all this, when I was a child and had a family and a shape of life around me, for whatever it was worth.

All this fed into the moment when the board walls had

burnt out and just the frame was there in outline, incandescent with fire, no longer a structure but an image, held briefly at the moment the material disappeared into the imaginary, the past disappeared into history: and then the whole thing fell in on itself and was gone. It was as if everything I knew and felt had been changed into something else. It was as if there was nothing left but what was new.

The next day, my friend and I reassembled the war surplus hut on the still-warm ashes with his son pitching in as well. It took two hours, fewer, and when we had finished it stood there sturdily as if to say the army had arrived, although in all truth its squared-off blank sides and the neat peaked roof above its single end door gave it more the look of a large dog kennel or perhaps of a very small church. It was thoroughly out of place, in other words an anachronism, and it took me a long time to accept it, to work it into my own private mythologies and narratives of being, my own personal *romance*. By the time I'd done so, many people had graced its graceless hearth. Young and old male and female artist and civilian normal and strange: all stayed there for brief or longer spells. And none of them for longer, and none of them more unusual, than the young woman I mentioned at my outset: the dweller in my army hut. Her name is Janet Frame.

She came into my life heralded by trumpets, or in fact by a car horn, two peremptory parps irrupting into my early Saturday afternoon snooze, followed ten or twenty seconds later by a *rat-a-tat-tat!* at the door. I'd got to the stage where I expected the odd visitor without welcoming them. Friends were another thing, friends knew to leave me alone till the afternoon as the sign by the gate instructed: *No visitors till 1.00 p.m., please.* Would that put them off? Not this one, it seemed. Still half-asleep from my post-lunch nap I was ripe for the plucking: and there she was before me as I opened the door, a plump-faced matron looking eagerly up at me, her eager vivid mouth already half-open.

Mister Sargeson? she breathed up at me. My standard nightmare visitor: age indistinct, medium to heavy tonnage, with a bosom like a bed bolster and her autograph book in her hand. I knew what came next: would I like to address her book club her church group her daughter's class at school?— Why no, madam, as it happens, I would not. I am merely a working stiff, as our American cousins put it, though I admit to finding the phrasing unfortunate. In the morning I work inside at my desk, and after a modest bite to eat at the kitchen counter you see behind me I spend the afternoon under the sun, working in my garden. At night I read and, occasionally and in a variety of ways, enjoy the company of others.

None of this of course was what I was actually saying to her, and, in all truth, it was taking me quite an effort to catch up to what it was that *she* was saying to *me*—

Your friend, I said, as if interested. Is she—?

I stepped down beside her onto the path, with its heat and its light.

Mm, yes, the woman said. I've got her out there in the car—

The name she mentioned was not unknown to me. Janet Frame, Janet Frame—I'd read something by someone called Janet Frame. But I was going to have to bluff this one out, by the look of it—

Yes, I heard my voice say. I'm bound to say I *have* read her—

But was it a single short story I was pretending to have read, or was I pretending to have read an entire book—?

Molly, the woman said her name was: I followed her up my path.

To exit 14 Esmonde Road one has to duck down through a hole in the hedge. Watching her do this from behind was not a sight for me—rather than skirts, for my own reasons I

16

prefer women to wear what they nowadays call *slacks*. I can't explain this to you, and on this occasion I tried not even to think of it. I tried to concentrate instead on the torrent of words that came back to me over the woman's plump, heaving, scented shoulders.

And there, on the other side of the hedge, I had my first glimpse of Janet. There is no way to convey its colour to you, by the way, I mean the colour of the car. I am not used to the dreadful things themselves and have yet to accept them: at best I expect them to be if not black, then brown or fawn, or possibly even dappled—horse colours, at any rate. What kind of animal might have the colour of *this* monster I really don't know: but there it was, and, in its maw, brooding in silence, there, too, was the young woman in question, sitting in its back seat and made so anonymous by dark glasses and headscarf that there seemed hardly any point at all in my coming out to meet her. Especially since, as her friend rapped briskly at the window beside her, she made not the slightest sign that she intended to acknowledge us, and instead just sat there, staring fixedly through the windscreen as if something very important was attached to the end of the bonnet that she alone could see.

A couple more stiff raps, and Molly turned back to me:

No, she said. It's no good. She's very shy—

I can see that—

But so gifted—

I can see that, too—

As a rule, I am awkward around women like this. The fact that I had my hands clasped behind me tells me now that, at some level, I felt I was back with my mother. And of course I was terrified I was going to be asked my opinion of particular stories Janet had written.

Now Molly had begun to talk about her own family.

Really? I said, to the astonishing information she'd just given me. The whole family—?

We all write or paint. My husband paints on velvet—

You can get some remarkable effects on velvet, I said.

So you see, she said, we're very concerned to help her develop her talent—to get her back on her feet—

Ah. *Back on her feet*—so she'd been off them. *That* rang a bell, a tiny tinkle, in my memory. There'd been a setback of some sort, somewhere in the past. I had no idea what it involved—tuberculosis? An abortion? Piles?—but I definitely remembered something tragic, something dark.

I probed further. So, I said. Quite a long illness—?

Through her twenties, right through her twenties, the woman said. It's been her art that's kept her going—

And she's better now—?

We're hopeful. The doctors are hopeful. She's recovering from a certain kind of treatment she's undergone—

I wasn't getting very far with this. In fact, given the young woman's immobility, her refusal to shift weight to left or right by turning her head to talk to us or even acknowledge we were there in the first place, the incoming information was starting to point in one particular direction.

She can move around all right—?

Oh, yes—she's very cautious, of course, she takes it step by step—

Yes, well, you would, wouldn't you—?

She says she sometimes remembers it as a ring of fire—

Quite, I said. Quite—!

And that is how I acquired Miss Janet Frame, promising-writer-in-chrysalis-form, genius-in-the-bud, and for an unspecified period of time my live-in house-or-hut-guest. Because, momentarily, I saw her as a fellow-sufferer, a comrade-in-arms in the unsleeping fight against the enemy that, like the Japanese at Singapore, attacks from behind—

Impulsively, emotionally, in an act of empathy for what the poor woman had been through and what faced her, I pronounced my own prison-sentence. With a sweep of an

18

arm in the direction of the macrocarpa hedge so sun-blazed from this side, I said—

I've got an old army hut in there, she can use it whenever she wants to write—

—and that was it. After it was done, after the niceties had been completed and I had persuaded the pair of them to bugger off and leave me alone, when I was back on the other side of my hedge and with my hand around the handle of a Dutch hoe I proposed to spend the rest of the day with, I came to my senses. Not about what lay in store for me—I'd had half a dozen youngsters in the hut over the four or five years the cottage had been built and at least one crim, and was used to people going in and out. I liked having them there, in fact I loved the company as a rule and some of them even stayed for weeks at a time. No: I came to my senses about my misunderstanding. It was not that I suddenly realised the truth: just that, once alone again and away from the press of strange women, I began to acknowledge how unlikely it was that a young person—anyone—might be incarcerated throughout the best years of her life for the reason that had madly crossed what parts of my brain were still functioning at the time. There was something more to Miss Janet Frame than that. What was it, what had gone wrong for her? And, in the meantime, *what was it that I had inflicted upon myself*—?

The thing is, you see, she couldn't have come into my life at a worse time. I'd enjoyed a long run of luck, lighting one story off another like a chain smoker, puffing on for nearly twenty years till, suddenly, just before she turned up, the tobacco ran out, so to speak, along with the matches. By then, of course, my transformation was complete: I mean the process by which the stricken, broken youth my father left behind at the family beach cottage all those years ago was somehow assembled, with what seems now like inevitability, into—well, the man

19

who fathered a nation's fiction. It sounds immodest to say it, I know, but that was the title bestowed upon me nonetheless, two or three years ago when I turned fifty: there I was, on the cover of the quarterly journal *Hammer* with my newish goatee beard, and there, running across the newish goatee beard, was the accolade itself. For what it is worth: I have no delusions about how widely my books are read in this modern-day Carthage in which we live. A writer? one of my neighbours said, when I started to get neighbours. We had you picked for a baker—you know, the hours you keep. They thought I was out all night tending the ovens!—a phrase, by the way, worthy of Janet herself: *tending the ovens*—

A year or two ago I published what was widely conceded to mark the pinnacle of my career so far, proof that the writing style I had pioneered was the Real McCoy, voice of the times we lived in, barbaric yawp of the common man, voice, no less, of a nation: a novel in two distinct parts, one playing cleverly against the other to achieve what a leading critic was convinced enough to declare *a brilliant conversation*, a dialogue (no less) between the divided selves of twentieth-century man. *Seven Heads of Grain*, my novel was called: reviewers and critics were unanimous that it confirmed my pre-eminence, if my pre-eminence had needed proving. Outwardly, I went along with all this as if the achievement had been what I wanted to bring about and the status what I deserved. But inwardly, I was never quite so sure. Inwardly, I knew too well that, in truth, the book represented the desperate, last-minute throwing-together of two different projects I'd separately despaired of for some time. The title, with its hint of feast and then famine—seven heads of golden grain and then seven withered ones—seemed too much, once I had chosen it: an unfortunate prophecy for my very self. As a writer I had prospered for rather more than seven years; would I now have just as many years of dearth?

And everything did, indeed, stop. It was the strangest

experience I'd had, what every artist fears most, perhaps even more than death. I was nearly fifty and I had nothing left to say. Friends congratulated me on *Seven Heads*, I got a letter from a lecturer in English at a university college deep to the south, then another from closer to hand. I read the handwriting and I read the type, I accepted the handshakes and smiled and nodded with a face like glass. Oh, several irons in the fire, you know how it is, I'd say, whenever they asked me what was coming next. Always busy. *But there was nothing.* Each morning I got up at six as usual and did my prefatory business, and then at eight settled into my hoop-backed chair as I'd done every weekday morning for nearly twenty years: and each time I settled down to my old Imperial, the machine stared back, its sheet of paper lolling out at me like an urchin's cheeky tongue. *England expects that every man will do his duty, Able was I ere I saw Elba, Every good boy deserves favour*: and when these forlorn sentences had been typed again a few times it seemed I was done for the day.

At moments like this I'd be reminded that John Calvin had not lost his singular capacity to manifest beside me. I'd lurch up desperately from the desk, push past his shade and fling out into a garden made foreign to me by the fact that as a rule I hardly ever saw it between eight in the morning and one in the afternoon: a garden disarrayed, blown apart from its original order and purpose by the ill wind of artistic mortality. Down at the fence-line I'd stare wildly at my bulging compost boxes, at their rotting vegetation, the biscuit-coloured foliage, the wreaths of blackened seaweed, the eggshells and lemon peel and tealeaves I'd flung the night before. Was it in there, is this where life came from? And off I'd go sack in hand to the mudflats and the mangroves at the end of the road, looking for whatever more I could get together to make *life* start happening again, sea lettuce dead fish driftwood for the fire: an elderly codger to the outside observer, a tattered coat upon a stick, with no distinguishing marks upon him save his evident failure to make headway in life.

Harry, you see, has been gone for some time. My on-again off-again come-again mate, met (make of this what you will) in my Christological year but also in what might be termed the most casual of circumstances (not to mention at the dead of night; though as far as details are concerned I think I'll leave it at that for the time being). Not the first such thus met, either, not by any manner or means, and not the best favoured in the more obvious of ways; but, without the slightest doubt, in all the succession of Bills and Dans and Daves and Toms met and matched and marched off again during that prolific and generous period of my later youth, the one who seized upon me in some complicated way I can (of course) never quite understand and which has never quite let go of me since. What to make of it?—that moment when the eye settles on some gnarled old brute and never leaves him again (I can see him in my mind right now, as I write this, like a private snapshot), and the heart gives its old familiar bounce in its birdcage of ribs? I'd experienced it before, that particular combination, but not the growing realisation, after his first visit and then his second, that something was settling itself between us far more complex than the usual run of things.

I'd already begun to assemble my array of old codgers at that stage of my life, even before I came to realise that that was what I was doing. They lived in huts and lean-to shacks all over the countryside, mementoes of an earlier time when the land was still being broken in and you could live rough and live single, getting through with odd jobs on farms or the edge of townships, shooting rabbit and possum and the occasional farmer's sheep. Some of them had come back from the big war, the first one, the one that had put paid to the times they lived in, put paid to an entire century: and they were the ones who kept away, they ran off whenever I hove to with my bag of produce—cabbages and carrots and what have you—that I'd leave by their door, hoping for the best, hoping that in due course they would relent. In the fallen flesh of their bodies I could relish the vestiges of their younger selves made beautiful by age—refined, matured, sweetened. In these older men there was often a strange, special ripeness. I hope you will try to understand what I mean.

For a long time that was how I wished to be, to live the way they did and, when I wrote, to write their world for them, to put their lives into words. I kept on, and after a while I got some of their stories out of them, with some I even ended up a sort of mate—as I did with old Solomon, my fisherman friend who lived forty miles up the coast and whom I visited regularly for many years, as I will tell. Theirs was the world I would eventually burn up in the family hut.

It was long before that moment that Harry came along. How can I explain him to you? Harry never failed you: never failed to disappoint. Put him in front of you and I would see the dismay on your face. Is this all? you'd say or think when you saw him: just any old bloke you might find on any tram, or standing at the bar of the Mon Desir with his hat set back on his head and one foot up on the brass of the foot-rail, eyes squinting in the drift of smoke from the rollie in his mouth: is *this* the man you said you'd give everything for, the man you said completes you? Well, as it happens, it is: but I see that I can explain him to you only by explaining other things, by looking away from him in order to show him to you more clearly. For Harry was made up of a hundred other people, Harry was the accumulation of a life's work. Harry was a sum.

My very first Harry, then—not *ur*-Harry, you understand, since something prior to, something *originating* Harry is inconceivable: Harry was Harry. But call the youth in the following account a version of Harry if you like. No need for any names, or for any particular details of his provenance.

Let me take you back to the Easter Bible camp I used to attend each year of my childhood and my youth. We studied in groups, nine or ten of us, each with an older boy to act as leader. Our spiritual guide at this time I now remember was perhaps sixteen or seventeen to my thirteen or twelve. We followed him around all day, dogs to his god. Of us all, I remember, I was the most devoted besotted infatuated and craven. I was pre-pubescent, I think (we got that sort of thing over and done with rather later in those days): but then sex had nothing to do with it, at least not sex of the obvious gasping rutting sort. Of the *other* sort, the kind I understand now, the kind that is in my garden as I write, the kind I grew my garden *for*—looking back now that I have learned to see it, *that* kind of sex was everywhere that day.

Here we were, then, gathered in front of him in the shade of a tree at noon. *Forgiveness*, I remember him saying, as he leaned forward into the semi-circle of earnest precarious bare-kneed youths disposed on the grass around him, each one tender as a pushed peach, as the poet says. What does Matthew have to tell us about forgiveness? the young god asked. Behind him, beyond the tree, the grass gentled down to the sand the beach the surf the sea, as on an island. That is how I remember it. Year after year we came to this cove twenty or thirty miles north of the city; the uncomplicated landscape rolled away from us north and south. The voice of Royston—there, I've let a name slip after all: though we called this particular youth, appropriately for a young monarch, *Roy*—the voice of Roy turned it into something else, something even better.

Forgiveness has to be immediate, one of the kids piped up; not me, because in the presence of this young god this young *Christ* I was struck dumb. Were there twelve of us at his feet?—I knew not: only that I couldn't get enough of

24

him. And now here came his parable. I'd heard it already that morning on the edge of another, earlier group: the story of the woman whose husband was struck dead by a flying golf ball on the ninth fairway. I knew the words by heart. I watched the movement of his chiselled lips the whites of his evenly spaced teeth the glans-coloured flutter of his tongue: *She forgave him straight away.* Again the pause, again the look to left and right. And, here it came once more: *She forgave him straight away.* His sleeves rolled high to his shoulders, tightly, sailor-style: from their cloth, under the slight salt bleach upon his skin, a vein ran precisely perfectly pleasingly enticingly down the exact front of either arm, to reticulate in the mystery of his wrists. I couldn't turn my gaze from them.

Who—?

Ah: but now Scones has spoken up. Our Doubting Thomas: charity in action, one of the handful of boys from broken homes who'd been given the chance to get away and better themselves for a week or two in the company of the children of the well-to-do. Rubbish, we secretly thought them in our mercy, and pitiable too: but of them all every last one of us agreed that Scones was by far the farthest fallen. I remember the general horror in the camp the first time his bladder and then his bowel betrayed him, the sound of his terrified *unh-unh*, the dread-filled whimper we learned to anticipate as the grace-note of each new disaster. And why *Scones?*—because those are what he'd promise us if we didn't tell the pastor or his minions that his body had let him down yet again, if we didn't betray him to the hellish middle-aged bitch who was the matron at the camp:

Don't tell them I shit meself and I'll bring yous all some scones—

Now, though, Roy is leaning earnestly towards him:

The woman whose husband had just been killed, he murmurs, his angel's face gentle with forgiveness.

25

But what she forgive him for—?

She forgave him for killing him—

But if she killed him, then he'd be dead—

A general shifting and stretching of limbs in the grass, someone whispering a word to someone else: a spell was being broken. Roy leans forward to his Doubting Scone again, his face lambent with patience—with forgiveness its very self:

There are *three* people—

He is holding up that number of fingers in what looks like a slightly obscene gesture:

A woman and two men—

It sounds like the start of a dirty joke, *There was an Englishman an Irishman and a Scotsman*—

Three—?

Scones screws up his eye at him—making the most, I suppose, of a muscle that still works. It's forty years ago, but I can see him now with his hand up like a salute to shade his brow, his left eye wrinkled in foggy disbelief, his fallen flyblown face radiating porcine agnosticism. I remember, too, the smell of ammonia and the ghastly yellow peril from which I sprang away as it pursued me across the bench seat I shared with him that first morning at camp, and I remember myself rearing up and betraying him to the authorities as fast as I could, raising the alarm, dumping him in the cactus, making damn' sure no one confused *him* with *me* and to hell with his scones—

Now if Janet were writing this we would already be long past the point at which we discovered that Scones *c'est moi mon semblable mon frère*. But I was a child and full of children's natural evil, utterly devoid of the compassion empathy insight and what have you that she managed to accumulate in her writing. I look back at my young self now: *j'accuse*. Let's just say it took me rather longer to rise above my animal status. For, of course—you've guessed it—*he* it is who was my first Harry, and the young messiah my first great disappointment.

Beautiful, yes, young Royston, like some induplicable ideal I was to glimpse in bits and pieces over forty years, in this man's colouring, that man's voice, someone else's teeth or mouth or wrist or hand: or in a gesture, like the funny quick double nod my old fisherman cobber Solomon gives whenever he has found a new way to respond to a question by saying nothing at all. Royston had that, and this, and the other thing, too: and it all added up, I came to realise, to nothing very much at all. His godliness had swallowed him whole, his Bible had snapped shut on him, foreclosing his life, entombing him young, and a couple of years later he melted away overseas on missionary work that (for all I know) still drearily consumes him in some godforsaken jungle somewhere in the world. In the years since, down here on the ground, I've kept on meeting bits and pieces of him walking around in other, lesser people, busily sinning.

And Harry—my on-again-off-again present-day Harry? Well. There was a moment—in the time when he was coming to grow on me, when it was slowly becoming apparent that here was someone arrived in my life who made all others seem unnecessary—there was a moment when Harry caught my eye. There'd been no particular intimacy, as I recall it, we were in the ancient hut together fully clothed and I was letting him have my considered opinion on some issue of the day, things weren't bloody right and no one was doing anything about it, that sort of thing. And I looked across to where he was sitting and where the sunlight fell in through the window and upon the bed, and saw his arm was held up against it, and saw him wrinkle up his eye at me. That's all. *That's all*—? Well, quite enough, as it happened. When the humour is upon us we are as strangers to ourselves and know not what we do. The heart has its reasons, as the Duchess of Windsor's publishers recently had her tell us, and of which (to bring attention back properly to the equally incomparable Blaise Pascal) reason knows nothing

27

at all. He was looking at me straight, Harry, just as his sad, incontinent prototype had gazed up hard at our Bible class leader many years before.

And I did not fail him as I (and, indeed, in the end, young Royston) had once failed poor doomed Scones. On Harry's used, marked, lived-in body I had already seen, in the throat and the set of the shoulders, and more than in these in the fall of the arms and the trace down the front of each of that hidden cord of vein that breaks in the wrist, the ghost of the young, impossible god. But it was in his eye that I saw everything else, all those things that made him human: his frailty, his need, his ignorance, his (yes) *incontinence*; and as well as these all the things he had slowly built on top of them ever since in order to survive and get by: his self-sufficiency, his self-containment, his readily available unavailability. *Here I am*, his winking gaze seemed to say. *All a bit of a joke, really, in' it? Gunner join in—?*

That was all, but it was quite enough to cleave me to him body and soul for the rest of my days, and to enter on a bond that no one understands, my closest friends, not one of them, to this day. As far as I'm concerned, Harry is free to come and go whenever he likes, and come and go he has done for nineteen years, turning up without warning or with little more than a scribbled letter-card a week before, and setting off again in due course with as little notice given. Out of the blue, a rap on the door jamb: and for the next few weeks or months he is with me, an affable, laconic, accepted presence in my life once more, someone to step past or over in my tiny fetid original cabin as I folded my bed or swept the floor, or, later in the day, crawled beneath his cot to slide the evening meal into the cooker. And someone to sit there after dinner as I scrubbed at pots and dishes or tried to write or read, someone set up in his cot with ancient gig-lamp, specs on his nose and a racing mag gripped between his earthy, earthly paws.

28

Best of all, though, was when neither of us did those things and I'd worked on him a bit to get him going: and then here they came once more, in that gravel-filled smoked and pickled voice of his: the stories of his life. The bomb that blew up the brothel in Cairo (*ten men killed in action*): the billet where the horse had stuck its head in the window and eaten up his breakfast in front of him (*true dinks, Frank, right under m'nose*): the fellow who'd been shot through the cheeks while sucking an orange—sometimes it was a lemon—and been left with no more damage than a pair of dimples, one on either side (*and did the girls like him, Frank, he couldn't keep 'em off him after that*): another sniper-shot that had parted someone's hair right down the middle, front to back (*God's truth he threw away his comb*): the erotic dancer in Alexandria who knotted her endowments for the young troops as part of her act (*wouldn't want to get hitched to her*): and so on. And then the racing stories, of nags dosed and hobbled, even (he insisted) painted an alternative hue in order to qualify for a lesser race (*had a good finish*); of the cup-winner they'd had to hack to death with axes when it went berserk on a ferry (*It was her or us, what choice'd we got?*). And so on into the night, all night through sometimes if I could keep him going. It was as if a favourite fictional character had come to life, had walked in the door and taken over—my own gnarled knobbled tobacco-scented Scheherazade. I couldn't get enough of him. He completed me. He completed my idea of myself.

And then, each time, in due course, at the conclusion of the unfolding of some private, inner process I had no access to and which was probably closer to what passes through the mind of a godwit or a turnstone when it decides that today is the day to leave, he would pack up his swag and go. He usually slipped his moorings when I was out so that he could avoid the awkward rituals of departure, which meant that I would come back home in the usual way and suddenly find

14 Esmonde Road minus Harry Doyle. Sometimes I'd have a premonition as I ducked through the gap in the hedge and crunched onto the crushed shells of the path, my rucksack heavy with the makings of a meal I'd expected to put together and share with him: and instead I would find myself enduring a cheerless evening alone at the kitchen counter spooning the food up in lumps while all around me the little dwelling cried out to me the loss of Harry. There'd be the familiar imprint on the bed beneath the window (or at least I'd think I could see it there, as on the Shroud of Turin), and the newspapers and racing mags, all neatly folded to one side of it, and in the kitchen perhaps a cup and saucer as well that I would always keep for a day or two like the Grail itself, its little wan puddle of cold milky tea a sort of chrism, the essence of our relationship preserved. And, always, as well as these, a note, on the table or the bed, usually in pencil on a scrap torn from somewhere, in his unexpectedly good hand, every letter slanted at the same angle and shaped in the way hammered into him by the priests at whatever school in Sydney had been his *alma mater. Well old dear*, he'd always begin. *Duty calls old son and its time to soldier on*—never much more than a line or two of this sort of thing, on its little scrap torn from envelope or brown paper bag, but each in itself quite enough, more than enough to be clasped to the breast for the next few days as I wandered about the place getting used to the fact that, again, once again, I was alone.

My friends reprove me about all this, and rightly, too. I disappear from their lives when Harry is in town, they say, and then, when he departs, I fall upon them to share my misery around. He uses me: they say that, too, which I find harder to take, although, in my heart, I know it's true, a little, some of it. It seems my lot, alas, to be used; it seems part of the deal, part of the need I have to be of service. Turn it the other way around, make me the recipient of the favours, and I wouldn't know what to do with them. I know enough about myself, at the same time, to know that none of this is anything special, rather that it is the presentable face of something very much less presentable, in fact the very thing that led me in my earlier years along a tightrope to Harry himself, met on the edge of a darkling plain that both terrified and drew me in. Both of us, of course, have left that nonsense behind, becoming over the years, if intermittently, a domesticated couple: Darby and, I suppose, John. And I know enough, too, to know the limitations of our situation, that to some large extent it is a one-way street. Many, over the years, have come to me, all of them expecting something, and none of them, I like to think, has gone away quite empty-handed. But there are times—those times when I come across yet another of Harry's farewell notes and realise that, once again, he has left me—there are times when I feel the emptiness of it all, the sadness of the way I've chosen. Of the way that has chosen me—

And that is what she came into, Janet, when she entered my life. Harry had been gone four months and I hadn't heard a word from him. There'd been the customary little farewell note when he slipped away, and the customary stab of pain and loss in the middle of my chest when I found it, and the tidyings and the tears that came next, amid the slow resumption of my solitary routines. Although as always his actual departure had taken me by surprise I'd some idea that he'd headed north, and I expected that this was the direction from which I'd hear from him in due course.

After about a month—the usual time it took for a letter-card to appear (or occasionally it was a stamped beer coaster or similar relic)—I began to check the letterbox regularly for him, and after a further month spent getting every kind of mail under the sun but the mail I'd hoped yearned and prayed for, I began to worry a little. After a third I was in a continuous state of mild panic: in nineteen years nothing

31

like this had happened before. He'd been away longer, up to six months in fact, but the longer he'd been gone the more frequently (though never quite *very* frequently) the cards had arrived. In these times there'd been other people he'd dallied with too, just as occasionally there'd been others for me in the course of that nineteen years: this was part of our arrangement, part of our confidence in each other, long tested long tried long proven. Now, naturally, that confidence began to quiver a little, as the days went by without a word and the questions started to ask themselves in the middle of the night. Had he found someone else, a better hole like Old Bill in the war-time cartoon? And would he simply abandon me to my misery like this if he had? Would he not at least tell me of his situation, to put my mind at rest? *Harry, still alive somewhere but living a life without me in it—*

And then, as the third month became the fourth, and the fifth beckoned, these petulant nocturnal jealousies turned to something else, something far more disturbing and forbidding for me to contemplate. They began to embrace the possibility that the *real* explanation for this long preternatural silence was that *Harry had died*—my greatest fear: not simply that he would die (I had long since imaginatively encompassed this fact, given I am ten years his junior) but that we would die apart, incommunicado; that he would simply disappear and I would have no idea where he was, whether he was alive still or dead like an old beloved tomcat slunk off to croak and turn to cardboard beneath a far-flung hedge somewhere—

When I think of this it's as if someone has walked over my grave: I can't tell you the feeling of it, the sensation of almost not-being that comes at its side. I just stand there when it happens, as I am standing now, staring out vacantly at my little green universe, and then come to myself to find I have a dishcloth in my hand or something equally ridiculous, a tiny blackened salt-spoon or a potato masher or something else from the shabby little domestic world I live in. It frightens me to recall that feeling of dependence and the sense of non-existence when the human being you've allowed to constitute so much of your sense of yourself lets you down in some way, or simply does the unexpected: even if it is, as it always is with Harry, more or less an expected unexpected. Had I known all those years ago that it would lead to these moments of utter disembowelment I can hardly say now that I would have been able to enter my relationship with him in the first place. Were they worth it, all those scattered pleasures? Was it true after all that love is a one-way street, was it true that, in the end, no one ever really loves a loving man—?

CHAPTER 2

As you can see, though, I'm writing again. It may not look much, but it seems I'm able once more to roll off my hard mattress at six in the morning and after the usual cursory breakfast go straight to my table and write. And with this first glimpse of spring we are enjoying now, sometimes I am up even earlier than that. Of course after what I've been through until just a month ago, the fact that there is anything at all, that my little kingdom has begun to be returned to me, seems not so very much short of a minor miracle—

As soon as I came back from the railway station I began to miss her. Maybe that was the real miracle. Her departure just a month ago, of course, was as overwhelming a nightmare as anything that had occupied the sixteen taxing months that went before it. Naturally I wanted to be sure she would be on the train and gone at last from my life. And as if she sensed precisely how important this was to me she resisted going, and became an equal and opposite force to every one of my endeavours to help her on her way. I took her to the post office and helped her transfer money overseas, I showed her how and where to apply for a passport—and then she lost her little indigo booklet with *Post Office* stamped on it at exactly the same time she lost the wretched passport itself. Or she mislaid them, I should say, because there they miraculously were a day or two later, side by side under her cot out in the hut as if she'd put them there, at the very spot where we'd both (I'm certain) bent our backs together and scoured four feverish palms across the dusty floor the day before.

Was she playing a game? And if so, was it with me or against herself? Certainly her panic seemed real enough when the two items first went astray, as was her delight when I spotted them once more in her little hutch, crowded as it was now with her huge black metal trunk (*J.P.F.* stencilled on its side in white skeleton-writing) and her suitcases and a haversack I'd given her, as well as the pumpkins I'd begun to stack there on the grounds (as I explained when she protested to me about them) that they had to go somewhere didn't they? No doubt wishing (if we are in the business of looking for unconscious motivation) to give her the hint that she herself was no longer needed in my army hut, that my regiment of vegetables was ready to take her place now she had completed her work there, maybe even preparatory to scribbling up some kind of collaborative pumpkin fiction for themselves.

No, there was no telling what she was up to in that hectic rushed anxious final period of our shared life, any more than there had been during the preceding long months as my penance wore on and on to its end. Inevitably, as I realise now that I am free of it, she was destined among other things to become ill in all this, and ill in all this duly she became, with a mysterious bug that afflicted her at mealtimes, the very point of each day at which hitherto she had shown such a capacity as whatever is the female version of a trencherman. My young friend Lyall, the Bard of the Abattoir as I call him, had dropped by with one of his packages *gratis* from the works (always wrapped in bloodstained pages from the *Herald*), and so I set out to get some meat into her by means of a quite fine cottage pie together with gravy and greens: but to my surprise she sat there pushing all this around her plate for five unenthusiastic minutes before she suddenly excused herself and lurched up and across and into the bathroom. In due course, after various noises off, she slid the door open again and slumped in its frame. I've been sick, she announced. I'm sorry but I really do seem to be coming down with something. And indeed she looked very much as if she had and was: if she was shamming she was doing a mighty fine job of it.

And so I left my meal to the flies, alas, and helped her to her cot. And all the time I wrung out flannels for her brow and tried to remember if I had any barley left for barley-water and time in which to concoct it, I counted out the days until her boat was due to leave and wondered: would I make it? Meaning, would I make it so that *she* could make it, to the Auckland railway station the overnight train Wellington the *Ruahine* and so forth, and thence irreversibly from my life?

And it is not untrue to say that indeed she did, but not without the kinds of further alarums and diversions that reduced me, at the end, to something approaching a nervous wreck. The night express sets off south at half past three each afternoon with its motley array of citizenry, and while the nation sleeps it noses its way through the break between the semi-tropical north and the great central plateau that marks the true division between the two islands and which might be thought to occur on an imaginary line that runs across country from Raglan on the west of our island to the Bay of Plenty on the farther coast. By the time some of us are stirring into our new day the train has long been chuffing its way through the tamer rolling farmlands and townships beyond the plateau and is getting nearer to its final destination in the windy precarious little town at the bottom of the island that is also, somehow, the nation's unlikely capital—where, as if in some grotesque inversion of the marriage ceremony (it was Lawrence Guigan who pointed this out to me, leering up from his wheelchair), Janet's father was destined to meet her and take her off my hands at last.

But as far as I was concerned this moment of divestment

would occur as soon as the train and its precious cargo began finally and irreversibly to move away from me and the Auckland Railway Station. So as we stood there I could barely take my eyes off the wheels, even before Janet got into her carriage at last and we were all standing around awkwardly and as is usual on these occasions not quite knowing what to say—in all this time I kept glancing at the engine the carriages the railwaymen and the metal rims upon which all depended, only turning back now and then to the desultory conversation—barely a conversation—that others were doing their best to accumulate. Margaret Guigan had driven us to the station in their little Morris motorcar, minus Lawrence but plus Janet, who was wedged in the back with her suitcases: and behind us Lyall followed all the way on a miraculous motorcycle-and-sidecar affair he had borrowed from a friend of mine, Janet's big black trunk sticking up beside him in the cockpit, and his goggles and helmet (whenever I turned back to check that he was indeed still there) giving him as ever an important, battlefield appearance.

And in the end we did make it, our little convoy, and Thwaites the historian-poet who thought he was a poet-historian turned up with Mrs Thwaites, and to my amazement Gordon Garlick the musical composer too, though he tarried for no more than five minutes as always and, as always, gave the impression that bigger things awaited him elsewhere. He bustled off, and then Janet's friend Molly bustled on with something of an entourage, she who had got me into this business in the first place: and on this occasion held up somehow and somewhere whose details disappeared in the natter of her explanation: and all the while I kept returning my gaze to the carriages and the passengers who were climbing aboard it, and felt a dread that suddenly they would start to move, that there would be a blast from the whistle and that tiny preliminary first lurch that always signals the start of things, and that off the train would then proceed without its

37

most precious item of cargo, the exporting of whom (as far as I was concerned at that moment) seemed the very point of the invention of steam locomotion itself—

Well, she almost managed to achieve that, getting on and getting off a number of times till I wondered whether she was in fact changing her mind at the last second and deciding to return to Takapuna and her sentimental education with me. I am pretty certain that that sort of escape was half in her mind, or wholly in her mind for half the time we were on the platform, and that when she was on the train she wished herself out of it and when she was out of the train she wished she was back inside. So that as it turned out the issue of where she would actually be when the train finally struck up became a close-run thing, the kind of gamble Harry himself might have placed one of his modest wagers on had he been with us. It was not a small matter of relief I felt, believe me, that as luck would have it she was in one of her onboard phases when that long-awaited blast from the whistle sounded and people started to call out to one another and the carriages gave that first premonitory lurch and shudder and then began to haul away slowly from left to right and the last farewells began. Miss Janet Frame was being conveyed from out of my life at last—well, out of my presence at least: I did not discount at all a continued verbal connection between us as long as the words in question were like small children, to be seen but not heard. Indeed I had encouraged her to write early and often, and in doing this found I was not entirely motivated by a desire for practical evidence that the geographical distance between us was increasing with the passing of each day.

For here indeed was the miracle of her departure, that as the train began to pull her away from me, and as I felt what I had expected to feel, the lifting of the unbearable weight I'd carried since March the year before and the opening up of my former life to me again, I also felt the last thing I expected to feel at that moment, a great gout of emotion. I watched her receding face, caught up as it was amongst the other faces at the carriage windows and the waving arms and the intervening bodies: itself in this tumult of farewells quite still and almost expressionless, the face of a child, of a young girl, of the lass who had presented herself to me at the door of my cottage sixteen months before in complete naivety and innocent expectation, and now being borne off into the wide and wicked world on her own and with not a soul to rely on. I felt this, and as I did so found myself becoming absolutely certain that among all those around me who waved and called and wished her well there was no other face she looked back at as she drew away: that her eye singled me out with such an intensity that I became to her the only figure on the long station platform.

Back at 14 Esmonde Road there was of course a final trick. As dusk settled in after we'd done a few things in town, Lyall drove me home in the now trunkless sidecar and shared with me an evening meal of sorts. Before he left we decided to take a look in the army hut for old time's sake. We both knew our Proust, or at any rate I did.

And there it was on the bed, the small fold of paper I realised as soon as I saw it I should have known to expect. The little room had been emptied all right, emptied of everything except her words. She'd left her language behind—I should have known, I should have guessed.

Famous last words—?

This from Lyall, behind me in the doorway.

She's always leaving me messages, I said. Her favourite game—

I unfolded it and looked. I handed it to him. He knotted his brow at the piece of paper:

Please arrange a suitable reception for the acrobat—

He handed it back to me.

What's that supposed to mean—?

I've no idea—

She left you a piece of paper saying *that*—?

I've told you, I've no idea what it means. It's a riddle. She'd make them up and I'd have to work them out, that was the deal. She left me one about you once—

He stared. *Me*—?

You. She made them up about everyone. I'll tell you yours some time—

What did she say—?

Can't remember. Sometimes they were quite easy and sometimes they were like this. She'd leave them around the place for me to find, in the meat-safe and so on, a different sentence each time—or just a phrase. Crossword clues, they're like crossword clues—

I waved him away. I was looking around the little room.

I'm too tired, I can't be bothered at the moment, I told him. You can screw it up and throw it away—

But he didn't throw it away, and after he left I sat in my armchair in the front room with the lights off as if no one was at home and with the piece of paper on the pile of books to my left. It was becoming too dark to see the writing but the phrase stayed in my mind, and it made me think of her on the train, rocking her way south in the dusk, completely alone amongst the sleeping families and the students and the businessmen playing cards and sneaking their furtive slurps of ale and spirits when the guard's back was turned. Miss Janet Frame, with her extraordinary personal story so utterly unlike the complacent everyday story of any or all of them did they but know it: although of course she always maintained during her time with me that this was not the case, that the only difference was that *she* was telling the truth about *her* difference while others hid theirs away: that we all carry some mark on us each and every one, though few are given the strength, she claimed (a strength which she seemed to see as involving a power of the imagination otherwise missing

40

from the population at large), to stand aside and really, truly live—

Well, now she had her chance, now she was setting out to do just that; and as I sat there in what was by now complete darkness but for the familiar fretwork from the streetlight, and with a gusty drive of rain drumming its lonely way across the roof, I thought of the child-woman who had spent a winter and a summer and half another winter with me, and felt once more that gout of emotion shapeless and grudging beneath my sternum. It was shapeless because I did not yet own it, because it surprised me and made me feel vulnerable and not fully in control of myself. And I begrudged it because it meant that even though her body had gone from hence her spirit had not; that just as much as Harry (and this was an understanding of which I had long since become slowly and reluctantly conscious), she was now a part of my very being, she was someone who had crept her way inside my sense of who I am and thus, in that respect at least, *would never leave me—*

A few days after her friend had come parping self-importantly up to my macrocarpa hedge with her special passenger in her car like Lenin in his sealed train arriving at the Finland Station, I spent time with my old cobber Solomon up the coast. He had what amounted to not much of a property on the sandy upper banks of the tidal creek at Pukapuka, about forty miles north of the city, in one of a series of many little bays on the southern side of that exceptionally placid expanse of water sometimes known as the Mahurangi. There he caught snapper, and also herring and a little further out kahawai, a matter with which I helped him as often as I could get away from the business of my own subsistence and make my way through the rolling farm country that presents itself once you push clear of the city and the market gardens and the orchards that surround it more or less.

But of course it was not just for his snapper that I kept up with him—

Exactly where in these parts lay the site of those Bible camps of my youth I find I've never been able to say, any of the times I bowl along in the passenger seat of the van or truck I've hitched my northerly ride in for the day, or far less often in a saloon or motorcycle sidecar. Sometimes if my ambitions lie far to the north I try a bus or service car, and in my younger days performed feats of prodigious effort on a borrowed bicycle. On one occasion I got myself very many miles north to a pub where Harry claimed to have found a job as well as work for me, surest thing he knew, I could bet the house on it if I could just get myself up there as quick as I could. Well, I did, and of course by the time I turned up drenched in sweat and as hungry as one of his beloved racehorses, he had fallen out with the publican and there was nothing for it but the long slow journey back home, the pair of us the bicycle and half a dozen yapping mongrels sliding about the tray of a city-bound farm truck for most of the way.

Solomon I hadn't seen for nearly a month, and I was saddened by his decline from my last inspection of him when I did: what I'd then thought was a cold had worsened into something else, as far as I could see, although he insisted he was on the mend. I had thoughts of the places you can get these old blokes into and best of all the old servicemen's home in town: but the more I urged this possibility the more he pulled away. So I tidied him up and left him comfortable with some vegetables I'd brought in my rucksack and two of the old man snapper he'd caught that morning, and made it the several dozen furlongs back to the East Coast Road at length where I thumbed a ride back home.

And it was on the way there while bouncing along in an old Essex Six converted into a truck that it occurred to me that Harry might be waiting at the other end. I'd been thinking of Solomon and his silences, and of the wound in

42

his left bicep that was like a navel, and of the shrug of fate that had stopped the bullet short of his heart. And I thought of Harry similarly surviving fate with his various shrugs of good fortune, and of the fellow next to me at the wheel, another old codger from a farm up north—what was *his* story, what bullet had *he* stopped short in his time on the planet? I thought how I might have got a lift with someone else perhaps, someone younger like the pair of callow boys I'd flagged down early that morning for my journey up the East Coast Road, townies returning to the farm they were trying their hand on as it turned out and the conversation began to go back and forth amongst us. Instead I'd found the enigmatic cove that drove beside me, a man of Harry's age and type, with wattled throat wrinkled gaze and lived-in features as well as the same air of much that was held in reserve. It had given me a belt in the chest when I scrambled into his cab, that familiar jolt of recognition: *G'day cobber*, he'd said around his cigarette and from deep in his chest, and then had said little enough else—

Of course I realise now I was thinking what I wanted to think, and I can also see that what I was thinking had no small connection to my unexpected visitation a day or two before. But at the time it was all promises signs and omens, the very air itself seeming to charge up with meaning the nearer we got to the outskirts of the suburbs. The old Essex was taking it hard, the steady *bang-bang-bang* of its motor anything but steady whenever even the slightest incline presented itself, and every now and then the gear stick slipped its cogs to a slight imprecation from my solemn chauffeur as he worked it back in again with a swift double stamp at the clutch. And each time he did I thought of Harry, not because of the mild curse that was passed—Harry in fact rarely swore—but because of the glimpse of the back of a gnarled hand, all red-blue-purple and with those tell-tale little flecks of black metal: and also because of the feast of seasoned skin and flesh I'd had that

43

day as I rubbed Solomon down after dealing to him. Surely it could mean only one thing.

Ahead of us the blue of the late-afternoon sky seemed to deepen and intensify, clouds the colours of mushrooms and salmon rolled in importantly from over the sea, houses and people seemed to fade into their own tiny irrelevance as they flickered by the window and the dramatic *mise en scène* that I fancied was assembling itself on my behalf began to push back at me. *Today was the day, I could count on it—*

Once I was back on my feet at Lake Road a strong salty breeze pushed me over the hump in Esmonde Road and to my gate. Nothing in the letterbox—but it took only a second for this fact to turn into a little bounce of hope. For my box was hardly ever empty, the postie always stopped at Number 14. Someone must have cleared it out—Harry? I pushed down the path to my little house, listening for the radio and the familiar dry nasal chant of the race commentator at Te Rapa or Ellerslie that always told me my man was back in residence, his gravelled voice about to come up at me once more: *G'day old son, thought you was holdin' out on me—*

But there was no one. I flung into the house, the bedroom, called his name, thrust into front room and then bathroom, tried the windows left and right. Everything was exactly as I'd left it at six that morning. I stood there, the wind out of my sails, the bumping of my heart slowing down, a wet smelly newspaper packet of fish still in my hand. I'd been so certain! I went out again and quartered the section, shifted the hose, half-heartedly kidded with the cats: no sign of him, squinting into the setting sun from beneath the brim of his trilby hat, rollie always one third of the way from the left corner of his mouth. I'd been so *certain*, as I'm sure I'd never been before.

Back inside I fell to filleting the two snapper I'd kept from Solomon's catch while the cats reared and squealed. Not long after we first met twenty years before, Harry slipped off on his first walkabout and after a while of waiting I'd simply given up on him, decided it had all been just one of those things. And then, suddenly, after three desolating months, he was back. He'd helped himself to the cot in my *beachside cottage* while I was away up the coast, so that when I came in just as I did today, late in the afternoon, reeking of fish and (on that occasion) expecting no one—there he was, feet crossed at the ankles, tobacco smoke curling around the edges of the newspaper held a little further along the lean horizontal body. The holes in the soles of his boots gazed up at me laconically like cartoon eyes: Harry was back! *G'day digger*, I remember he said to me as he crumpled the paper down to his ribs. It was an early evening cruelly like this one, its mood its feel brought back, perchance (once I got the pan of fillets onto the big solid front element of the stove), by the smell of the cooking fish: my reeking south-sea madeleines.

And then, as I was recalling this, a *tap-tap-tap* at the door—

My mind leapt one way and then another. Harry never tapped, he just turned up, manifesting about the house as just described, or (if I was already in residence) in the garden so that when I looked out of the window to check the water or the washing—there he was, like a scarecrow or one of the fruit trees down the back or the loquat trees at the front, something that had been there all the time, something that *belonged* although you hadn't quite noticed. On the other hand a tap on the door was better than no tap at all, and it raised the possibility however slight that it might be him after all, that fate might have changed its mind and delivered him up to me at last. Something of these thoughts flickered through my mind as I dropped whatever was in my hand, a knife or spoon I was using, and the cats scattered, and I was at the door and wrenching it open.

A woman's face looked back at me—

I stopped short, one hand on the doorknob. We stood, the

pair of us, *en tableau*. The hair, of course, no longer tamed by a headscarf, that great shock of it, russet, auburn, some extraordinary colour without a name, shot up and out and around and framed her face. And then the face itself, slightly square-jawed, slightly ruddy (I was starting to take all this in), a version of the body that served it, upon which hung a patterned summer frock that bared freckled shoulders and the sturdy arms and hands of a young farm girl. She was without jewellery: no rings, no bracelets, nothing at her ears or speckled throat—instead (I looked up at her) there was her expression, unforgettable, unmistakable, a flicker through her eyes and mouth, a look of such utter helplessness and terror—surrender, almost—no, it was gone now, and had it ever actually been there in the first place? Something barely apprehensible, something impossible to define but (I realised later) utterly determining of how I came to feel about her in the following weeks and months. In that time, even if briefly I find myself doubting it, I soon become certain again that something passed between us at that moment when we met: that something might have passed between us. What it was of course, what it might have meant, I have no idea.

Miss Frame, I said. I see you managed to find your way here—

And in she came. At the same time a colossal blowfly entered from behind her left shoulder and shot past us, and bellied and sawed its way across the room. It began to blurt about the lightshade.

In the front room, I waved my arm at the stove.

I've just been up the coast for the day, I said. Fishing—

I was backing off her: I found I was picking up newspapers, putting books in their place, sliding shut the washhouse door to conceal the water-convenience.

Hence the fishy smell, I said.

She was standing there, her hands behind her back like a little girl. Her silence made me feel I was prattling.

46

I'd leave the door open but it'll bring more flies in—

The blowfly was doing its business up high, battering from wall to wall. She looked up at it momentarily and back.

At last she spoke.

Mr Sargeson? she said politely.

I bowed from the waist:

The same—

My friend dropped me here—

The voice was a child's, her entire demeanour was a little child's, a little child who has been dumped at a friend's place to stay overnight, perhaps, and finds she has to make awful conversation with friend's dad. It took me off my guard. I had no idea whether it was real or not—well, it was real enough all right, but did she *mean* it? Was she acting or was it something else, some other kind of stunt?

I see—

I could feel myself beginning to get caught up in something.

There was a pause.

I've heard all about you, she said suddenly. I've read everything you've written. I think you're a wonderful writer—

This last was said with great sincerity, with a real and earnest intensity, as she looked up at me.

I do admire your talent, she said.

Very kind. Thankyou. Thankyou—

I wavered about, taken off guard. Then the usual polite refuge:

Tea? Would you like some tea—?

Her face reddened, almost as if I had suggested an indecency. It was an extraordinary display—the blood rose up her neck and face in great strawberry patches as if someone were thrusting it into her veins with a stirrup pump!

If it's no trouble, she piped.

Already I had the pan of fish pushed off the electric

47

element and the jug pushed on it. There were some scones in
the cupboard, made a day or so back but still plausible, and
I slapped on each of them a dab of the gooseberry jam that
Margaret Guigan and I put up the year before. I'd started to
rattle away as I tend to do in awkward situations like this,
talking about Margaret and her writer husband Lawrence
and his wheelchair with no idea what my young visitor would
make of it—until I spotted her lowering herself into my own
chair by the fireplace:

No no, I called out. Not there, that's mine—

I waved the knife at the day-bed under the windows in
the corner.

Try that—

She stood, and stared at it.

The divan? she said.

Whatever it's called—

It was a new one to me: but whether day-bed or divan,
she sat on it, smoothing her skirt beneath herself as she did.
She touched the faded seersucker cover that had once been
somebody else's curtains and would undoubtedly, in the
great scheme of things, become curtains again some day. It
was if she had never seen such an object before—a bed you
just *sat* on?

I brought her tea across:

Here you go, milk and two sugar. You've tried it with
honey—?

Tea—?

Russian-style. Tea with honey—

Tea with honey—?

Or in fact more often with jam—

Jam—?

This was slightly disconcerting, I have to admit—the way
she parried everything I said to her without any particular
input of her own. For one thing it made me feel I was prattling
away about nothing, which was no doubt true, but about this

far into most of my conversations I was used to someone telling me this was in fact the case, and expected a chance to riposte and enjoy a little entertaining cut and thrust. Absent this I decided to raise the tone a little, and so I mentioned the scene in *Dead Souls* where the whole business is described, the samovar the dish of jam and so on—

And naturally when I finished I asked her if she had in fact read the book—?

She looked a little abashed.

No, I haven't, she said.

I was astounded. Not read Gogol? I demanded—Tolstoy, then, there's tea in Tolstoy—in Dostoevsky, too, you've read Dostoevsky—?

Yes—yes—both—!

Tchekhov?—of course you have, everyone's read Tchekhov, anyone who fancies they can write has read Tchekhov. The writer's writer—the stories, anyway. Of course we're not reading anything if we're not reading the original, we're not reading the words, we're reading an impression. The rest's lost in translation—

I held out the plate to her.

Have a scone—

She grabbed at them so eagerly that some of her tea spilled. She was holding saucer and cup in her left hand and stuffing a halved scone into her mouth as if she hadn't eaten for a week! I kept the plate there as she took another half, and then, somehow and with impressive fingerwork, a third.

She tried to put the cup onto a stack of books that rose from the floor.

No no no, I cried. Not on books!

Didn't she know anything? I took the cup from her.

I'll find you a side table—

In fact I wanted to do something else as well, I wanted to find her little book of stories that I'd rummaged up in the local library and read at a sitting a couple of nights before. I brought it back from my bedroom along with the apple box I used as a bedside table.

I sank back in my chair and opened the book.

Tidal Pool, I read aloud. *Stories*—

She froze, a halved scone held in mid-air. She stared at me point blank. There was a slight tremor, or was she shaking her head at me *no no no*—?

From the local library, I told her. Read them last night—

Still the frozen stare, the stricken look across the room. I pressed on. She needed to know my assessment of them— surely this was what she had visited me today to hear?

Your stories, I began.

I paused to stir my tea the usual twenty times, aware, across the little rug between us, of her continued suspended animation, her continued dismayed gaze. She had even ceased to chew. I tapped the spoon against the side of the cup and laid it in the saucer.

Your stories have some merit, I said. There's some observation there, there's some detail, there's a world in them—

In truth I'd found them—well, not quite my cup of tea, you might say. There was some brilliant observation in passages, and a depth of emotional insight that was deeply poetic at times, quite affecting although less at the fictional level of creating empathy for her child-protagonists than between the lines, so to speak, in the implied experiences of the writer. Once again I wondered exactly what it was that had happened to her to produce such plangent notes at a tender age. Clearly there was a story behind her stories—

But one of them seemed of a different order to me, and far superior to the rest. Washing day, and a woman is caught up with the family's laundry and what have you—and a sheep appears at the door of the wash-house. That's all, but that's all that's needed to convey both an interior state of mind and an encompassing explaining world natural and man-made that were quite absent, I found, from the other stories in the little collection.

I thought it important to talk to her about it. I leaned forward.

Now, I said. One of these stories of yours—

She stared at me, looking terrified, her eyes unblinking as she waited for the death sentence:

—is particularly good—

There was a pause as she swallowed, but evidently with great difficulty.

But it's my least favourite story, she said, in her tiny voice. Of everything I've written—

But you don't know which story—

But, extraordinarily, she *did* know which story I meant:

The sheep story, she said.

She was still having apparent difficulty with the remnants of her scone: she dabbed her hankie at her mouth.

It happened to my mother, she said. A sheep looked in at her when she was out in the wash-house. She told me about it—

But you must see what's valuable in what you've written, surely—?

I can see what's valuable in it for me—

So I found myself having to explain her own work to her! Young Lyall tells me I tend to hold forth to my fingernails, and that is what I found myself beginning to do now as I sat back in my chair and fanned my fingers in front of me.

In that story, there's a real sense of the world, I told her. I presume that's what the sheep represents, reality presenting itself, economic reality, sheep don't get here by accident—

I flicked a look up at her for a moment, but her returning gaze was unreadable. I went back to my nails.

And there it is, I said. When she least expects it, when no one would expect it, suddenly it turns up and breaks into her fantasy—

A pause. It became a silence. The blowfly sawed across the room.

But it *is* her fantasy, she said at last.

And again there was that extraordinary stunt whereby the blood flushed up her body and into her face as if she had just said the most foolish and embarrassing thing in the world—

It's *all* fantasy, she said. There's nothing to break in *from*—

Where could I begin? Slowly, I started to set out for her what it was we're all doing, not just writers but of course those of us who find ourselves fetched up here in a time and a place that culturally speaking are on the dark side of the moon. *Introduce the landscape to the land*—an excellent phrase one of my friends used in a recent poem: I talked about that, and I used a similar phrase from a review I'd read a few years ago about *living with the land*. It's not that I thought completely like that, you understand, I mean I always knew there was something more to our project than just that first accommodation. But I wanted to make it clear to her that it *is* a *project* that the writer of today is involved in here, and that because of history we are obliged to work together to find a way of writing about what is around us so that those who come next don't have to do it, so that they may have what we never had, the beginnings of a local tradition to work in. And I did in fact think in terms of *terra firma*, the ground we stand on—that cultivated world outside my window whose green shade grew green thoughts and for whose continued growth my own generation (such as we were) must provide heroic, willing compost—

This is what I set out to her, and this is what she listened to as if palsied, giving no sign whether any word I said meant any single thing to her or not.

And that is the task of the artist, I concluded. As I see it, at any rate—

There was another challenging pause. I was aware of the fly, bouncing against a windowpane.

Suddenly she moved, suddenly she seemed to reassemble herself. I waited for her piping schoolgirl voice.

Instead, though, a different tone, almost a different person.

Words aren't little donkeys, she said, quite firmly.

I blinked at her.

You speak as if words are little donkeys that go out and bring back a load of facts for us, she said. Then we build a world from them that ends up looking like the world the facts come out of in the first place. What's the point of that—?

I was amazed at her boldness. I leaned forward again.

That's not quite what I meant, I said. You've caught part of it but it's not quite what I meant—

But it's some of what you meant, she said. Isn't it? And it's not enough, it's just not enough—

She looked away, through the window, at the green thoughts of my garden.

For example, she said, the sheep's a ewe—

She looked back again.

The sheep in my story, she said. She's a ewe. The woman looks out and sees a ewe looking in—

I thought about it, momentarily. It was indeed a Delphic utterance. I found myself reaching for the plate again.

Have a scone, I said.

She half-hesitated and then took one. We both sat there awkwardly, chewing at each other.

Well, I said. Anyway, there's potential there.

I swallowed tea and waited. I was hedging of course. It didn't mean anything.

A basis for a future, I said.

I waited. I swallowed tea. Still there was no response. How much longer was I expected to keep the conversational ball rolling without any assistance from her? Really, her behaviour was almost what you would call bizarre. And now she had her hankie out and at her face, a large mannish square of white she dabbed across her mouth.

She mumbled something and stood, and stumbled across the rug and towards the washhouse door and, I presumed, the water-convenience. She struggled for a moment, the door slid across and she was gone, wrenching it shut behind her in two frantic tugs.

I turned on the wireless radio to cover her privacies. The strains of Guy Lombardo and his Royal Canadians began to fill the room—d'you see what I mean when I say there are times when living here really *is* like being on the dark side of the moon?

Above my head, the fly had found the flypaper at last.

In two or three minutes, with much turning on and turning off of taps but not the slightest sign of flushing water, she was back. She seemed quite recovered, even refreshed. But there was no explanation. Instead:

Your lavatory, she said.

Everyone should have one—

But—

I had it lowered when the place was built, I told her. Modern lavatory pedestals are far too high. And then we wonder why we're all constipated—

How much did she want to hear? It was a topic on which I'd been known to clear a room. It was certainly not what I'd imagined we would find ourselves talking about on a first meeting—but then, neither was anything else that had gone between us in the previous half hour.

I decided to change the subject.

I'm sorry if I upset you, I said.

She was back at the corner bed, more formal now. She looked puzzled.

Mentioning your stories. You seemed—

Oh—no!

54

She tipped her cup against her face and back, quickly, as if to buy time. I had a suspicion the cup was empty.

I was ill when I wrote them, she said.

Aha—

Ill—?

A physical illness. A recurring physical problem I've had for some time—

And—do you find it hard to work—?

Whole months—

I remembered the silly business of a few days ago with Janet's friend Molly, and that mysterious phrase *a ring of fire* that for a moment I'd got so embarrassingly wrong. It was something obviously connected in some way with her difficult past, a clue to what it was that had happened to her. My curiosity was stirred, but it was becoming obvious to me that my young companion was not going to tell me the nature of her illness without a bit of prompting. Which of course made me even keener to find out what it was—

The silence lengthened. And so I used her own phrase back to her, I quoted it the way I would sometimes cast a baited line into the harbour from Solomon's dinghy and then wait to see what it came up with, snapper jellyfish or just plain seaweed—

A ring of—fire—? I suggested, and waited for a tug on the line. Would she pick up on it and take things further?

Well, pick up on it and take things further she certainly did, although not quite in any way I might have expected. She had another fake slurp at her emptied teacup, she put it back down in her saucer and for a moment she purported to look at something through the window. Then, as if to herself and with her face averted and her head slightly down, she began to murmur:

You do me wrong—

Was she was reproaching me?—but now, the old, familiar words:

*—to take me out o' the grave: Thou art a soul in bliss; but
I am bound Upon a wheel of fire—*

I managed the last line myself, and we recited it together:
That mine own tears Do scald like molten lead—

It seemed to delight her that we both remembered that
terrible scene where the exhausted Lear wakes from his
naked raging on the heath and in his madness begins to see
for the first time the truth of his world. For a moment all the
other nonsense fell away, mine and hers, and we were able to
laugh together, just for a second or two.

During the following long months she was to make much
of the redeeming power of literature and the importance it
had had in her life as a sort of lifebuoy, almost, as far as I
could see, as if there were nothing else to hold onto in her
world but books, words, imaginary things. There had been
no moment in my life that showed me the power of those
things—the power of art over life, the power of art to change
life—as that moment did.

Of course I was perfectly well aware, too, that she had
brilliantly steered me away from a topic she wanted to have
nothing to do with. I also remembered the line that comes
next in Shakespeare's great play. It was something I would
dwell on for weeks—months, right throughout her long stay
with me—the line Cordelia says to her batty pa as he comes-
to in his armed camp on the cliffs of Dover:

Sir, do you know me?

Did I know her?—did she know me? Who knew whom?

I left it there and pressed on:

So, I said briskly. How do you live—how do you support
yourself—?

This banality was nonetheless the key point: I struggled
forward in my chair—

I mean, do you have a tame quack—?

She looked baffled.

You know—a G.P. who signs your forms for you—?

She stared at me as if she had no idea what I meant, no practical idea of the problems she was going to face. And these things mattered so much!

I gestured outside, towards the pumpkin vines, the tomatoes, the lettuces and beans that fluttered and throbbed beneath the beat of the water sprinkler.

Look out there, I said. It doesn't sow itself. It doesn't weed itself. It doesn't water itself. The more time I spend on that and the cooking and the washing the less time I have to write and read. Even going down to Coldicutt's for bread wastes time. Writers are meant to write, they're meant to read. Everything else is just a waste—

I stood.

A writer should just get up and write, I said. Or get up and read—

But that's what I want! I want to live like you!

The words just burst out of her, with such force that they seemed to come from somewhere else, as if they could have no possible origin in the child-woman I'd been talking to. Her intensity rocked me a little: I scrambled to focus on my earlier theme. What was it I had been on about?—money, of all things, was that it?

You'll have to confront money, I managed to say. Alas, but it's true—

Across from me she seemed to have settled back down again. She was sitting forward on her seat, hands politely together and legs crossed at the ankles as if she was being photographed or interviewed for a job.

I pressed on:

It all comes down to money in the end, I told her. Money buys time. Can you imagine what it's like in a full-time job—I had one once, I was a solicitor, can you believe that?—not for long, just long enough to know I was in the wrong trade. I came to realise how much of life is waste, and that all that matters (I gestured at the pile of books by her chair) is *that*, producing *that*. And finding ways of keeping *that* (I gestured at the window, at my grassy green world outside) at bay—

But it's magical, she said.

The world is—?

She shook her head. This world—

She pointed through the window.

Your world—the one you've made here—

Now she was looking around the room.

When I came through the hedge, she said, it was like coming into a nursery rhyme—

The light, she was looking at the light in the room. I was used to it, of course, the strange dappled light of late summer softening into autumn, tinged green by my little jungle outside and become subtler, less bright, less charmed as the sun lowered. I suddenly became aware of it again, taught by her looking, perhaps, and aware too of that familiar time of day when a man has to be about his work in order not to think of darker things that don't require too much to be thought about.

I lurched up out of the chair, meaning business.

I see we'll have much to talk about, Miss Frame, I said. I could hear the mumble of the trapped fly above my head.

Now that I had become conscious of it, the light in the room seemed to be changing quickly. It was time she was gone, back to wherever she was staying.

I'll have to get you to chat with my doctor one day when you're here again, I told her. About some sort of pension. Are you going to use the hut out there? Write in there? When were you thinking of using it—?

She stared at me.

I'm in it! she said. I moved my things in this afternoon—!

It took a moment to register. I turned from the window. I could feel my mouth slowly falling open, like an idiot's.

Moved your *things* in—?

58

CHAPTER 3

And thus it was that Janet came into my little world and settled into the life of 14 Esmonde Road, Takapuna: although as things turned out it would be equally fair to say that the life of 14 Esmonde Road, Takapuna, was obliged to settle into her.

As I have said, over the years the modest little box behind my house has been home to a number of people of all sorts even including one who turned out, I discovered much later, to be a crim on the run, a man who in due course decamped from the protection of my rakes hoes forks and bags of blood-and-bone to the mercies of a coastal steamer and thus forever from my life. They all came and went, these waifs and strays, and a month or two would have seen even the tardiest of them do both: but when I realised what Janet had brought along with her I knew at once that I was in for the long haul.

It was not so much the abundance of what she had in my little hut that made me think this way as the modesty of it: as far as I could see there was little more to her than some books, an Olivetti in a portable case and a few clothes that required no more than eighteen inches of the horizontal broom handle nailed behind a curtain at one end of the hut. Evidently she travelled light, and somehow it was this that persuaded me of her cuckoo qualities—there was not even a suitcase in evidence, and her lack of a need for one scarcely suggested ongoing self-sufficiency to me, rather a need on the very edge of life to depend on others even for the bits and pieces, the salt-shakers and the electric irons and the washing baskets that are the stuff, alas, of a more settled life. Mine (insofar as I possessed such tiny domestic items) looked as if they were going to get plenty of use.

At our first breakfast together I set out the rules of engagement, by which I mean not the rules of eating together, of which naturally she had more than a little command, so much as the rules by which we were to share a property of no great size and a dwelling even smaller. Early to bed, I told her (*and up with the cock*, I usually added whenever I employed this phrase, though in my initial period with Janet I forbore from going that far: when in due course we came to know each other better and I let the whole phrase slip, she shrieked with delight). Breakfast at seven (meaning, I hoped she understood, that we would both get up about six) and all *facilities* available till 8.00 a.m.: *facilities*, said meaningfully, meant the shower-box the tub and the water-convenience through the wall. The period after breakfast, till 1.00 p.m., I made clear, was to be spent at our separate writing desks, working steadily revising thinking correcting and then, buoyed by that, writing afresh. Five hours a day, I told her, and no more, then lunch and the afternoon given over to those less literary things that need, alas, to be done.

Routine, that was what I was trying to get across to her. I delivered a bracing talk about responsibilities and disciplines. I must say I did myself proud, or rather I did my parents proud since at various stages of my monologue I was aware of first my father's voice coming from my mouth and then, less often but more stridently, my mother's. Between the three of us we gave poor Janet a fair old time, and now I look back on it I wouldn't necessarily deny that I might have been secretly hoping to make the idea of the writer's life sound so forbidding that she would give up on it and steal away, leaving me to stew once again in the pleasures of my solitary deprivation—

But she did no so such thing, and instead set about with a will to the business of apprenticing herself to the life of the writer, taking every item of advice and instruction at my word and performing it to the syllable the letter the comma and the last full stop. The early start to her day was no problem, she said, since she'd long been used to getting up at that time (*where*, I itched to know: a convent? Prison? Hell?), and indeed it seemed to be no trouble at all for her to make such a start, since she was often visible early in the garden or audible as she tap-tapped her way politely into the house to use the *facilities* while I was still in the process of getting myself up (*Hello? Hello?*). In these first few months her manner seemed invariably set each morning in that curious formality with which she'd first met me back in the last week of March, her clothing very much the same from day to day and of course there was always that extraordinary hair.

Initially, at least, you might say the ontogeny of each day recapitulated the phylogeny of our relationship, beginning as I have described and then losing formality as the hours ticked by and the sun hoisted itself up and across the sky. By lunch each day Janet had usually thawed, enough sometimes to accompany me to the local shops about a mile away where we took in the passing cavalcade of life as represented in the part of it acted out in the suburb of Takapuna. Often being there with her was as enjoyable (I had to admit to myself) as being there with Harry, with whom I used also to do this sort of promenading in the afternoon when he was in town, and who regularly piped up with this and that as we loitered. With Harry of course it was people not words that caught his attention, but with Janet it was the other way about. *Beauty Parlour*—she made much of that as we strolled past the local shops, with a witty line about the triumph of hope

61

over experience: *Beauty Parlour* along with *Master Butcher* and *Quality Meats* and *Sixty Minute Cleaners* (how minute would they be? she wondered) as well as one or two others. *Fruiterers* she liked particularly for its unexpected extra syllable, and before we'd got back to Esmonde Road on that particular occasion she'd rummaged up *poulterer* and *usurer* and *perjurer* to go along with it, as well as (later that evening and to her delight) *sorcerer*, with other possibilities following in the succeeding days—

By evening, then, we were often chattering away like caged birds. But it was as if with the coming of each new day she had to relearn us both anew, her life and the general business of living, with its nasty day-to-day necessity of having to do with people. Eventually she relaxed, so much so that I found myself obliged to make a new rule, that she chatter less in the mornings and instead explore the possibilities of sensible conversation and even of measured silence. Of course when I learned more of her story and where she'd been and what she'd had to put up with, I understood better why she was as she was. The wonder to me then was not that she'd survived so well, but that she'd survived at all.

At breakfast we always ate porridge with a yeast curd I made from a germ someone had given me long ago and which I persuaded to renewed life in my hot-water cylinder cupboard each evening. This business fascinated her, and I often found her checking its progress in the middle of the day as if it were a sick kitten or bird she was caring for instead of a tiny bug that did no more than bring about the distinctive tang of soured sweetness that greeted our respective palates each morning at the kitchen counter. There was always porridge and toast as well, and sometimes honey and always something or other that Margaret Guigan and I had put up in bottles the autumn before or the one before that, and as well and always, tea, and sometimes when it could be managed even a cup of coffee though only the kind made from a chicory essence. For lunch there was soup, from a pot I added to and added to and which had long ago developed a secret yeasty life of its own that didn't need to be looked into closely, and for our supper further vegetables depending on what was in season and augmented by anything we could manage to add, fish or eggs or (when the Bard of the Abattoir had made one of his irregular visits) chops and bangers and from time to infrequent time even a roast with accompanying potatoes and what have you, always an event in itself whenever it occurred.

Coming as she did from the benighted south (is that in New Zealand? I'd asked her when she told me where she'd been born), she was amazed by the variety and abundance of my garden. Back home *vegetable*, she told me, meant turnips cabbages swedes and what have you: and here she was, confronted by the mysteries of curly kale yam and kumara, and even the taro I have been trying to grow. But she was also intrigued by the ends to which I put some of my vegetables, and my promise of wine made from my pumpkins of a season or two before had her open-mouthed—you could make real wine *yourself*? From *pumpkins*?—Well, I told her, we would soon find out, since my self-appointed wine-maker Lawrence Guigan had assured me that our brew was maturing nicely in his garage and had even suggested a tasting party at 14 Esmonde Road in the not-too-distant future. In my private view the future he proposed was insufficiently distant, but Lawrence was confident in the success of his local product, as he tended to be in every other thing as well.

But as far as Janet was concerned, of all the vegetables I grew my peppers seemed the most interesting. She'd never seen or heard of them before, and till she picked a ripe one up thought them some kind of tomatoes—

Peppers, I told her.

She sniffed at it.

Are they—peppery—?

Ah, no, in fact they're slightly sweet—

Why are they called peppers if they're slightly sweet—?

They're not all sweet. The less ripe ones aren't. The green ones. They ripen red and then they're sweet. And the yellow ones and the orange ones—

Yes, she said, but why—?

Because of history, Miss Frame, I told her. And whether we like it or not. They acquire their names through history—

I had something of our earlier conversation in mind, you understand, the one we'd had the day she moved in.

Hence the disappointing gap between what a word says and what a thing is, I told her.

She looked properly put in her place, I remember thinking. But as it turned out she wasn't, because the next day it all came up again! She set off for the shops after lunch with the string bag she always took with her and which usually came back crammed with books from the local library: but when she returned this time, and much later than usual, it contained not words but a large paper bag full of *walnuts*—

I was at the counter, chopping up a fresh pile of peppers for our evening meal.

Walnuts? I said.

I had to buy something, she said. He had no idea what I meant. The greengrocer. About peppers—

You asked the greengrocer for peppers when I've got them here—?

The name. I asked him about the name. Capsicums—

Caps, the greengrocer had said, apparently. What kind of caps you looking for? They're green like a bell and then they go red like a Christmas light, she'd told the poor mystified fellow. In the end she'd fled with the walnuts—

I tried to explain about jalapeno and pimiento and pippali, she said.

And what did he make of that—?

He told me the library's down the road—

64

But evidently the library was where she'd just come from, with her load of new words to inflict on the unfortunate greengrocer. I went on chopping as she talked. In her quest for whatever it was she was seeking, she seemed to be trying to tell me, she'd ended up with—Sanskrit.

It's the closest we can get to the Indo-European, you see—

The ur-language, I said. You'd be very pleased with that—

I was chopping beans. By my hand a pile of peppers in a colander were glossy, waxy, promiscuous. She picked one up:

They're so light, she said.

Try a green one—

And I pushed the cut beans aside with the wet blade of my knife.

They're twice the weight, I said. They lighten as they ripen, there's less and less to them as they go on—

I rolled a green pepper towards her:

And thereby hangs a tale, I said.

She lifted the pepper. She waggled it by her ear:

It feels dense, she said. As if it's got secrets—

There's nothing in it. What are you expecting—?

I can hear something—

There's nothing inside!

I reached out and took it from her.

Here—

I cut it, end to end. I laid the two halves on the chopping board.

See? Empty—

Together we stared at its ruined interior, the untouched, moist suede of its ribs and their fins of pale seeds. Then my knife went *chop-chop-chop* on the wooden board and the mangled crumpled wet slices fell on top of one other. She stared and stared at them, I remember, as if I'd killed something. This meant nothing to me at the time. I was getting used to some of her ways, but had no idea of course what these vegetables would come to mean to her. How could I, how could anyone?

Instead of happening at that point in muted form, our first crisis came later, after several months, and was much greater. By this time she'd learned to relax somewhat: so much so that as I have said, she became over-eager and started to talk too much as she consumed the modest abundance I supplied. I began to wonder whether she had some kind of difficulty in that area, especially since at these times there seemed to be little substance to what she was saying—observations about the weather the shops the postman and the shenanigans of the two cats: that sort of nonsense. Cats had played a significant part in her formative years, it seemed, and she'd taken an interest in my two mogs and especially in the fact that they were nameless—as I was quite happy to keep them, since as far as I was concerned they were farm animals that earned their keep solely by involving themselves with problems of infestation and thus were in need of no special identity, any more than they required a special supply of food. But the question of providing them with names became a staple of our morning conversations, if conversations they could be called, and an array of unlikely feline names came up for consideration during several days: until one morning at the kitchen counter I could stand it no longer and found myself obliged to remind her of the seriousness of her calling.

There is more to life Miss Frame than idle chitter-chatter about shops and cats! I can remember telling her, sharply (*chitter-chatter* being one of my father's phrases and one that took me by surprise when it popped out of my head like that).

And then of course when I saw her reaction I wished I'd held my tongue, because it was as if I'd hit her. There was nothing I could do to prevent the tears from coming—hers, I mean. Off she took them to her room, from which it was the work of a couple of days to get her back out again, with covered meals left on her doorstep accompanied by a soft tap-tap and a few mollifying words muttered at the level of the keyhole: the first of what was to prove over the following many months a series of such oblations I was to find myself making, as for this reason and that (or indeed sometimes for no reason at all that I was able to see) she went into a decline and as a consequence took to a bed from which I found myself obliged each time to charm her yet once more.

But on this first occasion she emerged a morning or two later a different woman, as if her forty-eight-hour *purdah* had done the work of fifteen years and pulled her forward into an early middle age. She seemed slower, more thoughtful, more measured, but all this without any sense of contrivance: and as if to tamp in the notion that her change was real and in her body, that body seemed slightly shorter than before—yes yes I know, ridiculous is exactly how it looks to me too, now I've written it down: but I am quite convinced all the same that whilst in absentia she had in fact lost a modicum of height, as if the gravity of what I'd told her had literally dragged her down an inch or two and into sober thoughts. Of our falling-out there was no mention, nor of the questions of maturity and application which I had raised: but when I asked her what she'd done in her time away from human commerce, she said one word that suggested she'd taken it all to heart, the little I'd said in haste and the considerable amount I'd said at greater leisure in the days and weeks before.

Writing, she said, and left it at that.

Writing—!

I spluttered curd on my porridge and began to stir it in. Her news wasn't easy to hear, to tell the truth, given my own desolation in that area. But I put on a brave face:

67

And what is it that you're writing, may I ask—?

She looked away.

Nothing, she said. Nothing much—

Nothing will come of nothing—

But she didn't bite.

I'm really not sure what it is, she said. It doesn't have a name—

That was it—that was all. She was writing, and she wouldn't tell me about it. It was a superb sort of revenge if revenge is what it was meant to be. I'd told her earlier on, a little, of my own personal situation, that I was absent an important friendship and that this absence had had the curious effect of circumventing the writing process for me: this account was not untrue, but in fact it was a very simple shorthand for the much larger and more baffling processes that had taken hold of me. It was all I'd been prepared to say, though, and the real point I was trying to make was about *discipline*: that for all the apparent hopelessness of my situation at present, nevertheless I turned up for work (so to speak) at the same time each morning and went through the toils for four or five hours even if there was literally nothing to show for them in the end. This was the kind of devotion she had to aspire to, I made clear to her, the kind of bleakness she had to expect to face if she wanted to become a writer, an artist.

But now, to my dismay, I found that she'd taken my advice!—here she was, just a few yards across my back lawn, on the other side of my washing line, countering the blankness of my page with the fullness of her own. No further from me than the far side of my billowing sheets and freshly laundered smalls, she seemed to have invited the very muse (well, her version of it, perhaps) who for months now and it seemed years had declined to pay me the slightest attention—and she'd done it so easily, without any sense of confrontation or struggle whatsoever!

A revenge superb indeed. Over the weeks I began to get

used to the distant clatter of her typewriter as I sat in front of mine. Some mornings mine was completely silent, as little written on it when Janet tiptoed back across the lawn for lunch each one o'clock as when she'd tiptoed out after breakfast five hours earlier. On other mornings a few dry pellets might emerge, so to speak, and I'd find myself staring at the hideous approximation of what would once have been a page of story, the start of something that felt springy and real and full of the potential of life—but which was instead a sentence or two or just phrases, better than nothing you might think but when experienced week after week as the sum of each day's work, far worse. There was clearly something terribly wrong, and with each lunchtime visit to the mailbox no promise of relief in amongst the bills and the letters: no Harry, not a sign or a word, not even a second-hand account by mail from some kind friend or acquaintance of a chance sighting of my far-flung muse.

And Janet, meanwhile, went from strength to strength. I soon grew used to hearing the clatter of her typewriter coming from the door of the army hut *after* lunch as well as before, whenever I passed it by in my afternoon gardening: or sometimes from the other side I saw her caught for a moment or two in the uneasy striated wartime glass of its little window, a rippling image of her head rocked back as she paused, her eyes uplifted as if seeking the brow of Calliope herself—and then, successful as it seemed, down to earth she'd come again with her inspiration, and yet once more her fingers would begin pounding it out into words as I watched. Well, it was only natural that I should want to know what it was that had caught her attention like this, not least of course because nothing of that sort was busy catching mine: and since I found that I was devoting not a little of each day to bringing about the conditions that seemed to be producing her unfolding creativity, I couldn't help but feel I'd something of a stake in her headlong masterpiece.

69

I'll read anything you want me to take a look at, I said as a preliminary move and as casually as I could. You know that, don't you—?

Oh, of course! she responded, over-brightly as always when she was taking protective cover.

And on she went to describe the progress she'd been making and the number of words she'd already written, the pleasure she'd gained from the task and how she would have something ready in a day or two for me to run my eye over, she was just going through it once again herself—by which time I knew not to believe a word of what she was saying and to see it as more of that cloud of unmistakably blue-black ink I'd already found she emitted whenever she felt I was getting too close to things, whenever events became too pressing, whenever she felt herself getting *trapped*—

There was a particular way in which she spoke when she was putting on this sort of performance, I couldn't help but notice, by the way: quickly and glibly and (oddly) almost as if she were sucking the words back in and trying to swallow them as fast as she could, rather than trying to cough them out for public inspection. This slither of sentences always concluded with a much more specific one spoken in a completely different manner, more clearly and directly, and which always ended with an invisible but almost audible exclamation mark—

I'll give you something by the end of the week! was how she concluded this particular episode of thrust and parry.

And of course by the end of the week there was nothing, which is exactly what I'd learned to expect after one of these displays. In six months she managed never to show me a thing, and, what's more (or, in this case, what was less), she never let on a word of what it was she was up to—I mean, a word of what it was that she was writing, whether a novel a book of poems or perhaps an account of her time immediately before she disturbed my peace (on the nature of which, by the way, she had proven no more forthcoming than she'd been over the nature of whatever it was that she was writing).

But as things turned out, I got something out of her after several months had gone by, after that first misunderstanding and perhaps about June or July of that first year. It happened completely by accident though, and as you'll see was not at all what I might have expected. This time I had nothing planned, no gambit or feint devised to draw out of her some idea of what it was she was up to. Rather my interest was in a large can of honey I'd acquired, somewhat unexpectedly, from Little Ben son of Big Ben, the two of them the father and son team that had helped me extinguish my parents' hovel and replace it with the army hut. Their nicknames represented not so much their physical attributes as their relationship as father and son. Big Ben as his name suggests was a Londoner, in fact a Cockney, a man of jockey build though with no particular connection to the racing industry known to me: Little Ben, in contrast, was a locally grown young giant, over six foot of him, and at twenty with plenty to grow into yet. In all my long acquaintance with this pair I had never set eyes on a Mrs B. or heard one mentioned, any more than I'd heard reference to the possibility of any alternative children—or, indeed, a name to the religious discipline they appeared to practise with such decency and reserve that I assumed they must be Quakers. Whatever it was, the two of them father and son lived it through an Horatian life at Torbay, where their hives shared land with fruit trees and a few each of goats chooks and sheep—the latter part of a remarkable plan to spin their own wool, of which I'd heard a great deal over the years from the father without seeing much hard evidence that it was more than an idea, although from time to time the son, dropping by to lend a hand (just as I sometimes thumbed my way north to

71

do the same for them in return), assured me the business was begun, or nearly.

And now here he was on my doorstep once more and handing me one of their occasional cans of honey—No no, there was to be no payment, the youth made that clear when I started the courtesy business of reaching into my pockets (which had nothing in them, of course): the honey came with Dad's compliments, though (now I mentioned it) a pumpkin or two would certainly come in handy if I had as many as that to spare! And all through this song-and-dance the same handsome smile, and all the time he smiled it his eyes never left off the sight of Janet, visible through two doors behind me—No no, he wouldn't come in, Frank, thanks all the same, he had to be on his bike, things to do, he'd promised to give his dad a hand with something or other that was pressing: and a moment later he was off with the pumpkins and a bottle of Margaret's goosegog jam plus just one more backward glance for the unexpected damsel he'd spotted in my living room. *Fair go, Dad*, I could hear him telling his pa as the pumpkins clumped onto the kitchen table back at home: *old Frank's trottin' a sheila!* And so on: it was the first time either one of them had caught Janet outside her hut, which she tended to retreat to, or alternatively refused to emerge from, whenever my various friends dropped by. So far she'd managed to avoid almost everyone I knew: but now Young Ben had spotted her there was no doubt the jungle drums would be beating double time!

So off he went on his motorcycle with the pumpkins in its little sidecar attachment, leaving me with two things, the can of honey, whose lid I immediately started to work at with a knife, and something equally unexpected, a sudden awareness that Janet could be attractive to men. For that is how I saw young Ben's response, not as simple surprise at her presence in my life but as something else as well, indicated by the way he'd returned his gaze several times to where she sat

72

framed by the living-room door as she pretended to read a book or a magazine. And so what followed was shot through with something new, not so much a sense on my part of her feminine attractiveness (which of course is a concept I have always been constitutionally incapable of understanding, at least in its usual physical sense) as a sense of her as a separate being from the one who'd entered my life breathing emotional suffering vulnerability the need for protection and of course a yearning love of Art and Literature. It was a surprise: the thought of Janet existing in the world out there: I hadn't quite expected it.

Now, I am as capable as the next man, naturally, of conceiving a world without me in it, and of my friends and acquaintances in that world getting about their business perfectly well in my absence—that after all is how it will be when my time has come. Here though was my first glimpse in that self-less way of Janet—and the moment at which, I humbly realise now, looking back, she first began the long process of becoming real to me. Which may be one of the main things this story is about.

But then, as soon as Ben had gone, and as always seemed to happen with Janet, things took off in an unexpected direction. I'd hardly got the lid off the honey jar, from which I proposed to treat myself to a long, lingering scoop to dribble across my porridge, I'd hardly detached the thick film of yellow beeswax from the surface and dug a spoon into the feast that lay beneath, than she spoke:

Mr Bear, she said.

She'd been watching me. The words just seemed to pop out, as much a surprise for her as they certainly were for me—

I paused, the tip of my spoon in the honey. There was a moment of silence.

Mr Bear—? I asked.

The porridge, she said.

73

We stared at each other.

Ah, I said. I see—Goldilocks—

—and Pooh Bear—

—right, right, Pooh Bear has the honey—

I wasn't quite sure what I was doing in this strange little conversation, to tell the truth. But then it got stranger:

And then there's Professor Bear, she said.

I stood there.

Professor Bear—?

Little Women. And *Little Men*, too—

Light dawned. Oh, *that* kind of bear, I said—really, the way her mind worked sometimes baffled me. Professor Bhaer, the German in Louisa May Alcott—of course. Yes, I said. I remember him. *That is a poser*—d'you remember him saying that? *That is a poser*—

I do! (Always the same eagerness when she found herself talking about books.) And you remind me of him sometimes, she said. He was their tutor—

I decided to put the honey on my toast instead. And as it trickled down I set about sticking a pin into things for the hell of it:

Sententious New England claptrap, I said. But not without its charm—if puritanism is capable of being charming at all—

I looked slyly across at her.

You're not a puritan, are you—?

No, of course not! she cried, that invisible exclamation mark giving her away as usual.

Why, of course you are! I told her. We all are!—it's in us, we can't get away from it, none of us can—it's the curse of this country! Even someone like me, raised in puritanism, shot through with puritanism. Like you, like everyone. And so what is there left to be? A puritan anti-puritan—

It puzzled her, I could see that. I bit into the toast and its golden manna.

74

A puritan anti-puritan—? she wondered.

Someone who's caught up in it all but outside it at the same time! Someone who knows he's caught up but knows he can't get out of it. Then you become—I don't know—an anatomist of folly. You take this world with all its mindless restrictions, its—*obsession* with other people's sexual business—and you turn it on its head—

I slurped at my teacup and slapped it back in its saucer.

I mean, was *your* childhood like that? I demanded. Was it like *Little Women*?

No. No, it wasn't—

Then there's your task! I told her. That is what you must do—it's the task of every serious writer in this country. *Tell the truth about puritanism*—

Because that is what I could see in her damned sheep story, for goodness' sake—it was plain as day what she really needed to say, yet I couldn't get her to see it herself! And so I set forth, my mouth full, my spoon digging out more honey and dribbling it onto a second slice of toast as I spoke, words crunching forth as I tried to get her to see what it was she'd been doing in that story and what it was she really needed to do in the larger business of writing. I remembered again that earlier conversation I'd had with her on this topic and how it hadn't gone too well and I'd therefore let it lapse. Well, here it was, presenting itself to be thrashed out between us again. Perhaps (I remember thinking) the business would go more smoothly now we knew each other a little better.

But once again, as I'd found tended to happen with Janet, things took a puzzling, unexpected turn. She began to talk about St Cuthbert.

I didn't feel I'd over-stressed the puritan thing, and I'd certainly tried to concentrate on the crucial point as I saw it, that what we write owes something to society, that it comes out of society—society, life, whatever you want to call it—

and goes back into it again in an endless cycle: none of this startlingly new, naturally, but all of it apparently fresh to her and equally apparently not particularly comprehensible at that. But the fact is that we *do* live in a world, for God's sake—all of us, whether we like it or not: and so it seemed crucial to me to make her understand the dangers of solipsism, not least since (as far as I had been able to judge) she seemed to be well on in the business of writing whatever it was she was putting together in my potting shed, and for all I knew might have been barking up the wrong tree all the time she'd been doing so!

But now here we were, suddenly, translated to the Abbey of Lindisfarne in the sixth or seventh century A.D.—

I listened to her, fascinated, and, I have to admit, not a little knocked off my perch. I am not unfamiliar with the chronicles of the great Bede, of course, and with the account he gives in them of the unworldly saint whom Janet had mysteriously and unexpectedly fished up for me in response to my urging that she live and write more in the world. And *fished up* St Cuthbert was in a sense, given the particular stunt of his that had caught her attention. I could feel the excitement in her voice as she got onto it, the story of how in St Bede's account St Cuthbert had been spotted in the night making his way to the sea nearby to pray and, battily, marching straight ahead into the water without a pause as his voice went on and on preaching to the waves!

Yes, I said when she paused.

He was standing in the water and—

I know the story—

But then—

Yes yes, the otters—

She seemed a little dashed. Her breakfast lay uneaten before her.

Well, that's the important part, she said. The otters. They came up to him while he was preaching—

She fiddled with her teacup.

And then they dried his feet for him, she said.

It's a typically sanctifying retrospective account of its time but a story I must admit not without its charm, the pious saint's oratory being presented as such that the local sea-otters turned up to hear him out and then, once he was ashore, were thoughtful enough to dry and warm his feet for him. I seemed to remember other stunts involving an unexpectedly beneficent and obedient natural world in the story of St Cuthbert, and felt around for one of them to try and revive things—wasn't there some business with an eagle as well?

That brought him the bread? Janet lit up again. Yes, there was! But it's the otters that are important. He'd been standing up to his waist in the water and preaching to the waves, and they swam up to him, two otters, they came of their own accord—

And that's important—?

Yes! Yes—!

And you could see it was, and you could see her trying to tell me why. It suddenly occurred to me that she seemed almost to be thinking in another language, Russian or French perhaps, and translating it for me, feeling for the *mot juste*, the word that would work the trick. She pressed on bravely.

The thing is, she said, if we had the kind of language St Cuthbert was speaking, we wouldn't have to talk about it. About the language—

You mean Anglo-Saxon—?

Perhaps—

She nodded to herself: she was staring at the jar of honey between us on the counter.

But anyway, she said. A language where there's such a tight fit between what you say and what you're saying it *about*—

Pause. She looked up, but not especially at me.

That the first creates the second—

The first creates the second—?

Now here I was, repeating her, the way she usually repeated me!

You speak—and a world comes into being—

Right. Right—

But it wasn't right at all—I'd no idea what it was she was getting at. It really had developed into an unexpected conversation, this, and into an early morning out of the ordinary.

You speak a world, she said. Yes, that's what it is—a language that *uncreates*—

She'd been working it out in front of me, working it out for herself as she sat there. I waited. She looked at me for a moment and then away—

A language that rolls back the reel of time and reverses the Fall, she said. So there're no more gaps between us, people aren't strangers any more—

I stared at her: she stared back. It was not especially comfortable, but the words thrilled through me: *the reel of time, reverse the Fall*—

A language that will heal us and make us whole, she said. Heal and make whole—?

I was letting the words sink into me. *Heal and make whole*—

Language as utterance—

I waited, but it seemed that was that. I began to collect myself, I snapped myself out of it. She was bewitching me—a counter-attack seemed to be called for.

And that's where you're going to get this from, this language of *utterance*? I asked her. From Anglo-Saxon—as recently as that—? Why not Latin, why not Greek? Or Sanskrit? Why not Indo-European, if you're going to go right back up the family tree?

I dismounted from my stool and began to fill the jug at the sink. We were in for a long morning, by the look of things.

The jug went on the element. I mounted my stool again and resumed:

And all of them socially produced, Miss Frame, I told her. Every one of them. However magical they might seem now we look back at them, however exotic, in their time they were just plain old words, and most of them, I think you'll find, bleared and smeared with toil. The two go hand-in-hand, sad to say, talking and trading. Disappointingly prosaic, but that's the hard fact of it—words and work—

The trouble was, though, I knew in one part of me that she was right. St Bede's St Cuthbert was a wonderful yarn after all, the kind of transforming bulls' wool we can never do without and a perfect example of Janet's sacred imagination at work. A part of me knew that. Another part of me, though, with a completely different kind of knowing, knew with the same intensity with which she knew she was right that she was *wrong*. In the light of this kind of knowing her ideas looked half-baked, and when you pressed at them the way I was starting to press at them they began to look silly and immature: and, particularly (this is what really bothered me), they looked devoid of social responsibility. If she wanted to live and tell a kind of truth, in a world that was worthy of the word and where there was some sort of shape and purpose and *meaning* to things, what was the point of trying to get away from responsibility, to get away from society, to get away from *people*—?

Meanwhile, by the way, she was making no attempt to counter what I'd said and in fact had fallen so completely silent as to give the impression that she was barely present at all. And so a conversation about language and communication had brought about a deep silence between the two people who'd been having it! The jug of water on the element began to chuff and wheeze, sweat gathered on its spout. I pushed the open tin of honey across the counter towards her and found I was raising my eyebrows in her direction. She caught

79

this sign language and abruptly nodded back, as if she was waking out of some dream about St Cuthbert and the otters: she straightened and seized knife and toast.

We sat there at the counter, Janet and I, finishing our breakfast while the water boiled, as far apart from each other (I'd imagine) as we'd ever been since her arrival. It was as if our language had been sucked away from us. In its place there was the sound of the water in the jug on the element, seething bubbling rattling as if there were nothing else in the world but itself, and there was the size of the room, and the light coming into it—and then, suddenly, a clatter of sparrows on the roof, shrill, harsh, almost deafening. The world, pressing in at us. When I stirred my tea it sounded like someone rowing a boat.

As you can imagine, I dwelt on this strange episode for some time after it happened. And the more I did, the more it worried me. What if she was writing nonsense—what if I was inadvertently encouraging my house-guest to spend six to eight hours of her day (more, sometimes: sometimes I had to *urge* her in for her supper) devoting her energies to something that was of absolutely no value whatever? I'd known of cases like this, particularly among the naïve young, where a year of earnest writing had produced three hundred pages of equally earnest claptrap. I'd written such tripe myself when not much different from the age Janet was now: indeed at one point of my febrile self-deluded barminess I'd thought I was writing a significant original work of my own creation when what I was actually doing each solemn day in the public library was copying out word for word the published work of someone else!

These thoughts possessed me as I sat out each terrible morning in front of my typewriter, and stayed with me through each afternoon while I did my winter work in the garden. Of this, given the large amount of time I'd already devoted to it in the absence of my muse, there was little enough left: but I pressed on nonetheless with the business of strawing the rhubarb to quicken a few early sticks and covering the newly planted peas and beans with prunings from the fruit trees. The cabbage stumps of late summer had produced their little secondary heads, and I cut these to put on the table the only fresh greens we were likely to eat for a while. Then there was always the business of planting the seed trays for that moment in early spring when the weeds begin to grow again and tell us it is time once more to harden off the tray plants and begin the business of seeding.

Doing all this, of course, took me around and about the army hut, from which issued more often than not the relentless machine-gun fire of Janet's typing. No part of my garden seemed proof to her racket except the front, nearest the road, which with its bit of lawn and clump of loquat trees needed the least attention. Necessity condemned me, then, to the rear, and therefore to the unending reminder of my fallen status as mere artisan of the body and no longer of word and thought: and (it seemed to me) the unending reminder, too, of who it was who'd usurped that role. And so we worked together, Janet and I, my hands busy in the seeding trays on two old kitchen tables I'd wedged against the rear wall of the hut, on the other side of which her fingers were even busier on the keys of her Olivetti. As the days went on and the trays accumulated with their rows of little plants I would take peeks at her through the buckled wartime glass of her little window and see a rippling Janet at work, her back impressively straight and shoulders square, head slightly forward and brow knotted as her brawny practical hands punched words relentlessly across her page. So nearly incessant was her clatter that the occasional break in it drew my attention: I would look up sharply when this happened, and see her caught in puzzlement for a moment or bent to one side to consult what I imagined were notes she'd made on her well-planned path through her work. And then back to it she would fall, and to the steady, rhythmical *ratatatat* of its execution, each thump a blow to my very heart.

Given all this dogging me day and night, the thought of trespass became inevitable. At some point I began to consider the possibility of creeping across the Rubicon of my back lawn and into the hut while she was elsewhere. Can you blame me? It was after all, and when all was said and done, my hut—well, this was one of the ways in which I justified the thought to myself. The other was to convince myself that Janet had almost certainly done the same to me already, that is to say she'd almost certainly (I found myself deciding) had a good look around my little demesne when my own back was turned. Why would she not? As you can see, she was increasingly manifesting herself to me as rather more than first had met my eye, and in fact as someone it would be even more difficult to sum up in a word than is the case with most of us: and in turn with my various absences (including a trip up the coast to Solomon that proved he was getting no better over the winter, by the way), I'd given her plenty of opportunity to pry.

In truth there had not been the slightest sign throughout this time that she'd actually done so: or, to turn the notion on its head, in effect she had done nothing else and therein lay my privacy. For the cottage was never locked, and whether I was in it or out she required access to my facilities morning noon and night and had them freely—indeed it was at night that I occasionally heard her come into the very room in which I slept, since it was onto my single bedroom that the cottage's only outside door let. I'd rigged up bed-sheets to provide a sort of makeshift passage from outer to inner door (Frank's Back Passage, Lawrence Guigan christened it), and lying in my bed on the other side I more than occasionally heard her tiptoe in and then, after a few minutes and the flush of the water-convenience through the wall, back out again, never disturbing the sheets of cloth that hung between us. There was no mystery, in other words, with everything open to her and nothing withheld—and, given the tragic state of my productivity at the time, precious little to withhold anyway: with the ironic result as it seemed to me at least, that I felt most fully clothed when caught most nearly naked.

Her hut, on the other hand, was accumulating mystery each time I passed it. There were those glimpses through the window, as in a flickering picture at the cinema, and as if her public fame were already upon her, of the artist at work: and since on sunny days she often kept her door open I could see her through the doorway as well, a quarter turned away from me as she hammered obliviously at the keys: and saw, too, a pile of green paper by her left hand and tried to guess as I ducked away with barrow fork or spade how many pages it represented. It seemed so long ago now since I'd produced a comparable heap that I could scarcely estimate where she might have got to in hers—a hundred? More? Fewer, surely fewer—and back I would trundle my barrow for another sideways glimpse at a mound of accumulating greenery far different from my mere clippings and sweepings, and larger (I felt sure of this) by an appreciable amount each time I saw it. A hundred, surely there were a hundred pages beside her typewriter by now. Dear God—!

Then, one afternoon, inevitably, she dropped her guard and left the hut and property. Not far, only by foot to the local shops with her string bag of library books: but she left me with the pumping heart of an adolescent freed to his own grubby mischief. Her door was open: I tried to ignore the fact as I walked past it with tools and barrow. And in truth I had urgent things to do, since the frame for my runner beans had toppled of its own weight in early autumn and it was long past time I did something about it. I was still cramming my mind full of worthy concerns and comparisons like this when I found my body had taken me to the hut nevertheless,

83

to the gaping door, to the threshold of whatever it was that separated Janet and me—and there I stopped, at the broken step in front of it, and went no further. It seemed clear (and I felt this with intense relief) that I could never trespass, that whatever happened I would never betray her, or indeed myself, by going in. And so I stood, looking into the tenebrous light of a space that seemed to me almost sacred: like a glimpse, perhaps, into one of the cathedrals I'd seen all those years before in northern Italy during my *wanderjahre*—

Within which inner sanctum it seemed, all the same, that there was nothing much to be found. Of *things*, of course, objects, evidences of the resisting world, there were plenty, but none that made any immediate sense to me: nothing that added up as I first stood there (and thus in truth, I suppose it could be said, plenty that might be thought adequately to represent Janet herself). To the right her bed, no more than a cot but neatly made up, and to the left her desk with the Olivetti firmly cased and (as far as I could see) paperless—in fact the entire place was free of significant paper, I saw as I quizzed it, and with no tell-tale piles of completed typescript or even single scribbled sheets that might give me any clue to what it was she was up to—notes, I mean, or a plan or even a diagram. Instead, as I say, things, the golden foil from the bars of chocolate she used to buy, neatly smoothed and stacked save one or two pieces torn off and twisted into those tiny make-believe goblets children shape over the end of a finger, a slew of walnuts from a brown paper bag, a photograph of a group at the beach (I peered: which one was she?), a pair of scissors, a scatter of pencils, a large puff of cotton wool, and then, here and there around her typewriter, little scraps of paper torn from the green foolscap sheets I'd recommended for the protection of her eyesight. And that was all.

Well—not quite. There was a smell—no no no, I don't mean that badly: a scent, almost, there was a faint scent of

84

something that started to come to me as I stood at the door looking this way and that (and also, every few seconds, across my shoulder in case I was about to be taken by embarrassing surprise). My eyes quartered the place and my mind dealt with nothing else, until the smell began to insist on itself and I realised it was there, that I had already been dealing with the puzzle of it in some part of my being before I became fully conscious of its presence. It lingered, insistent, asking me questions, asking me a question: decay, perhaps, but decay that had turned to something else, sweeter and more nearly inevitable and omnipresent, *in* things like an essence, and vegetal, something which made me wonder for a moment if it indeed came from within the hut after all—

I looked about—and there it was, explaining itself in front of me: a pepper on the windowsill—

Now, when I tell you it must have been about June or July that I was making this unauthorised intrusion upon Janet's life (three or four months after her arrival and a day I remember as having a stony, unchanging light and those ever-present drifts of rain that sweep lightly across the isthmus at any time of year) you will begin to have some idea what it was that I was looking at. If I didn't make half my living from growing and harvesting the damned things during the summer months and into autumn, I doubt I would have known it for what it had become in the middle of our winter. A pepper, without a doubt: shrivelled, blackened, probably half its original size now but a pepper nonetheless, put on the sill to ripen perhaps, and then left there and left there to become something else, this memento of itself and of whatever that something else had come to mean to the occupant of my hut. That and the slew of walnuts on the desk did their trick, and here it came as if unbidden, the thing which as I slowly began to form my version of these events once I was back in the cottage and, later, in my bed that evening, came to seem more and more to be the very thing that I'd gone there to find in the first place. A shrivelled capsicum!

For it took me back to that strange conversation about the peppers that we'd had not long after she came to me, and her trip to the poor old greengrocer and all that it entailed. Naturally, thinking of the peppers made me think of the business that I've just related, about St Cuthbert and his otters. And of all things, that made me think back to Sir Thomas Browne, and a marvellous passage I read once in his *Religio* where he talks about *the wingy mysteries in divinity that have unhinged the brains of better heads than mine*, and the need to approach these mysteries through reason, not experience. What I have always taken that passage to mean (quite apart from anything else he might have intended by it) is that experience unmediated is experience with no meaning in itself at all. Well, here was experience unmediated if I ever saw it, and as I lay there I could feel the pull of it, the lure of its giddy, frightening mystery.

So you can see that by this stage of my adventure with her, and without her having shown me a single page of her work, she had me well and truly caught up in her baffling, curious and plain old *odd* way of seeing the world. I could still make no sense of her, it's true, but at least I was starting to feel there might be some sense to be made. But at the same time there was that pull of the opposite, towards—who knew what?

And most of all I was starting to see there was no doubt that the way of her thought was completely different from any way I'd ever thought myself, and I could apprehend that if it *did* make sense and it *did* work out for her it'd lead to writing of a sort the exact opposite of how I wrote myself— irony of ironies, since I can clearly remember telling dear old Harry one night years ago as he sat up behind me in his cot perusing his *Friday Flash* that I'd just discovered a way of writing completely fresh and new! Well, her way would be different, it seemed, and, curiously, the business of the peppers and the walnuts and the otters was a part of it, I was becoming sure of that. I was becoming sure that those things and the bits and pieces of writing on her desktop were, all of them, part of something new she seemed to be working out for herself—

And I found myself thinking again, as I lay there in my cot at night on what Sir Thomas would undoubtedly have called the *spear side* of the hanging bed-sheet, of the phrase that had kept returning to me ever since it first came into my mind:

Sir, do you know me?

Madam, I do not—

CHAPTER 4

And then on the other hand there was another Janet, someone who was so completely different from the first that she could hardly have been the same person. Always of course there was the unfamiliar female presence that obliged me to turn on the wireless radio each time I visited the convenience and put up the wooden seat again and again during the course of the day as often as she let it down. And there was the everyday houseguest who put spoons in the knife drawer and forgot to hang the tea towel up, and worst of all got in amongst my books. But on the other hand there was the Janet who suddenly manifested quite soon after her arrival, when Margaret Guigan and I were beginning the annual business of bottling: as soon as *this* Janet saw what we were up to she dropped everything and got stuck into the picking of the nectarines plums and greengages and then the washing of them: and by the time we got to boiling the syrup and scalding the glass jars she'd almost taken over the whole shooting match! I exaggerate, of course (no one ever really takes anything over from Margaret Guigan once she has set her mind to it), but only to give some sense of the magnitude of the change that had taken place in my houseguest.

And in subsequent months she often proved to be the same—not with actual housework I can assure you, since (as with various other female artistes I have known over the years) housework was not especially to her taste: but I mean about the kitchen, in which I found that from time to time she'd suddenly and abruptly fall-to as if someone had thrown a switch and turned her into the very Angel of the Hearth. Baking was one of the activities that unexpectedly appeared at these moments, at which times I'd find my kitchen commandeered and the floor crunching with sugar till I had to rummage out dustpan and brush. Where she got such ingredients from I have no idea, since chocolate sugar syrup and (often) even butter were hardly ongoing staples of my cupboard: but mixed into sticky rows they would be slid into my long-suffering oven, and in due course out they would come again, transformed into ginger crunch and Chinese chews and Anzac biscuits and other oddly-named gewgaws from the Edmonds cookbook—which household Bible she claimed, by the way, to have carried with her for years in a pink embroidered bag alongside a couple of other volumes whose names she would not divulge to me, as mainstays that had kept her going: though through what particular experiences, as I have said, she would not say—

Now it appalled me how little I could resist these confections when once they appeared, and how eagerly my friends fell upon them too, whenever they came by to visit and found that Janet had been slaving over a hot stove again. In fact it was the prospect of the wine-tasting party I'd mentioned to her soon after her arrival that first set her off. I'd no sooner told her that a handful of people might be dropping by the following afternoon for conversation musical entertainment and what have you than she seemed galvanised in the manner I have indicated, with the result that by the time Margaret Guigan, Lyall Neary and a couple of others were manhandling Lawrence's wheelchair down my pathway for our afternoon (and as it proved, evening) of entertainment—there they were, still cooling on their trays at the open kitchen window, the biffs bangs crunches and chews that Janet had spent an overheated afternoon manufacturing (yes, their names really are quite extraordinary). *Ah, Bisto!* was Lawrence's contribution as he was jostled over my threshold sniffing with his head thrown theatrically back, and *Your lodger?* his wife's as she managed his wheelchair in. Of course I tried to make out the fancy grub was my own work, but as it turned out no one was specially interested in where it had come from because what they were specially interested in was where it was going.

And as I joined in the gobbling and the licking I couldn't help feeling what the lady novelists call *a twinge of unease*, something to do in this case with the self-indulgence of it all and particularly the way the sugar the cocoa the coconut and all the rest of it sat so ill with what followed straight afterwards, the home-made pumpkin wine which Lawrence had brought with him and begun to force on people straight away—the latter Margaret's phrase, by the way, though I do have to admit my guests seemed unanimous in their belief that the wine disagreed with the baking and not the other way about. By the time of the little gathering I am describing, the slightly disconcerting orange-grey sludge that was once my pumpkins had long ago been deposited into a cocoon of muslin through which, over a period of weeks, my precious drops of wine had made their way. For surely wine is what it was by now, I kept telling myself each time I visited Lawrence's garage and checked the rows of bottles, each regularly tweaked a quarter turn as the wine-maker had confidently advised. Surely Mother Nature was taking its course inside each vessel and I was about to be rewarded with what would be her veritable essence, something as little intervened on as possible and truly a natural elixir of life.

In fact as it turned out our pumpkin wine was a sad disappointment, although I kept a brave face and drank off a couple of glasses with a simulation of gusto. But young Lyall, who had once survived much of a bottle of illicit Hokonui whisky in my presence not long after I first met him, fell silent after a couple of swigs of my product and retired to a corner to reflect. There was no doubt that fermentation and then the subtler processes that followed had turned the liquid into something other than pumpkin yeast and sugar: but the question remained whether *what* it had turned it into was something better or something significantly worse. Bit cloudy Frank, was Lawrence's verdict as he swirled it in a wineglass he'd brought along, and then he put it to his nose. What d'you think? I asked anxiously after he had taken a few snuffs, although at heart I'd always thought he was a bit of a bluffer in matters of taste and refinement if not the arts. Retained its nose, he said, whatever that was supposed to mean, and then he swigged it back and held it in his mouth. Well—? I demanded, and there was a pause as he swallowed. Well at least it's not vinegar, he said. At least there's that. He held the glass out to me for more. But does it induce oblivion, he said. Always the question with wine—

Well, induce oblivion it certainly did, though at the time I couldn't see there was more to the business than that because I hadn't seen the true nature of the battle which (in effect) was being fought out that night between my home products and Janet's. Now, of course, a year later and as I look back through everything that was to happen between us, it's obvious enough to me what it all might be thought to stand for. But back then as the food and the drink began their contest during the course of the evening it seemed no more than a matter of pride. First Lyall crept outside around ten or eleven and then Gordon Garlick and after a few minutes his boyfriend as well, the fancy pup he'd brought with him from the varsity. It's that rubbish you've been eating, I said, as after quite a bit they came trailing back in one by one—well, as Lyall and Gordon came trailing back in one by one, since the fancy pup stayed stranded outside. Still having a spit, Lyall said, watching through the window. Well what'd you expect, I said, if you insist on eating food that's got no goodness in it whatsoever? And when Margaret said that fears of nutritional over-refinement hadn't appeared to stop me from wading into the biffs and the bangs myself, I countered with the view that it was the scientist in me that had driven me on in my explorations. At least I knew when to stop, I said. When to stop! she said. It was you that led the charge!

All this was rather undermined I have to admit by the fact that at this stage I had a twinge or two myself lower down and was beginning to wonder what it might all be starting to amount to. And it was further and far more significantly undermined when Lawrence suddenly and without warning let fly. Get that will you, he said, and began to dab feebly at his front. He always tried to carry things off whenever he disgraced himself like this: but really there was no joke for Margaret and me in the following half hour or more of tidying him up as well as the wheelchair and surrounding floor. We had to fling the door and windows open, and at that time of the year too: in which process by the way we were able to glimpse Gordon's varsity ragamuffin prettily posed on all fours at the base of the loquat trees like Narcissus looking into the pool, although undoubtedly considerably less pleased with what it was that looked back at him.

It was plain my little party was ruined, and as we mopped and rinsed and squeezed I couldn't let go the notion that it was Janet had done the ruining with her precious sweetmeats. But when I revived this thought Margaret would have none of it. Oh what *nonsense*, Frank, she said from beside me where we knelt and scrubbed. I didn't touch your rotgut and I'm the only one not affected. *I'm* not either, I said. Yes you are, she said. You're rumbling away like the hot water cylinder, you'll explode any minute and then we'll have to do all this again. And then *How're you feeling?* at her husband, who was laid out on the divan to which the two of us had manhandled him from his little chariot. She went on dabbing at the floor. Those cakes are delicious, she said. There's not

92

a thing wrong with them, *I'm* not throwing up am I. Yes but combined with the wine, I said. Oh, nonsense, Margaret said. She seems very domesticated to me, very talented this Fame girl of yours. Frame, I said. Janet Frame. And she's not a girl she's a woman. Frame, said Margaret. Anyway where is she, this *woman*, why isn't she here, where're you hiding her?

And that was a very good question indeed. Even at that early stage it was no surprise to me that Janet had slipped away when she heard the sound of the Guigans' car door, since as I've said slipping away is what she'd tended to do whenever visitors turned up. A door slamming the sound of voices the crunch of foot on seashell path and like the witches in *Macbeth* she made herself air into which she vanished. This had been so consistent a pattern that for the first few months of her time with me I didn't bother to mention her existence to most of my callers since in the social sense she seemed in fact hardly to exist at all. But the Guigans knew about her and Lyall too after a fashion since he'd glimpsed her a couple of times at a distance, and indeed it was he who brought us the startling information on this occasion of the party I'm describing and the drinking of the pumpkin wine that she was, as far as could be determined, really and truly off the property. No she's not in the hut, he said when I told Margaret that that was where she always hid so that was where she'd be. But apparently Lyall had had a look in the hut since the door just happened to be open, and he said that she just happened to be gone. Scarpered, he said. Flown!

In point of fact she'd pulled this kind of stunt before, when I'd caught her ironing. This was another of those unexpected transformations that would occur when suddenly and without the slightest warning it was as if Calliope had turned into Aunt Daisy herself with her handy household hints on wireless radio. I'd no ironing tackle of my own, instead wore my clothing gathered like fresh fruit from the bushes on which I spread each garment after every wash and where they usually dried to the colour of snow. Less often I'd skip the wash entirely and hang my clothes on the line unlaundered, to be rinsed for a day or two by sun and wind. Well, when I came in one day she'd all these items gathered up as well as a thing or two of her own, and was working away at them with a tiny iron clutched in her sturdy unadorned hand—she had a blanket across my little table in the front room and was pressing one of my tea towels on it, if you please! Good God woman, who irons tea towels? I asked her, after a little pause to get used to the fact of her intrusion since that in a sense is what it was. What next, the carpet? Carpet? she said, looking around my bare boards, and as occasionally happened there was a slight doubt that she was quite in on the joke.

Anyway, that is how we handled the occasion, with me showing no offence and Janet telling me her friend Molly had bought her the iron as part of a campaign to help her *settle down and find her feet* and that the only reason she had accepted it was that it was supposed to be a *travelling iron*. Just as she liked shop signs she always enjoyed those wonderfully rich and empty phrases people use in their everyday lives, and gave them a special arch emphasis whenever she said them. In this case she was particularly intrigued by the notion of an iron that might suddenly decide to pack itself up and take itself off in order to see the world. Where would it go? I wondered aloud as I began preparing our evening meal: and after we both agreed it would be *pressing business* wherever it was, off we took the fancy together (*Ireland, Iona, the Gold Coast, Silver City, Preston* and what have you) until we made the link between *iron* and *irony* and wondered a little about that. And it wasn't until somewhat later in my time with her that I understood the significance of *that* little journey, as I will tell you a little later in *this* one—

94

But first comes the appalling moment a month or two later, alas, when in I bumped from lunch at the Peking in town, a leisurely hour reading in the Progressive Bookshop and then the ferry trip across the harbour—and found her ironing one of Harry's shirts! Now, I'd got used to finding her occasionally at work with the pressing and the folding, just as I'd got used to the steady unpredictability of the absences of these episodes and the weeks that went by with both of us wearing clothes not unpleasantly crumpled. But here she was, pressing the *travelling iron* into the pale blue plaid of one of the shirts Harry had left behind, and something far less playful was let loose in me. *What in God's name d'you think you're doing*—? was out of my mouth before I had even thought it.

We stood there, breathing at each other, not moving.

Naturally, Harry's relics always lay about the place as they'd done for twenty years and more, and equally naturally Janet came across one or other of them from time to time. Early on for example I found myself fumbling along in a conversation about horse racing that she'd astonished me by bringing up herself, when I suddenly realised that she'd mistaken me for an enthusiast of the turf on the basis of a stray *Friday Flash* that Harry had left next to the convenience. She'd just been trying to please me!—and that was the first really good laugh we had together, or at least that is how I remember it, as I and then after a moment she realised we'd both been bluffing and that neither of us cared a jot about the very topic both of us had been precariously rubbing up together for five minutes or even six, each working on the basis that the other had an interest in bloodstock throbbing along their veins. I've never been near a racetrack in my life! she said when I asked, and I explained in turn that despite my best efforts my only interest in them was less the form of the nags than the form of the former jockey who from time to time escorted me to watch them racing, both of us in our Sunday best as we rubbed shoulders with the Great Unwashed.

But Harry's clothing minus Harry seemed to be another thing. That it was so came to me only as I stood there in front of her holding his shirt in my hand, with its frayed collar that he'd turned himself with laborious needle and thread—I'd snatched it from her, I must have: here it was, bunched in my fist. She looked utterly terrified and I can't blame her: something in my strange over-reaction terrified me, too, welling up as it did from parts unknown. What in God's name was she doing: but, then, what in God's name was I—?

We stood there.

I thought I'd press your shirts for you, she whispered across to me—barely even a whisper. I thought you'd be pleased, she said.

We stood there, neither of us knowing what to do. Then she propped the iron at the end of the table and switched it off at the wall.

Excuse me, she said, and slipped out. She was behind me and gone. She disappeared.

And that is what I mean: she *disappeared*. I do not use the word lightly. She dematerialised from the planet Earth as far as I was able to see, and for the rest of the day evening night and dawn could be found nowhere on it. When I first began to realise something of this I searched the house. Then I tried the section front to back, and knocked on the door of the hut, and went out and stood on the road and even walked a length of it in one direction and a length of it in the other. One of my neighbours was at his front lawn with a mower as I went past, and I paused: had he seen a young lady passing by? Young lady? he said, and took a bit of a look at me, I thought. No, he hadn't seen any young lady wandering past. Nor any old ones either, he called after me. And so back into the house I went, and up and down the garden again, and after that of course I was knocking at her doorpost once more and, still hearing nothing, pushing at the door gently, tap-tapping as I went and half-expecting to see her inert form up on the bed, life taken. But no: no Janet, and it seemed indeed no life to take. She'd gone, gone utterly, like one of those Indian fakirs who are rumoured to be able to disappear up lengths of rope and into the sky. I even had a look up there when I thought that particular thought, into the late afternoon haze and the higher cirrus, and if I had in fact spotted her up there looking back down at me like the man in the moon I'd have been only somewhat more surprised than I was the following morning when—there she was, after the inevitable tap-tap and *hullo* at the door, ready for her breakfast!

Where did you get to? I asked as I spilled the porridge into her bowl. At first she affected not to know what I was talking about and it was as if the business with the shirt had never happened. But I pressed at her. Yesterday afternoon, last night, I said, as I did the business with the yeast and the honey. You weren't here, when did you get back—?

I was here all the time, she said. So there was nowhere to come back from—

Well, I didn't see you, I said, and I was looking around for you.

Then perhaps you were looking in the wrong place, she said, calm as could be and working a spoon at the surface of her porridge. Perhaps you should have looked at the edge of things—

The edge of what things, I wanted to know.

Words perhaps, she said, and looked up at me as she supped her porridge. Perhaps I slipped out of the language and you couldn't find me, she said. Perhaps that's what happened. There's always places where words stop, you know, they can't go on forever. Words stop and then there's nothing because the words make the things—

Well, this was all a bit too fanciful for me and not a little strange as I'm sure you can see. I fell silent, but as I worked away at my porridge I had to admit that if anyone could do what she was talking about it would be Janet—because she had so completely and utterly disappeared the night before, that is what I am trying to say. The absoluteness of it frightened me a bit. It brought back the feeling I'd had forty years before when Signor Bosco and Son visited town and caused Archie Scott to disappear. I still remember the gasp of the audience when the magician opened the door of his cabinet onstage and we all saw that Archie had gone, our little classmate who'd volunteered to get inside it: the sudden lurch in reality, the translation to another dimension—besides, what would his family say, wouldn't they miss him? And the world he talked about afterwards, when once the magician had brought him back and we were able to ask him nay *beg* him to say where it was he'd been—*that* never went away either, not completely, not the pure wonder of it when first he told how once inside the magic cabinet and locked away he'd heard the sound of singing, a veritable choir in the heavens beyond him, and how he'd had been carried up towards a light, an intense white light, before—suddenly—waking up back inside the magician's box.

It changed over the weeks, this version of his travels to the stars, as we followed him around the playground and begged him to tell it to us just one more time and he began to launch further and further into the cosmos and meet stranger and stranger creatures along the way: but as his believers dropped off one by one I it was who remained loyal to the end, so much did I need to feel again that belt in the stomach, that urge to believe there was more to things than the daily world presented to us.

Naturally, when in due course and with no little reluctance I entered that daily world, I tried to put those things away as (alas) we are instructed by our betters to do. And I made a pretty good fist of it, I like to think, gradually drawn as I was by my reading and my day-to-day experiences and especially by the reassuring way each seemed to reinforce the other in what seemed like a measured progression towards the confirmation of what was around me. This world, once I began to understand it, was obviously a bit short on heavenly choirs and intense white light: but on the other hand it proved to have subtle attractions of its own, ironies delicacies and patterns some of which I've already described. Harry's apparition in my Christological year seemed wondrously to confirm it as a world *fallen but foursquare*, full of compensations once you learned where to look for them. And it was to the recording of these modest, unassuming riches that I'd begun to devote my art.

But here once more, suddenly, courtesy my curious houseguest, was the world of Archie Scott—and once more that feeling, that primitive yearning babyhood twinge that comes when our earliest needs are touched on. I finished my porridge and went about the business of making toast: but all the time a boy again, more than some of me, however I might have appeared to the gaze of others. Could she see that, though, did she know?

And it was about that time, and almost certainly in consequence of the unfortunate business with Harry's shirt, that I first tried to explain to Janet the man's significance to me.

Now I want to tell you about a mate of mine, I began, and went on as best I could to square the conversational circle by telling her everything while at the same time not really telling her too much at all. In truth I just wanted to get the business of my over-reaction behind me so as to seem less strange, to myself as much as to her. So when Harry's here, I told her as I tried to sum things up, we—live together. In the hut? she wanted to know, and when I said yes, sometimes, she said so he's a writer then. Not really I said, and tried to explain. I told her a little of how we'd met, Harry and I, a very little, and of how things had developed since then, the great deal that we shared and the great deal we kept to ourselves: and particularly I told her of our habit, strange to some, of spending lengthy periods apart. Throughout all this she listened (as I remember it) with the puzzling mix of expressionless fascination I'd already learned to expect from her, an attentiveness conveyed in some other way (you might say) than by the muscles of her face. Part of it was conveyed in her reply, given after a full minute of reflection:

So he's your copy, she said. You write, and he's what you write about—

Well, it's obvious enough to me now what she meant, but when I heard these words I thought for a moment she meant Harry was a copy of *me*, that we were twins of a sort, and it brought me up short because in our nineteen years together I'd never had pause to think of us like that—the joy of him had always been that he didn't require thinking about at *all*, except in the obvious doggy day-to-day ways: I mean that he didn't need to be detached from the medium he came in, he didn't need to be thought about as a separate thing. In fact he couldn't possibly *be* detached and that was the point of him, he was part of the *polloi*, he was part of the very stuff of life. Harry was the material I wrote about, he was what I copied, since there was little need but to get all of him down as he was, so to speak, Harry and everything else he stood in for if I could manage it. And in fact that was what Janet actually meant, as I'm sure you'll have seen from the start.

All the same that first brief impression of unexpected twinship stayed with me, so that over the next few days and weeks I fell to wondering what *was* the true nature of the relationship between the two of us, Harry and me, and whether he really was someone separate or just a copy of some sort. Of course it was not the best moment for these questions to be put to me given his lengthening absence from my current life: in that growing gulf the implications of his silence could ferment and ferment like the yeast in my cylinder cupboard, and were capable of yielding the same sour taste in the end. If he wasn't a copy, then who was he and did I really know him after all? And if he *was* just a copy, what was it that I'd been writing about for nearly twenty years, him or me? Was it all 'out there', as I'd assumed, or was everything actually where Janet herself seemed to me increasingly to believe it was, 'in here'? Were we in fact, each one of us, just making things up all the time, and had I been wrong throughout my entire career—could it be (the thought began dismayingly to offer itself to me) that all this time it had been *me* and not *her* who'd been barking up the wrong tree?

Well, she turned up for breakfast the morning after the party the pastries and the pumpkin wine, just as she'd turned up for breakfast after her first disappearance. What with the strangeness of the reply she'd given when I asked her where she'd been that first time I took care not to mention the matter after the second, but the topic came up anyway, buoyed by her apparent eagerness to talk about the party and the very things she seemed to have gone to so much trouble to avoid. Yes, much appreciated by all, I replied when she asked me how her cooking had gone down, although I didn't go into much detail about the various ways in which it had come back up again and the possible role of my home-made wine in bringing that misfortune about. See, it's all disappeared, I said. Not a single thing left for the tins. People seem to like your recipes. Well, the recipes just came out of a book, she said modestly, and fell to her breakfast.

And then, after a second or two:

Was that Mr Guigan in the wheelchair? Last night—?

I went on briefly with my porridge. I'd told her about the Guigans as I had told her about most of my friends over the several months she'd been with me, and she'd even been forced to make fleeting conversation with one or two of them when taken by surprise and unable to find cover in sufficient time. Little Ben was one, as I've noted, and Lyall another, a couple of times, till she was able to flee in confusion: and I've mentioned her heroic performance with Margaret Guigan the preserving pan the Mason jars and the fruit, when for a higher cause she sustained human contact for an entire afternoon. Of Lawrence she was well enough aware and at that point might even have actually met him at some stage and his wheelchair as well. But what was going on here, what was she doing asking me a question like that if she'd just spent the night at the edge of things as she'd earlier claimed she was able to do—if she'd disappeared off the planet, why was she suddenly trying to draw attention to the possibility that after all she'd been on it all the time? What was she up to, what game was she playing?

I decided to hedge my bets.

Yes, I said. Always has to be carried in, poor sod—

We bowed our heads over our bowls. For a few moments the work of our spoons was in tandem, like oars. What next?

He called you a Jew—

I stopped and looked up:

Lawrence did—?

He said, *I wish the old Jew would stump up for an outside light.* When they were carrying him out—

Where had she been to hear that? But I held steady:

The chap who built this place for me was a Jew. Perhaps he meant him—

It made the motorbike man laugh, she said.

Ah, yes—Lyall Neary, he helped carry Lawrence in and out—

Now this really caught her attention. Her spoon stopped: she looked up: *Neary?* she said. It seemed to excite her.

102

Yes—

I stared at her.

Is that really his name—?

Yes. Lyall Neary—you heard it before, or something—?

N-e-a-r-y—?

N-e-a-r-y—

What a wonderful name!

Is it—?

Well—think about it—

I was baffled.

Neary—

Still baffled—

—it's nearly—

Ah—!

Nearly *nearly*—! I said.

We both sat there laughing.

See? she said. You have to look near the edge of things—

It was very satisfying, I must admit, even though as far as I was able to see at the time it was just a game. She clapped her hands with delight, and in fact I'd never seen her quite as happy in our four or five months together to that point. *Lyall Nearly, nearly: nearly Lyall Nearly.* Well, now—

The thing is, though, that what Janet gave me like this turned out to have been a remarkable insight. As I sit here now trying to sum things up its accuracy as the young man's epitaph almost overwhelms me. For, as I have come to realise in the time of Janet's stay with me, Lyall Neary is indeed *nearly*—nearly an artist, nearly a writer, nearly a decent human being: truly a nearly-man. Before she came into my life, I had begun to wonder, reading his strange unpublished half-prose half-verse scribbled on the backs of things, whether he might in fact be the coming man, the young writer whose appearance would validate everything of a preparatory nature that had been done over the years by pioneers like me. In the time since, it is not untrue to say

103

that I have come more and more to wonder whether in fact
the idea of a coming man has anything whatever to do with
(as you might say) the price of fish. But if in fact it *does*, and
has some meaning after all, then I'm bound to say that more
and more it is becoming obvious to me who that individual
might really be—

Meanwhile, having delivered herself of this profundity
about Lyall, off Janet went in her angel-of-the-hearth routine,
collecting up the breakfast dishes and assembling them in the
sink behind me as I sat at the counter thinking the things that
had begun to press in on me. There was the smell of soap in
hot water the cluck and clatter of plates and bowls in the sink
and the sound of her humming to herself—and to me it felt
like a performance, unnervingly enough to make me stand,
suddenly, and leave the house to get away from it. After all
my earlier work there was little enough to do in the garden
after all, as I have related, and I stood there doing it, glad to
be loitering amongst the wintering vegetables and watching
the house until she came out. Her solidity and cheerfulness
unnerved me: worse than that, they seemed *intended* to
unnerve me. I was beginning to feel well and truly caught up
in something—

For a long time my life had been pretty straightforward:
for months now I'd got up each morning, mooched around
checked the letterbox kidded the cats and then let the absence
of Harry wash pleasurably over me. It rinsed through
everything that remained to each day, giving a depth of
richness to its colours and sounds and plangent tonality to the
simplest of its objects and events. Washing the dishes after a
lonely meal, for example, was a chore elevated to the feeling
and delicacy almost of an operatic aria, one from Puccini
perhaps, with me a hapless Cio-Cio San to Harry's heartless
American lieutenant—yes yes, all very self-indulgent I know,
and ridiculous, I know that too: and all of it nothing, nothing

at all to the frank joy I felt each time I heard the crunch on the seashell pathway and saw that my own elderly and somewhat dishevelled Pinkerton had actually returned to me once more. I do know the difference between my various kinds of happiness, and I know which one I truly prefer.

Against this certainty, though, Janet seemed now to be leading me away from myself and out onto quicksand. Or was she?—looked at objectively, she'd done nothing: nothing beyond giving me a right royal gingering-up, that is. Over the years, as it happens, I've never been short of friends willing to tell me I am over-susceptible to this sort of brooding and who are also of the opinion that I need the help of no one else in order to bring blossom and fruit to the great unpruned tree of my wild imaginings. And maybe that was true, maybe I *had* been giving myself the ding-bats, maybe I *had* been leading myself up the garden path, who knows? But whatever the answer, it is not untrue to say that in due course it was up the garden path I found I was leading myself once more, I mean the actual path that led to Janet's hut, in a blind half-thinking repetition of what I'd done that time she slipped away to the local shops and these same unhealthy thoughts took me to her very threshold: though not, on that occasion, beyond it. But whereas her trips to local shops and library were a regular event that always gave me a precious hour or even sometimes two in which to regain a little equilibrium, this time it was across the harbour and to the city that she'd promised to take herself, and hence it was the entire afternoon and early evening that threatened to be liberated for me—and disastrously so, as it turned out and I will tell, since this longer departure followed immediately on the conversation I've recorded just a moment ago and the dark imaginings it reinforced in me. To put it in Harry's poolroom parlance, she'd left the ball over the pocket. All that was required was for my Caliban self to knock it in—

Which is a way of drawing even my own attention aside

from the crude fact of what it was that I really did that afternoon when Janet turned her back. Deceitfully, furtively, I *entered the army hut*—I did what I thought I'd never do, I crossed her threshold, I stood with pumping heart in the sacral light I'd but glimpsed the last time I'd been there in her absence, I breathed in that strange, vegetal smell once more, faded now, almost a fancy that left the original pepper a spectral presence on the windowsill, presiding over the things I was gradually seeing it had come to represent: words, I found words. This time there was nothing hidden away from me: or so it seemed as I rummaged and fumbled through the leaves and scraps on her tabletop, the little fragments of green paper I'd seen before and which turned out now to have sentences scribbled on them, each in her distinctive blue-and-black schoolgirl cursive with its loops and dots: *Drink me* written on one of them, and on another *Mind your own beeswax*, and on others just a single word: *worsted* and *gypsy* and *hawk* are three that I remember—

I hadn't been sure what I'd expected to find when I went into the little dwelling, but then, suddenly, I found it—me, myself, my name, looking back at me from one of the scraps of paper! Not *Frank* or *Frank Sargeson*, however, or even *Mr Sargeson*, but, disconcertingly, one word: *Fwank*—

I couldn't have been more taken aback if I'd found she'd drawn me naked with exaggerated cartoon genitalia. *Fwank*—a condescending diminutive, or possibly a fond one, or (given the concatenation of letters that followed the initial) even sexual: but whichever it was, it was obviously her version of me, myself in her world, first real evidence I'd been given that I had some kind of status in her private inner life. But was this all that status amounted to?—was this the best she could do with *the father of a nation's fiction*, the man who'd taken her into his life and dwelling to teach her how to live think and write: consign me to a comic turn on the margins of her project, a scrap of paper along with all the trivial jottings doodles word-kites and so on that fall off the sides of a main text as it pursues its headlong career?

Well, I could have made more of this, much more, since betrayal and self-pity are two of my strongest stimulants and I'd barely begun to feast on this unexpected windfall. But it was about this point that I was deflected to something else, the pile of green paper that lay unprotected beside her typewriter, the topmost sheet, the lines of typing, the words themselves, each letter with a hint of blood-red at the bottom from the striped ribbon she always used. Fiction, I realised immediately: fiction that rendered two men talking, or (I read on) mostly one of them talking to the other about the aging process and what it was doing to his body, the devilments of advancing senility and what have you. The other man said little: and why should he be required to speak at all, given how well the author had rendered the voice the character almost the *appearance* of his interlocutor, through phrasing intonations and all those other little tics and mannerisms that begin to give the effect of a living breathing human on the page? All in all it was a bravura performance to be achieved within the space of a single sheet of foolscap, green unlined—

I don't recall at exactly which point of my descent down that page it was that I began slowly to realise why her rendering was so lifelike and what it was she was up to, but it was his final confession to his young friend (as I imagined him to be) that clinched the deal as far as I was concerned. The two men are discussing the challenges of ageing and the frailties of the flesh, particularly in certain matters of some delicacy. Well (Janet's unknown older man confides to his listener), *he* can still manage to take a stand. The question is whether or not it is a firm stand that he manages to take.

For several seconds I was stalled, just standing there and staring at the words on the paper in my hand. Then I dropped the sheet and plunged out of the hut, my ears and cheeks aflame. There was nothing for it but the vegetable patch: there I grabbed the hoe and began to jab it amongst the cabbages and the cauliflowers, now well into early maturity, their green pale against the soil around them. I tried to calm myself. I remembered exactly the conversation I was having when I said those words, to Lawrence Guigan when he and Margaret popped in for lunch a month or two before. Margaret had left him with me while she drove to the local shops, and in her absence Lawrence and I started up a spirited account of our aches and pains, his of course far outweighing mine since a motoring accident had reduced him to a wheelchair soon after their marriage, meaning that in truth there was a very real doubt whether he was able to manage anything at all. Still, we had these conversations from time to time and I always played along with them as if we were a couple of young bucks equally urgent in the business of getting a shot away, as the saying goes, even if it was tacitly agreed that we tended to fire our ordnance in distinctly different directions.

In part I have to admit I was being nosey, trying to find an answer to the question that had dogged me since the pair of them came creaking into my life—Margaret, a handsome and clearly sensual woman, even I could see that, pushing in front of her Lawrence, a husband bunched up in the wheelchair from which he only ever moved when she managed to lug him out and throw him on their bed. And then what? was always and unworthily the question that followed in my mind when I thought of this scene, a curiosity that other friends, when I raised this issue with them behind the Guigans' collective back, always condemned as libidinous and shameful. Quite so, I used to reply: nothing is private to a writer, nothing is out of bounds. Nevertheless, on this particular occasion with Lawrence I had taken care to pitch my conversation in a direction I imagined might eventually bring out the details I sought, and just in case his accident

108

had indeed reduced his ordnance to small arms, so to speak, I made out to him that sometimes in these matters he was not completely alone—a kindness that had been returned to me now in this shocking manner, this invasion of my privacy far surpassing my own invasion of hers in entering the hut to find it in the first place.

Janet must have been listening outside my window. It made my blood run cold to think of it. If on that occasion, of course, when else, and what more had she heard when she did? I jabbed and jabbed with the hoe—my God, she was playing ducks and drakes with me! The sweat came in big drops. And to leave the page there on her desk, of course, meant the obvious thing, didn't it—that she knew I'd find it, that she knew I might be checking up on her? Damn her! She had me snookered, she had me really trapped: I couldn't confront her about it and I couldn't put it out of my mind— couldn't go one way and couldn't go the other!

I stopped hoeing and stood still. Of course: I was one of her fictional characters. I was caught in one of her stories, completely at her mercy, completely under her control. It shocked me to think that for some months she might have had her teeth into me like that: what might she have been saying of me, what had she overheard, what privacies had she spied? Many times over the years, of course, I myself had put people I'd known into stories, family members, friends and acquaintances—even strangers I'd taken a fancy to as having some kind of literary potential, some quality that spoke to me in the fleeting seconds of our passing acquaintance. In some cases I rubbed these people up a bit so that no one would know them and in others I let them stand on the page for all to see, relying on human vanity to ensure that no one actually recognised himself thus exposed. But now the tables were turned, the biter was bit—so *this* is what it was like to be written, to have a creator, to be *possessed*—

There was something so unhealthy about this thought that

for all its sweat and heat my body gave a single shudder, as if a big cold hand had suddenly gripped it from above. I'd fallen under the spell of her words: she spoke, and I moved, she spoke again and I stopped, caught as I was now within her language—a word myself, caught in her sentences, caught in her fiction: *Fwank*. For the first time I was seeing a way of using language that was different from my own, so very different that mine looked naïve silly childish by comparison. Where I had preached to her the task of recording the world bit by bit in its social layers and functions, what men said what men did how they looked and (by implication) the larger things that made them do so—here was a different, darker contract by which *the writer controlled the words on the page to control the very world itself*—

Strange as it was, all this, and briefly as I glimpsed it amidst my tiny vegetable world (and difficult as it is to get down on this page right now in a way that you will get a sense of), I knew it contained a kind of truth. It was the most unpalatable of all truths about art, that told of its unhealthiness, its reliance on neurosis, its closeness to paranoia, its intimacy with wild dreams of conquest and ultimate meaning—

And it was somewhere in all this, in a process that must have lasted only a second or two, that I was a wake-up to her story about St Cuthbert and his otters. Two phrases went through my mind: *I am her otter* and then *I am her other.* I laughed out loud—the pleasure of it! I sound like Janet writing this, I know: but that is the point, she was turning me into herself, and for a moment or two it felt no bad thing. I could taste the drunkenness of the quest, the potty rightness of it, the wonderful wistful magnificence of the desire for a world drawn to the artist by the magical power of the word, birds trees leaves fields folk and farm animals all of them made obedient to our writerly commands. That's what St Cuthbert's *spell* did in St Bede's story (itself in turn another sort of *spell*). He preached, and in swam the otters: or, as Janet

110

might have it, he preached and in swam the whole damned world, caught by *language*, reeled in by *language*. And it was only through this tiny *spell* in Janet's other, these moments suddenly bound into her strange, remarkable, extraordinary mind, that I'd been able to see it.

I'd like to be able to say now that this is the point at which I realised my responsibility to her, that I snapped out of her spell straight away and realised she couldn't go on like this, that if this was what she aspired to she could only produce goblin fantasies of no significance whatever—and what publisher in this day and age would have to do with nonsense like that? I did indeed snap out of this spell (so suddenly and completely that for some time afterwards I was unable to retrieve the insights I have tried to render just above), and in due course I did in fact do my duty by her, as I will tell. But I am ashamed to say that what I did next, and out of nothing better than a desire for vengeance because it seemed that she had bested me, was to try to turn the tables on her, try to play her at her own game. If I could no longer write on the page, I decided, I could do at least as well in the world itself. With what sad results, alas, you will now see—

CHAPTER 5

Margaret Guigan has just departed, after a Saturday afternoon spent helping me clean and tidy the hut now Janet has gone from it. In truth there's been precious little for either of us to do, something Margaret remarked on as the two of us began the business we were really about, storing fruit we'd put up in bottles a couple of months ago when Janet was in the early stages of agonising over the thousand things she knew were fated to go wrong for her as she prepared to pack her luggage and depart. The jars of fruit have been stacked in my bedroom and the front room, along with a dozen things her unexpected arrival squeezed out, pumpkins and garden tools and bags of onions and what have you, all items it will be my pleasant task to restore in the coming weeks to the order that formerly reigned around me (or at least it is my old man's fancy that such unlikely order was once the case).

The pristine state of the army hut astonished Margaret as she swept my broom at nothing very much at all, and she wondered aloud whether Janet had cleaned the place herself before she left. I made the obvious retort that Janet would know a broomstick only if she were to fly it, and that got Margaret's dander up as of course it was intended to do. Now now, she said. Janet's a remarkable woman, you've said so yourself—how many people have written an entire novel in this place? Then her broom stopped knocking and bumping and she looked hard at me. Remember she had you to put up with all the time, she said. Well, that rocked me, I can tell you—I could hardly believe my ears! Put up with *me*? I said. *I* had to put up with *her*! And when I asked Margaret what she thought it had been like for *me*, she said everyone in Auckland knew what it had been like for me because I hadn't let off moaning the entire year Janet had been on my property. Sixteen months, I said. All right sixteen months, Margaret said, that's even worse, sixteen months of whining. She started sweeping again. You were both so manipulative, she said. Well, I couldn't believe *that* either. Manipulative? *Me*—? I stood staring at her. You played so many games, she said, both of you, you were as bad as each other but it was her I felt sorry for in the end. Sorry! Don't feel sorry for Janet, she's as tough as old boots, I said. Besides, I don't play games. Margaret's head came up at that: Come on now Frank, you play games with *all* of us, she said. Go on, admit it. *Me*? I said. *You*, she said. Name one, I said. Just one. And *that* wasn't the smartest thing I could have found to say, as it turned out.

The strange Christianity inflicted in my childhood is never far away from me: and so when I took the next step after my covert penetration of Janet's privacy, I couldn't help but feel as if *the devil made me do it*. There's no telling what Satan will get up to after all, given that he has a sense of humour: it's the main thing that distinguishes him from the stern Calvinist God, who, on the whole, I've found, has none. Satan on the other hand I've found to be domestic and local: you put him behind you and lo!—he shoves you into doing what you really wanted to do all along. That, for some time anyway, was my explanation for the sequence of events that took place in the days weeks and months after I began to believe that in effect I was becoming one of Janet's fictional characters. In other words these events seemed like

113

my punishment for turning the tables on her, which as you will see now is what I tried to do—my punishment (I thought for a time, in that childhood way) because I'd tried to play at being God.

Of course I'm glad to say that now, with mature reflection and the passage of time, I see myself simply as having broken my own rules and no one else's—I mean the rule I'd thought was sovereign in my work, that one observes and records but does not especially intervene. And glad to say too that I prefer to see these events not necessarily as a punishment at all but as an education: although the latter was an understanding that took its time to come about, I can tell you, and you might well say that on that head I'm still in the classroom.

What drove me to make the intervention you are about to see, alas, was the unending racket of Janet's typing. Starting each morning from the hut as I began my grim vigil at my desk in the house, it rolled on till lunch each day and then more often than not resumed in the early afternoon as I've told. Then some days it began to carry on further, after our meal and into the evenings like some terrible tintinnabulation out of Edgar Allan Poe. Each and every blow she struck at her keys was in the absence of one of my own: but following my covert visit to her hut and what I saw there, the inevitable next assumption began to suggest itself to me, that each blow was in fact the *cause* of the absence of my own—that every touch of a key she made was a touch stolen. For what else would explain her reluctance to let me see a word of what she was writing but the fact that every one of those words was about me?—my life, the stuff she'd obviously been picking up at my table but also behind my doors and beneath my windows (all of which I kept more firmly shut these days, by the way, along with my mouth as far as I was able)? It was as plain as my hand in front of me: she'd moved in and taken over, not just my house and my board but my self, and not just my *writing* self but my *whole* self—who knew

114

what details she'd helped herself to, who knew which of my furnishings and friends had ended up on her page by now: and (worse) *who knew what she had invented*?

These thoughts increasingly took hold of me day and night until I began to feel the strange sensation that she was literally sucking the life from me. And as if to rub my nose in this bizarre illusion, there she was at breakfast each morning, bright as paint!—as I myself increasingly struggled to the kitchen counter, each long troubled night leaving me farther and farther behind on the breakfast front and often barely beginning even the primary business of fetching the yeast from the cylinder cupboard and skimming its froth before she appeared. In short, I had become a shadow of the man whom Janet first met a few months earlier, a host now in the worst possible sense of the word.

All this seemed to her no matter, though, merely a happy challenge it was long past time she turned and met. Down I was to sit, she said, and for a change *she* would wait on *me*, I always made breakfast for *her* and now it was time *she* did her bit—would I be happy with porridge or would I like to try something new? The something new, the time she suggested it, turned out to be *pain grillé français* as she called it with full Frenchified intonation, bread fried in an egg mixture in which I detected a dash of nutmeg or was it mace and if either of these then where oh where had she got them from?—not from my barren cupboards, of that I was quite certain, since following winter months they tended to contain not so very much one might go so far as to term refinements. And little enough in the way of necessities either, if we were to come to that and especially to the curious matter of freshly-laid eggs: but nevertheless here were two of them on the counter, and produced with such pride you'd think she'd laid them both herself!

Well, I had to do something that would stop this night-mare or at least turn it off the path that it was taking, and as fate would have it the opportunity to do so presented itself in the form of Lyall Neary. For here he was, dropping by after dinner one weekday evening, his pockets as usual like the widow's cruse and his fist full of verse or was it prose who could tell?—but anyway it was the usual stuff with which he used from time to time to make his various assaults on greatness, and from which he began to read aloud now, pacing my boards as my more prosaic fork chased the sausages he'd provided me around the frying pan in which they sizzled as an impromptu and unexpected second course to the meal I thought I'd just completed. And all the time he declaimed and I fried, the Gatling gunfire of Janet's typing proceeded from her hut, thinned by distance, the fizz of my cooking, Lyall's declamations and a healthy north-to-northwest breeze: but nevertheless still audible to the point that (when Lyall's reading and my fulsome and unreserved praise of it were done) I drew his attention to the phenomenon.

He cocked an ear and listened. I was right, he reckoned, she was really giving it curry, what was the story? Well, story indeed, I said, I reckon she's writing a novel, and then I proceeded to give him something of a version of what had been going on between the two of us the last few weeks and months. Obviously she could hardly be listening at my door and window while still typing in the hut, but all the same I'd become so jumpy about being overheard these days that the version I gave him was somewhat bowdlerised despite myself, as well as whispered in his direction across the counter rather than being stated in a normal voice. I made it clear that I was at my wit's end nevertheless, not only writing nothing but feeling drained in a way that was new to me and which I couldn't understand.

All the time I spoke, Lyall methodically ate his way through the sausages on his plate one by one. The last he held up on his fork.

Give her one of these, he said, that'd sort her out.

She's eaten already, I told him.

No no no. He waggled the sausage at me. *Give* her one—

Oh, I *see*—

I stopped in mid-sausage.

Give her one—? I said.

I was surprised by my reaction, not at the apparent suggestion that I should be the giver of the sausage in question (something for which I lacked the necessary spice, so to speak), but at the thought that Lyall could think of her in these terms at all. Normally, as I have indicated, I couldn't get enough of this sort of talk, and his adventures with the fairer sex were episodes narrated to an eager audience whenever I was about. I would never tire, for example, of his ongoing story of a generous lass called Verna whom he saw from time to time in Napier or was it Gisborne, and with whom he claimed repeated feats of such inventiveness that I began to wonder at the possibilities of a link between his constant exposure to raw blood and muscle in his day job and the heroic nature of his nocturnal explorations. My mother always claimed that the nature of their work was what made butchers far too cheeky: *Too close to the meat* is the phrase she used, a belief that led to my being employed in a prophylactic manner, along with my brother, to collect the weekly order in her place. Then, when adolescence claimed us, she suddenly introduced a weekly meatless day: Remember Belgium, she used to say, it does us good to go without from time to time—this went with my father's proposition that one should always leave the table feeling slightly hungry. Well, perhaps this was the nub of Lyall's problem, perhaps he needed to remember the heroic deprivations of our gallant ally in the earlier war and forget his wretched purloined meat—?

She's not like that, I found myself telling him, primly. She's not that sort of girl—

He chewed at me a moment. Course she is, he said. They're all up for it, you told me that yourself—

Now in all truth this was true, and in fact a recurrent theme in my conversation: *The wren goes to 't, and the small gilded fly does lecher in my sight* (though as far as Lyall was concerned he was more the soiled horse that comes up a few lines later)—anyway, human frailty in general and our tendency to the horizontal in particular have been frequent themes of mine, since it's always seemed to me the commonest purpose of our existence is to find new ways of getting one another into old beds. Should my hut-guest be the only one to be excluded from these recurring rhythms of nature? I've already told how Little Ben appeared at my door with the honey, and of the curious progression of thoughts and themes that was consequent upon his gift: and I thought in particular now of the way his eyes had lingered on the distant princess he glimpsed through my inner doorway, and the sudden sense I'd had then of how Janet might seem to another set of eyes than mine. And it was thinking about this episode in the following days that had me turning my mind in another direction completely.

What if I were to set her up with one of the two of them, Ben or Lyall? What if I were to play the part of Pander in such a way that she ended up with one or the other of them to the advantage of both participants, I mean Janet and whichever man might better fit the bill—to their advantage, and (now the idea was beginning to unfold itself in my mind like a rich Turkish carpet rolling down the steps of some imaginary seraglio) to mine as well?

Which of the two of them, though? With Ben there was that distinctive taste of honey brought about by the disciplines of his family's modest faith. Would that appeal? After all, I'd wondered from time to time at the possibility of a religious past in Janet, albeit one where the quaking was of a different nature (upbringings of the hard religious kind often explain tormented adult lives, I've found: an observation I feel I've earned the right to make). But whether that was so or not, it seemed to me their unworldliness was not in doubt, Ben's and hers, and that *here* was the obvious bond between them—granted, his simplicity was not at all of the same order as hers, which gave more than a hint or two of complex hidden depths as you've already seen: was this where his solidity would come in, would his steadiness right her rudder for her and give her ballast too?

Or would those same hidden depths require something more exciting, and was that where the other man would find his place—would staid bookish Janet prove not so staid and bookish after all, did she conceal a secret wish to be drawn into the dank meaty undergrowth in which young Lyall lived his life? And whichever outcome were to be the case (my figurative Turkish carpet here reaching the bottom of the seraglio staircase, as you might say), was there not a possibility that in due course either man might steer her away from me and, in the best way possible, right out of my life?—a scene I imagined taking place with myself in benign attendance, of course, the author off to one side and paring his fingernails so to speak, since at that point I would have succeeded in writing Janet into a fiction of my own imagining, turning the tables on her as it seemed she'd turned the tables on me!

And since fate had first put this idea into my head by delivering me Lyall and his fateful sausages, what I decided was to let it take its course: I would work my scheme on whichever man next showed up at Esmonde Road, Ben or Lyall. They were both fairly regular visitors, and so life itself with one of its usual shrugs would provide the raw material: on it I would stamp my subtle pattern. It was just a matter of waiting to see which man chance served up to me. So it was that when I heard the familiar motorcycle roar starting to make its way into my mind a day or two later, I knew that, one way or the

119

other, I was in business. But which way? I peered through the little kitchen window and waited, breath held: heaven or hell, honey or flesh?—and *Lyall* it was who came bowing his way through the overgrowth of the front hedge, and looking up and catching my eye and winking at me as if he were already one of my characters and looking forward to whatever role it was I would require him to play. He was to be my protagonist, then: excitement over stability!

At this point Janet herself, I recall, was at off at the local shops and library and we had the place to ourselves as I began to prepare my master-class. I had already decided how I would proceed in either eventuality. But again it was as if Lyall were in on the business, because he brought up the subject himself as he pushed in through the back door. Nice'n quiet today, he said, and jerked his head towards the army hut. Off shopping, I replied. And so I was able to start straight away in the business of making her irresistible. She was a talented young woman, I told him, and certainly the most gifted to have occupied the hut. Great promise, I said, but of course promise always comes at a price. What d'you mean, price? he grunted. Oh, you know what genius is like, I said, and began to tell him a few of the difficulties I'd been having: not that my account would have been unfamiliar to any of my friends, so often had I given it. But I knew him as a man who liked a challenge, so I didn't stint in details that would make her seem complex and difficult but also intriguing and interesting, a little different—a great deal different, surely—from the Veras and the Vernas who had so far littered his life.

And so fluent was my account as I babbled on, and watched a new and hitherto-unknown Janet form itself around the real one as I spoke, that I found I'd gone beyond myself and told him that she had a past.

He sat up. A past—? he said. What sort of a past—?

I stopped short. In truth I had no real idea. By this stage of

Janet's time with me—and I remember this conversation as being several months into it—I'd made a number of different attempts to dig out more concerning her whereabouts before she turned up on my doorstep. But she emitted as much blue-black ink on that as on any other matter. *A period of private research* was one response to some of my early probing, and *a working holiday* another. In that period I'd come pretty much to the conclusion, though, that her behaviour suggested she'd survived something, and that the something she'd survived was some kind of hospitalisation. Don't ask me where I got this notion. It hung between Lyall and me, unspoken, a single word. *Hospital.* Could he see it, did he know what I was thinking? *Hospital.* We caught and then avoided each other's eye. I let the silence linger. Then:

A past, I said, as enigmatically as I could. Up to you to find out—

A past, he said. Christ, you wouldn't know it—

He sat there rubbing his chin. You could tell I'd hooked him. Now it was time for my masterstroke.

Steer clear of her, I told him. That's what I reckon—

He flicked a look up at me. His brow knotted. Steer *clear* of her? he said. What d'you mean, she's a bit of a hard case?

And I'd got him, I could tell. He sat there, crouched forward and with his fingers still on the cigarette he'd crushed in my seashell, his other hand against his mouth as he thought it through. I'd started something with him and Janet.

Well, so pleased was I with myself that I told the Guigans about it when I called at Clarence Road with vegetables that weekend.

I think I've fixed Janet up, I said, and outlined the details.

With Lyall *Neary*? Margaret said when I'd done. He's not suitable at all, Frank, what are you thinking of? Why don't you set her up with the young Paine boy if you have to interfere like that, what's his name?

Lordbepraised, said Lawrence from his wheelchair, they're all called something silly like that.

He's called Ben, I said. The same as his father. No he's too soft, he couldn't handle her.

Anyway, Margaret said, what d'you mean, you've fixed her up?

And I was more than a little surprised, I have to say, that she couldn't quite see it as I did, I mean that she couldn't see the link between my thinking of something between Lyall and Janet and that something coming about. As far as Margaret was concerned I'd confused sequence and consequence: the two events, thought and deed, were unconnected and there was no promise of any kind of development. And as far as Lawrence was concerned it seemed it was the business of the names that had his attention and nothing more:

What d'you do if you drop out of the church? he asked suddenly. You know, if you stop quaking—change your name to Lordbefucked?

Lawrence, Margaret said.

In fact for the next few days and weeks nothing out of the ordinary happened that I could see or hear. Janet came and went, from house to hut, hut to house and house to hut again: I sat each morning listening to the clatter of her machine as I contemplated the utter silence of mine. By now it was every afternoon that she typed, not most, and most evenings instead of some. I sought refuge from her racket at the sand-spit, looking for flounder and gathering seaweed. The local library saw even more of me than was normally the case, I took the Bayswater ferry across the harbour nearly every day and found things around the city to invite my soul. Back in the garden I found that any sudden sound had my immediate attention: any sound, that is, unconnected to her wretched clatter. When would something happen, when would the plot thicken?

Then one night, late, something jolted me awake. I sat up in my bed. There was someone outside. I could hear someone moving outside. The back door though closed was, as always, unlocked for Janet's night-time convenience should she need it, and at first I thought it was she whom I could hear. But there was no sound of her on the other side of my hanging bed-sheets, not the squeaky opening of the door on painful hinges or the sound of her tiptoeing in with her usual exaggerated caution. Then (my heart beat faster) it occurred to me that this could be *Harry come back at last* and of course I stepped out of bed smartly at the thought of *that*: although to tell the truth I'd never known him to show up so far distant from the serving of a meal. Out I went all the same with an old coat over my night attire, and straight away got a cat against my shin for my trouble. And I hadn't done much more than reach down and start to kid with him than I heard a voice, out on the road—

It was two in the morning, just a little after, I'd checked the alarm clock when I woke up. Not eagerly, I moved bit by bit along the back of the house and up the bedroom side, where there was grass. At the front room corner, near the loquat trees, I saw shadows on the lawn and nothing in them: and when I finally crept to the gate and through the hedge and (very reluctantly) out—there was Esmonde Road aslumber, its mighty heart lying still in the smokeless air, as you might say, in one direction its sleeping houses and, in the other, the dark mystery of the mangrove swamp at the end of the road.

Naturally I probed Janet on the matter at breakfast. She was as unreadable as ever, but scrubbed and fresh and in good appetite as she settled to the porridge and the curd. Had she passed a refreshing night, I asked her?—and it turned out she'd slept like the dead. Had she not been woken, then, by anything at all during that period of oblivion?—and it seemed not even Peel's 'View, Halloo!' could have done the trick. No such luck for me, I told her, and went on to elaborate on my two-in-the-morning adventure. Cats, she said, cat noise wakes me all the time, especially this time of year. But not last night? I wondered. Not that she could remember, was the gist of her reply, and then she fell to her bowl of porridge again and its usual monastic accompaniments. That good appetite I've already mentioned was partnered by good spirits, too, it seemed, a point on which I later reflected to myself for the possibility of inner significance: and as I did so, it didn't take much of putting two together with two for me to settle on Lyall Neary as what was needed to make them four. After all, if he wanted to pay a covert visit at the dead of night he needed only to kill his motor down at the Lake Road corner and push the Army Indian to my gate, and do the same the other way about when once he left: had he still the legs for it, of course—

And so when I happened to run into him at the ferry terminal a night or two later I asked him straight out. I told him I'd heard a noise outside the house the night before last and that I'd gone to have a look. Did he know by any chance what it was that might have been going on—?

He leaned back against the wall of the terminal building and gave me a hard look through our cigarette smoke. Had I seen anything? he wondered—not a thing, I replied, but brother, I *heard* plenty. What sort of things did I hear, then? he wanted to know—so I explained that it had been hard to make out any particulars but there'd been a bit of noise. I could swear there was something going on, I said.

He looked at me hard again. Good thing you couldn't see in, then, he said.

Well now—I could hardly believe my ears! I stared at him, I stared at him—so it was true, then, it was Lyall in the hut with Janet in the middle of the night—that was what he meant, wasn't it? I could hardly believe my *ears*—

Really—really—?

124

He smirked. No names no packdrill, he said. You know the story, Frank—

Naturally I fished for further details: but he was unforthcoming in a way I hadn't found in him before:

You know the story, Frank, he said, no names. Don't worry, I'll spill the beans one day, I'll let y'have the whole bloody tinful!—just don't tell her you know anything now or you'll bugger it up for me—

No no, of course not, of course not—

That night, though, I couldn't settle, I couldn't settle at all for trying not to imagine the scenario that must surely have taken place. After I'd spent a night more than half awake it was only my intense curiosity the next morning that enabled me to put up a show of alert attentiveness when Janet came in for her breakfast. Cats again? she said when she saw my unslept state. Something like that, I replied, and wondered what irony might be in her words. Shall I make the porridge, then? she suggested, and apologised for having no eggs available that morning. And all the time my mind was whirling about the room, just whirling—had I *really* started off this story that seemed to be taking shape—?

Then, a day or two later, an extraordinary development occurred. Janet stopped typing. We'd had lunch after yet another morning of feast for her and famine for me, and when she returned to the hut following the meal I expected her to resume her devoirs in the usual way. But in short order she reappeared at the hut door in her royal disguise of headscarf and sunglasses, and a light fawn coat she'd told me her friend Molly had given her. I'm just popping out, she said. Out? I asked, like a fussing aunt. Are you sure? Yes, she was sure, she just needed some fresh air. With one knee on the divan in the corner of the front room I watched her through the window as she ducked through the gap in the hedge. Alas, in all truth the lunch had been lunch in name only and I suspected she might well be popping out for one of

125

the many bars of Caramello chocolate whose outer wrappings I frequently found in my rubbish bin. But on the other hand she might not, and as the author (so to speak) of the events that seemed to be developing, surely it was my responsibility to follow her and determine whether in fact they continued to develop? Surely it was, and I'd even taken the jacket from behind my bedroom door and placed my beret on my head to that end—when, as if I had been pushed there by some external force, I found myself sitting at my desk instead.

There, I stared at the blank page I'd confronted all the morning, whose upper corners continued to droop back sadly on either side of the metal support bar. I scratched at my thumbs with my fingernails, I rubbed my palms together: what was this—this pricking-of-the-thumbs that I hadn't felt in—how many weeks months and years was it since I last wrote something that felt as if it had some truth and integrity to it? My fingers began to press at the keys, in front of me my Imperial started up again, for all the world like an ancient Spinning Jenny suddenly summoned back to life after two hundred years. Stiff levers creaked typeface up and over, ribbon began to punch paper, soon a steady thumping clatter settled in and my heart was beginning to flutter high in my chest. During my bleak morning sessions I occasionally experienced something like this, and there were times when my fingers even ran away with me completely and half or all a page was filled up within an hour or two. But then it always took a hundredth of that time to confirm the worthlessness of what was on them (and also to remember that as far as I was concerned, a full page in a morning was a very bad sign). What was happening now was different, though: strange, because it was so long since I'd felt it, but familiar once I did—like those occasions in my life when a long period of abstinence was replaced by an unexpected fulfilment and I would find myself marvelling once again at the way the body reminded itself of the rules of life while the soul looked on.

Now here it was again, the Platonic version of this rule, and my soul watched and marvelled at what my body wrote—

About what?—about a trio of women, I am surprised to be able to tell you. Not unprecedented in my work, of course, which has its womenfolk as you will know, but enough of a rarity to catch my attention as they appeared before me on this occasion: and never before so many of them or so signally unaccompanied by their menfolk. What was I doing, where was it all coming from, what was this monstrous regiment that was taking over my green foolscap page?— no matter, here they were, three of them, marching in from the margins and undoubtedly, all of them, simply who they were and individuals I would get to know in due course. And who cared, as long as their origins however distant and unexpected were in the world and in the life I'd been living in that world? As to anything else: with any luck, that would declare itself soon enough, this gift from wherever it was such gifts declare themselves, and after the initial familiar business by which these things appeared in the good old days: first the life, bustling onstage, and then, slowly apprehended, its purpose.

By now an hour or so had gone—no, more: I saw by my clucking old alarm clock that I'd worked for nearly two!— and I'd got myself a fair old pile of paper stacked beside the typewriter, which is of course a figurative way of saying that I'd written on a single page very many more words than I might for some time have expected to produce in a normal working day. I counted in the usual way, the number of lines times half the number of words in first line and last: five hundred and more—well, now! I positively reared up from my chair in delight at *that*, and stood there massaging my bony backside back to life in a room that sparkled with early afternoon light and under a roof clattering with happy sparrows. It felt like the good old days when I used to surface involuntarily from my task to find that once again and without planning I was right on time and could turn to the kitchen with thoughts of the rest of the day unfolding cosily in lunch a nap the garden and maybe an evening stroll, all the while knowing that ready for eight o'clock the following morning there lay a little growth of written life for me to address in my usual way, a word taken out here and a comma supplied there preparatory to another fruitful morning. I walked on air, I smiled to myself, I hummed about the kitchen like the cat that licked the proverbial cream. I was still wearing my beret, I found.

Janet returned an hour later, earlier than I expected and not visibly changed. I eyed her for clues—dishevelled hair, a lipstick smudge, clothing out of place—and finding nothing, resorted to the sardonic and the jovial. Chocolate, Miss Frame? I said: and she caught herself and gave me the most furtive of looks across her fawn shoulder. How can you tell? she wanted to know—and I explained about the wrappers in the rubbish bin. You can't keep secrets from me! I said: and *that* earned me a special look, I can tell you. I could all but see her wondering whether I'd been in the hut during her absence, and as soon as our little intercourse was done I noticed that she darted in there, as if to check her private things—

It really did seem as if I'd stopped her in her tracks and at the same time started myself up again in mine, for over the next few days and then a week and then more the machine-gun racket that usually filled the property came from my Imperial alone. For three or four early hours each day I clattered happily away at my machine, and then bounced up to prepare lunch and out to the garden after that, or to the local shops and library. Like Prospero's our little isle was full of noises: but not one of them came from the army hut.

At first I revelled in the business, of course, having suffered dearth so very long, and found myself eager to meet again each morning the gay trio who'd so suddenly absorbed my attention. Of course, given my recent experience of finding myself on Janet's page, it was natural that I should pay attention to the question whether she had crept onto mine. Had she?—well, it is not untrue to say that a detail here and there might under certain lights be thought to resemble some of her own: but the real delight of what was happening once more was the autonomy of it, the lack of will involved, the joyous sense of life being created on the page while I looked on amazed enthralled and humbled. But what then of that other life, the one occurring around about me: and particularly, what of Janet?—well, to outward appearances she seemed pretty much the same, turning up for breakfast each morning, returning to the hut till one and then back to the house for a further meal, retiring to the hut once more after that and to her self-inflicted *purdah*. For all this time, the rattling volley of my work continued to be equalled by nothing whatever from her side.

A little more than a week of this and I began to feel concerned. She skipped a meal, then two, and my basic instincts began to be aroused. Was she ill, I asked her, did she feel poorly?—she was quite well if a little tired, she told me. I made so bold as to ask after the current state of her writing—was there a reason perhaps that I couldn't hear so very much activity with the typewriter these last few days? Ah, sadly her typing activities were in suspension owing to events beyond her control. *Events beyond her control*: did she mean funny business with Lyall? But as she went through the usual business of assuring me yet one more time that she would have a draft of something or other ready for me to run my eye over any day now, I realised that once again she'd been open and communicative to all appearances, and yet once again as a result she'd engulfed me in that cloud of unknowing which seemed to be the given of all my dealings with her. I kept my eye on her each breakfast-time appearance to see if her body could give me clues instead, but apart from a slight darkening beneath the eyes that came and went (and which for all I could remember might have been there when she was at the height of her powers), there was nothing to give her away. Any sign of a physical illness and of course I'd have made the usual moves when any guest of mine falls ill, with thermometer hot water bottle barley sugar and what have you: but there was none. Each night I checked the hut from my solitary rear window. In the dark it sat a few yards away like a wooden sarcophagus, mute and occupied, the slight sea winds of that season moving the fruit trees nearby and working branch and twig against its roof in tiny repetitious squeaks. I'd stopped her in her tracks all right: a veritable *teinture de vice* to savour along with the notion that my schemes and machinations might after all be having *some* effect out there in the world, even if not quite the effect that I'd intended—

Then the plot indeed thickened. I've a person to meet in town, she said after lunch one day, completely out of nothing as she left the room and in an over-the-shoulder manner that suggested she meant me to ask for details. Well!—that *did* attract my attention, as you might imagine: but I feigned a cool indifference and let her slip away unquestioned, though I watched her nevertheless from the little kitchen window as she slipped through the gate once more in her royal disguise. In truth I could hardly contain myself at this confirmation that my little plot really was taking on a life of its own. Characters once created take you where they will, as everyone must know (that is, after one gets over the initial shock of finding out their all-too-human nature): but her recent withdrawal had concerned me. Now here was some action again! I gave her a minute and then slipped to the gate as if to check the mail, but instead took a quick trot over the hump in the road: and there she was, down at the corner already with her firm stumping tread just taking her into Lake Road—but turning *left* instead of *right*! So there really *was* something up, there was no doubt of that if she was heading to the local shops when she'd told me she was off for the terminal and the city! I grabbed my beret and rucksack from the cottage and set off after her.

But I lost the scent when once I reached the Takapuna shops, and found myself wandering about like a child. Since the library seemed the most obvious place she might arrange to meet someone I looked around its rows of shelves and checked the reading section and the stands of newspapers, and found nothing but the usual denizens of the deep. Then I tried Oliver's Café and Coffee Bar, where once or twice we'd taken a cup of tea together, Janet and I, when life seemed far less complicated for us both and I was merely an elderly gent setting an anxious young woman on the taxing path of life. But no Janet there: nor in the steady regression of little shops the local village offered from Oliver's on down, and which I looked into one by one until I found myself standing in a Sunshine milk-shake bar of all places, where the two young folk who stared back at me from one of its garish stalls were definitely not Lyall (as I expected of course her *person* would surely be), or Janet herself, nor even Janet forlornly on her own and sucking at the straw of some hideous raspberry shake in lonely compensation.

She seemed to have given me the slip. I turned and began to stroll back, my empty rucksack light against my spine. I peered into likely shops: was she in Lane's bakery?—she was not. The Takapuna Fish Supply, behind the constant waterfall that kept at least the inside of its window fresh? Not there, either, or in Buchanan's Ladies' Wear, whose corsetry display detained me far less than fifteen seconds. Well, what about the place next door, where the product sold was something even more ephemeral: for it was that very beauty parlour whose name had caught Janet's eye before

131

any others when first we tried the shops together back in April or was it May—

And there—in the back of the shop, turned away from me as she sat under the big bonnet of a hair dryer—was Janet! *Surely, surely* it was her: though I'd had no more than a glimpse as I passed and peeked and I hadn't broken my step until the shock of it caught up with me and hit me and made me stop. Janet, having her hair done in a beauty parlour—?

I crept back, I bent and shaded my brow, I tried to see to the rear of the salon again. Surely not, surely not—but now one of the hairdressing women looked up and at me with a frown and I had to pull back from the window and duck away. Not *Janet* in a beauty parlour, though, I thought as I walked off, Janet of all people, she with whom I'd used to laugh so much at the wonderful concatenation of those two words as we stood before this very shop and watched the succession of elderly battleships sailing in through its doors and then back out again fully rigged. Well no, I decided, it couldn't possibly be *her*: her friend Molly maybe, she who'd started this benighted business off in the first place, but never Janet. And all this present natter, by the way, just to cover time spent loitering in McKenzie's nearby before returning to the *beauty parlour* for one more furtive peek—at a shop that now had no customers, it turned out, and its two *beauticians* left to their own Platonic devices, though not so much so that the one who had scowled before could not launch at me one more terrifying grimace—

Well as you might imagine, once back at 14 Esmonde Road I was all agog when next I set eyes on our heroine, which turned out to be later in the day, at the time when usual thoughts turn to matters culinary. Instead of these, though, I thought of her, and checked the letterbox a dozen times (still nothing from Harry, by the way) until eventually I spotted her coming over the horizon, and then I slipped back and began to busy myself indoors. And then—here she was in front of me once more, headscarf firmly tied, though with no sign in what she showed me, when once her dark glasses were removed, that any particular attentions courtesy of those beauticians had taken place. In fact I stared so long and hard that I embarrassed her, to my shame, and had to reassure her that the problem lay in my eyes and not in what they looked on. Advancing age! I told her, and took my glasses off and put them back on again to no especial purpose: but all the while the headscarf stayed in place, and the longer it did the more convinced I was that there and there alone lay the transformation whose rituals I'd peered into an hour or two before like Aladdin in the *Thousand and One Nights*. What magic these rituals had conspired who knew or cared: the fact of them could not have been more obvious had she flung the scarf in my face and revealed the sculpted locks of Betty Grable. She was up to something—*they* were up to something, she and he, the two of them, nothing could be clearer—and no author could have been more delighted at such obedience of heroine and hero to his plans.

So that when she told me she was going out it was no surprise. Oh and by the way she wouldn't need an evening meal, she said, from the path between house and hut. Really? I said, looking down at her from my back doorway, my face as blank as Fu Manchu's. I might be a bit late, she said, cautiously, looking up but not quite enough to catch my eye. Take as long as you like, Miss Frame, I said, it's your life (that last a little touch, by the way, I very much enjoyed).

And as I turned back into the house I was barely able to conceal from her my self-regarding smirk. Thankyou Mister Joyce!—James, I mean, and his business of the disembodied author who stands to one side, detached from his created work as he pares his fingernails and his characters live out their seemingly independent lives. Well, for this unfolding work of fiction that godlike figure was *me*, of this I had no doubt, so confident was I now in the momentum of the events to which I'd given an initial, barely perceptible push: but which appeared now, as I looked on, to be steadily unrolling themselves of their own volition like that richly patterned Turkish carpet I'd imagined cascading down the staircase. So confident was I in fact that I took care literally to stand to one side and let this little chapter complete itself, not even deigning to go to front gate or window as the rumble of Lyall's approaching motorcycle announced itself on cue at half-past six that evening, fell away a little on the other side of the hedge for half a minute as (I imagined) he scooped up his passenger, then, after Janet had mounted the pillion (I could see her awkward movements as I stood there in my bedroom, eyes closed), rose into the departing blare that took her off to—well, whatever it was came next in this adventure I'd set in motion for her, for them, for the pair of them. Elsewhere, was the point, and maybe in the short-to-medium term even a ticket to permanent departure, for who knows the ways of the human heart?

Thinking these necessary thoughts I fairly buzzed and hummed as I fell to the business of cleaning my few pots and plates from my evening meal, sorting out the cats, bringing in my garden tools under a fading evening light more than half gone now, and, finally, picking through my bookshelf for an old favourite with whom to celebrate the peace and silence that had suddenly engulfed my life once more. After all, what better for an artist than art, and what better for art than the eye of an artist?

And wasn't it Dr Johnson who said that, if we speak exactly, we are none of us in our right mind?

CHAPTER 6

Words, meanwhile, accumulated on my page—I don't mean these you're reading now, written a full year after the events they describe, but those that seemed vouchsafed to me in that new sulphur-flare of creativity I've described as possessing me after so very many months spent in fear that *that* particular part of my existence was over, and thus all my life gone pointless finished and to be spent in utter darkness. Proven wrong as it seemed and filled once again by whatever divine or secular breath it is that gives these things to us, I felt pleased and at the same time guilty: the first in the obvious way I've given some account of, and the second equally obvious since I've surely shown how much convinced I was that some kind of curious exchange had come about between me and my involuntary guest. This conviction was deeply Protestant in its nature: by its light one was either damned or saved and there was nothing in between. The more I battered the keys the more Janet's silence went on, and the more Janet's silence went on the more I battered the keys: and the more I battered the keys the more I wondered whether this new dispensation meant that I was saved and she was damned, I mean in the artistic sense. And if I *had* been saved as it seemed, why had I been chosen, and could she be saved again and I be damned once more?

Despite this evidence of the thoroughness of John Calvin's work in my earlier life, the pages mounted, to the point where they required a small stone to keep them in place and order on my desk. The usual story length was soon exceeded and the excitement of a longer work seemed promised me at last. If not quite running over, my cup seemed certainly more than half full.

As to what was on those pages I was writing—ah, now, that was another matter. Obviously, over the years I'd become not unfamiliar with the nature of inspiration and particularly with its resemblance to the course of love—I mean those early transports of delight common to both ventures, the certainty (in the case of writing) that the new venture will be the work that works at last, the one that sums your vision stamps your mark and brings you fame and fortune. And I also mean what comes next, the end of the honeymoon and the slow coming to terms with what is really there, either the realisation that a fair measure of hard work might just bring off a passable effort, or more often than not (alas) the realisation there is nothing much there to be brought off after all, and that this is the end, so to speak, of the affair. *Came the dawn*, as the words on the cinema screen used to tell us before the talkies—well, in my sudden new venture, and rather later than is usually the case for me, after perhaps a week or two of happy and hectic typing, I reached that dawn.

And when I did so, and read what I had written with undeluded eyes, I found I had no idea what to make of it in either direction. It seemed to me neither bad nor good. For one thing, as I've said, the creative pattern this time around had been rather different from before—for me, as in matters of the heart, the writing process tends to the prosaic: initial raptures in both ventures tending to be of the modified variety, like those of Nanki-Poo. While capable of early excitement in both kinds of attachment as I've shown, at heart I am very ready as a rule to see them both as plain old work, each of them a matter of getting on with what you've got and making a fist of it. I write from the head in order to write from the heart, if you see what I mean, and not the other way around as many others do. Often I make a plan of what I want, listing things to put into my work in full awareness that an increasing number of readers critics academics and what have you are waiting to pounce and pull them back out again: perhaps (I've sometimes thought) I should post them each the list and save myself the trouble of writing the novel? But instead I plug on, more Trollope, you might say, than Coleridge with his opium pipe.

To put it simply, I am not used to being swept off my feet the way I was that winter-spring. Once again the word *possession* comes to mind. The words were there, but they disturbed me—I who was writing the wretched things, or at least writing them down: for the question where they actually came from was more and more an issue as the pile of pages mounted. Who *were* these people marching onto my page, and why were they women, or (to be quite accurate) why was my main character—she who came nearest to the sense of speaking in my ear as I wrote—not a man? I remembered Janet's words about the need to look at the very edge of things, and wondered whether this was what she had in mind—I who thought I'd made my name standing on the margins myself, and speaking for the life I found there. Well, here was something different, requiring to be dealt with in place of all the Bills and Jims and Daves who'd earned my full attention to this point. Here was something very new.

Janet, meanwhile, baffled me. At first the relenting of her attack upon the keys was the astonishment I have told, and the opening of my floodgates seemed an obvious result. Any early guilt I might have felt was washed away in the excitement of that moment and what followed, but as my pages mounted up and my life seemed to resume its former shape or something near it, I began to think of her and the guilt returned. Was I stealing from her now just as I'd feared she'd been taking from me before? Did her natural reticence and awkwardness conceal a great despair, was she enduring something like the miseries I'd gone through but not letting on? Although by this point a little of the true nature of her unhappiness was becoming known to me on the half-guessed half-intuited basis I have shown, it always seemed to be well beyond my reach and little to do (as far as I could see) with anything local and personal—to our relationship, that is, to the odd collision of cosmic billiard balls that had knocked us both into the same dark corner like this.

But it seemed that she was not unhappy, there was the mystery of it: in fact, I'd hardly seen her better. Of course the supplementary thought then offered itself, that she'd had no time for art because she'd been too busy acquiring copy, so to speak, at the busy hands of the Bard of the Abattoir, and this led to the further thought that such regular activity might account for her fresh complexion and relatively positive outlook on life. There's nothing like regular outdoor exercise, after all. Of these explanations or something like them I was now convinced, although I heard no more of him than the arriving and departing blare of his motorcycle every second night or third. For nothing of his interest now lay unrevealed: here he was, audible if not visible, blatant and brazen in those early evenings like a Roman taking up his Sabine prize. And then in due course off he would go, usually an hour or two later and never more than three. The early nature of these exits surprised a little, but his failure to pop his head in my door did not: after all, the last he'd seen of me I must have seemed to him like Prospero protecting his daughter's virgin-knot.

Thus Janet and I settled into a routine as regular as it once had been, except that this time the creative boot was on the other foot: although as I say she seemed far less concerned by her silence than I'd been by my own. But now it became the case that hers began to concern me, though I have to point out (for fear my motives start to look too worthy) that it was the nature of her nocturnal activities that had my interest as much as the whereabouts of her creative muse—well, rather more, to tell the truth, given my ongoing and regrettable excess of interest in that side of human nature. But when I began to probe, first subtly and then not very subtly at all, she turned my queries aside with her usual great blasts of blue-black ink. She was tidying up something for me to see, she'd soon have something I might look at, she felt she'd reached a significant stage of development and was preparing to push forward: in other words there was nothing that I hadn't heard before in some unfruitful form or other. As far as anything else was concerned she cut off further enquiry, and a polite mention of Lyall's name, with which I'd hoped to bait my hook, brought a snapping response to the effect that she hadn't laid eyes on Lyall in several weeks. Which might to some extent have been true, it occurred to me, given the darkness of the evenings in which he was turning up, but was otherwise hard to make any sense of other than as a whopping great lie—

And then, following one of these sessions of give-but-no-take, she did something that surprised me: she dashed out into the hut and brought back her knitting. Now, despite the other domestic achievements I've indicated as causing me various astonishments to this point, this was unexpected. When had she found time to produce the large rectangle of rough grey-brown wool she held before me?—was *this* what she'd been up to in the hut after all, and thus the only fruit of my attempt to help her transform herself from civilian into artist: eighteen inches of plain-stitch in the shape of a pullover front? And whom might it be for? But when I put voice to this latter thought the young lady became (I thought) quite coquettish and told me, well, I'd have to wait and see, wouldn't I?—although in holding it up against me as if to measure its fit and thereby demonstrating its outsize

139

qualities, she let slip what might be argued to be at least the very rudiments of a clue. It's a gift, she said, for someone I admire very much. Oh yes? I said, and tried to sound neither arch nor smug at knowing whom she meant. For someone who's been very good to me lately, she said, and rolled the knitting up around its needles. I'm glad, I said. Very glad! And surely as she returned to the hut she must have been struck and puzzled by just how glad I seemed to be on her behalf, and on behalf of whomever it was that she admired so much—my generosity must have seemed overwhelming, and indeed it was, for it overwhelmed me as well. A good fit for Lyall, is what I felt, of course.

Looking back now, I find myself astonished at how pleased I was with the way things seemed to be working out: was it time (I remember wondering) for me to reveal all, to show my hand in bringing about this consummation? And I decided not, for who knew what next step it might take— why, the business I'd begun was barely started. Where next, where next—? What else could come of that simple sentence or two I'd trickled into Lyall's ear that seemed to have caused so many things to happen?

Then the weather changed. I don't just mean out there, under the sky: I mean in here, in the house—or to be more precise, inside the hut. The times I've recently described turned out to have been a sort of Indian spring, so to speak, a little patch of balmy weather that teased a scattering of blossoms from the red-leafed plum tree next door and from my peaches: and after that there came a week of passing thunderstorms that thrashed their branches almost bare again. Through streaming panes I watched the havoc in my garden. Branches rocked and swayed, infant leaves and blossom flew the air, confetti strewed the ground and stuck to window-glass till the next blast washed it off. A tempest like this was somewhat out of season, although of course, sunshine or no, on a peninsula a little rain is always to be expected and it might be said in truth that there are no such things as seasons at all. But thunderheads like these were omens of an especially hot summer: or so old Solomon used to reckon (and when this thought came to mind I blushed to think how long it was I'd left him in neglect: not even a single letter-card had I sent his way for longer than I cared to think).

For me though they presaged something else, a different change of barometric pressure as Janet withdrew inside her hut. It took me a little while to note the alteration of her mood, and when I did it was natural that I tried to link it to something that was happening outside herself. Most obvious was the weather as described, since the sudden cracks of thunder certainly had me on edge, not to mention the electric quality given to the air at such times. Yet not even the lavish chiaroscuro of the climate could explain the degree of change in her when once I'd concentrated on it. Had I offended, then, was I again the culprit?—and now here I was once more taking covered plates of food to the doorstep of her hut and trying to find a way of keeping off both cats and rain. *Miss Frame, Miss Frame,* I hooted by the doorknob as if that was the way into her strange heart, and I rapped my knuckles not very eagerly on the doorpost. But apparently Miss Frame was not receiving visitors, although whenever I slipped out to check dishes left the night before I found that little remained on them save knife and fork. It took me back to the earlier side of the winter we were coming through, when she'd first begun to hide herself away like this. How would she emerge this time—*when* would she emerge?

Then, suddenly, that old two-plus-two of mine came back: how long was it, pray, since a motorcycle had disturbed my evening peace? Days? A week?—of course, of *course,* they'd had a tiff, Lyall and Janet, they'd had a row, hence his absence, hence her gloom!—so now it was two-*minus*-two, and not for the first time 14 Esmonde Road was home (it

141

seemed) to a broken heart. I was ready to share her burden and (naturally) to tell her even more of mine, but when I tried to bring the topic up during one of her rare visits to the house it seemed she was in no mood for comparing notes. She bit off my attempts to mention the possibility of men in her life and in fact all attempts to mention anything whatever: she was in and out, and left the sense that other matters occupied her mind. To tell the truth, once witnessed like this the impression she gave was not so much of despair and utter hopelessness as a determined focus on objects far removed from anything remotely tied to me.

And then after a couple of days of this and maybe three, her typing started up again.

At first I didn't hear it, any more than I took note of the flies bees and wasps that made their random way in and out during summer months, sawing across the room and knocking against windows before they found their long lament upon my flypaper. I was staring at that morning's page of work, which presented me with puzzles new and baffling, and which had brought itself about in bursts of staccato gunfire rather than any steady rhythmic rattle of the keys in that almost-heedless writing I'd returned to these last many days and weeks as they were proving themselves to be. There I was, in one of the gaps that had lengthened in my typing as I gazed and wondered at myself and gazed again, and all the time like Claudius's poison the Janet-sound had been trickling in my ear unnoticed: not enough immediately to wake me from my trance as I crouched with fingers raised to strike the keys again, but enough to buzz and tap and fizz into my brain—until suddenly I was conscious of it once again, that steady rattle-rattle-rattle coming through the open back door once more, after all this time: here it was again, that terrifying *furor scribendi*—

I sat there at my desk. Janet, typing again—

At one o'clock she presented herself for lunch the first time

142

in at least a week, and seemed in slightly better spirits as she sat there at my counter. I'd nothing better than bread and cheese to offer (though is there anything better, by the way?), which I augmented with a dozen pickled cucumber slices to mark the occasion of her appearance. But despite my slight attempt at ironic celebration she had very little to say, and parried my questions in her usual expert manner till we were back in our aboriginal silence once more. Then, suddenly:

You're underwater again? she said.

And she flicked at me a look she sometimes gave that quite unnerved me, just a quick little flirting stab with mineral eyes that, once done, was all in my mind: had she looked at all, had I imagined it, did she mean something by it if she had?

Underwater? I asked.

I hear you typing. Is it something new, are you just started—?

Oh—I see. Yes, yes, I've been blessed again, thank goodness—

Though of course now she too was back at work and in the state of mind she'd reduced me to by this stage I was very much in doubt whether once back at my desk I would ever write another word again—

I'm very lucky, I said.

Or spinning—

She looked away: this felt unaddressed, unowned.

That's what it's sometimes like, she said.

I waited. I'd learned that this sort of thing with Janet was what sometimes amounted to an explanation. But whether an explanation of her resumed writing or of the state of play with her motorcycle companion or of something else that lay beyond my ken, I had no idea. Had she caught up with my machinations, perhaps, was this what she was sidling towards in her strange indirect way, had Lyall spilled the beans to her? One never knew, one never knew a thing.

She said, I'm in mourning—

I'm sorry to hear that, Miss Frame—

I waited.

It seems you can't spin underwater—

Well, this was far too deep for me, and I had to stand and gather up the plates to cover the impossibility of reply. As with all things Janet, it had a certain sense to it but only while it lasted, and afterwards was as baffling an arrangement of words as one might expect to hear. I think that I've reproduced them fairly here and without the tendency of which I sometimes stand accused, to make rather more of things than things necessarily require to have made of them. But she had me a little concerned as she left me for the hut, I can assure you, and some may see why, as I watched her leave, my thoughts went back to my earlier conversation with Lyall, when the word *hospital* came bobbing up between us and neither man had known what next to do with the thought of it—no more than I knew on this occasion after lunch, when as soon as the thought bobbed up once more, back down I thrust it once again—underwater, I suppose, if that meant anything at all. Who knew, who knew anything, who knew what it was that was down there—?

As far as my work-in-progress was concerned my misgivings proved to be prophetic, for the following morning I found a struggle to return to where I'd been a day before—for whatever that was worth, it must be added. Those staccato bursts of typing I'd fired off the last week or so changed place too, defecting to the hut as Janet began to rattle and pause, rattle and pause, while I just sat and listened to her doing so. After a while I tried to fire a volley or two in return but then hove to, as baffled by myself as I'd ever been. It was someone else's work in front of me, it wasn't mine—a sense that is usually replaced, as the day matures, by the old familiar swoon back into things, that picking-up of the traces, that writerly falling-in-love-again that becomes a day's work. Not this time for me though, and not (if I were to tell myself the truth) for several days now: for several days, in fact, I realised as I read and re-read what I'd been writing, I'd been fumbling along, kidding myself, improvising. For weeks I'd typed and typed with (as it seemed) almost nothing in my mind, barely a thought in my head as the pages accumulated happily beside me with their unexpected tale of female life: and then the misgivings began, and the pauses in my typing, the bursts of puzzled activity and the long silences between. It seemed the writerly pricking of the thumbs I'd felt not so very long before was proving no more, in the end, than what might be thought the equivalent of an unwriterly thumbing of the prick—

After an hour of thoughts like these I could take no more. I stood and moved away from the writing table. There was a sputter of Gatling fire from the hut, like a flurry of rain, barely as long, then silence, then another rattle. It occurred to me all at once that rather than being rivals fighting for supremacy Janet and I might be in the same boat, that all the signs suggested she might be becalmed as much as I. The possibility of disappointment was no new thing for me, but could I stand the thought of hers? For myself, I feared the growing thought that everything I'd done this winter since that first fine excitement might prove to have been some kind of hoax inside my head after all, that I might return to the utter desolation of her earlier time with me. But the thought of the same disillusionment for her seemed far worse. My own motivations in the time that Janet suddenly became such a fixed part of my life were not always (as I've tried to make plain so far) of the highest order, and it has not been easy for me to own them as I've tried to do. But to think that she might be passing through that worst of all writerly crises, that *that* was what she'd been moving towards and through these last several days—the thought of this was more than I could bear. I at least had had my successes to look back on.

But where were hers, and what would she do if I was right and she proved bereft—what would *I* do?

These thoughts meanwhile had taken me to the back door of the house, where I stood waiting for her to start typing again. It had rained lightly, with that wondrous smell of metal left behind in the air. From her no sound, though, and so I stepped down and strolled the path, first around the rear corner of the house and to the gate and letterbox, since it occurred to me that just such an omen-free morning as this, when I'd been completely and unusually devoid of thought of him, would be precisely the moment to receive a word from Harry. Absent art, and that would be exactly when he'd strike (you can see how such a thought might form itself as I went along): this notion had often occurred to me before, but, as had also occurred before with equal frequency, I was wrong and the box lay bare of any sign or squeak from him. As always—every day, every day—this lack struck a light sharp blow in my chest, with all those implications I dared not countenance too long and with them the not-unrelated thought (once more) of that other old codger of mine up the coast whom I'd put off seeing or dropping a line to for—how long now? And after a few seconds I hastened away down the path and from the realisation that the number of weeks since last I'd called on poor old Solomon was now no fewer than *ten*. I hastened from the thought, and towards the cause (as it unworthily seemed at the time) of that neglect:

Who sat (I discovered as I strolled past her open door) knitting—

I strolled to the compost boxes at the bottom of the garden, paused and returned to her door. On the desk in front of her I saw pages of green paper that she was reading: this is what she looked up from, knitting all the while with a soft persistent click-click-click. I wavered and stopped— an unthinkable presumption for a working writer, I know: but was she in fact working? And as I did, she paused for a moment and held her knitting up towards me. It dangled from her pins, a rough homespun recognisably in the business of becoming what she'd claimed it was—I could see the shape of a jersey front now and sculpted curves for the shoulders, and the vee of a neck appeared up high: almost the torso of a headless man. Then down it came again and the needle-ends began once more offhandedly to wag. All done without a word, by the way, as if the gesture was sufficient in itself, and the knitting stood in for every other thing in the world that required explanation. Naturally I thought of Madame Defarge at the guillotine.

And so I began to turn my thoughts to Lyall, as you might imagine, for if Janet had nothing to say of this mystery, then he would have to fill her place. So much then for my recent authorial pretensions, you might think, as I scurried about trying to unravel the very plot I myself had started with a whisper in his ear: but if I thought of this at all back then I have no recollection what I came up with for a conclusion, whether it seemed inevitable, part of the wild goose chase our own work leads us on or the silly conceit I think it now. What I do recall is the sense that things were darkening around me and that only he could help me clear them up: and so I set about the usual round of calls I made whenever he went off like this, as seemed to have been the case. From one or two the usual response—so I was still alive, then, Harry must be back for me to have been out of circulation so long, had I been overseas?—and to each of these tiny sarcasms I made my customary emollient replies. But no sign of Lyall, not even via Gordon Garlick, off whom he used to sponge from time to time: the killing season's starting soon, Gordon boomed down the phone at me, he'll be off in the freezing works. Which means he's out of town of course—

So that, it seemed, was that, leaving me to deal with Janet on my own devices and with my growing fear that her continuing silence and solitude were very forbidding signs

147

of something worse to come. If the irony of my situation escaped me then, by the way, it certainly does not escape me now: I who'd set events in motion had been left to deal with the results alone. Rightly so, rightly so—except that as it turns out the events in question were not quite what I presumed them to be at the time, and the story proved to be much stranger than boy-meets-girl-and-boy-departs. For, first of all, an evening or two later—within a week, I'm sure of that—the motorbike returned, and left me sitting in my front room with ears on stalks, so to speak, as first its motor cut and then the familiar heavy male tread went down the side of the house and along the back and I heard voices, not clearly, and the thump of the hut door. It was later than usual, about nine, and I stood there quite amazed, so sure had I been that on this head I'd got things right and that nothing more was left to know.

The start of chapter two, you might say and in a manner of speaking—but should I start to read it, that was the question: I mean by slipping out to see what might be floating on the dark cool spring night? Surely an innocent evening stroll might yield a word or two to a passing listener, words that might do much to explain the state of play now Lyall (for this is how it seemed) had motored through the early night from who-knew-where (the nearest freezing works out of town were a full fifty miles away) to claim his—what? But before I could do anything of this dubious sort, my lesser self was saved by the simple event of the slamming of the hut door a second time and the sound of those heavy feet proceeding along the back of my house once more—ridiculously soon, far too soon to correspond to my imaginings, for barely a minute or two had passed since their thumping arrival. I was out in a second, pulled along my path by a heavy bodily crash and thump ahead of me and another around the corner of the house as the man in question stumbled off towards the gate, thrashing into bushes as he went—and there, there, I saw

148

him for half a second, doubled over as he went through the gap in my hedge and out. A man, definitely, and surely (now here was the motorbike, kicking and kicking and starting up at last) Lyall, returned to the scene of the crime—?

I flung out and down the path, I rounded the corner of the house and slithered through the hedge—I think I called his name out—

And what I saw departing, just cresting the hump in the road and falling away on its other side, was a motorbike and sidecar, and the man I saw on the motorbike was, without a doubt, Little Ben—

Well, this knocked me for six as you might imagine. I've made much, in this account, of my schemes and the pride I'd taken in setting up my little plot—too much, perhaps, since the mind when heated is a stranger to the same mind cooled, and there is much of my thought and motivation in this period that is simply no longer there for me to know. For all that I've chosen to render myself at this point as Prospero on his island, anyone can see I was far from being very much in command of it at all. So my first reaction to what I glimpsed that night (after the initial shock of it, and once I'd got myself back inside the house and was thinking a little straighter) was relief: I'd seen a real person rather than a phantom, and something that was happening rather than something I'd imagined. That thought kept me in my mind rather than going quite out of it, and in fact I see this now, for all that was to come next, as the first moment in which I began to come to earth from all this nonsense I'd caught myself up in. I clutched at the younger Ben, so to speak, and down to earth he brought me—

But not immediately. It was no small business to take aboard the meaning of what had happened and the thought that Janet's evening visitor was other than assumed. What was Lyall's game, telling me (more or less) that he had been the cause of Janet's evening exercise—or was that true but had she developed other interests now he laboured on the mutton chain far away, his heart in bits and pieces? Or (another thought) was it in fact the case that she'd been balancing both interests all this time and playing off Army Indian (so to speak) against motorbike and sidecar—were there more, too, had there been a plague of different vehicles unbeknownst to me, a veritable motorcycle jamboree? And could any of this madness possibly be the work of any Janet I thought I knew, even given the well-established facts that none of us ever knows anyone anyway and that the longer an acquaintance endures the more this is the case?

The next step and the beginnings of an answer were obvious enough and no more than a phonecall away, a matter which given the time of night meant it would be the morning's first task after a short stroll to the Lake Road phone box. If Young Ben proved bashful as to his nocturnal activities once thus rung, it was possible the older Ben would be more forthcoming: and besides, the lad for all his size was still a juvenile and needed saving from the temptations I could see spreading before him like the contents of one of his blessed honey-pots—well, this was the kind of specious nonsense I was thinking at the time as I tried to rationalise what I intended while preparing myself for bed. And it disappeared from my mind completely as I folded back my covers and saw a square of paper underneath, on my bottom sheet.

I stood with my hand holding up the bedclothes and gazed and gazed. What in the name of hell was this—?

I picked it up and turned it over:

A fruit in the middle of its location—

I stood there, staring at her ink.

What on earth could she mean—I say *she* because who else? It was her writing, and as to the business of putting the thing there, she'd been on the property all day albeit largely incommunicado, and had obviously ducked in and left it in

150

my bed (*in my bed*!) while my back was turned. But *why*, what was she trying to say, what did she mean by it? It rocked me, it seemed so strange, so incomprehensible—but whatever the explanation, there it was, the hard, odd fact of it, something new to keep me from my sleep when once I lay beneath the covers, and cold comfort for another long demanding night. And then, in the morning?—obviously she'd know I'd found it, and the fact of it as much as its contents would lie between us till one or the other of us brought it out into the open: as yet one more oddity to be addressed, yet one more baffling complication.

Late in the night I heard the house door creaking open on the far side of the hanging sheets from me, ten feet away. If I was asleep at all—who knows?—it snapped me awake. Often, she slipped in like this to the water-convenience and barely disturbed my slumbers: in the morning she would apologise for having woken me when in fact I'd slept the night away undisturbed. Now as she came in I lay there with eyes popping and arms clutched to my sides. I couldn't help my reaction, unworthy as it was: couldn't help but hold my breath till she crept back past the far side of the hanging bed-sheets a minute or two later and the door was closed behind her once again.

Or I may have dreamed all this—

And the next night, God help me, the motorcycle was back. As far as confronting Janet about the note was concerned my decision to take the coward's way out had gone untested, as Janet didn't stir. I left her a covered plate after lunch and another for her evening meal, and never has crockery landed on wooden step with smaller disturbance to the surrounding airwaves, I can tell you: and when I slipped out at eight both were there, cleared and stacked for collection in the usual way. The thought did cross my mind that her mysterious note might be some kind of thankyou for these meals, but any further reflection of this kind went out the door when, once again, the roar of an approaching motorcycle disturbed the denizens of Esmonde Road. Once again it sputtered out on the far side of my hedge, and once again the cats scattered as Ben (I now assumed) thudded along the side and rear of my little house. Once more, voices, and the *clump* of Janet's door—

I waited. A couple of minutes went by then three then four. I opened my own door and slipped out. Past the hut there was a hose I could fiddle with for a moment or two while I watched—and what more innocent activity (despite the late hour) than to coil it up and in doing so approach bit by bit the tap it was connected to and thus the hut nearby: and the life within? There was a momentary frustration as I discovered that Janet had made a sort of curtain out of a cloth or frock of hers that blocked the window: but a moment of excitement, too, when I noticed that it had been disturbed enough to allow a tiny gap near its lower hem and consequently a glimpse of what went on within. I gave barely a sideways glance as I carried the hose past—that was, after all (wasn't it?) what I'd come out to do, coil the hose: but what I saw had me back for a better look, and then, for all the shame I felt (which amounted in truth, as ever, to no more than a fear of being discovered), a third. And even these visits to her pane and the postage stamp of light beyond were not enough to satisfy my gaze. For there was Ben all right, but Ben sitting obediently with his hands held up while Janet wound from them the skein of wool they held apart for her, and a busy ball of wool grew in her hands: Hercules to her Omphale—

In the days following this nonsense I made a deliberate effort to resume my former ways of life, I remember, and began once more to cross the harbour regularly and to town as if trying to put the recent past behind me by reclaiming my more distant one. I yearned to resume something of my lost habits, not least the harmless sniffing after books in the public library and in various bookshops spotted about the city, and then the taking of an evening meal at the Peking in Wellesley Street where the elderly Chinaman owner sat at a table by the door watching his sons and daughters doing all the work and two slices of bread were served free with every meal. Once again the old fellow and I enjoyed our comically different versions of the English language, and once again I could stroll through the early evening streets afterwards and down to the ferry building the jetty and home. How normal this life seemed when once resumed, and how much I wanted to embrace it again and tear away from the tangled web I'd woven, or that had simply woven itself for me.

But instead, towards the close of my third or fourth such visit, I found that web still hanging in wait—for when I arrived at the wharf, there was Lyall down below me on the terminal steps, one of ten or a dozen waiting to board the ferry and in his heavy black jacket looking disturbingly, I thought, like a spider. He was three-quarters turned away from me: he looked dark and unkempt: I leaned on the railing and looked down on him as I listened to the slop and slap of jetty water. For a moment I thought to walk off again and kill time in town until the next boat left, thus leaving behind me unaddressed and unresolved the whole wretched business I associated with him and Janet. But what if he was headed across to Esmonde Road with the purpose of seeing her again, or even to give me the time of day?—and with that thought I found myself pressing down the steps towards him, slightly dismayed (I have to admit) by my lack of self-restraint, my sheer bloody nosiness and where it had a habit of taking me time after time. It was as if I could never get away from the nightmare because the nightmare was inside me: and yet I knew Lyall's presence offered as good a chance as any I had to tie up loose ends. I told myself this—or I tell it now, looking back, trying to make sense of myself as I was a year ago and more, trying to understand the decisions I made then.

I moved down the steps and towards him, and seized his wrist—

He twisted around towards me. Frank, he said. Long time no see. And it turned out he'd come a cropper on his motorbike and been laid up a couple of weeks. So that's why you haven't been around lately! I said. Janet's missing you. Of course that was pure invention but it seemed to have an effect. *Missing* me, he said. Is that right? He seemed a bit thrown by the thought. Well, aren't you off to see her, I said, indicating the ferry, which was now filling up with folk. Isn't that where you're going? But he said no, he hadn't that in mind particularly, it was the question of his bike, which was over the other side waiting for him on the Bayswater jetty: apparently it had been fixed up in some friend's yard nearby. Gordon Garlick? I suggested, and we both had a bit of a laugh at the thought of old Gordon in overalls and with unlikely oil on his hands. But we were uneasy together, Lyall and I, and I thought of the times I ran into Rex Fairburn waiting for the ferry in exactly the same place and had to talk to him when things were so bad between us. As far as Lyall was concerned, though, I thought quite apart from anything else he looked down on his luck and up against it, which of course had me wondering about the state of play as far as his amorous interests were concerned.

On the ferry we stood side by side at the rail while the wake fanned out in the still dark water and the engine went *put-put-put* beneath our feet. Lyall said he'd been killing time at an Evelyn Ankers flick and we talked about that for a while. I said I preferred her beau, a brooding pup called Richard Denning, and he said Richard Denning wasn't in this film. It was a Western, he said, as if that made a difference. And then he got onto what he always got onto in conversations about his favourite movie bints, the question of the relative mammary endowments mother nature had disposed among them, and I brought up the question I always raised at times like this, namely what his obsession with issues of size betrayed about his relationship with his mother. You leave my mother out of it, Frank, he said. The two things aren't connected. What two things? I said, and then he said I was reading ideas into what he said, I was seeing meanings that were never there in the first place. Well, with this sort of talk we warmed up a little, though of course we had to keep it down on account of the folk who were standing nearby and who'd take a dim view of the kind of stuff we were saying if they overheard it.

And then because things felt a bit more like the old days I took the plunge and brought up Janet's name again:

Janet, he said, and looked away. What about her—?

Well, I said. You were having a good time there weren't you, the two of you, weren't you getting to be friends—?

It was hard to know how to put it because it seemed to be a slightly touchy issue.

I saw a bit of her, he muttered, but you could tell he wasn't happy to be talking about it. There was a darker side to him that I'd sometimes sensed before, and I could feel it now, coming through. But then I come off the bike, he said, and I had my hands full with that—

So when *was* that? I asked. And he said he didn't know but he supposed it was the end of July. You said two weeks just now, I said, and he said, well no, it was more like a month now he thought about it, he'd had two weeks in the hospital and he'd been out at least two weeks now or maybe three—

Well, this bemused me more than somewhat, I might say. The thought that he'd been crocked up in hospital and hadn't let me know was hard enough to take, with its lost opportunities for bedside vigils and the attendant thought that someone I knew who was sick might be able to do

155

without my help in that way. But consideration of this was put aside by another thought emerging, which was that if he'd got the date of his accident right, then there were very few days and weeks left back then for him to have spent with Janet. It was difficult working things out just there and then and on the spot, but the more I ran it through my mind the more it seemed to me that if he'd had his accident when he said he did, in point of fact there was hardly time enough before it (as far as I could reconstruct events) for him to have spent any days and weeks with her at all. This deduction left me in two minds, one urging discretion on what might have been a painful business, the other full of memories of Lyall's own indiscretions in past matters of the heart and his tendency not to leave any detail unspoken if in fact such details were capable of being confined in words. Sometimes when he was spilling the beans on his escapades with some lass or other I'd had to ask him to stop!—well, to slow down a bit at any rate, so I could catch up with particular details.

Naturally it was the second of those thoughts that had its way.

He stood there looking at the horizon when once I'd put to him the gist of my calculations and what they implied. Well, maybe it's less than that, he said after a while. I don't know, I don't keep a bloody diary do I—

Well, when you last came by my place, I said, do you remember that? And he said yes he did. And you told me you were, you know, I said. I told you what? he said. You said you were—and I couldn't finish the sentence because suddenly it sounded silly and wrong to say it out loud, suddenly it seemed so crass even to be thinking of Janet in the way that I'd been thinking. *You* know, I said. You told me you were stamping her card for her. He stared at me. I did not, he said. Yes you did, I said. I said no such thing, he said. *You* remember, I said, and I was beginning to wonder at this point whether

156

I remembered, whether I might have flipped my lid at last and was only just beginning to realise. But I had such clear recollections of how he'd said it was a good thing I couldn't see what was going on—though when you put it that way (I began to realise with some dismay), what was it that he'd *really* said, what was it he'd actually committed himself to having been up to—?

I checked my watch: we were halfway across.

I might've said something like that, he said, when I insisted on my version of events. But it's a fact, it's a good thing you couldn't see, that's all I would've meant. People shouldn't go spying in other people's windows—

On this point he was quite right of course, but he said it so loudly that two or three of the other passengers looked around and I had to hush him down a bit. Keep it down, I said, I wasn't spying on anyone. And then I set out my version of events in full, how I'd thought he'd turned up each night at Esmonde Road when I heard the motorbike arrive and that he'd taken his pleasures and then been on his merry way. When I'd finished, the mounting sense I had was of course dismay that I could have got so very much of this account so very wrong: but the main point that seemed to irk him was when I brought the matter up concerning young Ben's role and the possibility that now seemed very real, to the effect that what I'd taken to be the sound of Lyall's motorbike each time it turned up had been in fact the sound of Ben's. *That* heap of shit? he said, and once more I had to hush him down as people turned their heads towards us. You mixed up my Army Indian with that heap of shit he rides? Keep your voice *down*, I said as people looked around at us. But he decided to take it as far as he could, it seemed, as if my failures in matters mechanical gave him not only the edge in the matters we were discussing but also the moral high ground as well. That heap of shit, he said. I can't believe it—

But now he'd shown this attitude I got my dander up as

much as I'm capable of doing and as happens from time to time though never often, and I found it was me that was having difficulty keeping my voice down. Well, I said, if that's the case how often did you see her, did you see her at all? Janet? I could see him wavering. I can't remember, he said. No come on, I said. Of course you can remember. No I can't, he said. He turned away. I could feel enough from him not to pursue it. I tried to calm myself down. What was it we were arguing about, anyway?

There was a silence, a minute, two minutes, with the throb of the engine beneath our feet in every second.

I saw her just the once, he said suddenly.

You could tell he didn't like admitting it. He spat it out at me.

I saw her after you told me, he said. You know, after you told me she was keen. Well, you got that wrong—

How very much I regretted that foolishness now. I tried to say something but he cut me short—

I come in one night, he said. Late. Tapped on the door of the hut. Christ, you'd've thought I was Jack the bloody Ripper—

He turned away from me. Above the fade where the sun had gone down the slightest curve of a moon hung. *Put-put-put* beneath the decking—

Well? Then what happened—?

Suddenly he turned back to me. She's fucking *crazy*, Frank, he said. I could see his fists gripping the rail. She's fucking *mental*—

The way he said it scared me, terrified me. I could feel something cold crawl up my back, beneath the skin. I could feel myself tensing, lower down.

What d'you mean? I said. She's certainly unusual—

Unusual—? She's—

He fumbled his hands around, his body twisted as if he was in the grip of something. It certainly did nothing to settle

158

me down, seeing him like that, in fact it fair put the wind up me. I couldn't swallow properly.

She's not all there, he burst out. No, that's wrong—there's too much of her. I dunno. Jesus—

He turned and walked away, still touching the rail. The shore was looming up with its lights, you could hear voices on the jetty.

You never know what you're going to get when you're with her. One minute she's normal, the next she's—it's like you're with the, I dunno, the Duchess of fucking Kent or something—

Did she turn you down? Is that it—?

He flung himself against the rail, against the slight inward swing of the ferry as it began its berthing curve.

Turn me down? he said. Christ, Frank, I never *got* that far, I never knew where I fucking was—turn me down? I wish she'd had a fucking *chance* to turn me down, I wish we'd fucking *got* that far—

Language—

We both turned: a couple on the far side of the ferry, the man with an arm around the woman as if shielding her. I could see his face in the half-light, under the brim of his hat.

There's women aboard, the man called. His woman was turned away. She was wearing a ridiculous little hat, off to one side above her ear.

Lyall took a step towards them. Get a fucking dead dog up youse, he called out. You want to make something of it—?

Lyall—

I grabbed at his arm. I got a fistful of jacket.

Lyall—

He swung around at me, back at me:

She's a *schizophrenic*, he hissed.

Put-put-put went the engine, and then silence as it shut off ready to berth. There was the swish of the hull against the water as the boat moved freehand towards the jetty. He swiped my fist away from his jacket and stood there, glowering down at me. Behind him the jetty loomed up.

You're living with a schizophrenic, *Frank*. A bloody *schizophrenic*—

Bump, against the pilings, softly but definitely, as always, and as always the slightest tremor, up through the legs. I stood there, gripping the railing, giving at the knees.

The moment he said it, everything changed. What did it mean—split personality, different personalities, something like that? But it was the sound of the word that was shocking, that and the way he hissed it out at me in the dusk. It was as if the passenger who'd just objected was really complaining about *that* word and not the swearing. It sneaked in like all those other medical words nobody likes to hear, *haematoma* and *carcinoma* and *coronary* and *thrombosis*. *Schizophrenia*. It had an irrational loading of doom that terrified me, rooted me to the spot so that I just stood and watched the crewman loop the hawser and the complaining man get off, his arm still protecting the woman, and after them another passenger, male, behind him, and another, and then Lyall himself, his broad-shouldered triangular back as he went up the steps, feet slightly splayed, to the top.

I caught him up on the road where he'd left the bike. He was bouncing into the saddle and kicking the stand free with a heel.

Really? I said.

Really—

He kicked the starter and the engine gave a premonitory snarl and died.

Hop aboard—

He kicked the starter again.

She *told* you—?

But I was lost in the noise as the engine coughed and Lyall caught it, coaxing it up with his wrist at the throttle till it

160

settled to its usual throaty roar. He yelled something: what was it? He pointed at the pillion. I shook my head. He kicked the stand away and pushed the bike forward. He yelled something again as he started to roll forward.

What's that—?

He yelled it out again. I walked beside him, behind him.

She's been in the bin, he yelled. He was moving away.

What—?

His finger made a twirling movement near his right temple:

The loony bin—

Did she say that? I was running after him now, but he was pulling away. Did she tell you that—?

There was a blare of gravel and he was going, his tail-light on-off-on like an angry winking eye. He was gone.

That night I doused the light and rolled myself up in my old Harry-smelling blanket with my mind full of the word Lyall had given me. It still shocked me, but in truth I'd no idea where its power came from. The more I thought about it the less sure I was that I really knew what it meant—did I think it was something to do with split personality because the 'schiz' part of the word sounded like 'splits', was it nothing more than that, was it as silly as that? It felt as if the word was keeping me out, keeping its meaning on the outside, keeping me away from itself and that's where it got its power from. I knew I'd have to find out more—

I lay there, aware of her twenty feet away and the back door of the cottage open as it always was and nothing between us.

Sharp in the middle of the night I woke up dreaming a terrible violent noise. Had it happened yet? I sat up on an elbow, sweating. I listened to the pump going in my chest. What had happened, what was it? I found the matchbox and lit the candle on the windowsill. After a minute I saw a piece of paper on the floor by the bed. I'd no idea whether I'd stepped over it getting into bed or it had been put there while I slept.

I opened it, and read her words:

His look is the beast that guides his chariot—

I thrust it away from me, I thrust its paper corner into the candle flame, I held it away from me as it flared and burnt, I held it against the heat on my hand, my fingers, in my nails, till it was a black charred curl that fell to the bedroom floor. I sat there trying to forget the strange, terrible sentence it had brought me. I tried to understand what all this was going to mean.

After a couple more minutes I was steady enough to creep out of bed and pull the curtain aside from the back window.

Out there, from a void, the army hut, looking back.

From a drawer in the kitchen I took the trimming knife Lyall had given me, the sharpest that I had, and carried it back to my bed.

CHAPTER 7

I'd always told the world that despite my august calling I was at heart no different from the folk on either side of 14 Esmonde Road or on the factory floor. I was just another toiler, albeit in a different kind of furrow from the rest. Yet all the time I'd ignored the vanity of writing for men and women who needed no one to write their lives. The truth is that the people who read my work and understand as much as I let them understand are a very select bunch indeed—university folk, teachers, a politician or two, other writers, artists and those civilians who've hauled themselves up by their own brittle bootstraps. Which is another way of saying that in number they are very few indeed, and that of my fellow men most are like the neighbour three doors down the road from me who let it be known a number of years ago that there was a fellow three doors up who'd done not a hand's turn in his life.

But my time with Janet told me something new about myself, and an irony at that. For it turns out I was right after all: I *am* no different from my fellows: we all share the worst of human failings, every one of us. I who'd always preached the need never to judge our fellow man and always to open ourselves to the variety of the human condition even in its strangest shapes and forms—I proved no better than the man next door when confronted by the prospect of an illness of the mind. From the very thought of it I fled in blind fear panic and confusion, and with just as much ignorance and misinformation as the rest of the round world. And from a *word*, what's more, uttered thrice like a magic spell that transformed everything once spoken, and a word all the more powerful for the lack of any content. For I was no clearer about it when I woke from whatever sketch of a night's sleep I managed after my ferry trip with Lyall than when he first poured it in my ear while we were aboard. But that was its power, I realised, as I sat on the edge of my bed: you couldn't break the word open. And naturally when I thought of that, I also thought of some of the things Janet had said along those lines earlier in her time with me, and tried to bring them back to mind.

She herself, though, Janet in person—now, that was a different kettle of fish. The thought of her now terrified me. Even in writing this down I am ashamed, please understand that, and fully aware of its absurdity of course: after all, I'd been sharing the place with her for nearly six months and for all our ups and downs (and in truth the more mystifying, nay disturbing, events of recent days and weeks) I was still demonstrably alive and unscathed—I was not pricked, and I did not bleed. What then was I afraid of? And as I try to find some kind of answer to that question now, a year and more after this dismaying and not especially edifying period of my life, the best thing I can point to is the slow, reluctant progress, from the unexamined life of my mind into its examined life, of my knowledge of her past. I've made much, I see as I look back, of my bafflement at her origins. But the truth is that, at some level, I always knew them: at some level they had percolated through to me, from gossip, from word of mouth, from the culture itself—somehow and in some way, I'd known from my very first encounter that she'd been in a hospital not so very long before, and that her time there had not been brief. Knew it, but didn't know it: had known it and tucked it quietly away. The very discretion and politeness that had

164

precluded my ever raising this delicate matter with her relied on the even more extraordinary discretion and politeness by which, it seemed, I had refrained from even raising it with myself. But now—*abracadabra!*—here it came, out into the light to be confronted, with all the attendant pains and fears of such an unwanted birth. At least that is how I reckon it now. I stopped pretending, even to myself.

That early morning following Lyall's revelation, of course, I had no such thoughts and survival was the only game in town. Before the slightest sign of life from the army hut I was gone, my plans laid: with my rucksack on my shoulder I was at the side of Lake Road before the sun had got much farther above the horizon than the hand I was holding out to the traffic passing by. I'd neglected Solomon long enough—well, this is what I told myself at the time, though even then I felt some measure of shame that my motivation was rather to leave my own door than to arrive at his. But while setting off to see him was obviously a ruse to put off the evil hour when I had to confront my hut-guest with my new knowledge burdening my mind, it is not at all untrue to say he'd never entirely left that mind, and that thoughts of him had lately turned to dreams, though less of pleasure than the guiltier ones of plants unwatered and cats unloved—

In twenty minutes I was aboard a cream lorry returning from the early ferry and heading north. As the suburbs fell away to left and right I sensed the last few days falling with them. My companion was one of us, another human, one more of those elderly codgers I happily came across on trips like this from time to time, with their collective air of much in the way of wisdom hard earned and held close. This old brute was a little more forthcoming than most, however, and had plenty to say on some of the great issues of the day, not least of which had to do with the management of public money on such principles that Rex Fairburn himself might have been approving had he managed to fit his long and lanky frame into the cab of the lorry beside us. Even without Rex, though, by the time my driver dropped me off within a manageable walk of Solomon's little beachside shack I was in no manner of doubt that the whole of our present time is but in suspension before the inevitable moment when the Social Credit Political League elects its present leader to the local House of Representatives. For it seems the millennium awaits no more than the parliamentary arrival of Mr Wilfred Owen. Then we'll see, the old fellow told me: and who can say he might be wrong?

But all matters of political economy disappeared from thought when once I'd completed the long slog down Pukapuka Road and scrambled down Solomon's track and to the bank of the tidal creek. As his little cottage came in view it showed evidence for the worst of fears: for it was shut and padlocked—this I could see as I all but fell the last few steps down towards it. In all my years of knowing him the place had never been closed up: in fact I couldn't even remember a door to it. But there a door stood in fact and faced me down, its four panels and their crackled remains of pale blue paint suggesting distant and finer origins. I hardly bothered to push at it or turn the knob: I've never seen a door more shut or a house more emphatically abandoned. I didn't even call the old man's name, instead took a look about the place with my heart pumping hard in my chest. And a glimpse in the window around the back was enough to finish the business off for me—his bed was stripped, striped mattress bared, a little chest beside it robbed of drawers. Outside, the bits and pieces of his daily life were gone—the nets and bags and pots and the accumulated driftwood for his fire, and, further away, the tiny wooden boat in which over the years we'd bobbed together further from the coast than I could sometimes see. I walked down the bank of the creek to the mangroves and tried to persuade myself I could glimpse him in it on the harbour water, that he'd made a full recovery behind my back and put his old life on himself once more without my help. But I knew better.

Well, this turn of events had me rattled as much as you might imagine, although like me Solomon had had long battles concerning his informal living arrangements and I wondered if the authorities had closed him down at last for too much furtive digging in the sand at night?—but a couple on a tractor up the road told me no, they didn't think so, they'd an idea there was a son had picked him up or maybe it had been a cousin or a nephew: a youth, anyway. The old fellow had kept to himself, apparently, and had been left to do so over the years: though when I listened more I was much in doubt they were talking of the same man, the farmer and his wife, they gave details so much at odds the one against the other. Hard work of course, pinning down one particular old fellow amongst the last three decades' rich supply of walking wounded, and I found even my resources of description taxed as I tried to fix the detail that would close the matter up. And little help when the farmer's wife began to form the view in the midst of things that the old chap had in fact croaked, she was pretty sure now we'd talked a bit that this was so, and that it had been the business of the visiting son cousin or nephew to remove the corpse: a view with which her husband was so much at odds, however, that I left them to it and still arguing as I swung my rucksack on my back once more and set off for the main road a mile away and more to start my journey home. Solomon, it seemed, had dissolved behind me when my back was turned. You can imagine what other thoughts took me home to Takapuna, and with the day barely started and all.

Now, as well as bringing about a delay in facing Janet, this morning venture north was something I'd hit on overnight as a feint to take me from the house in the long period of hours before the local library deigned to open up its doors to me: but the business up the coast had turned me around so fast I'd still some many minutes to beguile before I could start my project of research. I spent them eyeing up our Takapuna citizenry on the street. I tried to think of Solomon and where to search for him: and although he never fully left my mind it was a matter of some irritation to me that every time I looked at someone walking past, I thought of Janet and not him. More than anything else this seemed to stand for the imbalance her presence had brought into my life, between its old forms and responsibilities and the ones that had been thrust in their way: and as I sat there I grew increasingly resentful of this interference, as if it was her presence and not my inattention that had caused the rift between my old fisherman and me, and even (if the farmer's wife was right and the unthinkable now required to be thought) the possibility of his death. This of course was all of a piece with what I'd felt regarding Janet and Harry, the mounting sense that somehow she was the cause of his disappearance, even though that disappearance had long preceded her own arrival. Of course none of this makes any sense, but there was the point, that everything had done so until she came along—

To thwart these thoughts I fumbled up some change and tried the phone box in Hurstmere Road. It wasn't till I'd rung the number of the hospital and listened to the dial tone that it occurred to me that for all our long acquaintance I knew his single name and nothing more: Solomon, I told the matron at the other end when once she answered me. No, I don't know his other name, I said. I don't know whether it's his first or his last, either. Well, that was no help as you might imagine and if I hadn't done some skilful work afterwards with Button B and recouped my initial investment thereby, the entire business would have been a loss. They'd no one in there alive or dead who sounded like my man.

Appropriately to the warp I fancied Janet had put on my life, the library when it opened up at last seemed subtly, disturbingly changed, an idea so unsettling I tried not to entertain it any more than I was able. But the thought persisted that the circulation desk had been moved a little to the right, not by much but just enough to make me ask about it after I'd built myself up to make the approach I knew I had to make. Moved? said the young lass behind the desk when I raised the possibility with her. This desk? I don't think so. The shelves, then—? I wondered, and got such a look from her and the old dame at her side as well that I called it off and raised the matter that I'd come for. And once I'd got *that* off my chest, what with the start I'd made regarding the positioning of the furniture, I can tell you they were handling me with tongs. Psychology? the older woman asked me with a stare that had me wondering whether she might have known something of my distant hidden past. We don't usually carry books like that in a suburban library, we'll have to order them from the main library in town. What exactly were you looking for? And so I had to voice the wretched word, as low as I could, but then that blew back in my face because they couldn't hear my first two shots at it and I was reduced in the end to bawling it out loud and clear after all:

Schizophrenia—

Well, it didn't produce quite the widespread panic I'd expected, but it shut them up all right. I felt like a youth asking for French letters at the chemist's shop! It's for some private research I'm doing, I said, on illnesses of the mind. Yes yes, we'll see what we can manage, they told me, come back in a day or two—

As I retreated to the door she couldn't take her eye off me, the older one, as if by saying the word I'd owned up to having the very illness itself: I felt that everyone in the library, staff and customers, was thinking in much the same way, I felt as if a layer of skin had been stripped from me and that everyone could see the words I thought and the things I felt, as if I'd stopped being what I was and gone over to the other side in some way, and forfeited every right I had to being treated as a human being. In other words (I realised later), I began to feel what Janet must have felt pretty much every minute of the day. How had this happened? How had I been reduced from the magus she had made her pilgrimage to consult (*the father of a nation's fiction*) to this, a furtive figure scuttling along Lake Road with rucksack and beret—innocent only to the passing observer, just any old codger trying to get to the fruiterer's perhaps, or the dairy for twenty Capstan, or to the Mon for a jug and a counter lunch? And how much happier I, if indeed I'd been that man and nothing more!—if I'd been blessed with Harry's sturdy self-containment, say, with the happy infinity of his limited horizons, the never-failing freshness of his repetitious life, on the probable recurrences of whose chief daily pleasures—a fag, the wireless, a cuppa and *Best Bets*, a stroll to the local pub—one would get no odds at all. Instead I carried a secret, a thought, a word, a worry about myself—something that people, I knew, were beginning to be able to see in me. Of that I was sure, I was certain—

And now at last there was the business of Janet to confront. I was unable to write, of course, this latest bombshell having brought an end to all pretence my former working life was again upon me: and besides, the morning was pretty much done when once I'd quit the library and set off reluctantly for home. There, and without the slightest pang of hunger, I nevertheless found myself busily starting to assemble the rudiments of a lunch, as if some midday siren had sounded in my head and my body had taken to making decisions on its own: assembling lunch for her, that is, as well as lunch for me, even though her recent appearances at any meal had been sporadic enough and despite the fact besides that if she did show up I'd no idea how to talk to her any more, no idea what on earth to say. And yet here I was, busily stirring the

170

stockpot on the electric element, slicing the loaf I'd bought at Lane's and setting out plates and cutlery for two. The mindless whistling that came from my lips while I was doing this suggested that my body had hit on feigning nonchalance as the best way around possibilities of impending social embarrassment: but what to say to the fact that when I listened to myself I found the tune I hummed was Uncle Toby's Lillibullero?

Well, it's not untrue to say the song that once sang a king from three kingdoms served in this instance to carry me through Janet's appearance when once it came. Since dawn I'd built myself up so much for this moment that when I heard her at the rear door and then saw her at the inner one I leapt with fright, so much so that she stopped short and stared at me as if I'd lost my mind. I fancy a knife or fork went clattering on the floor, but I wonder now if that is an embellishment of narration—no matter: it serves to render something of the state of mind I'd reduced myself to at the time. I remember giving her a thin, terrified, lipless smile: I must have looked like a skull.

Meanwhile, as I say, it was Lillibullero that rescued me somewhat—

Lawrence Sterne! she said. *Tristram Shandy*!

Right! I said. Correct! All over-bright of course, and rubbing palms together as I spoke—nay, sliding them, for all the perspiration the moment had induced: and I felt my face begin to grimace into another ghastly twisted smile. Thinking back to this moment I'm put in mind of the story of the woman who was caught in her bath by the local peeping Tom, and didn't know what to do and so waved politely at him as he peered in her window at her innocence: and he completed the comedy of his trespass by solemnly waving back—

I have to say, though, I was more than somewhat lost in admiration at Janet's knowledge: after all, which of *you* can start to whistle the tune now it has been named, or name it when you hear it played? On the other hand (and with Janet it always seemed that there was another hand), I'd stopped whistling it as soon as I heard her foot thump on the saddle of the cottage outer door, and there was a real doubt in my mind that she could have heard me there: which raised once more the nagging question whether she'd been about my windows in the minutes beforehand. An unworthy thought, of course, but reinforced by the fact that (I realised) my latter-day vigilance in the matter of keeping them closed against such possibilities had fallen away to the extent that, there beside me and unnoticed, my kitchen window yawned agape—

All this though was swept away by the enthusiasm with which she settled to the business of Uncle Toby and his tune. It turned out she knew the latter from her father's pipe band in Oamaru, and the oddity of their choosing to play such a Sassenach boast while wearing the kilt gave us something more to talk about. But Sterne it was who dominated, since there had been few things to equal the wonder she'd felt, apparently, when once *Tristram Shandy* came her way. And since that had been pretty much my experience too when first confronted by its wonderful farrago of blank pages black pages misplaced marbled end-papers and of course the sheer delight of that story that never quite begins while never quite coming to an end—why, who would have said, if watching through that open kitchen window, that we were not some elevated sort of Darby and Joan, she and I, lost in our perpetual talk of art and literature as we were, and I as keen to give to it as she—?

So that it was a jolt, once soup and bread had disappeared and I stood and turned to the business of filling up the jug, to remember all at once the burden of the day and particularly the hectic panic-stricken flight I'd made to Pukapuka that morning in order to avoid the very person I now sat prattling with at lunch: a person, what's more, who was giving every evidence (I had to admit) not only that her recent slump was over but that such episodes were something she'd always been a stranger to—and more than this, that questions of her larger state of mind were not in need of raising in the first place. She was in good form, in other words, so much so that as the water in the jug began to chuff and wheeze behind me I found myself settling down at the counter with her once more and starting to tell her of my earlier adventure. Of Solomon's existence she was well aware, of course, given that she'd eaten fish I'd caught with him earlier in her stay. But although I did not scruple, as I outlined the business of his decline and my neglect, in giving hints sufficient that she might reflect on the role her distracting presence had in my dereliction, it seemed to be something else entirely that caught her interest in my account. So much so that by the end it seemed she couldn't wait for me to reach it, and as soon as I did, here she was:

It's obvious, she said. It's obvious what's happened—

It is—?

It's what happens when you forget people, she said. They stop existing—

You mean they disappear—?

No. No. They stop *existing*, they don't *exist* any more—

Now, you have to understand that in this exchange there was no way of judging the nature of her message, whether by its tone or through the details of her expression. It was given as a simple statement of fact unmarked by anything that might have pointed up the irony it might have had or any other shape or weight. In other words, I'd no idea how to take it, any more than I'd had with earlier suggestions she'd made concerning material reality and the possibility of escaping it.

As I thought these thoughts she went on with what provoked them, to the effect that memory was the key to

173

everything and that to remember the past you had to keep on visiting it: going back kept it all alive, she said. If what she meant was things and places I found that I could catch the drift of this, but I had difficulty seeing its application to other parts of the world, to human beings in particular, unless of course they'd died and you visited them in the ground. But when I said this, she was emphatic. It was all memory, she said, every single thing, and memories had to be kept alive— if we didn't think things and write them down, well, then everything would disappear.

That's what's happened to your Mr Fisherman, she said. You stopped thinking about him, and he's stopped existing. You should have written him a letter now and then at least, that would've kept him there—

With everything she said I found there was a sort of aftertaste as when they put something in the tap water: you don't notice it when drinking, but later it comes to you and lingers. The strange remarks she made about Solomon were to haunt me for some time without ever quite making sense, and at the same time without ever being susceptible to pursuit and dismissal as complete and utter nonsense. Her mind worked in strange associations, intuitively, inductively, and I am quite certain that many times she was not yet completely aware of the significance of what she was giving utterance to herself. She guessed her way towards her meanings, perhaps, and this gave her statements both a prophetic quality and a sense that they lived beside great truths rather than in the heart of them. And as you will soon see, the fact that such a sense was also in her work was something I was about to discover.

For as I thought the thoughts I've rendered here, she'd changed her tack. About her there was a sense of slight mystery, as if she was working her way towards something. That remarkable effect was on her now, I noticed, by which her face changed colour as a sign of the advent of finer

174

feelings, and I wondered what was up as first her neck and then her face turned pink then scarlet. Sideways, she always came at things sideways: she'd started to tell me something about butterflies. Butterflies as early as this? I wondered. But she was certain—a butterfly had flown in the window of her hut just now. Surely not until next month at least, I said, and added that if she'd seen one as early as this, then it was a good job I'd yet to plant out all my cabbage seedlings. I meant it as a joke to deflect her silliness, but she took me seriously: no, not that kind of butterfly, she insisted, not the white ones. Apparently it was a Monarch—it had come into the hut looking important, she insisted, and it obviously wanted to tell her something—

Well, as far as I was concerned the conversation had fallen away badly at this, and what she was saying was clearly nonsense of the sort that often had me fed up, what with so much of the real world requiring to be dealt with. I stood and turned to the business in hand, the crockery and what have you: and behind me she went on prattling, which is all I thought it at the time. An omen it was, this butterfly, apparently, though as far as I was concerned everything in her world was either a talisman of sorts or nothing at all worth caring about.

But then she said a thing that had me lifting up my head again above the sink.

Finished? I said to her. Well done—that's taken quite a while—

There was a bit of a pause and then she said that she supposed so. I returned to my dishes. It seemed very long to her, she said.

Is it a long chapter, then, I asked. Is that what's taken time—?

Oh, it doesn't have chapters, she said. It's not like a normal book, really, because it's—just—well, it's not a normal book—

175

Well, I said, what is it that you've finished, then—?

She stared at me. The book, she said. I've finished the book—

I stared at her.

You've finished writing it—?

Yes—

The entire book—?

Yes—

I was thunderstruck!

You've written an entire novel in—what—five months—?

I suppose so, she said. I suppose it's been that long—

An *entire novel* in five months—?

Yes. Except it's not a novel, it's something else.

She looked around herself, as if the word she wanted was on the floor or the wall.

It's an—exploration, she said.

I stared at her. An exploration, I said. Well, what's that? Is it—

I fumbled for words: God, how being with her worked me into corners like this, made me think in ways I hadn't thought for years—

Is it made up? I asked. Is it fiction—?

Oh, yes. It's all made up—

I thought of the scrap I'd read in the hut: what part did *that* play in this exploration of hers—?

And how long is it? I asked.

She shrugged. I haven't counted, she said. Forty, fifty thousand words—?

Forty or fifty thousand words, and they're all made up? I smiled at her. Well, then, I am glad to be able to inform you, Miss Frame, that you have written a novella—

She stared up at me from the kitchen counter. It's not a novella either, she said in her strange, scared, apologetic little way. It's not anything, it hasn't even got a title—

Well, I carried this exchange off all right but in truth it

176

rocked me, I mean the thought that since she'd turned up back in March she'd managed not only to write but to write as much as *that*: and in amongst the alarms and distractions we'd managed between us, to boot! I'd had that little gibe at her for the length of it (a pettiness for which I flayed myself when alone and in bed that night), but in truth that hoard of words seemed to me a fine and even an amazing achievement however long she'd taken. I'd always struggled to sustain my longer narratives, and the vignette worked-up and the observation expanded have always remained my truest strengths—I've already mentioned the need to cobble two shorter works together a year or two ago to bring about the effect of a longer, the work that by the look of things might well be my last such reckoned any kind of success of esteem. And then, as I say, for her to have brought her project off as well, I mean to have *finished* it: that knocked me back too, since coming to an end of things—knowing that the end of things has come—is no more easy for a man of my seasoning than for a young lass of hers. Oh well (I thought), we'll see if it's any good: for I assumed that now she'd spilled the beans she'd let me have her manuscript straight away, for judgment and advice—especially now I'd told her (for all her protestations) what it really was she'd written.

It was somewhere in the business of settling this information in my mind, as I dealt to the dishes and she wiped them by my side, that I opened the meat-safe near the bench we stood at. I expect I was putting back the loaf of bread or something like it—and for a moment I resisted what I saw in there. Another folded square of paper lay inside. I shut the little door and went on talking, and carried the business off, over the remaining four or five minutes it took to get shot of our little chore of housework and Janet back inside the hut. But it shocked me when I saw it, as if something unclean had flown out at me like a brown viviparous blowfly caught feasting on my meat. It was as if that other world I feared so much had

177

suddenly appeared again, overwhelming the conversation we'd just had with all its moments of reassurance—and then, too, there was the horror of the fact that all the time we'd spoken thus she'd known it was in there and awaiting me: known that, and known I didn't know it. And it was the thought of this that chilled me most, the sense that all the time we'd lunched together she'd been watching me and waiting, possibly wondering whether I'd spotted it already and was covering up: but always in control of the exchange that was taking place.

I dared not think about it more than I'd done. I made myself open the meat-safe door again once she was gone. All strength had left my upper arms as I took and opened the little speck of folded paper and read the four words she'd written on it:

Meaning all volume satisfies—

It stayed with me as I went back to the local library the following day. I was desperate to find an explanation. Once inside the door I had that sense again that shelves were slightly askew and the newspaper reading area in the wrong place—weren't they?—and I stood a full ten seconds trying to recall the whereabouts of a reference section I'd had my head in just about every week these last fifteen or twenty years: more, more. But this time I kept mum about my strange disorientation, and tried to present a bluff appearance at the desk as a harmless bookish old gent. The young woman I'd talked to the day before didn't help things when she seemed not to recognise me for a second or two. You've been in here before? she asked. *Been in here before*—I practically live here! I'm a local identity, I wanted to tell her, for my beret and rucksack if nothing else in this world of trilby hats and briefcases and fixed ideas. *You* remember, I said to her, and then, reluctantly, mentioned once more the business of illnesses of the mind.

And it seemed she'd found me some helpful books in the central library, after all. You'll have to read them in one of the offices, though, she said. Some books we don't allow in general circulation—

And so it was I sat at a table in someone's office near the rear of the building with books that seemed like Strontium-90, as if the very fact of them might cause panic in the streets. I started to read, a few pages here and a few pages there and then in greater detail: and as I did, and began to apprehend what might be thought their radioactive qualities, I felt my lips slowly unzipping till my mouth hung open like an idiot's. The terrifying thing that Lyall had told me about wasn't hard to find: in fact much of the wretched volume seemed to be taken up with that word and its possible meanings. And dear God what a nightmare they seemed to be! The very books themselves were bad enough—the little pile of them, buff and grey volumes each (I found as I worked my way through them one by one) with its arid version of what might be expected of persons afflicted in their minds.

But the *idea* of such books felt bad, too: the thought that men and women with the chance to write—who might even be given the extraordinary, the unimaginable gift of *being paid in order to do so*—would choose to spend their time day after day and week after week writing about the terrifying world the authors of these particular texts had chosen to show. And then to *live* in that world, to be required to gain that knowledge in the first place, amongst such unhappiness and suffering, amongst people doomed, incurable, sentenced, people in truth as damned as the ones in those newsreels we used to see ten years ago in the local cinemas, part of the stupendous horror of the last war— well, *almost* as damned as they: except that for these latter-day souls, the ones whose existence I was now glimpsing in the textbooks, the sentence was *to live on and on and on*, and with no one to tell the world their fate save the bleak soulless technicians who wrote the books. The forlorn, the lost, the damned—

The violent, too: this was the other thing I saw as I read. A man would take his life in his hands working with some of the cases I saw that wretched morning. The photographs were bad enough—one of the volumes had shots that made my blood run cold, of poor benighted creatures in the very depths of what a human being could become. Just to look at them was more than I could bring myself to do: and yet I found myself staring and staring at them, unable to stop, taken beyond anything I could have expected of myself, mesmerised by the horror of them, the travesty of humanity they showed and the story that their images began to tell me. I slammed it shut at last—it was as if the damned thing had bitten my hand! But I had to stop what the book was telling me, all of the books, I had to stop the story they were telling—

Back in the main library I stared about. Nothing had changed, and everything had changed. It was exactly the same as before, and that is what so terrified me. Its ordinariness, its *everdayness* terrified me. Now, amazingly, astoundingly, all seemed shipshape, the overwhelming sense of discord that had greeted me when I came in had disappeared as if it had never been, so much so that I felt disturbed at having felt it in the first place. For (I looked around) of *course* the reference section was where it always was, of *course* the shelving stood where it had always stood, of *course* the usual old lags were dotted about in their usual various places: the old bloater who came in for the *Times* each morning and left at exactly half-past ten with a bearing that suggested a military past, a distant neighbour from down the road who was often in amongst the hardbound magazines and this morning was in amongst them once again. I even thought my young librarian briefly caught my eye as I looked about, and smiled as if reassured: yes, I was there, yes, I was *in my place*. I played up to her, I smiled and nodded as I went out—part of her normality, part of the solid day-to-day expectedness of things, its ruddy foursquare quality. I could be counted on: but could she look at me and tell, could she see? For I was changed, a veritable ice age had passed since she had seen me coming in ninety minutes earlier.

You understand it is only in these dramatic and in fact rather Janet-like terms that I am able to render myself at the point I'd reached as I walked out of the library and, slowly, with deviations into as many shops as I could find to delay the evil hour, back to hut and cottage. Even now it is difficult to deal with the things that had leapt up from the unclean pages of those volumes I had read—or looked at, or dipped into, whatever word it is that serves to describe the experience I'd just submitted myself to. For it is not untrue to say that, as far as those matters are concerned, as the old song goes, *I was that soldier.* That is the thing, you see. I think back to my young self when I moved into my parents' beachside hovel all those years ago now, an act which at the time was the only thing left I could think of doing since I'd run myself into the ground and there was nowhere else to go—the police were after me my family was after me and my friends were in hot pursuit. And I no child, any more than Janet was still a child when she went through what it was now becoming plain she'd been through.

In truth most of those two sentences are made up of wild exaggerations, I see now that I have written them: but it will give you some sense of the fix I was in when I tell you that the part that's truest is the first part. I had fallen foul of the law. No, I'm not going to tell you any more than that. I'm meant to be telling you about my time with Janet.

I am not one of those who need to be told that each of us is to some degree damaged: that is all I am trying to say. But because the knowledge that we are thus afflicted is always somewhere in my head waiting to be remembered, I take care not to invite its attention. The whole point of the life I have evolved at 14 Esmonde Road since that terrible desperate day when I found myself washed up there as if from a shipwreck is to forget that past. The whole point has been to make a life that gets away from those terrible memories and keeps at bay their horror, each day, just on the other side of the brittle walls around us, on the far side of any fence or hedge. That is what they are for, fences and hedges, and that is what I saw again the moment I lifted my eyes from those hideous textbooks and swept my gaze around the library shelves, that is what I saw again as I crept my way through the shops while delaying as long as possible my return—the terrible truth that for every second of every hour the utter ordinariness of the everyday cries out what lies just behind it. Each time your neighbour agrees across the fence that *this is right* or calls out *you can do mine next* when he spots you mowing your lawn is a shriek from the abyss: the same abyss I'd peered into that morning in the bookshelves. Every civil act, the butcher counting each brown penny of change into my palm to tell his honesty the car stopping to let me cross the road the postie waiting by my letterbox to hand me my mail in person *looks like rain yes this is right*—these are travesties, every one of them, candles in the wind ready to be blown out by the slightest change in the weather. We teeter, all of us, hands linked, on the very crust of hell—

Well, you can see that I'd got myself into a fine old lather by the time I stood at the letterbox watching the postman crank his heavy bike off towards Lake Road. The fan of mail he'd left in my paw was nothing but bills, the Electric Power Board and so on, and rubbish offering me eternal life. There was nothing for it but to face the music—was she on the property, though, or had she disappeared again, conveniently this time, giving me enough breathing space to recover from the morning's excess, if recovery were possible? I tried the three rooms of the cottage, I pushed around the section for her, I stood on tiptoe before the crazy eye of her window and spied a hut empty inside. How did she do it— she hadn't passed me on her way to the shops as I returned, and she hardly went anywhere else, except sometimes south to the ferry. But hadn't she crossed the harbour recently, a matter of a day or two back, and if so would she go again so soon? Possibly, possibly, I was beginning to convince myself as I walked back up the vegetable garden path and by the door of the hut: possibly I would have the place to myself for an hour or two while I sorted myself out. I could feel my back straightening and my muscles beginning to relax a little.

And then, suddenly, there she was in front of me, rounding the corner of my cottage as I rounded the corner of the hut! She was walking towards me with a brisk heavy tread, scarfed head down and string bag in her fist pulling her shoulder to an angle—dear God, she'd been shopping nearby all the time I'd been sitting palsied in the library reading (in effect) the story of her past: she'd been going about her daily business amongst that great mix of ordinary people as I plunged into the abyss. I remember the thought of that overwhelming me, I remember feeling that it didn't make sense, I remember thinking that I couldn't fit the two things together and that they needed fitting together *if only I knew how.* Now of course I do know, now of course all this seems very different to me, I can tell you. But at the time it was as if the Great Chain of Being itself had come unstuck—

We slammed to a halt, ten foot apart. The two of us stood there stiff as kindling, we stared at each other like a couple of trespassing cats. It was almost as if we'd run into each other naked—and *that* is a considerable thought. But it wasn't what I was thinking at the time: at the time I was in a blue funk, at the time my mind was full of what I'd been reading not so very many minutes earlier, at the time I was seized by a panic that appals me now to think back on it. I searched her face, her eyes: and she was puzzling the latter back at me as if it was *I* who was the source of the problem—as if it was *my* behaviour that was in question!

Is something wrong—?

For a moment I wasn't quite sure which of us had spoken: it was my question to ask, after all. I was aware of her bag, and the brown parcels from Coldicutt's I could see amongst its bulging strings, and also what looked like Chinese gooseberries pushing out their ugly unshaven little Oriental mugs at me.

Mr Sargeson—?

I stared. I tried to imagine her in amongst the poor lost creatures I'd just seen in the photos, I tried to imagine her as one of them. I gazed into her eyes. What was I doing, what was I looking for—a mad glitter? After a moment I realised I was looking at her as if she were a photograph herself, an illustration to an idea, a proposition. I'd lost the humanity of her as easily as that!

I realised I hadn't spoken. I fought hard to speak—

Yes, I found myself saying. Yes, yes—

It didn't make for a good start to this new dispensation in which Lyall's single terrible word and then the pictures in those textbooks had come between us. I remember her puzzlement, and that she somehow made a way around me on the path and to the hut. How strange I must have seemed to her then, and in the next few days too: until, inevitably, the crisis came and there was some relief to the horror that had begun to grow between us. That this was so is clear now I have some distance from it and also a knowledge of all that happened afterwards, I mean in the remainder of her long stay. Looking back, I have the sense of how precariously the errors grew between us in that time: in tone misunderstood, glances misinterpreted, clumsy words or phrases. After two days such tension built between us that anything could set it off, and it did. I snapped at her over lost spoons and misplaced books. She burst into tears over nothing at all, and then over having burst into tears. Soon the only words that passed between us were those on the scraps of paper I continued to find about the place, more messages from an abyss that seemed to open deeper and deeper as the days went on. *Tense inside in groper species*, one of them said, I remember, and although the fear had gone that finding the first of these had engendered, there was still the sheer strangeness of them to deal with. They seemed so utterly impossible of purpose, so impossible of meaning—

During the day I took every chance I had to escape them elsewhere—friends long neglected were astonished to hear my rap upon their door, and after making their initial sarcasms endured my long complaints about my burden. Give her the boot, they often said: and in return they endured long explanations of my need to clutch the asp to my breast. Back home I avoided her as much as I could by staying in the garden, crouching sometimes when I heard her on the path, freezing till I heard her door thump shut again. Once as I dug down the back near the compost boxes I stopped to catch my breath and saw her watching me from the hut. She used often to sit on her doorstep watching me work, all the while fiddling with the leaves of the plants near her door, tugging at them, sucking their stems, chewing them like Tom Sawyer or Huckleberry Finn—once, not long after she turned up, I had to stop her blowing on a seed-head: can you believe that, blowing on a dandelion puffball? Where d'you think that's going to end up? I called out to her, and she seemed genuinely not to know, she seemed genuinely surprised that I should ask: I expect she'd been making a wish or some faery thing of that sort. I suggested that if she was so keen to spread future weeds in my garden she might care to spend some time pulling the present ones out. But now—now she was just looking at me, her arms folded tightly against herself and her head forward. I realised she'd been watching me in this unflinching way for several minutes, and the sweat stuck my shirt cold to my back.

But the nights were worse. Any movement had me awake, and if I heard her slipping in the back door beyond the hanging sheet I lay there wide-eyed and thrust against the wall until she'd gone. Two nights of this were enough for me, and then I decamped to the front room and Harry's bed. I convinced myself I was safer there, though from *what* I couldn't have told you had you asked me at the time. The trouble was I kept it to myself, you see, not my general grief of course but the particular business Lyall started off and what followed it. It was one thing to complain to friends till they reeled away from me exhausted, but it seemed to me quite another to let slip the darker stuff he'd told me, and particularly that word, and those pictures in the textbooks—it seemed wrong to talk of that, almost as if I were to spill the beans on something close between Harry and me (and you can imagine what I felt when I found myself thinking in *those* terms about me and Janet). My scruples on this head are the best I can salvage of myself from this wretched time: but apart from them I was stranded and alone, prey to my own thoughts, writing letters left and right my friends told me made no sense whatever once received. You're giving yourself the willies, Frank, one of them wrote back. You need to get out more, you need to get out of town—

Good advice, excellent advice, and something I wish I'd heeded. But instead of doing that I hid my knives, every one of them, and that's what tipped the balance in the end. The sorry business began perhaps a fortnight into this long fiasco when suddenly I noticed one of them was gone, a trimming knife Lyall had smuggled from the local works for me. There was nothing special to it in size but I liked its balance in my hand and the very thought of it, the *work* in it, and always kept it sharpened with a stone. Well, when I looked for it to trim some flounder a friend had speared by the sand-spit of the harbour and dropped off to me fresh one day—it was gone. At first I was unconcerned, but as I opened drawers and doors and then widened my search to the living area and beyond a thought and then a panic grew. Other, lesser knives remained but that particular one was gone, it was clearer and clearer to me as I moved about the house and then (had I used it outside and left it there?) the garden. It had vanished. And for all I tried to resist it, an idea began to insist on itself to me, that the disappearance of the knife was not at all unconnected with what might have been argued to be the precarious state of Janet's mind. I blush to write this now, of course, and I must acknowledge too that regarding the actual whereabouts of this knife, the sharper of my readers will be ahead of me at this point: but at the time and given the state I was in, there was no other explanation to the events that were (I thought) unfolding than those I've outlined here.

Thus it was that I arrived at my mad solution to the problem. At first I thought to ask my neighbour to keep the remaining knives for me so I could slip next door and use them there, but the difficulty of doing that soon presented itself to me. Obviously the knives had to stay outside the house but on the property, and it took few further seconds of reflection to settle on the sole remaining area for concealment. And so down by the compost boxes I dug a hole in the earth I'd newly turned over, a couple of feet deep and no more, and rolled the knives in sacking and put them in there—not just the knives but (this will show you how my mind was working, or not working, at the time) such other things as a wooden mallet I inherited from an aunt for softening uncooked meat, and a potato masher from the same source: as if Janet might have used the latter in the night to reduce my addled brains to the state at which a little melted butter and a dash of freshly-ground pepper might have improved them!

After these frenzies, then, what else might happen, do you think, except that Janet would spot the absence of this cutlery, and that she would point it out to me, and that I would find myself incapable of providing any explanation? All this happened, and once she'd drawn the obvious conclusion from the embarrassed fumbling of my excuses, there was a quick, final unravelling of things between us. I presume there was a visit to the local phone box at some point, since the following morning (after an evening and night whose horror could not be conveyed to you) a strong double rap at the back doorway announced her friend Molly, she who'd landed me in this business in the first place: and I'd hardly called out Janet's name when behind her Janet herself appeared, but Janet transformed and dressed for travel—Janet, struggling out of the hut in coat and hat and dragging an unexpected suitcase knocking and bumping behind her. My heart leapt: dared I think she'd had enough, dared I think she was going for good, was I to be rid of her at last? But as she stepped clear of the hut rational thought returned to me: she carried no typewriter in her hand or even native-style on her head, and therefore gave no clear sign that this was in truth to be the end of our particular and devastating road. Instead (as Molly vouchsafed to me while the three of us gaggled up my path and towards my gate and her wretched little car) there was to be a trip south, to the family and the safety (as far as I was concerned) of the other island: something Janet had just decided to undertake on the spur of the moment the night before, she said, since it had been so long since she'd seen her folks!

I let much of this go in one ear and out the other, naturally, as I absorbed the practical facts of it as far as I was concerned: a two week period was indicated, meaning a fortnight of bachelordom for me, fourteen whole days left to my own devices while these two car-drove down to the capital and then Janet took the sea-going ferry south and, for a time at least, disappeared from out of my life. It was so unexpected, a blessing I could never have dreamed of and (I fervently

188

hoped) a God-sent time in which, with any luck, I might start to put my ship to rights and work out a longer-term strategy for freedom (and this was something on which I'd had an idea or two, I might point out, in the course of dealing with these my last few trials). Ahead, fourteen glorious days of unanticipated silence, fourteen days in which the most difficult thing to do would be to decide what to eat.

All these thoughts, then, were rubbing up against one another inside my head, so to speak, as I went through the rituals of farewell on the north side of my macrocarpa hedge. After these were done and Janet's bag was loaded and doors slammed at least a dozen unnecessary times I expected the car to lurch off forthwith: but there was a pause and a conference inside, and then the passenger window suddenly came cranking down, and now here was Janet's hand thrust out at me—a box of chocolates after all this, the lover's gift, all wrapped and bound with string?—surely, surely she couldn't be doing anything quite so vulgar—what was this, a peace offering?

I reached out for it, and found something else instead.

It was her book, her manuscript, being delivered into my hand, bound in quarters like a gift and complete with blue ribbon and knotted bow. It was a gesture so unexpected that I simply could not fathom it at that moment. But the object filled my hands with fear.

Your novel! I said jovially, falsely.

It's not a novel—

Yes, yes. Quite. A—a speculation—

An exploration, she said.

An exploration, yes, now I remember. An exploration. Well—thankyou, thankyou. I'll try to read it—I'll certainly read it—

It was terrifying. She gave me no look or sign more than I have recorded here, instead cranked the window heavily back up in a final sort of way—and then the car was moving, they

189

were off, first in a slowly clumsy turn that found the shingle on either side of Esmonde Road and then, precariously, towards and over the hump and the distant corner. I watched them until they disappeared, and when once that was done I turned back to the house with her little parcel in my hands. What was in it, had she given my very self over to me and left me to read about it in some final gesture of revenge? I'd thought myself freed, but she was still with me, inescapably— was that it, was that what she was trying to bring about—? I slumped on my chair inside, my bubble-dream of freedom thoroughly pricked.

And then Harry turned up.

CHAPTER 8

Just like that—I glanced through the bedroom window and there he was, out in the garden! No warning, no fuss—the way he always did it, the way he always turned up: suddenly he appeared, suddenly he was back, suddenly he was home and standing there in front of me. For a moment I couldn't believe it was Harry, it didn't seem real, it didn't seem possible—unusually, I hadn't even been thinking of him, in fact I'd hardly been thinking of anything at all, my first few hours of solitude having so played on me that by the time he appeared, a little after lunch, I was barely more than a blank page. And into that gap, that *absence* he'd inserted himself, so that it felt as if he might have been hiding somewhere around the garden all this time, kidding me, waiting for my attention to drift away before he made his move. Or had he been hiding *inside* me: had I dreamed him, had I made him up, brought him to life myself the way I'd surely invented my strange hut-dweller?

I rapped my knuckles on the bedroom window-pane. *Harry*—!

He was standing on my path looking at my vegetables and surveying the section as if checking that everything was still as it should be. His trilby was pushed back on his head, his little paunch thrust slightly forward, his hands placed carefully and slightly behind his narrow hips. You could tell he heard me as I rapped the glass and called out, and again when I did it again (*rap-rap—Harry!*). But he ignored me the way the cats ignore me when I call to them, taking his own time, turning to me just when he was good and ready. Then, when he *was* ready, and turned—there it was once more, his kind old wrinkled old dear old Aussie face, the eyes squeezing up in amusement as he spotted me, just a crinkled double wink like the old tomcat, and he gave a tiny nod but as if to himself, as if he was confirming the details of my little world: yes, everything was in its place, the hut the house the vegetables and even silly old Frank himself, standing over there in the back-room window. And he turned back to the lettuces and cabbages again, his bony elbows spread wide to a sharp double point at either side.

And the lettuces were all I could think to talk about as I came up to him out there in clumsy blundering strides as if I were wading through water, as if I couldn't work my legs fast enough to get to him. Inspecting the lettuces? is what I came out with—you can see I was properly knocked off my perch to say a thing as daft as that. Look, they were going to seed on me, was the gist of what he said in his familiar gruff Harry Doyle voice. Turn m'back and what do I find, he said, you're growin' a head on you—

I pumped at his hand. I wanted to grab him there and then, all of him, I wanted to smother him in hugs and kisses: but I knew that with Harry you had to take your time. As he turned away from me again, though, I held onto his hard old knobby black-and-violet paw for as long as I could. Harry, back at last—and he was *right*, last season's lettuces *had* paled and wilted, their seed-heads towered up before us in a row of little minarets. I'd hardly noticed, but now I did they seemed to sum up everything of the terrible last six months and more—the time since I'd begun to realise that he was missing, and the time since *she*'d turned up, his unexpected alter ego. But now *he*'d turned up in turn, now he was back!—I pulled away and blew my nose. There were so many things I wanted to ask him. First of all where had he *been*, for God's sake—?

But instead I spouted some more of my silliness about the vegetables, time for sowing, that sort of thing. As I've just said, you had to take it slowly with Harry, particularly when he's just returned to the nest. Had a few distractions, is what I managed to come out with in the end. I'd take my own time, I decided, to tell him about Janet. A *sheila*—? he'd say when I did. Y'got a *sheila* in the hut—? I knew that that's what he'd say. But what else would he have to tell, what was his news, and above all *where had he got to* these last nine months—?

And it turned out he'd been back home all this time visiting family in Sydney!—or so he'd have me believe as we settled down on either side of my kitchen counter and following his usual rites of passage on entering the house. I had no idea he'd any family left to visit!—whenever he'd talked about them in the past he'd described them all as falling off the twig one by one from his earliest years till he was left to wander the earth a poor motherless orphan: something along those lines. Now, as I served him up a cup of tea and worked flour in a bowl with a little water milk and rising, here he was, serving me up a brother and his unexpected family in return, all with names and lives I knew nothing about, not to mention an uncle I'd never heard mention of before either. Cyril he was, his mother's youngest brother though possibly as the story went on Cyril was the unexpected brother's name and this was an equally unexpected Uncle Ces he had in mind. ('And you wouldn't credit it, Frank, his surname's Poole! Ces Poole!') It was hard to keep track of all this as the tea went down and the yarn unfolded, episode by episode—and it *was* a yarn, I knew that, as the big solid element of the stove heated and the flour mixture went on.

All Harry's yarns were just that, not so much a pack of lies as alternative ways of telling me about his current flirtation

193

with the truth, conveying less the hard facts as they came along than what was contingent upon the hard facts, the interesting bits of dust and fluff they accumulated along the way. And in that it was precisely this sort of day-to-day detritus that fascinated me as a writer, I reckoned Harry a fellow artist of sorts as I have said, and certainly my master in spinning a tale by spinning another tale around it and doubling that with something else again. A bullshit artist, in short: at the end of each performance you felt like standing up and breaking into a round of applause, as I was yet again tempted to do when once he'd brought this his latest *tour de force* to a conclusion and was sitting there in front of me draining his third cup or was it his fourth, his little finger crooked satirically as ever while he drank. And all the time his tiny chook's eyes winked at me over the cup's rim as he tried to work out how well his yarn was going down, whether he was going to get away with pulling off yet another long shot once again. Which of course he did, as he always managed to do—

Oh yes he'd done well, there was no doubt about *that* as he returned cup to saucer and himself back against his cushion, once more with his favourite audience before him along with the pile of scones I'd cut and buttered while he spoke. He'd got away with it again—charmed the birds from my trees the teeth from my head and the leg from my iron pot: all the while letting not a solitary thing slip concerning where he might actually have been these many long months and what it was he'd really been up to during them, and certainly without answering a single one of my questions. It was a bravura performance all right.

And when we got to the point, and I asked him why he hadn't written to me in all this time and told him I'd been beside myself with worry and what it was I'd been afraid had happened to him, there was no containing his surprise. No letters?—why, he'd written to me once a week without fail, on aerogrammes provided by his munificent Uncle Ces or was it Cyril. I hadn't got them? Well, once a fortnight, nothing surer. Not *one* of them? He sat back in the chair and shook his head, the epitome of surprise.

Well blow me down, Frank, he said. You sure—?

I'd have noticed airmail, Harry, I told him. D'you think I wasn't looking out for you? Every day—?

Well, that took the biscuit, you could have knocked him over with a feather, he'd have to go and take a tablet: and so forth. I had no way of knowing whether this was all part of the farrago he'd been putting together this last half hour or the truth the whole truth and nothing but the truth, the final evidence that he'd actually been as far away all this time as he'd claimed. But evidently dozens of aerogrammes had been dispatched in my direction—hundreds, even—despite the fact that each one had been a tax nay an utter *drain* on his epistolary resources, he for whom a single letter-card or beer coaster had long been quite enough to contain all the news he was capable of assembling at any single point: but each aerogramme faithfully licked sealed and stamped, apparently, addressed to F. Sargeson Esq.—more satire here— of 14 Esmonde Road Takapuna Auckland N.Z. and sent off into the world. He even persuaded me out to the letterbox the aerogrammes were certain to have landed in as if that was the place where things had started to go wrong, and as we opened and shut it and opened it again to make sure of its innocence and poked the ground at its base these absent missives became more and more substantial, more frequent and more crammed with information than any square of pale blue tissue ten inches by seven-and-a-half could possibly have been imagined to contain. In fact it seemed (as he elaborated his position) that he'd poured out on them his very essence, giving me at last the elusive core I'd yearned so long to hold to mine, the quiddity of his being, his very and utter soul. Unfortunately this seemed to have been mislaid by the New Zealand Post Office.

And then he looked up at me with his shrewd little rooster's eyes. Must be that dame of yours, he said.

I was thunderstruck—how'd he know about Janet? She'd be down in Oamaru by this stage, don't think I didn't know exactly where she was likely to be at any given minute of my day. I'd been saving her for a trump card to whip from behind my back when once he'd finished laying out all his blarney before me, not because I thought her presence would mean anything in particular to him but simply because I wanted to have something he didn't already know about, something that had occurred outside his welter of knowing winks and nods and grins. But he'd outfoxed me again!

And it turned out he'd been on the premises at least twenty-four hours. As he led me down the path again and across to the hut I realised that was where he'd been last night, and that he'd been observing the place from at least the morning before and probably longer than that. He must've turned up when I'd been away on the coast or across the harbour and found I had someone aboard and so lain low, sleeping rough perhaps in the local public park until he'd sorted out who my guest might be and the nature of her relationship to me. Minus Janet's presence I had been delighted at the chance to put her little universe from my mind as I tried to regain and restore my own, and all the while I was doing this he must have sat in the hut keeping an eye on me, weighing things up till he felt he could make his move. Weighing *her* up too, as he showed me when once we were in her door—for he had taken over her little dwelling, pretty much, with his swag on the floor and his jacket over the back of the chair, his shaving kit next to her typewriter and the twist and toil of the bed-sheets indicating what was probably a slightly less uncomfortable rest for him last night. Until, eventually, satisfied that my departed guest represented no probable long-term threat to him (and also that she was a 'sheila' and therefore no possible personal rival), he had emerged.

196

But seeing him there in the tiny, private world she'd made of the hut strangely affected me. It reinforced that sense I already had that the two of them, Harry and Janet, were connected in some way. The outer resemblances were obvious enough when I thought about them—their self-protectiveness, the caution with which they went about their lives, the way Harry had hidden before manifesting himself, even the way they both took a sort of refuge in words, he in both his artful reticence and the elaborate persiflage of his yarns and she in the equally worked-up silence of the page. But it went deeper than that. In some complex way they were both crucial parts of my life. Of Harry I had known that of course for many years: but of Janet, not at all. It disturbed me, it shocked me, it completely took me aback. I slowly began to see, to my astonishment, the last thing I could have expected, the truth that just as he had absorbed much of my life in the past she would absorb much of it in the future, and that (although in completely different ways) I would be as little able to get rid of her as I'd ever want to get rid of him.

Harry had never quite taken to the house as he had to the old shack that preceded the army hut, something I remember as very genuinely astonishing me at the time I noticed it was so. But the fact of the matter was, I realised in due course, he'd needed the very restrictions the house had been built to escape in order to reinforce the subtle delicacies and restraints the two of us had evolved so that we could share our earlier life. The shack was our earlier relationship, you might say, and its smoking embers therefore a challenge to its recasting. Well, plain old practical non-symbolic Harry seemed still to be getting the hang of this, and eight full years after house replaced hovel he continued to make a great show of occupying it, as if it was still spanking new and not already showing even in that relatively short space of time more than a few sad evidences of human inhabitation.

And so whenever he turned up like this there was always his initial comedy of declining entry to the house outright and offering to doss down rough instead, in what he always referred to as *the Starlight Hotel*. And when that song-and-dance was over and I'd actually managed to persuade him in, there was the next charade, in which with exaggerated care he removed his boots at the door and then high-stepped about on tiptoes as if the floor had just been waxed and buffed rather than suffering no more than the occasional lick with linseed oil between irregular wipes and sweeps. And then the business of marvelling at the sudden apparition of things he'd in fact long been used to, the wireless radio the built-in bookshelves the very books themselves—had I *really* read all of those, every single one, well what a clever fellow I must surely be, far too good to be kicking around with such a simple unlettered cove as himself: that sort of thing. And then the studious opening of each window door or drawer he used, and the same again when once it was time to close them. Even when he'd tired of these performances there was always his more genuine puzzlement in front of cupboards—where things were, what went where, he was still blowed if he could follow my fancy new routine, wasn't I turning into a bit of a toff with my flash and snooty ways? Yes, I'd definitely hopped the fence and crossed over to the Tories, it was something bound to happen all along, he could see that plain as day now: why hadn't he rumbled me long before this?

As a rule I would never tire of this sort of thing, indeed I'd feel a bit short-changed if he missed out a particular word line or movement from the last such performance he'd put on. As part of my realisation that he'd been happier in the shack I'd understood after a while that, however slowly and laboriously, his new routines were growing in place of those subtler ones that had helped us share the smaller dwelling, and I was anxious he re-employ them each time he came

198

back to the house the better that he might settle himself into an environment I knew he would never fully adjust to. For I realised he actually *did* feel a little awed by my translation over the years from hunter-gatherer hut-dweller and subsistence-farmer to something rather better than any of those estates, both as a more nearly conventional (though still not so very fully conventional) citizen and of course as *the father of a nation's fiction.* Of my work he knew nothing by the way, as one might expect: or at least he knew *almost* nothing, since I had once persuaded him to read a short piece of mine of which he'd slyly said, after several evenings of mumbled reading stertorous breathing and muffled expressions as of a man in pain, that my achievement had been so extraordinarily good in it that for fear of future disappointment he would never need to read a single further thing I wrote! All well and good, naturally, and of course a little entertainment all in itself: but what was he going to make of Miss Janet Frame when once she returned to me in thirteen days time, I wondered, she who represented every single thing one might imagine as being opposed to his irregular ironic and democratic way of life? And what in turn was Miss Frame to make of *him*, he who from her quite different point of view might be thought to embody every single thing she wrote in order to escape?

Well, after he'd polished off the scones and had yet another cup of tea, there was nothing for it as far as Harry was concerned but that we should hunt down those missing letters. I was happy enough to leave the whole shooting-match rest on the grounds that I'd had my share of entertainment from the matter: but no, he would hear of nothing less than a thorough search since it was his word that was on the line and there was nothing to a man once you took his word away, what was there that could possibly be left of him once a fellow did that? This sort of cock-and-bull kept us going as we strolled about the place with hands in pockets and feet stirring at objects on the ground, a ritual I realised was required of us both in order to put the whole business behind us and get on with less important matters.

And so it was that at the end of this performance we found ourselves back at the letterbox once again and rummaging in the corner of the front hedge that was adjacent to it just in case the aerogrammes had somehow blown in there: or at least Harry had a rummage, for it was he who emerged from its dark and glossy fronds with a brown bag in his hand.

He held it up. A little stream of white grains trickled from one corner.

He licked his finger and tried a few of them. He held the bag out to me:

Sugar, he said.

And indeed it was, coarsely ground white cane sugar, in the kind of bag that Coldicutt's packed. I stared at it. Sugar from Coldicutt's—? I stared and stared, because of course there was something coming through to me from wherever it is that everything always adds up, and all the time I was attending to the things it was trying to tell me Harry was going on about what I must have been doing to the hedge to make it crop in bags of sugar. Must've been feeding it better than hay, he reckoned, because it certainly wasn't horse shit coming out the other end: by now he had his entire upper body in the hedge and was handing back to me another bag from further in: almost empty, this one, but containing a brown chocolaty grit that proved after a quick dab on the tongue to be exactly that, chocolate, and then there was another and yet another being handed back to me—I forget now what was in which but they were the same sort of things as the first two and none of them the only such in the hedge because when Harry got his head out and told me to stick mine in I saw various items inside, little bits of this and that sitting in the crooks of the dark inside branches like a tiny solar system all of their own.

200

And as you might imagine, when I'd pulled my head out of the hedge my mind had begun to work away pretty hard at all of this—some idiot child of the neighbours perhaps, stealing stuff and stowing it away here—the local kids, stuffing away bits of uneaten lunch?

Harry looked at me shrewdly. That dame of yours, he said. Not givin' her enough tucker—?

He plucked the cigarette from his mouth and blew a trail of smoke across his face.

I was rocked. He'd said what I'd been trying not to think: but of course it *had* to be Janet, who else in the world would dream of doing something as odd, as *strange* as this? The front hedge was obviously where she hid whatever she didn't want me to find—and of course, of course: *that* was where she hid *herself*, too, whenever she did her disappearing act!—all of a sudden I was a wakeup to that particular stunt as well. What in God's name else had she got hidden away in there—the real Archie Scott perhaps, sitting patiently amongst the branches, still waiting to be called back into Signor Bosco's magic box? Moncrieff and Hood, the missing airmen?

I was back in the house by the time I was thinking all this business through, and the day outside was in the early stages of shutting down, and there was the thought of my first meal with Harry—which had me tickled pink, I can tell you, to one side of my seething thoughts. But the thing was (it began to occur to me as I peeled the spuds), it wasn't *me* who'd worked out these ideas about Janet, it was the business of Harry's missing aerogrammes that had done the trick, almost as if finding Janet's little cache was the direct result of his cock-and-bull yarn. We'd gone out looking for one kind of nothing-very-much and had come up with another, Janet's hidey-hole. Wasn't that it—?

This is what I put to Harry later on, as we ate together at the little card table and a log of willow chattered and spat in the grate as logs of willow tend to do. I told him the full long tale about Janet and some of the things that had happened, like the business with the peppers and (as far as I was able to understand them at that early stage) her strange notions about words and things. I also mentioned her long spells in hibernation and her sudden changes of mood and even (as it sometimes seemed) entire changes of personality, along with her apparent ability simply to disappear into thin air so that it was as if she'd never existed in the first place, and then to reappear in front of me as solid as a pound of butter. I finished up with the notion that had come to me after his find out by the letterbox, the idea that the place she'd gone to hide whenever she pulled her disappearing trick was inside my macrocarpa hedge—

All the time I spoke he sat there with his little sharp blue eyes flicking up to mine every few seconds while he ate, up and back down again.

When I finished he sat there in front of me for a further moment as he dealt with another tiny bone. He looked at me again. I waited for his response. Here came the bone, fished out with his fingers—

Now why'd she go and do a silly thing like that, he said.

And as I recall it now, this single sparse statement had the effect on me of a good hard jolt that shook me awake and made me see the nonsense of the past many months and the fancies I'd been living in them. How could I have entertained any other thought at all, how could I have even imagined it for a minute? Harry had spoken. Of course on occasions like this what mattered was never quite the substance of whatever it was he'd found it in himself to say, since on the whole, whatever it was, it was little enough and squeezed out hard, like juice from a lemon. But that is exactly what gave his words their tang, and made me gobble up their freshness. Now, in the light of subsequent events, it all looks a bit more complicated than that: *one world at a time* as the great man said on his deathbed, meaning (for present purposes) that the

202

transition between any two states of understanding is never as clear-cut as I am making it seem here. But at the time the impact seemed of a transforming nature, or at least that is how I remember it. Suddenly, and for the first time in very many months, my feet were standing on solid ground once more.

Now, looking back on it, I think of Sir Thomas Browne again and those wingy mysteries he talks of in divinity that unhinge the brain if too long dwelt upon unreasoned. That was what I'd had in Janet's hut back in June or July: and that was what she'd brought into the rest of my life with her unpredictability, her unreadability and these mystifying scraps of paper she'd been leaving about, with their strange riddles that at their very best sat on the edge of communicating something important but in the end told you nothing very much at all. Sitting at the table opposite me as he rolled his first post-dinner cigarette that night of his return, Harry seemed to me the opposite. He seemed as he always seemed, foursquare as a fencepost: if not quite the embodiment of reason itself, then certainly representing reasonableness, as in the *bald-headed man at the back of the omnibus* I remember from my legal clerking days representing average decent common sense in the world out there. And so, seduced by the familiar gravel of his voice and by the joy of his return, by the way he seemed to have set the clock ticking once more, I proceeded to betray Janet to him bit by bit, feeding to him morsels of her as I'd fed to him morsels of the flounder whose bones lay now scattered on our plates. Those cats, I said at one stage, she's even named the cats, and I pointed to them as they twirled and yowled amongst our legs: and when I told him the names she'd actually picked I did it in such a way (I have to admit) that made him as mystified as I knew he would inevitably be: which was one of the shabbier things I did that night and in the course of the following thirteen days, by the way, since when she first told me the names she'd chosen for them I'd been truly lost in admiration of her wit and learning.

But in amongst my cheapskate embroidering of my story, I'm bound to say there was one thing I found I didn't tell him, strange to relate. Now I look back I see this unexpected access of discretion on my part as the life-line that held me and Janet together at that point, the taut and fragile thread that meant there was something—*something*—that still held firm between us. On instinct, I didn't tell him about the little notes she left me. They were a private matter that we had together, a matter still to be worked on solved and understood. How did I know that about them then—?

And finally we were done that night, Harry and I, and there was the business of kitchen matters to be attended to, the fire kicked in and the Tilley lamp doused: for whenever Harry was in residence and night came down I would indulge him by ignoring the possibilities of electric lighting and keeping the night at bay with the same old oil-lamp that once had lit the aboriginal shack for us (and on a number of occasions nearly set it ablaze before its time). Whenever he is in residence the lamp sits there on the counter looking like Sherlock Holmes's fateful gasogene, a cryptic emblem of the almost Oriental other-world of winks and nods and nuances that Harry brings along with him: emblem of that lost colonial world I banished with the burning of the hut.

But now you must believe that after these attentions, the good Lord for the time being spread his enormous shielding hands over 14 Esmonde Road—

Of course I realise it must be a complete surprise to hear me speak like that: but I've said before that whether or not I wish it to be so, it is very easy to revive in me the sentiments of my Christian past and replace my hard-won adult vocabulary with something far more infantile cosy and familiar. I have besides no other but this childhood way of telling of the peace that creeps upon me when my old companion is back in my house and all is well, for the time being, with the rolling world.

Now: at this point I have a suspicion that some of you are hoping for something more, details perhaps of what it is that might pass between Harry and me when long months of waiting on my part meet long nights of requitement on his. It is not in the least misleading when I tell you, though, that there is nothing whatsoever for me to tell—not of the sort, that is, which (it concerns me) some may have in mind to be discovered to them. But (you say) down-to-earth practical everyday Harry—for all his blarney surely there is little room there for anything more than earthy earthly here-and-now body flesh and bones? Meaning, surely there are only simple details there that might all too readily be told? Yes, to some extent that is true: and how could it be otherwise given the nature of the contract on which we met all those years ago, whose essence was nothing more and nothing less than the possibilities of the kind that two strangers might be capable to make in brief exchanges conducted within our brute material world (exchanges which by the way I feel no compunction in revealing were always of the most satisfactory nature given the enterprises undertaken)?

And which of the two of us would ever willingly forget anything of those earlier years if it meant forgetting too the early morning search under bed and bedside apple-box for wherever it was that Harry's teeth had got to overnight?

But as I've told before, matters began to grow between us within a very short time of our initial chance exchange, and I have already tried to give a rendering of that moment (as I care to remember it) when they began to do so and I found myself invited into a world I've never willingly since left, one in which whatever it is that I am becomes wholly made of whatever it is that makes Harry up as well: which is why that querying of my relationship to him that Janet made a few months before this return (and which when it happened made me wonder for the first time whether I really knew him after all) had such a remarkable effect on me for the day or two I allowed it to overtake my thoughts. Absent Harry (and present Janet) I was all too much a prey to over-probing thoughts like hers that had lived too long inside a single airless human head: present Harry (and absent Janet) all thoughts were body-thoughts again, *my* thoughts, and my old embodied Harry-world breezily alive once more: no need to think too much, time simply to get on with whatever it is that seems to pop up next.

Now, here's a good example of the latter: Harry's trick early in this his most recent stay with me when he very much added to my general astonishment at the world by offering to weed the lettuce-bed of the very minaret-lettuces he'd first remarked on, as well as of their accompanying encumbrances. Here was an unprecedented gesture on his part that really had me baffled, till I twigged what it was that he was up to in the longer run:

Time he lent a hand, is how this particular nonsense began, for he knew that over the years he'd always left too much for me to do alone: now at my advancing age (yet he is a full decade my senior, remember) he'd decided he was good-and-ready to show willing and to pull his weight as well—if I could just give him a hint first, though, of how such weight might best be pulled? And so out we went to the vegetable garden, the two of us, and down on one knee I sank and tugged a weed or two from the rich volcanic chocolate of my garden soil. *That* was the way it was done, I made clear to him as he stood behind me: for in matters of horticulture it is an immovable truth that if you want the job done properly, hand-weeding is the only answer. He agreed enthusiastically as he leaned down behind me on the garden path, hands on knees: but he felt a little further demonstration was still required of me—certainly he was starting to get the hang of things, although he thought he would never master the astonishing speed and skill with which I worked: could I just display these to him a moment longer? And so it went on to the end, of course, with me on all fours plucking out the lettuce-hulks and the weeds one by one while all the time Harry paced me from behind, his mitts safely clasped behind his back as he filled the air with admirations of my skill. And thus in twenty minutes or so the job was done, I by now in on his joke and completing the entire shooting-match for him with no little enjoyment: and in full agreement as we stood there admiring his handiwork that when it came to gardening, the proposition was indeed true that hand-weeding is the only answer. (Which raised the issue, he slyly added a little later, of what the question was in the first place?)

Of Frank and Harry together, then, no other details are available much better than this: for what details of our commerce could be told that are worthier the hearing? Of two solemn old brontosauruses, perhaps, their speckled heavy limbs entangled as each explores the other's sharky flesh for joy dulled then numbed then lost by long familiarity? Far better the truth, if it is the literal world you require: which is a thoroughly secular business of getting the old fellow dossed down on the divan for the night, and sealing off with rolled towels the windows that are above it, and keeping him propped up because of his catarrh but still flat enough because of his back, filling a hot water bottle for his chest, always an issue at this time of the year (I'd already noticed a dry little cough that was bothering him), and slipping his old enamel chamber pot beneath his bed. Then, knowing better than to try indulging any overt display of affection, what always occurs each night instead, almost what you might call a deferred passing-brushing kind of fingertip-handshake, meeting-point of all the irony in our long shared life and all the warm sincerity as well.

And after that, amid bouncing shadows, the Tilley is taken out and doused in my room next door—

207

Where now occurs the point I savour most in all my life, that inexpressible sense which takes me as I sink at last onto my own hard bed when its grimness is softened by my knowledge that all the things of my little world have come at last in place: out there the garden, waiting for another season to begin, the little plants beneath their glass, others safely under straw: in here the house pretty near in ship-shape, its cupboards filled with the little treats I always save for times like these: tobacco, jam, a tin or two of salmon, pickled onions cucumber and dill, the jar of Gentlemen's Relish someone gave me an age ago and of course and always a cache of the boiled sweets that Harry favours when once he's had his dinner. And the slightest sigh or murmur through the night will bring my bare feet to the cold floor to contemplate once more the giver of this benefaction, who lies, when I come to him, beneath the streetlight's grid of patches in the enlivened dark, his beaky figure sprawled in sleep bringing thoughts of a *Pietà* (and who is this who comes towards him but a mother?): his rasping snores his orisons, the incense for this chilly worship the scent of Tilley paraffin.

Of such is the Kingdom of Heaven on earth.

During the night the rattle of his chamber wakes me several times. You all right, Harry? I call. Goin' good, cob, he tells me back each time, and coughs and hawks his phlegmy cough.

This then was the curious background against which I read Janet's masterpiece, as I to my shame ironically thought of it and was in the habit of describing it in passing to Harry until I began to read a page or two and realised what it really was. Of the contrast between their two worlds, hers and his, I could not of course have been more fully conscious as I picked at the love-knot that tied the packet of her pages together—*my* two worlds too, I suppose, and inevitably drifting closer when I'd spent so much of my life trying to keep them far apart. As far as literature was concerned I'd had this moment before and many times as you might imagine, since people (particularly the younger variety, I've found) rarely hesitate to demand I read their work. If you only knew! is what I usually say when they tell me of their hopes, and I take care to dwell at length on the frustration loneliness poverty and neglect which in all truth have been the lowest common denominators of my last twenty years. If you want that, I say, then there it is: but far better learn a trade. And so once again each time I find myself speaking exactly like my father many years ago, and once again each supplicant politely hears me out: and then invariably presents me with his work.

All this to say that nonetheless, every time I find I'm reading something new like this, there is a moment of pleasure excitement and anticipation no past experience can ever dash. Someone read *Crime and Punishment* for the first time after all, and someone first read *The Pilgrim's Progress*: I mean beyond their authors, of course. There is a Russian story of a man who when asked to read a friend's new manuscript and finding it within minutes to be self-evidently the beginnings of a great masterpiece, got up and changed his clothes to something more suited to the occasion, evening attire or military uniform perhaps. Well, all these things I thought and felt as I began to read Janet's nameless work (she'd just gone bang in as if it were writing itself), my feet at the grate of a fire burning the last of the winter's wood or nearly, and Harry to my left propped up in a snoring doze that had his mouth ajar but specs still on his nose-tip, while behind me the wick of the Tilley was twisted up as far as it would reach to help my reading. And in that position I became her first reader, till the paraffin ran out at last and I had managed fifty pages, by which time (and in fact much earlier in my reading) I found I had a considerable amount of careful re-thinking to do, about her world and mine as well, and even about my good companion.

CHAPTER 9

Today an aerogramme at last from Janet in London, first proof she hasn't revived her disappearing act and left the material world completely! She's been there a fortnight now according to the date she's typed inside, but a little longer according to the date-stamp on the envelope. The gap between the two speaks to me before the words inside: Janet on her own and out there in the world—she who once told me she couldn't post a letter without screwing up her courage and making a dash for it through the terror of her private emotional rain. And indeed she says there was a crisis on board ship, whose rolling movement she claims still follows her through the streets of Hounslow where she's found a room for herself as well as an irritating Irish landlord: and before that there was another crisis of some sort at her first hotel. In other words she seems to be in form. Despite that, though, she's been wandering freely about the Great Wen, it seems, and amongst other things has found for me somewhere a small expanse of water she claims is named Cock Pond. I thought of you immediately and had to go and see it, she writes. When I did I wondered if you would like to take a dip? This last liberty by the way is new to me and a little surprising: on certain things at least, distance seemed to lend familiarity.

Seeing the pale blue airmail letter when I opened the

letterbox took me back to Harry's promised abundance of communication that day a year back now—very nearly—when he appeared amongst my vegetables and there began for me the working-out of the strange business a mere sentence or two had got me into at its start (my mention of the army hut to Janet's friend Molly being the obvious point at which I judged this long carnival to have begun). Between the two of them, Janet and Harry, there are so many links like that, so many little echoes and rhymes—or positives as against negatives, themselves making a link of a magnetic nature. For example her letter arrives full of information while his with all their hope and promise never came at all, never even existed in the first place: but Janet is supposed to be the ethereal one and Harry the man of the here-and-now! He goes and she comes, and then the routine is reversed and out he pops again as soon as she disappears—like the man of the little wooden couple in those weather-barometers that never show them both at one and the same time (and which, curiously, always seem to reserve the role of announcing a change for the worse to the *male* of the species).

Yet how could a pair of people be more utterly different than these two most obviously are, and am I right to make the tale of it I'm still trying to put together long after they've disappeared? Did I really upset the apple cart when I foolishly tried to set something up with Janet and Lyall Neary, or was the sudden revelation of her past just an accident lying in wait to happen? And what was I to make of the business of Harry showing up when he did, as soon as Janet had turned her back, so to speak: and even more pressing, what was I going to make of their collision, which had to happen when once he entered the plot and which seemed so much destined—fated—when once he did? And above all, does it really have the meaning it still seems to have as I sit here now that all is done and dusted—the meaning it seems to have *at times*, that is, when at other times in truth it seems to have none at all—?

It did not take so very many days of Harry's much-anticipated return to 14 Esmonde Road for me to see that all was not as well with him as once had been the case. That dry cough of his which woke me up at night and kept me hovering during the day was a long-familiar worry but one that never seemed to change: and who was I to make him modify his ways when I need as much as any in the world to modify my own (a fact he'd always point out to me whenever I began to roll a cigarette)? Naturally this didn't prevent me from trying out my various remedies, since in all truth any eagerness I might have to get someone to a bed has usually tended to refer to my desire to play the nursemaid more than anything other. And since Harry was usually a pushover when it came to a bit of hand-and-foot attention of this sort, it dismayed me more than somewhat when I first proposed a little bed-rest and found he pushed away the thought as angrily as he did. Nothing wrong with *me*, mate, he said, and turned away. I'd offered him a vapour rub and then a heated flannel tied around his middle, but he was in no mood for that or for any other help I might give him. He sat there rolling a further fag in a manner not to be taken lightly.

No: the change in him was larger and it was subtler than any switch of this or that behaviour might be thought capable to arrest. Possibly he was right to decline my attentions, then, and possibly what I was witnessing after the longest time we'd ever had apart were no more than before-and-after snapshots in a long process that closer commerce usually hides. It jolted me to think this. Harry was at this point in his early sixties, and in the last stages of the long march towards the universal pension. The hole he seemed now to be in I've seen appear in other men of his age and I expect to fall into it myself in ten years time when and if another decade adds to this baffling daily nonsense of being alive. A man works a long time in one life, and even when a chap like Harry manages several lives at once, the common theme of each of which is keeping work at bay, the toil of so much effort can leave just the same marks after fifty years as on a lesser man who has worked his life away in the same old mode of gainful employment. He once admitted as much when I suggested he settle down to one thing and one thing only: but it wouldn't challenge him enough! was his reply—he was still a relative youngster, he wasn't ready to quit on himself like that, it'd be a crime to waste his extraordinary health and vigour on the kind of sissified malingering for which a city job might call (though none such had in fact been mentioned). Why, it took the strength of ten to keep his own at a cutting edge: what did I think it was like for him to live on the brink like this from day to day as he watched out for the threat of meaningful employment?—he was worn out, he needed a weekend off, his nose was never out of the vacancy columns of the paper, did I think he actually *liked* carrying the daily weight of the *Herald* on hands and arms the way he did? Not to mention the need to get up early each morning in order to pinch it from the neighbour's driveway in the first place—

And by the end of this wonderful bit of sustained nonsense he had me almost convinced (as I remember it) that he was right to live the principled life he did and keep himself in tune for the big opportunity he seemed incapable of doubting lay in wait for him at any point (and which was never entirely unconnected with the investments he regularly made at the local betting shop).

On this his latest visitation, though, his impersonation of Mr Micawber appeared less frequently than before, and the same kind of disappearance was true more generally for the very thing that had most made him Harry over the years, that quintessential defining snook he cocked at the world as his signature and which set my heart a-beat whenever

I realised that here it was again, he was going to show it off for me once more and I was in for yet another round of royal entertainment, almost always (naturally) at someone else's expense. I mean the sort of comedy I've mentioned as his constitution—the kind of act he performed with those lettuces in my garden within an hour or two of arrival, for example, when he had me doing his weeding for him while he looked on. But within a day or two of that first little joke I realised there seemed to be in some of the subsequent stunts he pulled and the touches that went along with them a sense of effort that was new, as if he had played the part of Harry far too long and was growing tired of watching himself having to do it yet once more. Not always: now and then would come a moment that was vintage Harry Doyle, and then I would stow away all earlier fears: he was still the man he'd always been after all. But soon would come another moment more unguarded when I would catch him out, as it were, and my old fears would return. He would seem not so much tired of it all (I decided) as hollowed out, preoccupied, not himself.

How much of this before it became inevitable that my earlier fears and doubts returned? Where had he been, and was it my concern? At all levels our relationship was founded as I have told and as must be coming clearer too on what was left unsaid as much as on what was openly stated. It must also be obvious that such a dispensation always favoured *him* and not *me*, given that I'd long known letting him have his head was the only way our two-in-hand might work. But how much I wished to hold him back! And (equally and opposite) how much he needed to be free!—so that here was revealed the inevitable slip-knot that lies at the heart of any long relationship, the insoluble problem we spend our times turning to and turning to again until the work of a partnership is what we mean when we say a partnership is working. Here it was once more, pulling on my hand. Except that Janet suddenly intervened, and after that things were not quite the same as once they'd been—

Of this she reminded me after a week of her absence, with a letter-card from down in Oamaru, its appearance in my letterbox bringing echoes of Harry's phantom correspondence and that rattle between their names I was coming now to expect. More strange messages, I wondered as I read her now familiar handwriting: or anger at the implications of the strange behaviour I'd shown before she went? This letter-card was from a different Janet, though, the one the family probably got when she returned to them—Mother had been baking, Dad had had no luck with his fishing: that sort of thing. It occurred to me to slip it into the hedge for her eventually to find when she returned, tit for her tat: but instead I forgot it in some other way itself forgotten. Harry was the main act now, and the question of what would happen in a further week's time when she came back I left unaddressed. With his return my real life seemed resumed, even my current worries with him part of a familiar material reality he brought along, since ongoing worry was an important factor in the reassurance his presence gave me: in a perverse way, it was always a relief for me to find my old anxieties still alive. In other words, one was always concerned as far as Harry was concerned.

And meanwhile there he was with a pillow at his back and *Best Bets* on his lap as he sat in his customary afternoon position on the divan below my front corner window. From this eminence he would take the late afternoon sun, casting the occasional look out at my front garden to report on anything that might have been happening in that not-very-considerable slice of the world available to him through the gap in my hedge. As I stood at this gap holding Janet's letter-card I saw him looking out at me like this, and it concerned me that this was one of those hollow moments I'd begun to notice in him when it seemed as if there was nothing very much for me to read in his usual winking gaze. And then of course the cough, which I could hear from outside even though the breeze was in the trees and enough to make the phone wires hum and swing above me. You've got me worried, Harry, I thought.

And that's when quite suddenly the idea of the loquat trees popped into my head—there they were in the garden not far from Harry's front corner window, their thick dark glossy leaves nodding at me as if to say yes, yes, they'd always been there, nothing's changed. Dear God, but I'd got cut off from my little world of late!—those leaves were bowed and bursting with their clustered green-and-yellow-golden fruit: and yet I'd hardly noticed them until now, the very fruit I always waited for most eagerly of all since it comes far earlier than the rest, a full season sooner, winter-and-spring to the summer-and-autumn of almost everything else. By the time I was thinking these thoughts I was among their branches and seizing a soft fat little globe from within their leaves: the flesh was perhaps a week short of readiness, it seemed to me, but when I bit into it the juice still burst on my tongue like the very start of summer. As I chewed and swallowed I pulled the rest of it apart and counted five big dark seeds inside. Loquats are ready, I called to Harry in his window, and he gave me back half a nod as I held the bitten fruit up towards him. But it was not really the fruit I was after, it was the leaves: for from the loquat leaf (as I'd recalled thirty seconds earlier) you may make a tea that is capable of bringing about all sorts of marvellous things. From the loquat leaf quite apart from anything else you may make a cure for nasty coughs and chest infections: the very infections it seemed to me afflicted Harry.

When was it in the business of grabbing handfuls of leaves that Janet's words came back again? How does it work, this business of attaching words to things, and is that in truth *how*

216

the business works: or is it, as Janet seems to claim, the other way around, words first then things, then—everything—?

A fruit in the middle of its location—

I plucked and clutched at leaves.

A fruit in the middle of its location—

I pulled my jersey out and up like a scrumping schoolboy, and began to fill it with leaves and fruit.

A fruit in the middle of its location—

I stopped. I suspect that you have already got to the trick of it, most of you, and possibly many pages back to boot. But I was living in the thick of things, I was caught up in the mess of it all and to me the moment of understanding seemed very nearly something out of *Revelation*. More than that, it was quite a terrible shock to seize the *thing* when finding the *word*, as if the first was the seed of the second—it was like a collision, so much so that when it happened the loquat I'd just picked seemed to pop out of my hand as if it had been shot from my grip. It bounced away in my unmown grass and lay there to be looked at and looked at and thought of, a thing-in-the-world. For indeed it is not at all untrue to propose that in the middle of *its location* is a fruit: the very fruit that I was picking lies in there, forever caught in the amber of those two words. The *word* enclosed the *thing*, *became* the thing: and as I thought this I was going back a few months in my mind, to that extraordinary conversation (conversation?—had I been required to speak a word of it?) early in Janet's stay with me. What was it she'd said then—the fit of words and things so that—what was it? So that one creates the other? I'd have to ask her, I'd have to tell her I'd worked it out, her words were riddles and I'd solved one for her at last: I'd have to tell her that, by God, she was right after all!

But right about exactly *what* I was considerably less sure as I took into the house a fruit-filled jersey that was bouncing like a woman's and as the golden little orbs tumbled from it to the kitchen bench. The tea was easy enough to make, after

I'd crushed the strange grooved leaves between two spoons: but as the jug seethed and worried on the front element it was the loquats that had my attention. Had I ever looked at fruit so hard before, had I ever looked at *anything* so hard in my life? For it was as if each one had been revealed to me in some way—not simply as any old fruit but *this* fruit *here*, *this* year's crop, *my* fruit that had grown on *my* tree out in the world beyond *my* windows: and which somehow had been returned to me through Janet's strange, strange act of naming them for me as if for the very first time. And it was barely a step from thinking this to thinking that there was a destiny to what was going on (for the possibility that something might indeed be going on was becoming very firmly lodged in my head by this stage)—that in some way Janet had led me to the tree, her words, however hidden from me at first, somehow preceding my act of seeing it and picking its fruit, but (I was becoming clearer on this now) somehow melting away, too, once they had done their work, releasing these extraordinary things in front of me, just loquats, just the loquats, just *these* loquats, redeemed and shadowless, like fruit in a painting—

Of course I didn't work it out nearly as neatly as this straight away: instead there was the chuffing of the jug as it began to boil behind me and the business of the loquat-leaf tea and after that the further song-and-dance of getting it into Harry, the object of the exercise in the first place. He was on the divan with his eyes closed and although I am not sure he was really asleep, when I tapped his shoulder he set up a great fuss at being so rudely woken—he was well away there for God's sake, I was as bad as the Irish night-nurse that woke the patient to give him a sleeping draught, now what was he being expected to take down his gullet this time, and besides, where were his makings? Your tobacco's on the floor, I said, and settled to the business of trying to cure him. Oh, a very different business this, I sensed, this rumpty old world of Harry Doyle compared to the extraordinary world it seemed Janet had just revealed to me beside it—*inside* it, *within* it: that was the point. Just *what* was she going to make of him—? And all the time I fussed with Harry and dabbed at his chin I was thinking as you might imagine of the other phrases that she'd left for me about the house across these strange winter months: *His look is the beast that guides his chariot, Meaning all volume satisfies, Tense inside in groper species*: and what were the others: and what did they mean? For now the first one had cracked itself open for me I realised that surely they must all mean something and the fact of that must mean something bigger still. What, though, what, *what* did it mean—?

As soon as the loquats showed me their seeds like this I went back to Janet's package as you might imagine, and read her novel draft from end to end once more, and with new eyes. I'd read it once, quickly and to the accompaniment of Harry's snores as I have told, but this time I was more leisurely about the business. A race meeting somewhere to the north had taken him off and left me to her world—and hers it very much was, as I reminded myself from my first reading and my first impression of it. That sense I often have when I read a youngster's maiden work that I could help here and I could help there—well, there was no need for that. Here was a woman who needed no help. Now, I must make clear I don't necessarily mean that as happily as it sounds, because parts of it disturbed me and all in all you might say it was not my cup of tea, or even quite (as far as I could tell) a cup of tea at all. Please try to understand. Gordon Garlick told me once the story of a Schubert symphony, possibly the Great, and how its first musicians could hardly find a tune in it. Well, finding one in Janet was easier the second time through (though never outright easy), and the idea of her work as a symphony is no bad way to get a sense of how it felt to read, so unlike any normal thing it was that I'd seen and nearer poetry than prose—in fact parts of it were actual poetry, I mean set apart and meant to be read as such. And all one piece as a result, you might say, with no one part you might take away and leave the rest intact.

Above all, there was no stopping it, if you see what I mean. It had the feel of history behind it, the feel of the twentieth century in it, the feel of our times. I mean despair. I often think of Fairburn now when I think of Janet, he whom I sometimes glimpsed on the ferry as I've told, a man who with his endless thirst for belief had spent many years in the philosophers and theologians, not to mention his deep acquaintance with the poets and the novelists as well. How much learning he had, and how little use for him it was in the end, he who had the particular cast of mind that needs not so much to believe but to believe himself believing. As I read her, I could see the same large discord of experience in Janet, and the same capacity as a consequence to clutch at meaning and to cleave to things too close: but I could also see the crucial difference, that she had learned somehow to push despair away—not to ignore it, and not to be consumed by it as Rex, alas, has finally been consumed: but to play with it, to play a tune on it that she can hear even if no one else can hear it yet. And thus in a historical sense (and I hope I can get my meaning across to you on this important point) she was the only right and proper inhabitant of my army hut, while Rex and I and Harry too I suppose—all those of us who'd reached a certain age—we all belong in truth to the rotting hovel my parents left me, the one I'd burnt to the ground: to the hut and the world it represented. I speak in a figurative sense of course. In that sense, we're all still back there: all of us save Janet.

But for one thing, with which I'll end this little interlude. In Janet's nameless work I could see myself—I could see what she'd read of me and taken from my earlier stuff and made of it, and I could also see something of what I had written these last few days and weeks as well. And if hers was not quite my cup of tea or not a cup of tea at all, then my *own* new work had exactly the same strange and unexpected taste. Once I'd come to terms with her extraordinary presence in my life—the strange fact of her, her inimitable *Janet* quality—I understood her to be my pupil, come to me to learn her trade do her work pick up tips and keep her place. This was despite my arid state of mind and fears of complete extinction: I might be done, but I'd done much, and as I understood it I was passing on my life to her, the fullness of my achievement. And she would have none of it, if you please!—she had a life of her own, it turned out, and had no need of mine or very little. What she'd done she'd done herself, her very own strange sad intricate piece of work, the kind of thing it would probably take years to comprehend, years to like and admire properly. And yet it had in it *now* the recognisable sounds and moods of the world around us, its discords disharmonies disturbances dissatisfactions: all of them turned into something else or in the business of doing so. And she was taking me with her, that was the extraordinary truth of things it seemed, and all of this she was doing without speaking a single word.

My first intimation that Janet had returned came from Harry in his lookout position on his front room divan. *Tart's back*, was the verbal telegram by which he transmitted this particular information, and then he fell again to a brooding contemplation of his paper and its pressing issues of current equine form. And although tart she definitely was not, returned she undoubtedly was, as I could see when once I'd hurried to the back door: where I found her standing in the gap twixt hut and house with suitcase in hand and herself as breathless as if she'd just walked every inch of the very considerable distance between here and the benighted south, a measure of some many miles more than five hundred.

I said her name and she as redundantly mine. I asked

how she was and she said that she was fine, thank you: then she asked after me and it turned out I was doing fine as well!—here we were then, definitely Mr Sargeson and Miss Frame once more as we slipped into each other's sentences once again, while standing gaping at each other and with no way of knowing which of us was warier of the other. Janet was back: and what's more, so was the man whose presence my instincts were increasingly telling me somehow complemented hers and which also weighed on me as I stood there breathing hard as if I, too, had completed at least some of her long journey with her. The triangle was completed, the game had changed, neither of them was a figment of my mind after all, here we were all three of us on the magic island once more: what now?

Well, I let them run into each other, shall I say: she in the first place having no reason to expect that he might be in residence at all, and he in the second having no evident enthusiasm for making the acquaintance of anyone who might distract him from the business in hand: for *Best Bets* still held him captive like the picture in Wittgenstein. And to tell you the truth I was so foxed by the entire situation that I simply gave up and let things happen, which meant that almost straight away she came upon him as she ducked into the house and then the front room on her way to the water-convenience—came upon him sitting in his pomp on the living room divan, his blanket on his knees, his racing guide held high.

I could see the shock go through her, the momentary check to her stride and her head ducking down as she slipped aside and into the bathroom and hauled the sliding door hard across with a slapping bump. As I turned the wireless up for her benefit I found myself imagining the usual change of her appearance taking place in there that I'd seen at times like this—I mean the blood rising to her neck her cheeks her ears and so forth—and the terror she must be feeling. I should have warned her, I should have warned her: but of what, what would Harry represent to her—?

His eyes meanwhile flicked up at mine and stayed there.

Now Harry, I hissed. Be a gent—

His head and eyebrows lifted up behind the wisps of cigarette smoke as if he was amazed I might consider him capable of any other behaviour than sheer perfection. And then there was that amused tomcat crinkle of the eyes and he sank back to his booklet. He was very much there today—had the loquat tea worked its wonders on him after all, perhaps?

Well, Janet took her time, so much so that there was a number of chances for Harry to meet my gaze again in the amount of it she took, and, once, to tap his wrist in order to indicate the passing of the minutes. And when a good fifteen of them had disappeared he began to speculate aloud on what it was that might have been detaining her.

Round the S-bend by now, he hissed.

Harry, I said.

No, true dinks, round the bend and out to sea—

Keep your *voice* down—

Or tunnelled out, he said. Like a bloody rabbit—should have reached Foxton by now—

At which point the sliding door rumbled suddenly open and Janet stood there before us again, terrified. Harry's eyes flickered back to his book.

She froze there helplessly in the door: which way to flee—?

Miss Frame, I said. You'll remember me mentioning my good friend Harry Doyle—

She stared at him. Her top lip went back slightly—did it? Or did I imagine so? Of words she spoke not one.

Harry looked up and tipped an imaginary hat at her. Lady, he said. How you doin'—?

She stared at him with who-knew-what thoughts. Floating, she said, in her tiny voice, and stared some more.

It took him by surprise, I could see that even if another might not. I could see him fishing up a response:

Floatin'? he managed after a bit. That right—?

I stepped in.

Janet's had a long journey from down south, I said.

Harry's cackle, broken by his gluey chest and a forest fire of coughs. South, he said to me when he'd reassembled himself. Foxton, d'y'mean? Down Foxton way—?

Harry's got a thing about Foxton, I said to Janet. Take no notice—

It was true but too complicated to explain here: something about a painted horse. Anyway, he wasn't allowed back in Foxton any more, not on the racetrack at any rate.

I was rubbing my hands together, I noticed, like a headwaiter.

Janet's a writer, I said to Harry.

Harry stared at her. You told me, he said. Poetry—

Fiction, not poetry—

She stared at me, at him, at me again.

Pterodactyl, she said.

There was a silence. What to say in return—?

Excuse me, she said.

And she slipped towards and through my bedroom door and to the back passage and her freedom. The hut door thumped. I stood there.

What she say—?

Pterodactyl, I said.

What the hell's she mean—?

Pterodactyl—

He stared at me: you bloody arty-farts, I could hear him thinking: it was one of his phrases. Well, that's a deep one, is what he managed in the end. Bit too curly for me. And he returned to his booklet.

A bit too curly for me, too, to tell the truth, although I realised now of course that like her riddles it had to mean

224

something. There was no chance to ask her over our evening meal, either, since she didn't favour us with her company as Harry and I settled down in due course to whatever it was I'd mustered up that night. As it turned out (I looked around for her after the meal) she'd done what I should've known she'd do when confronted with another unexpected figment of reality: she'd gone to ground—but not, as it happened, in the hut, whose door was open and interior empty but for bed desk and suitcase when I tapped politely on the doorpost. I tried the vegetable patch, which was almost invisible in the dark, and was there myself discovered by the cats, at work on moths. Out then to the gate I wandered, and stood under the high rickety rattling lampshade of the streetlight, hands in pockets while a slight breeze tried at my shirt—was she hiding there beside me in my shaggy macrocarpa hedge, crouched amongst the interior branches and peering out at me as I stood beside it? Could she see me but I not her, always her favourite contract of relationship? Should I call her name out, should I go even further and thrust my head right inside the hedge the way Harry had made me do a couple of weeks before? And if I did and found her within, what would I say?—that I'd solved the riddle about the loquat, that the words had seemed to come first, or both the word and the thing together? That I had begun to enter the strange world she was presenting to me, to the point that—here I was, a grown man talking to a hedge like some suburban version of Jack and the beanstalk?

I pulled away, I walked away, suddenly aware of what I must have looked like—if indeed there was anyone at all who might care to watch me on a blind suburban road at seven o'clock on an early October evening. Innocent enough, I suppose, to the exterior view: and yet there was always that guilty boyhood fear that inner thoughts and deeds were visible to the censoring eye of society: and what thoughts! For she really had me shaken at this stage, and I found myself struggling to regain once more that simulation of ordinariness I'd learned to achieve all those years ago and which had proved to be such a rock in my life when I was fighting off the very things I'd found within myself that Janet seemed determined now to wake up in me again! Yet (I knew this as I settled on my haunches behind the army hut and turned to the task next at hand, the business of splitting wood for tomorrow's fire) there was no getting away from the *conundrum* of her, the strange and baffling challenge that her presence posed, since what she was setting me was no more and no less than the very riddle of her state of mind. It was obvious that there was more, much more to this young woman than I'd begun to fear at the end of that terrible journey on which Lyall had taken me across the River Styx.

Thus I was able to face her much more easily now she was back than in that lost, terrible month before she'd left to journey south: and it is not impossible that a sensing of that very slight relaxation on my part did the work of bringing her the same measure of relief. This is not to say that all was once again as free and easy between us as things had sometimes been during the days of our very earliest commerce (for all the many unexpected moments that occurred in that time), just that when I next heard her at the back door of the cottage I no longer felt that dreadful surge of fear in the middle of my chest that had caught me not so very many weeks before whenever she came upon me as she did. And, as I will relate, things were about to get better than that, not least because, in amongst all my other concerns and worries, I'd hit upon a fine solution for one of the more ticklish not to say more peculiar of my problems, that of how to broach the matter of the riddles and the loquats, still a business sufficiently idiosyncratic (you might say) as to require careful preparation. And then, all of a sudden, quite late in the evening of the day she returned, I had it: and fell to bringing it about, as you will witness in a moment or two.

The following afternoon she came into the house, flicking her eyes about the place for Harry. But he had left some time before, his trilby hat at a jaunty angle as he ducked through the gap in the hedge and out.

Gone, I told her. Town. Business—

Business? she said, as if I was really keeping him hidden somewhere, in the meat-safe possibly, in order to spring a nasty surprise. *Him*—?

An investment matter. Concerning bloodstock—

She brought herself more fully into the room, like one of the cats, on guard, still looking around, still keeping to the wall.

He really isn't here, I said. And he really doesn't bite when he is—

She sat down carefully, smoothing her skirt over her bottom the way she'd done on that first day: on a chair, I noticed, and not the divan.

He reminds me of my father's friends. She said it suddenly, as if it'd just occurred to her. The men Dad works with on the railways—

Work, I said. *Harry*—?

I used to take Dad's tucker-box down to the yard for him sometimes. His lunch. They used to look at us. The men. At me and my sisters. As if they *knew* something—

She looked away.

Oh, I don't think Harry actually *knows* anything—

She ignored me. It was as if they knew something we didn't, she said. Girls. Women. I've felt it again. Down there, these last two weeks—

I waited. In fact I knew what she meant, of men in general if not particularly of Harry. For all my concealments and conformities, that awareness was always present, of the rage and fear when men get themselves together in large numbers

and there comes about the business of controlling the urges
that arise through sheer confusing proximity of male body to
male body, urges of which most of them, as far as I can see,
have not the slightest beginnings of an idea at all. I've always
felt that punishing people like Harry and me for this problem
is an irony, by the way, since surely it is people like Harry
and me who in truth have found the only solution to it.

And Mr Doyle's like that, she said. He watches you—

Ah. Well, Miss Frame, he may well watch you, but I can
assure you it's not in quite the same way—

It was terrible—

Harry was—?

Down there. My holiday. I'm never going back—

By now I had learned of course to expect these lurches of
attention, if not quite yet the trick of joining them all together
into a seamless narrative. Nonetheless I could see a sort of
thread emerging here.

All that anger, she said, but not to me.

I waited.

I used to see them waiting at the end of town. The
swaggers. There was a sort of park they'd gather in, and then
off they'd go. I used to be afraid of them but now I know I
should've felt jealous, they were leaving—

I was surprised: she'd told me her home town was her
special place: her novel was set there in part: it evoked its
tiny small-town life in a way that suggested considerable
nostalgia. I presumed the town had lost its charm for her
now it was living in the present tense. I had other fish to fry,
though—or, as it happened, a pie to eat.

Why *pterodactyl*, I asked her. You said it to me. Yesterday.
When I told Harry you wrote fiction not poetry—

Oh. Yes. Fiction not poetry. It just popped out—

Yes, but why—?

Because it's in dactyls. *Fiction not poetry*—

I ran it through my mind—and indeed it was, it is—*fic*tion

228

not *poetry*. She was quite right. I should have expected that she would be. There remained the question of—

And he terrifies me, she said.

Harry does—?

It just happened in my mind. That's how it works—

How does he terrify you—?

But a look of such anguish appeared on her face, in fact a look I'd never seen before amongst the considerable repertoire of facial expressions she'd shown in her time with me, that I decided to change the topic. And I had the very thing to do that with, thanks to my labours of the night before. I sprang up: I took the covered dish I'd placed in the meat-safe overnight and put it in front of her. I removed the cover:

Ah, she said. For tonight—?

Yes, but what is it—?

She looked up at me. A pie, possibly—?

Yes, but what *kind* of a pie, Miss Frame—?

She peered at it and sniffed. Well, she said. A fruit pie—

Ah, yes, but what *kind* of a fruit pie, Miss Frame—?

And then she twigged. I don't think I've ever seen anyone quite so happy over anything this side of a child at Christmas, anyone so utterly delighted as she was in that first moment of realisation—she slapped her palms together in front of her face, she even managed a sort of dance in the chair while still somehow remaining seated in it. I was suddenly struck by what an extraordinary smile she has, how *well* she laughs, how much she seems to like being happy when somehow despite her best resistances happiness comes upon her. Well, naturally, I was caught up in all this excitement and couldn't wait to tell her how I'd finally made the connection. She listened as I ran through it, with the same rapt attention with which she sometimes listened to music on the wireless radio. The only part that surprised her was the fact that loquats come into fruit when they do. She kept staring out of the window at them.

Those loquats there? she said. You used those ones? Are you sure you haven't hung them there just to make a point—?

They've hung themselves, they fruit in early summer—not everything comes out of tins and bottles, I told her as I stowed the pie back in the safe for the evening meal. Or books either—

You realise that pie is like the riddle?—they've both got *loquat* in the middle of them—?

Ah—no, I said, hadn't realised. I checked the front window. (Was I *really* hoping Harry's return would be delayed?) But you're quite right, they do—

What about the others? *His look is the beast that guides his chariot*—?

She snapped her fingers. And an extraordinary thing happened as she did:

Ben! I said. He steers his motorcycle—

It just came into my mind as she snapped her fingers—I was shocked by the involuntariness of it, and the whiff of Signor Bosco, too, from all those years ago.

Her face lit up. Correct! She seemed galvanised, she straightened up, she slapped her hands together. He's like a young steer—

Ben is—?

That's what he reminds me of. The way he looks at you—

He stares at you like a young steer—?

—while he steers his motorbike—with his head down and that middle parting—She made a quick gesture at her brow. The horns coming away on either side—

I could see it straight away—of course: she was right. But if that is what he was, a thought now occurred to me:

What about the other end—?

The other end of the motorbike—?

The other end of the steer—

What about it—?

230

Well, you wouldn't want him to be a steer, I don't think—

Why not—?

He'd have no—

I looked away and coughed into my fist as if delicately. And to my amazement, suddenly she twigged—

No balls—! she said.

It just popped out: she clapped her hand against her mouth.

I gave a great yelp of laughter. That's it! I cried. It made me slap my palms together in delight just as she'd done before. He'd have no balls! And I slapped them both together once again. That's it—!

It was something of a breakthrough between us—as the entire business proved to be, of course, I mean the slow process of understanding her own particular language, learning to enter it, taking the first steps towards the way in which she seems to think. It was as if I'd moved from my own world towards hers—into it, even, right into the world she lived in and which made up all her meanings for her. The other two riddles she had to explain to me, I mean the two I'd found: for it seemed she'd left out more of a paper trail than I'd realised, and in the next few days I came across more bits and pieces along with new ones she supplied. They were both about the book, she said, and that was what she was trying to get across to me: in other words, the fact that she had finished writing it. And *literally* in other words: *Meaning all volume satisfies* meant 'fulfilled', apparently, while *Tense inside in groper species* gives up to the determined puzzler (she assured me) the word 'finished'. And you can imagine how long I sat there in the following days and tried to work out how they might come to mean the things she said they meant: though she admitted to me they were both imperfect in conception. She was still learning her craft, she said, still learning simpler ways of complication.

231

Which (as you will see) begged the question of her purpose in the first place. But when I asked it—well, she turned things back on me, and became as complex as her riddles. And here I found myself hoist high at last. For as I dodged her sprays of blue-black ink I clearly saw when all was said and done my own machinations lying at the foot of everything gone wrong—I mean my setting Lyall on her trail and the growing chaos after that, whatever it involved. Naturally I was reluctant to spill the beans on the formulating part I'd played in *that* particular *folie de grandeur*, but as long as I kept quiet on it I was forced to do the same for explanations of my following behaviour, I mean my reactions to the very things I myself provoked. So much for the magus-author high above the fray: here was I, then, just another bewildered character seeking answers, reduced to dropping hints and waiting for responses if they came, and baffled by her large expansive silences. From which dribs and drabs I gathered, little by little and not easily, the following facts: that Lyall had indeed dropped by the army hut but was gone soon after never to return, and that wild horses could not persuade her to tell me more of what had passed between them on that one occasion: but that whatever it was, to judge by the revulsion with which she spoke the little that she said, it involved nothing of the sort of activities he had bragged about to me, however indirectly. Here was an explanation, through the fog of her indirections, of his colossal rage at her. Hell hath no fury, it seemed, like a meat-trimmer scorned.

What then of the other business, I mean the constant return of Little Ben's motorbike as had clearly been the case?—and in fact it had *always* been Ben (she brightened here as she began to tell me), and it turned out these visits came down to nothing more than the making of the jersey! Hercules to her Omphale indeed, he had spun her wool and tried to teach the same skill to her: to little effect, apparently, for in the end he'd done the work himself while she'd watched. Given the nature of his background I had no doubt that all of this was true, and as I turned it over in the days and weeks that followed I gave increasing weight to the meaning I've just mentioned, the strange tale of the ancient hero's unmanning and the younger Ben's strange embracing of the very things that meant. I don't mean he knew the slightest thing about this reference, of course (or that like Hercules he was reduced to wearing women's clothes!)—I simply mean that I could see much in him a woman like Janet might enjoy and trust. And I could see in the way Janet talked of him that this was exactly the case: and by turning all this inside out, I could also see by implication something of what Lyall must have represented to her when he turned up at her door, the smell of him, the danger. He stank of drains, she told me, not on this occasion but offhandedly some time later. And he did, too, except it was not drains that were the cause.

So there you have it—the truth behind my wild romantic thoughts. Other answers slowly took some shape during the following weeks as we worked through the business of her book, she and I, for as you will see that was what came next, that and one or two other things that were not small. Those long yawning silences on her part, though, that had represented to me the triumph of my Imperial?—no more, it seemed, than the time she spent in reading through her finished work before retyping the odd page here and there. Her silence and her misery, signs to me of impending breakdown and collapse?—no more than pangs attendant on any act of giving birth. In other words, nothing I'd done had had the slightest effect on her, none of my imaginings had any basis, and all my intervention did was set off a random shot on a billiards table whose outcome was the terrifying word Lyall hit me with that night a month before, and all that followed. You can imagine the effect on me these understandings had as they accumulated inside my mind, and crystallised into an explanation that explained, a story I could believe in.

They did so far more slowly and less clearly than I've rendered here, I might say, and like flowers were at their best at the height of the day. The night played havoc with them sometimes, and occasionally I would find myself awake and lathered up as if we were back in the thick of things, she and I, in that abyss of misunderstanding we'd lived in during the winter. In those nights, however briefly, it was as if nothing had been explained at all and reason was impossible: the old terror was back on me and I sat up in bed thinking *why, why, why*—but every time this happened, in due course *came the dawn* and everything was restored. That moment when we first shared her language became the turning-point again: the day we were no longer Mr Sargeson and Miss Frame to each other, for example, a change I remember as something that seemed to sum up all the other things that changed between us, or the things that might (I sometimes think) have changed had we remained indeed just that simple pair of labels, *Frank* and *Janet*—

But then Harry turned up again.

CHAPTER 10

It is part of the reticence I treasure so much in Harry that I have very few notions of the details of his early life more than those I've sketched so far in passing, all of them based on information blurred by his passion for inexactness. Given that my own early misadventures have compelled me to similar measures on occasion, I am in sympathy with his delicacies regarding his past. But they mean that more than a little guesswork is required when it comes to the business of judging his earliest motivations, and sometimes I find myself obliged to take him less as induplicable Harry Doyle than as a specimen of a larger genus, *Homo Harrius* if you like. Solomon is of course another such, one more of that great plurality of blokes thrown up by the first of the two wars and the century that made it. Though their number has been thinned by the usual silent artillery, they are still very much about the place and part of our national distinctiveness: self-sufficient, womanless and almost as if brought about by some kind of universal male parthenogenesis, they can be found at any pub racetrack football ground or gymnasium as if drawn there by the sweat of their communal exertion. I've never decided whether my failure quite to get involved in either of our overseas military adventures was my good fortune (as I normally reckon it to be) or the loss of a formative and final experience in the rites and inner meanings of this completely masculine world.

The point I am edging my way towards in a manner itself inexact is how Harry came to walk the side of the street I met him on, so to speak. And bound up in *that* question is the one I'm really after, which is to do with the womenfolk. In my own case as you might have gathered I tend like Harry to be a man's man and to find the company of women beside the point, by and large—by which I mean simply that they have no necessary part in the mode of life I've chosen or that has chosen me. Already you have seen something of my difficulties with what I would term a certain kind of woman, I mean of a particular style class and temperament and even (at times) a particular mode of attire, and it is not untrue to guess a link here to people with whom I've shared earlier parts of my life. One of the punishments of advancing age, I've found, is in those unwelcome mirror-glimpses of these ancestors suddenly beginning to look back at me from my reflected face, with an eye here, a lower lip there, more often a fleeting set of face that brings back childhood fear and anger whenever it appears. These apparitions of my family's distaff side sans hairnet and steel-rimmed spectacles make me wish that (for all his limitations both abstract and literal) I'd taken more from my father's branch as my more fortunate brother did, and escaped these material reminders of my maternal past.

Yet here I am with Janet in my life, and of course with Margaret Guigan too and half a dozen others of the fairer sex regularly about the place as well. From time to time these women tell me that I have my little ways—for example (according to Margaret), the frequent needling use of that very phrase *the fairer sex*. Their further accusation that I am odd concerning the business of women wearing skirts I freely admit, since it is a difficulty I cannot explain to myself beyond supposing it part of a larger aversion displaced. And I have been rapped across the knuckles (very nearly literally, as you'll see) for what I'm told is by far my worst failing, a tendency to bully women when pressing on an argument (once again Margaret is my informant here and the phrase is hers). Sometimes, she says, I even make them cry. That I do the first with man or woman is undoubted, since I am a man of strong opinions and I like to make my case: and that my interlocutors have on occasion had recourse to tears is as much true. But to conjoin the two as cause and effect seems nonsense to me—although the time I put this riposte to Margaret was the time she took the frying pan to me at her house and pretty near chased me from it, the house I mean and not the pan, although I'm sure that at the living moment she'd rather have had me in the latter and sizzling over a hot flame.

Which brings me to my point, though, on this head, which is that I like a woman to have a little character. Janet as you will gather I am still working out for myself and I have yet to place her fully, so to speak: but in respect to Margaret, in all truth I can't imagine her very far from me at any time. In what has gone so far you'll have picked up something of how we deal, she and I, and the tendency towards the robust in our exchanges that has led us twice to be confused as man and wife in public. (Because we bicker, I told her: because we never touch, she said.) *There's* something to think of, and sometimes I have done so, erasing her husband from my thoughts, his chaperone presence I mean, and wondering what would then be left of us. The invisibly triangular nature of relationships is always known to me, and the way an invisible ma or pa will get between a couple as a presence all the more haunting for being in phantom form—there are six people in every bed, after all, though only two of them may be visible. And somewhere in there is my explanation for what happens next when thoughts like these arise, which can be expressed only as a version of those mirror-moments when my mother and her sisters appear in front of me: except there is no mirror in this case, only a woman unprotected by a husband's presence: close, but always distant: available, and thus unavailable to *me*—

But in Harry's case it's as if women are from another planet. From time to time of course, although not so much nowadays, there's been bragging talk of his army youth, the general brothel stuff he claimed they all got up to together in Egypt forty years ago when the blood fizzed around their veins. But in truth I've never seen him near a woman in my life. He has no more use for them than a tone-deaf man for a brass band, and would likely be the last taken for anyone's husband at a party. Over the years many women have come and gone at 14 Esmonde Road, the ones I've mentioned and others I haven't—in the army hut, for example, whose longest inhabitation until Janet broke the record was by a young woman who had serious ambitions to be an engineer, if you please! My old friend G., whom I haven't mentioned until now, occasionally turns up with her dogs. And of course so many of my visitors have wives, young women all too often post-war pregnant, which brings an added dimension of bafflement to Harry's life, though he always likes their little *snooks*, as he calls the smaller children when they turn up, and they seem to feel pretty much the same way about him. He has a trick with matchsticks that holds them open-mouthed: me too, sometimes, as I watch—

When he coincides with my older female visitors, though, by and large he tends to ignore them. He does this not impolitely but as if they exist in a different dimension from the one he lives in, like images on a screen or pictures in a book. Like me he seems slightly more at ease if the woman in question is, as he puts it, spoken for—with Margaret, for example, he almost manages a relationship of some kind, although when I overheard him telling her one of his long baroque yarns one day (something to do with the definition of a tight spot which I think had a rather regrettable conclusion) I realised that this involved a high degree of forbearance on her part.

But with the would-be female engineer just mentioned he was up the creek without a paddle (which is one word different from how he might put it). With her and many others he managed to avoid offence, as I say, but as a rule he does this by avoiding everything else as well.

And thus he is a different bag of tricks from me, and much more like that vast ambiguous male majority I've just mentioned as keeping a lip-curled distance from half the human population, as if all the things men might need are available in themselves and *the fairer sex* at best no more than some kind of evolutionary deviation. And not simply nature gone wrong, but sometimes red in tooth and claw as well: men whose bodies still carry the marks of their endurance on the battlefield seem terrified in the presence of a woman and at a loss for what to do with them and where to look—they turn as if to suits of armour in both disposition and comportment, stiff of limb and of course with visor well clamped shut as well. At various times Harry has demonstrated some or all of these possibilities when threatened by the proximity of what he refers to (variously) as *dames bints sheilas* and *tarts*, and tends to arrange things so that he will find himself as rapidly as possible in the nearest refuge that promises to be free of women, be it betting shop hairdressing saloon or the bar of the Mon Desir.

I bring this up now and not sooner because it didn't become an issue until Janet's arrival made it so. Naturally, his presence in my life has been a puzzle all my friends confronted one by one as they entered it: who *was* this old bloke propped up in the corner during Frank's literary soirées—some elderly relative I was obliged to do time with for form's sake, some needy neighbour in receipt of my legendary hospitality? An unusually ill-informed and first-time visitor once asked me the question straight out: who *is* that dreadful man, Frank, what on earth's he doing here? By and large I was forgiving of these reactions, knowing as I did that Harry is as an excellent whisky is reputed to be, something of an acquired taste, and also that over the years a number of my coterie had indeed taken the trouble to sip at him and in due course seemed genuinely to enjoy his earthy, smoky taste. And in truth most had heard of him and his role in my life before they had their first collision, so to speak, and thus were not entirely unprepared for the shock as taste hit taste and caste bumped into caste. Nor was he unprepared for them—that initial tipping of an imaginary hat he made to Janet when they first confronted each other in my house was the grace-note to all meetings he made with my arty-farts: satirical, of course, but like all satire offering substance if substance were required: if the recipient expected politeness, why, there in front of them was politeness its very self, politeness personified and raising its hat in their direction! Much of Harry's repertoire amongst my friends involved the acceptance of this gesture and what then followed, a contract by which he was allowed to walk his own curious tightrope before their disbelieving gaze, together with all those balancing gestures and rituals by which he managed to keep himself aloft. All in all as I've indicated, a performance in itself: the performance of Harry, by Harry, but not (I like to think) entirely *for* Harry.

Janet, though, simply had no way of reading him. That first meeting, when she ran into him on her return from the south and then barricaded herself beside the water-convenience before surrendering once more to the unforgiving gaze of men, seemed to exhaust the possibilities that lay between them. His imaginary hat was doffed to no purpose, and she saw what her eyes told her was in front of her: that, and (by the same means of involuntary displacement, I suspect, to which I've just admitted in my relations with a certain mode of woman) worse. When first I realised this, my spirits were briefly raised and I unworthily anticipated the prospect of her complete departure and the field being left to Harry and to me. But this thought lasted seconds once I recalled my debt to her or more properly the one I owed myself through her existence. She'd come to me for the everyday domestic shelter that I'd of course provided, but she'd come to me for shelter of another kind as well. And until the business of her publication had been sorted out, as far as I could see my debt was unacquitted. Fine words, you might think, in which case I leave you to decide in due course whether or not I've earned the right to say them. But finer still to my mind (not to mention rather more surprising to me) was my growing realisation that if I looked into my heart, and quite apart from matters literary, I was not yet quite ready for her to quit the property. So unexpected, this thought, that when first it offered itself to me I stuffed it to the back of my mind straight away for later contemplation, or preferably for none at all.

Instead I approached the business of resolving things with her and Harry. This was urgent, given their presence in a house of small proportions on land that offered only so much further space to hide in. The latter-day tendency to invalid behaviour that Harry manifested (albeit without admission of actual invalidity) meant that in effect the entire front half of my little dwelling was out of bounds to Janet for much of any day and all of every night: and since access to the water-convenience and what have you was made by way of it, the entire building was in effect forbidden to her when Harry was in residence. How she coped in that respect I do not know of course or need to know, but in those first few weeks that Harry was *in situ* she hardly ever took the risk of coming in that I could see. The serving of meals, too, became complex and then worse, a nightmare, and at one point I seriously considered managing them in continuous shifts, the way Lyall told me the canteen runs at the meat-works. In the end, though, I approached the matter in accordance with my conscience, and started with the single fact that linked her manuscript to the problem he presented her: that her difficulty with Harry was a textual difficulty and thus a business of reading, or of learning to read.

First though I got the matter of her literary future off my chest. As is my habit in these situations, I was direct but not unkind: 'No butter no sugar and no vinegar' is my motto. Besides in her case there was nothing in particular to be unkind about and much to indicate the opposite approach. That she had a future as a writer I'd already made clear to her, of course, as often as I could. But that it was now much closer to the present as a result of her endeavours in the army hut I made as plain as any fact could possibly be made. With the same principles of discipline and fortitude, I told her, there was nothing she could not do: within reason of course. But first the business of publication: did she have anyone in mind to send it to? If so, should it be aimed locally or overseas, the one more possible, the other a longer shot? And did she feel herself prepared for the rigours of reception thereafter, not to say the attentions of the reviewer? Was she prepared, in short, for a form of public life?

And here our Janet turned even more subtle and complex than was usually the case. Publication?—it seemed she'd had no thought of going so far as actual *publication*, since what she'd created wasn't even a particular thing, neither fish nor flesh nor good red herring for all that she could tell. As she'd made plain, it was just an exploration on paper that she'd undertaken not least to see if she could complete the project, which of course she was pleased to have done as much as she was delighted by my praise of the result. But actual *publication* had been the farthest undertaking from her mind when she was writing it: the entire business had never been more than a form of private research, little more than a pastime: and so on. Ah yes but you mention *completing* it just now, I said, which suggests it is a particular thing in your mind that has had some kind of shape to be achieved: as indeed it is to the happy reader, since as I think I've said, not the least of her accomplishments was to allow her work to be read as a single and complete experience, with beginning middle end and nothing else—

Thus I wore her down little by little, and won her reluctant agreement that her typescript should be sent off without delay. A title might be nice, I suggested, and there were one or two things further that I thought required her attention, which she gave them straight away—chapter division was one of them, I recall, and I recommended suitable points at which such interruptions might be weighed. But when it came to the question of where to send her work it seemed that after all her ambition outweighed her general fear of life, since she was able to show me a recent letter from a reputable publisher to the south which responded to one of hers sent some weeks before it and urged her to send the manuscript forthwith! So much for all my blandishments, and yet more evidence if evidence were needed that in all matters still she was what my father used to call *a tight chest of drawers*—

In another week, then, there we were, the pair of us, in front of the post office in Hurstmere Road with the packet held between us as if we were both its parents and set to launch it off in life like a first child with a gold sovereign in its pocket. I took my hands from it and she as quickly passed it back to me—

But what if they don't like it? her child's-voice said as we paused in this little game.

Why then they'll send it back and tell us so, I replied. I put it in her hands again. And then we'll try another publisher and if necessary another after that—

And I think I said something too about casting bread upon the waters.

Then, as if of its own volition, as if sucked into the mail-slot, down our package went—a quite awful moment for both of us, I might say—and landed deep inside with a muffled, irrevocable *thump*—

We stood there for a second or two, and then we turned away.

Now, I said. Harry—

I chafed my palms together as we walked.

What about him, she said.

A little matter of further reading, I suggested.

And as we walked back to Esmonde Road I tried to bring her around to another way of thinking on this matter. As it happens I had in mind a separate thing as well, not just the urgent business of reconciling the two people I shared my life with at the time but the addressing of an aspect of her writing that had been much in my thoughts as we'd shared the business of getting her typescript up to scratch and ready for the dispatch we'd just given it. The thing was this: that for all the remarkable achievement of her first extended venture in prose fiction (as I always insisted to her it was), for all the evidence that it pushed away from any established tradition so far and yet was moored still within that tradition and gave back to it, enhanced it, there was within its unfolding story a remarkable reliance on herself and family for a subject, on them and on friends and neighbours as well: in short, on what was already known to her. This proposition, when I raised it now as we walked together down Lake Road, she readily agreed to as if her practice were a normal thing.

Now, I'm as aware as any of the notion that all art is a form of autobiography, and as I've already made clear, from time to time I've found myself relying for both character and story on those around me and in my past. But few of those I thus immortalise would know it when confronted by the page, and it is not untrue to claim I've had the pleasure of receiving compliments on the plausible literary invention of a character of particularly compelling unwholesomeness from the very human being through whose existence that creation received its primal germ of life! Of course human vanity plays a part in this sort of misrecognising, but the creative mind plays larger still, since long before the page it brings about all manner of transformation beyond the conscious mind of the mere scribblers who write it down: and I am surely not the first and only such—nor last—to marvel at the apparent independence of the life that thus results, the wondrous verisimilitude that is managed in parts of one's own mind to which one has no kind of access whatever. Where did *you* come from—? has been my not-infrequent inner greeting to such creations when once they have appeared before me as like to human life as a new neighbour peering over my fence or hedge and giving me unasked the time of day. At moments like this we are all readers not writers, and someone else (*who* though, *who*—?) is doing the creative business for us.

Well, to the likelihood of all this she had no difficulty assenting as we walked along, although I took care as we did so to keep my voice down when in earshot of the passing population of Lake Road, and it certainly came out to her with far less polish than I've rendered it here as having: inasmuch as it has any at all. I decided, too, not to mention one of the key parts of my argument, the evidence of that sentence stolen from my mouth and which I'd read on that typed page in her hut. What better evidence that she poached things straight from life unchanged?—but it turned out there'd been no sign of it in her novella, and besides I was unwilling, understandably I think, to be reduced therefore to admit my act of penetration by bringing the topic up myself. Which, against the dispiriting content of the stolen sentence itself, is the manly way I prefer to describe it here—

Thus by the time we reached the hump in Esmonde Road this breezy morning in early October, as far as the matter of the art of life and the life of art was concerned you might say I'd shot my bolt. We stopped there, both of us apparently reluctant to return quite yet to house and army hut, and I could think of no better point to redirect our thought to Harry and the possibilities offered by his existence to enhance her human understanding, and hence her craft in creating character.

But her expression changed immediately I mentioned his name once more.

Mr Doyle? she said, and looked away. Breeze fluttered her headscarf.

Harry, I said. Himself—

What do you mean—d'you mean I should *write* about him—?

Not necessarily—no, not at all, that's the point, the point is not to write—

Not to write—?

Not to write immediately. That's the point, Janet, that's what I'm trying to tell you. The words don't necessarily happen first—

Well, I can tell you she looked at me when I came up with that!—but I pressed on, so urgent did it seem to take this opportunity of arguing what was obviously at hand, given the proximity of something that seemed to me (the more and more I talked) a perfect example of a meeting-point of life and art. Broaden your horizons! I heard myself advising her, to my regret on later reflection: but as far as I was concerned at that moment I was in for a penny and in for a pound, and by the time we reached my letterbox and had filleted its interior of mail and stooped our way through the hedge-gap and onto our familiar property again I'd managed far worse than that, I mean in the use of clichés I would now associate more with the pre-pubescent desolations of the Boy Scout movement than with any higher calling—so low did I go in the art of persuasion it's a wonder I didn't urge on her the merits of nocturnal boxing gloves and a chilly morning shower! If I'd shot my bolt ten minutes earlier out there on Esmonde Road, what was the state to which had I reduced that figurative mechanism by the time we reached our respective doors, hers to the army hut and mine to the little cottage?

As I closed mine behind me, though, I realised the worst part of this exchange was that she'd agreed to everything I'd said in it. For example, I'd suggested that as a start to things the three of us might share a communal meal that evening, she and Harry and I, and that for it I might make something special, insofar as doing so was within my compass. But everything you make is special, she murmured at that point (and my suspicions should have begun to be aroused with *that*): and demurely she agreed that yes, the proposal was an excellent one and was there anything she could do to help? No: this is a celebration, I reminded her, thinking to tie her down to it a little more. This is a day not like other days— hard things to write, novels, a fact which I reminded her is not recognised by everyone: and even harder to write at her breathtaking speed.

And to my great astonishment, after I'd expected up to the very last minute that some kind of feint or dodge might intervene and keep her safely in her hut, there was Janet presenting herself at six o'clock that evening as in the good old days, and ready for the special feast I'd managed—which was in truth no more than a string of sausages raised to the higher purpose of bringing life to a casserole, itself in turn enhanced by the very first serving of the newest of new potatoes from my garden. For dessert there was the last of the loquats, of course: although their season was never long and these were a little past their time I thought Janet would appreciate the reference they made. I explained that I'd have liked to drink to her success with my home-made pumpkin wine, now well on in the second life our latter-day attentions had given it, but that I was well aware of Lawrence Guigan's strictures regarding any further approach. Perhaps it'll be ready for the day your book is published, I said, which enabled her to say for the tenth or twelfth time that we would never see her typescript more: and while I reassured her for the tenth or twelfth time that this was not necessarily the case, I rummaged down from the cupboard a bottle of mere local wine instead.

Top shelf, I said, and poured some into our celebratory jam jars. At least it'll keep the cold and 'flu away—

But as soon as Harry came in and we all settled up to the counter for the meal, he seemed to take some kind of exception to my choice.

What's the big idea Frank, he said, and turned the bottle this way and that inside a sceptical fist. Gettin' a bit fancy aren't we—y'horse come in or something—?

For God's sake, Harry, it's just Lemora, everyone drinks Lemora—

Not me. Not this rotgut—

It's a red-letter day, I told him. We're celebrating. Janet's posted her manuscript off to a publisher!

Typescript, Janet murmured.

He stared at her, in pretended amazement.

That right—both of them at once? Well, whaddya know, sister—

He seemed determined to put a dampener on things and I couldn't tell why. When I tried to fill his jar he put a protective hand on top of it.

It's rotgut, he said. Too bloody sweet for a start—

I briefly mentioned two or three of his favourite drinks including stout and raspberry, a mixture that always represented to me the terminus of what a man might reasonably be expected to put up with on the road to social bonding. But it seemed that as far as he was concerned our inexpensive lemon wine represented the very same dead end, and not simply in matters of taste either but in its negative social implications as well. In short, his refusal was a principled one. As far as he was concerned we were getting above ourselves, Janet and I, something he gave no voice to at the time but which he made apparent enough to me when I caught his eye (and here I found my long familiarity with him a guide) as Janet and I clinked our jam jars together and together drank to the success of her enterprise.

To my great surprise—for it was something I could never have calculated despite that long acquaintance—I seemed to have touched a nerve in him, but precisely where it might lead I couldn't quite decide as we fell to our sausages and new potatoes. If he'd never drunk it how could he know it was sweet, how could he claim not to like the taste? And if on the other hand it offended his working-man principles to offer him wine, surely the fact that it was done free of charge presented at least a countervailing principle to a man who when confronted by the irritating niceties of paying his way at the counter of any pub has tended to be what he always refers to in other men as *a bit of a cold bot*? Or (a sudden thought) was it in fact purely a matter of jealousy on his part that was operating now, as green as the mint that graced the ivory-coloured potatoes and all the sharper in its tang for not being necessarily under the inspection of any awareness on his part?

(And here I have to pause to say that those new potatoes were as wonderful as any I could remember taking from my soil.)

In due course and inevitably, while his mood further settled in the manner that I've indicated, Janet and mine began to move collectively in the opposite direction. Predictably enough, the Lemora loosened our tongues a little and then somewhat more than that, and together with the excellent food before us (by which I refer almost exclusively to the work of Mother Nature in its preparation) made of us as merry a couple as ever I could have imagined ourselves capable of being in any of our darker days: indeed merrier by far. When I say this I don't mean we drank ourselves to the point of later embarrassment and regret, of course: simply that like the wine of Shakespeare's Brutus it *buried all unkindness,* or it seemed for the moment at least to bring about the prospect of some such accommodation.

The trouble began, though, when I said those very words, about burying unkindness, and Janet spotted the reference straight off and challenged me with another, the familiar proposition that *a good wine needs no bush,* which I was able immediately to fix to its seat near the end of *As You Like It.* But then she floored me with some lines from *Richard III,* as she identified them to be when once I'd given up on the matter of identifying them, and after that she pulled my leg good and proper given the fact of their reference to the doomed king's failing *alacrity of spirit.* Then I fired back with one from *Othello* that she pinned down straight away, of course, after saying that as far as the wine was concerned she was definitely not *exclaiming more against it* like Cassio in the play!

And then suddenly Harry was leering at me.

Need a bit o' bush? he said—

It stopped our prattle all right. For a second or two the pair of us just sat there, Janet and I, not knowing what to do. I am no choir-boy as I'm sure you are able to see, and it was embarrassment for her that held me up rather than embarrassment for me: as far as I was concerned and in the normal run of things I would probably have ignored such a comment or in truth enjoyed it—in fact had it just been Harry and me present he would never have bothered to make it, since his words were so clearly aimed at Janet and at Janet alone. He was picking up on the line she'd just quoted, of course, but he fired it back at her smeared with a lewdness that in truth was rare in my day-to-day experience of his behaviour. Something was clearly up with him, something that injected into the evening what I realised after a few moments Janet must have seen in that first benighted meeting of theirs a week or two before—to do with sex, a certain kind of sex, a male sexuality she didn't see in me, this despite my greater openness to women—*because* of it, that was my next thought, *because* of that openness: whereas what she saw in him was another thing entirely, something I have spent much of this present chapter in trying to pin down but can't yet quite put proper words to—

Immediately this unpleasant line of thought began to present itself to me it began to dissipate again, a process urged on in the moment I caught Harry's eye across the counter and found him winking at me in his sly old familiar old watery old way: and in a second it was possible to conceive of seeing him once more as just himself, wry old entertaining Harry, dabbing at his lips and his floury tongue as he eased off the stool, away from us and towards his packet of makings on the divan: Harry the rogue, Harry going too far as usual—

Take a turn outside, he said, and slipped away, already rolling himself a cigarette—

I knew he was off to the Thompsons' property down the road, where he'd found for himself a swayback horse and a couple of goats. It took another second or two for me to realise the meaning of that conspiratorial wink and the nature of his parting gift. I could tell that she could smell it too, Janet, I could see her expression change, I could see the colour start to pump up yet again in neck ears cheeks and upon (if I dare) her bosom—and I felt myself colouring a little too on her behalf, and so flung myself up as if determined action might deflect her attention as well as mine. I snatched up plates, I indicated the farther end of the room for her, I pushed wide a window as off-handedly as I could. Was there something on the radio we might listen to together, I wondered, or did she fancy a brief walk down to the mangroves to help the meal go down such as I'd never thought of suggesting to her before? I was in short a very tornado of embarrassment, loudly doing my best to cover up my shame at Harry's breach of taste and etiquette as well as my shame at my own shame, since all the time (although without any particular coherence) I was aware of certain inconsistencies in my reaction: I mean the way I'd taken the role of Janet's protector when with other women I often threw them to the dogs at times when things got out of hand like this, and had even spoken out on the need for consistency of behaviour between the sexes in all things as a matter of urgent principle.

This was the sort of oddity that Harry brought up in his own defence when I tried to have things out with him later in the evening. By this stage all dishes were cleared away and Janet had resumed the safety of her garden fastness for the night. He returned from wherever he'd been with his old cheerful smirk, but I started right in at him.

What did he mean, I demanded, by causing such embarrassment, and at a time of celebration? Come on now Frank you've dropped a few yourself in your day, he said. Get off your bloody high horse, where's your bloody sense of humour got to, I dunno what's happenin' to you these days. That's not the point, I said. It's nothing to do with a sense of humour it's to do with time and place. And that remark you made. What remark? he said. You know very well what remark, I said. Christ, y'worried about *that*? He stared at me. I didn't start it anyway, youse two brought it up with your fancy bloody talk and that flash rotgut of yours. It doesn't mean what you think, I said, *a good wine needs no bush* doesn't mean what you took out of it. Well, what *does* it mean then? he demanded. And the trouble was I'd no idea what it meant when he shoved it back at me like that: which is an irony in several directions as I'm sure you'll realise straight away. I blustered on about bushes always being associated with wine, then got onto the business of his silliness about refusing to drink it. You're a bit fine-mouthed yourself, I said. Aren't you? I mean not drinking wine? If you've never had it how come you don't like the way it tastes?

252

But in return he made the undeniable point that I myself had never had a tart (as he put it) but I didn't much seem to like the taste of *them*—

Well, we went at it hammer and tongs for twenty minutes, with him telling me I didn't usually stand on ceremony, that as a rule I'd been the working-man's friend but as far as he could see I was starting to get the wrong sort of ideas about myself and it was something to do with this bloody woman, I'd changed since she came along, she was twisting my mind for me. How? I said. You treat her special, he said, you treat her like she's someone special, Christ, she's just a dame just like anyone else. No I don't, I said, though in truth I knew by now I did. You're different with her, he said, I saw it right off, first thing I was in the door a month ago. I'm not, I said. You are, he said. I'm not, I said, I'm the same with her as I am with every woman. You're not, he said. I am, I said. Well then, he said, what about Guigan's wife that time with the bloody marrow? It was a cucumber, I said, and a pickling cucumber at that. Well, would you wave *that* at your bloody girlfriend out there? he said. A bloody pickling cucumber—?

He stood pointing out the back, and I could see his steam was up as much as I'd ever seen it: but also that it would rise no further, not least because he was caught up next by a crouching, crunching fit of coughing—

Would you do that to *her*—? he said, after another minute. Little Miss Fancy-Pants—?

We stood there breathing hard at each other, and of course we were both of us terribly upset though it was probably more obvious in me than it was in him. He really did get my goat at times, though, and I told him so—

I don't see what's so bloody special about her, he said, but not as hard as he'd spoken before, as if the fight was leaving him. I don't see what's supposed to be so special—

She's gifted, I said, and as soon as I said it I thought how lame the word sounded and what a world lay between the two of us at that moment, me and Harry. She's just written a book, I said, an important book. It's a work of art—

And the reply he made at this point was the one that always came from him whenever that particular word was used, and always as if it brought a just and sufficient end to whatever conversation it was that had thrown it up:

Art? he said. Arse—

He turned away towards his bed.

So we made our preparations for the night in a silence that was audible. I couldn't get to sleep of course and to tell the truth I was close enough to tears. As a rule we didn't row that much, Harry and I, and I can't remember even now, looking back, when it was we'd last got that deep beneath the ironic tacks and turns of our customary navigation—there'd been a few storms in our early days of course while we were learning the cut of each other's jib, so to speak: but as I've made plain it was the habitual nature of our to-and-fro that was at the heart of things for us, and once we'd made our tacit agreement on particular patterns and rituals between ourselves, things were always pretty much settled. As in any relationship there were objects down below the water-line that didn't need to be disturbed, both in each of us and in what we shared together, and so we conspired never to trouble them as a rule. But we'd stirred them up tonight, there was no doubting that, and what was worse we'd added something to them without meaning to, and something new as well: whatever thing it was that Janet represented to the two of us, quite apart from the separate thing she'd become to me in the many months that had passed.

In effect, her presence was making him less known to me again and closer to the mystery he'd once been. In particular it raised the question, given the strength of their responses each one to the other, what was it that might have passed between them in the various times I'd not been present? Had he said something to her, had he done something to her, was there something that had taken place between them that I didn't know about? It seemed impossible on both sides: but wasn't the lesson I was learning these last few many weeks and months in just that very fact, that you don't know as much about people as you think you do? There was Janet, busy with one man as I'd thought when she was busy with another and, when the truth was told, busy with neither, or anything more than her knitting: now, what if Harry were to be revealed the other way around when once the layers peeled off *him* (if that were ever possible)? What if (the thought returned to me for the first time since his return) he'd been with someone else these last ten months, I mean not a simple dalliance such as I knew we'd both used more distantly to have from time to time, but something more substantial—a *ménage à deux* like ours? What if this explained the lengthy times he was apart from me?

Now *there* was another thought to take to bed with me. On this particular night, though, and as I should have expected, there was something else that proved an adequate nightcap for the evening—inevitably, after the mealtime's gruelling exchanges, another square of paper lay on my pillow. As I fumbled it up and turned my torch to it, I realised I'd half-expected it to be there all the time:

Sounds a bit like a small apartment you loaned—

CHAPTER 11

Still there was the problem of Solomon. A further telephone call to the hospital in town was no more successful in turning him up than a subsequent visit to their main reception desk proved to be. The further telephone enquiries they made for me as I stood listening to them at their counter didn't find him at any other local hospital either, any more than the work of a subsequent day and much of an afternoon spent at the library in town examining the details of recently deceased males in the local newspapers and listening for echoes in their names. In these there was everything and nothing at the same time, in that the regular recurrence of service numbers and other military details I read there evoked for me a single great generalisation, like a wave of history overwhelming me. Of course not knowing Solomon's full name didn't help much, something pointed out to me when I tried the central police station near the end of a long humid day I'd devoted simply to his cause. Just Solomon, said the copper at the main desk. Just Solomon, I said back. It's not a lot to go on mate, he said. A first name'd be nice. Well, maybe that's his first name, I suggested. Yeah well in that case it'd be a surname we'd be after, the copper said. If Solomon was his first name, see—

Something of this I related to Janet at the end of the day spent in the library. That she was much on edge waiting to hear from the publisher I could tell from spotting her at the letterbox yet one more time as I walked home along Esmonde Road. When she saw me approaching in the distance she scuttled back through the hedge-gap, and when once I'd made it to the door of the hut it was to find that she'd arranged herself with a book inside, from which she looked up with a fine display of having been interrupted whilst long lost to the world. I imagine her day had seen many such trips to gate and box, as well as many such bleak returns to the very same place in the very same volume. I might say that the silence of the publisher had *me* a little worried as well, but not so much for its duration, since in my own experience the publishing world lives on a different planet, Neptune perhaps or even Pluto, where time passes at a more leisurely rate. I was concerned more for the effect on Janet of a possible rejection: for the possibility that this would in fact be the case was something I'd become convinced of by now, a fortnight or more after the posting-off of her package—after all, as I've indicated, it was a very curious bag of tricks she'd sent them. Not that I thought it shouldn't be published, of course: I wanted the very best for her, naturally.

The business with Solomon was a useful distraction for us both, then, and the details of what might be thought of as the enlarging of his disappearance tickled her fancy when once I'd set them out for her. I told you, she said. You forgot him and now he's gone, what did you expect, he wasn't written down: and so on. Nonsense, I told her back, and let slip my plan to travel north again to Pukapuka soon, where I fully expected to flush him out. He's living flesh and blood, I said. He *was*, she said back. And now he's something else because you stopped reading him! A lot of cock and bull is what I thought of this, to tell the truth, but I declined to make that plain a second time around. I was getting a bit sick of these fancies (as they seemed to me), not because they were getting in the way of hard facts but because they threatened more and more to have something to them, and I was far from ready

257

at this point to give in to such a thought and the possibility they indicated of the existence of such a disconcerting world. Not kindly I riposted with the question I knew the answer to, namely whether the publisher had given her his decision yet, and that had the effect of shutting her up good and proper. And afterwards as usual I tore myself apart for my cruelty, and for the rest of the day made sure that as far as she was concerned I was quite as nice as pie.

If I sound irritable in this exchange it's for the good reason that I was, and the cause of that irritability was there for anyone to see. For surely the most obvious counter to Janet's faery world was in the slow decline of Harry right in front of her: after all, what kind of magic was it that would start to bring *him* around from that? During each day I followed him about, keeping an eye on things while trying not to look as if I was doing so, during the night I woke whenever he stirred. All too well I remember in the *Psalms* the proposition that *of heaviness comes death*, but here this remonstration seemed to operate the other way about as his body began to show (to my eye, at any rate) the slowing and then the drawing-down that awaits us all as the earth pulls us back into itself bit by bit at the end, and we dissolve there in the manner the Scriptures seem all too eager to reassure us will take place—and sufficient cause of sorrow in *that* sequence of events, I should have thought. In him the sheer *corporeal* nature of existence (ah, *that*'s the word I was looking for) was there in front of me to see, in his heavy tread, the stoop of his neck and back and the evident relief with which he sank down, after doing not very much at all, to chair bed or (once) floor.

As I've made plain already he wasn't an easy patient, a difficulty made all the worse by his reluctance to acknowledge the possibility that there might be anything wrong with him in the first place. Despite the cacophony of his hacks hawks spits and stupendous farts that acted as something of an alarm clock for the pair of us each morning (we were both early risers), his usual response to my query as to how he'd passed the night was in the phrase *box o' birds. Dead ones*, was the punch-line he always added at some point when once he'd reclaimed himself from further spluttering, and this was usually followed by a wheezing version of a sort of pub-laugh, one that had no real mirth in it but was all ritual and proffered fellowship as he rolled the first smoke of the day. What's a boxer-bird? Janet asked me after she'd overheard one such exchange, a question that enabled Harry to lead her on a merry dance when I invited him to clarify the matter to her: *little boxing gloves*? I heard her ask incredulously at one point as I listened from my bedroom.

That, alas, was early in his current rustication: as weeks went by he became less and less prone to fabulous inventions of this sort. The doctor? I eventually suggested, a proposal which (as I should have expected) released from him a long tirade about the perfidious work of quacks—why, his old mate Monty had been right as rain for years, never went to a doctor never had a day's illness in his life fit as a fiddle box o' birds: two visits to the bloody quack and strike me dead he was lying in his grave, God's truth Frank. Don't tell me about bloody doctors, he said as he turned away. I wouldn't take one of them bloody cats to twisters like that (and here he pointed to The Rat Man and Penis Envy as they went sidling by). Besides, I don't need a bloody doctor I'm not crook I got my pills, anyway these days a man doesn't need a quack, the quacks're all being done out of business by the pills anyway, that's all a man needs, pills. And here he'd hold up one or another of the vast array of bottles phials tubes and whatnot that made up much of the swag he was in the habit of taking with him from place to place. Dr Vincent's Pink Little Liver pills were a favourite, in matters of digestion the Bile Bean seemed to have no challenger, and then there was always his Milk of Magnesia with its dark blue bottle. Whenever I argued against these the virtues of silver beet spinach and other dark-leafed vegetables as well as exercise sunshine and Adam's Ale, he always seemed able to dig up from pocket or swag yet another snake-oil item whose effect he insisted had long been sovereign in maintaining his perpetually tip-top shape.

The fact that he was very evidently in no shape at all eventually drove me to a hard-earned trip to the doctor myself, where I confided Harry's symptoms as I understood them to a man who hardly ever saw me in my own right from one year to the next and had never set eyes on Harry at all. Well, he sounds like he'll have to come in, the doctor told me, I can't do much if he's not here in front of me can I? And in the end that was all I could get out of him, pretty much, although he did agree that Harry should give up the smokes. If he's coughing that much it's madness, he said as he scribbled out his account. He might well've got something on his lungs.

The quack said it's madness, I told Harry when I returned. He just happened to bring it up when I was in for my back. He says you might've got something on your lungs. But Harry was having none of this, of course, and pointed to the adverts in the newspaper that said that smoking soothes the throat. Look, he said. It's not the smokes makin' me crook it's the bloody smokes keepin' me goin'—

This was the first time he came near to admitting there might be something wrong with him, so maybe that made the expensive trip to the quack worth it after all. At least his declining appetite solved the problem of our troubled mealtimes, the prospect of eating seeming increasingly distasteful to the point that often when I placed plates on the counter he contrived to slope off elsewhere, either on a slow walk down the road to check the Thompsons' horse or in some spot down the garden where he'd catch the midday or evening sun till Janet and I had finished—as was the case for the cats, the compost boxes were a favourite retreat and I would often find the three of them together down the back, the cats and the old fellow himself, enjoying the warmth of vegetal combustion. Just as he was with children and horses, by the way, Harry was at his best with cats and dogs, treating all categories human or otherwise as if they were smaller versions of the equine species. What with him on the property as well as Janet my two old mogs had never had it better, and played each of us off against the others in the usual scheming way of their kind.

Well, it was while he was down at the Thompson property avoiding the prospect of further eating that the incident occurred which tipped him over the edge, so to speak, and to the point where there was no doubting any more the state of his health. As my cooking began to reach a climax he slipped off one early evening in what had lately become the usual way, but for some time after Janet and I had eaten the fruits of my labour in the kitchen and cleaned up the consequences of it there was no sign of him coming back: and so I set off down the road towards the mangroves to find out where he'd got to. And there he was, leaning against the fence of the horse-paddock and with his face as dirty-grey-and-white as the roped goat that still strained at him on the other side. Bugger butted me, he murmured as I came up: and then he fell into my arms. It was all I could do to get him home. And there you might say the trouble began.

Now, since our breakthrough-moment with the loquats Janet hadn't stinted with her little notes, though she tended to leave them in less subtle places than hitherto since the business of the curious exchange they'd brought about between us was a matter now open and discussed. In that time the *fact* that this strange business was important to her had become easier to understand than *how*: but bit by curious bit I'd come to understand that my ability to tell her what she meant as each of them turned up one by one was an important reassurance to her, as if by proving I was able to crack their code, so to speak, I had graduated in a school of thought of which you might say she was founder staff and head mistress. It was a different way of thinking, that was obvious enough, but although my entry to it seemed important to her I could tell there was more to the matter than simply that. It was as if, in some profound way, by understanding how her words worked I'd given final proof that I was worthy of trust in every other thing. It proved she was not so much alone as before, perhaps.

From time to time of course I disappointed her and she found herself having to drop some heavy hints. But her delight whenever I managed at last to work out some new challenge that had been stumping me for a while was exactly as I've described her response that very first time I got it right: unfeigned and itself a pleasure for me to see. These disappointments happened less and less as I understood more and more what it was she was up to with her riddles, and occasionally there were wondrous moments like that second time, when she'd snapped her fingers and the right word popped into my mind as if by magic: except that on these subsequent occasions the finger-snapping took place in my mind so to speak, and I was able to experience the pleasure of being able to hand straight back to her the slip of paper in question with the solution on my lips. And yes, I did feel close to her at times like that, as if I understood her well and we were both on the same side of the barricade that obviously loomed somewhat higher in her mind than ever it had in mine.

But at the time I've been describing, when I lugged Harry home from the Thompson place with his arm around my neck and found myself attending to him on his bed, it happened that one of her notes had been nagging at my mind for a day or two without significant result. *Kind hawks kill*, this one read, which I found I could make no way with: and since she'd left it on my bedroom windowsill I let it stay there as if I hadn't come upon it quite yet, the better perhaps to play the trick of seeming to find the answer straight away when once her uncreating words had popped into my mind as I knew they would eventually do.

But they didn't, what with one thing and another, and *Kind hawks kill* the words remained. Playing games with them was a matter as far from my mind at that stage as you might imagine anything to be, and instead I bustled about the place busy with the very practical business of getting Harry to rights, or at least into his bed and on the road to functioning once more. Like an Amalekite, it seemed, he'd been smitten hip and thigh, though whether the goat had actually broken something there I was incapable to tell. But since generally speaking he greeted any setback to his health and person with as much noise and fuss as possible and as if confronting the dreaded end itself, I took his taut and uncomplaining silence on this occasion to indicate the possibility that serious damage had occurred beneath the bulging ugly welt I found inside his clothing. In truth his waxy pallor suggested something rather worse, and for the first time it began to occur to me that he was sailing into very stormy waters indeed. And thinking *that* took me somewhere I'd never been before inside my head and never wish to go again—

So it was that the doctor made Harry's acquaintance after all, following my phone call at the neighbour's house and a long wait for him to appear. Oh this is your friend you mentioned, the doctor said to me as he stepped his way into the front room. You could see he was angry to be called out at that time of night and also that he didn't think much of our way of life either: from the way he was looking around you'd think we were living in the hen house and that our real home was somewhere else on the property. Now what's the matter, he said to Harry very loudly, as if the poor fellow was at least a

263

hundred years old, though given the way Harry looked at that point I can't blame him for assuming that. He's been butted by a billygoat, I said, and the doctor said, A *billygoat*—? as if he'd never heard the like before. But he gave Harry a fair old once-over, and as he went on he seemed less and less interested in the work the goat had done than in the rest of him, tapping on his back and chest and looking in his eyes and ears with his torch. At the end of it all he sat Harry back against his pillows and cushions and pulled the covers up so high I thought he was going to go all the way and cover his face as well and turn and give me the worst news possible there and then.

Instead he said, Your friend here's got jaundice—

I said, Jaundice—? I'd no idea.

Just need a tonic, Harry said. It was the first thing he'd uttered since the doctor had told him to say *ah*—

And we need to take a proper look at his pelvis too, the doctor said. He needs to be admitted, where's your phone—?

Tonic'd fix me up, Harry said.

Well, it was quite a business going next door at eleven o'clock at night which is what the time was by now, but somehow we managed to get an ambulance though it took forever and a day to arrive across the harbour on the vehicular ferry. And then there was Harry propped up in it looking as scared as hell and me next to him as they closed the door on us, and the thing gave a lurch and off we went, without the siren though which given the occasion I thought a bit of a shame. But the whole business seemed to me a fair old reminder of the important principle that in life you just don't know and you never can tell.

Soon get you fixed up, Harry, I said, though of course I didn't really know what I meant, and if anything he looked worse than when the doctor had first come in the door some hours before. Soon get you into hospital, I told him.

Tonic'd do the trick, Harry said.

*

It occurs to me you may be wondering where Janet was in all this unpleasant business: and the answer is that she was lying low in the army hut. For that I don't really blame her, since there was nothing much she might have been expected usefully to do, and given that this entire upheaval could be seen as pretty much another episode in the ongoing private matter between Harry and me, her withdrawal from it could even be interpreted as a choice involving a degree of tact taste delicacy and compassion on her part. But however you decide to see it, absent is what she was throughout, so that I didn't run into her until well on in the day after Harry's disappearance into the hospital. It was at lunch, which to give her credit she had the grace to prepare herself, even though it involved only the heating of soup and what have you—

What happened to Mr Doyle? she asked, and so I gave her a dramatic account of the night's proceedings, emphasising the fact that I'd had no sleep for its entire duration and only recently got back from Harry's bedside. I left unmentioned and for a further instalment the information that it had turned out there was nothing more wrong with Harry's coxal bone (as I'd discovered its proper name to be overnight, and as I was careful to name it in my account to Janet) than that the flesh adjacent to it had been given a beating from the billygoat. All this she took in as we ladled our soup, asking a question here and a question there as my story unfolded: but the thing that struck me as most curious in her response was that the central element of it, as far as she seemed to think, was not the disaster inflicted on Harry but the goat.

No, I didn't see it happen, I said when she asked me. I turned up ten minutes later. He was trying to make it home on his own, I thought he was a goner when I saw him—

So the goat just butted him, she said.

Goats do that, I said, they don't need asking. It's in the nature of the goat.

She flicked a look up at me. You said he got your goat, she murmured. Do you remember saying that?

I sat up. Had I?

You were having an argument. The other day. You said, *That's what gets my goat, Harry.* I overheard you—

I sat staring at her. After a long sleepless night and the worry over Harry, I found this not a good direction for things to be moving in. *Overheard* us—?

What are you trying to say? I asked her.

She dabbed her mouth with her hanky. Oh, it's an interesting coincidence, that's all, she said. Don't you think? He *gets your goat* and then a couple of days later the goat gets him—?

I decided to leave aside the business of quite how she'd overheard a private conversation we might have been having, Harry and I, in which the phrase in question might well have been used, since it was one of the phrases I tend to employ from time to time. After all, if she'd been in the shower box or using the convenience, say, and I'd been through the wall and raising my voice with Harry, for all I know she might have overheard us fair and square, might she not—?

It's just a phrase, I said. I was working a final knob of bread around the inside of my bowl as a way of keeping calm. I don't even know where it comes from, I said.

Yes, but isn't it interesting, she said. The word and then the thing—

Yes, but just a coincidence, that's all—

Oh, I don't think so—

I sat back and folded my arms. It seemed I was going to have it out with her after all.

So you're saying to me, I said, that if I hadn't told Harry he was getting my goat—which I can't remember saying, by the way—

But I heard you say it—

—you're trying to tell me that if I hadn't said *goat* the goat wouldn't have butted him, is that right—?

That's right, she said. Saying it makes it more probable, it allows it to happen—

Well, this was stuff and nonsense and I started to I tell her so.

I really can't believe that in this day and age, I said—and then I stopped, because I could feel my voice getting away from me, getting near the edge of control. *Really*, I said. If you just knew how it's been—

I was thinking of Harry as I'd left him, sitting up in the hospital bed with his nose all red and how I'd felt like crying when I saw him like that.

You don't seem to understand, I told her. He's an old man—

She stared at me. Yes, I understand that, she said.

He's not an *idea*, that's what I mean—he's human, he's a human being. He's flesh and blood—

She sat staring, waiting. I went on.

He's *real*—I mean it's all very charming, this notion of yours—words before things or whatever it's supposed to entail—but it's not very practical, is it? It's not much of a way to run the world when—when life comes rushing at you like the bloody goat—

And it was here, alas, that the words of that last riddle she'd left me popped into my mind, and then, a second later, out of my mouth:

I mean, *Kind hawks kill*—what in God's name is that supposed to mean—?

There was an audible silence between us: wind, bird chatter, distant traffic.

I thought you'd get it straight away, she said in her little-schoolgirl voice. A kind of hawk—

Well, that had me a little taken aback, to tell you the truth, because although I'd not been thinking about the blasted thing much in the last twenty-four hours and for obvious reasons, when I'd thought of it before that I'd gone at it in a

267

different way and puzzled at how a hawk could possibly be kind. But—a *kind* of hawk—?

But now she was standing up, she was leaving. Excuse me, she said.

I watched her through the door. She was obviously upset—but then so was I: and it wasn't till I'd allowed myself the pleasure of bathing in my own bile for an hour or two more that I let her state of mind begin to concern me once again. I wasn't myself, naturally, with so little sleep behind me, but looking back now I can hardly blame myself for feeling as I did. For all I knew as I stood there, Harry might have died an hour before at the hospital, and the doctor might be turning into Esmonde Road as I stood there rinsing the soup bowls at the sink, and on his way to break the news of it to me in person since I lacked the telephone. I'd spent most of the last nine months thinking Harry might be dead, without ever anticipating the possibility that he might turn up alive after all but *then* die more or less in front of me and more or less straight away, as he seemed to be threatening to do right now. Against the reality of this and just the *fact* of it—the fact of the human condition, I suppose you might say if it doesn't sound too pretentious—against all this, her precious notes and their riddles, not to mention her usual flummery of butterflies and puffballs and fairies at the bottom of the garden—against the human condition, all that gauzy nonsense seemed—well, precious, there was no other word for it, precious and self-indulgent. And after I'd woken several hours later from a lengthy afternoon nap on Harry's bed I found I didn't think very much differently about this when once refreshed—

Given the shape of things as they were beginning to crystallise in my mind at this time, the business of Solomon's whereabouts and his fate became part of the story of Harry, just as the story of Harry had become part of the strange contest of words and things that had settled down between

Janet and me in the long months beforehand. This is clearer to my mind now I sit looking back and sorting out my ideas—too clear in fact, as it seems to me that sometimes I give the matter of this contest too much emphasis in what I write. We were both living it from moment to moment though, I mean Janet and me—especially me, since in a very real sense (and it astonishes me even now to find myself writing these words!) by this stage it was becoming more and more evident that *she* was the one who'd been teaching *me*. But by and large we were both muddling through the unfortunate fumbles and misunderstandings of the sort that you've just witnessed. When looking back at one's earlier life like this, whether at a great distance or as I'm doing now from little more than a year after the events described, it seems that one need always remember that question Dr Johnson raised, about the rightness of our minds even at the best of times—all of us, every single one.

Thus it was that nothing seemed more urgent to my year-ago mind than the business of finding Solomon again, as if confirming him to be living flesh and blood would somehow salvage Harry too. Having tried the hospitals the papers and the constabulary I felt there was nothing for it but to try the old folks' homes as well, and the obvious place to start (it seemed to me) was with the ferry trip the bus-ride and then the trek that took me to the city's sole home for retired servicemen in the suburb of Mt Eden. This was the long business I've made it seem, and as it turned out its upshot was no better than my other quests had been—and also no worse, since once again there was everything there and nothing. There seemed to be some thought amongst the staff that I was looking for a place myself, an illusion I did nothing to dispel since it enabled me to wander through the marvellous oldie-worldie house that had been given up to its present higher purpose of providing shelter to men whose boots you might say I felt myself in truth unfit to clean.

And in amongst them I found Solomon all right, and Harry too, but several times of each, for the entire place seemed to be full of versions of them both!—here they were, sitting about in armchairs or propping themselves up on sticks, or persuading the bright green baize of a billiard table on which one of Solomon's doubles played a Harry lookalike while a third and fourth looked on and another pair limped past the window. Talking to them one by one reinforced the sense of a narrow variation from a broad norm, with Harry's seamed face here and Solomon's shy turn-away glance there, and every voice the same, darkened by tobacco smoke and detained by the collective habits of ironic deflection. My two old blokes were everywhere, and nowhere as well, having slipped through my fingers once again: and I have no doubt that if the dead in the newspaper death notices rose up before me the effect would be much the same as the one the Ranfurly Home provided—they'd all be the men in question, but at the same time they'd just be themselves, the particularity that proved the general. Into this principle Solomon seemed to have disappeared as if into the great majority of the departed, since not one of the old diggers had heard his name: and how to describe in detail someone who looked pretty much exactly the same as the man receiving the description?

Naturally, Solomon's strange disappearance made Harry's survival more important to me. He'd been attended to as much as the doctors at the hospital appeared to think he needed, and the dreaded verdict of tuberculosis had been avoided in favour of something more mysterious called a *low blood count*, which the quacks explained to Harry and then again to me without either of us making so very much sense of it at all: something to do with fighting infection, though, was conveyed as the essence of the matter. There were other things wrong as well, and the doctors made it clear that Harry would be weak and suffer setbacks from time to time, but that all in all he would respond to the kind of attention I made clear I was proposing to lavish on him. Such attention as he'd been given to that point seemed to be having some effect, and it first dawned on me that he might have turned the corner when I sat with him one evening at the hospital as the RSA visitors came up to his bedside with their gifts of chocolate and smokes for the former soldiers among the patients: to their query whether he was a returned serviceman or not he told them no, no, he wasn't, as it happened he was still over there fighting—

The question of getting him home from the hospital at the end of the week required addressing, and was solved with a pleasant day of work at the Bens' property in Torbay where I helped them clear stones and couch grass from a flank of their land in return for the loan of motorbike sidecar and chauffeur. A few days later the lad's contraption served to bring Harry back home, with me up, as Ben would say, clutched behind him on the pillion, and Harry wedged in the little attachment with blankets pillows and what have you and my hand hooked into his collar to keep his head from rolling about. He looked a scarecrow, to tell the truth, but on the other hand he was a scarecrow planted in my own vegetable patch once more, if you see what I mean, and I couldn't have been happier to see him there whatever crazy angle he might have been reduced to. And when I had him propped up with pillows and cushions on the divan once more and his blankets tucked over him, I felt the same as I felt that night he came home again many weeks before and I settled him down in exactly the same manner: that all was coming right with my world—well, I had *almost* the same feeling I felt that night, because after all, this time Janet was about the place.

Actually, I don't mean that as badly as it sounds since the last thing of which she could have stood accused at this time was that she was getting in the way. How she did it I'm still not quite sure but she managed almost to give the effect of not being on the property at all, I don't mean for selected periods of evanescence as before, where her absences sometimes felt like some kind of stunt, but for extended periods of time, days on end, as a lifestyle. Waiting to hear from the publisher was the problem, I supposed, though when I totted up on the calendar the number of days that had actually passed since that wrenching moment she and I had shared in front of the parcels slot at the post office it didn't seem so very extraordinarily many after all. But one such day would have been quite enough for her to endure, I suspect, and in the presence of many anxious days and (now) weeks she'd gone to ground, and the nearest I got to her was when I left her covered meals at the hut door and then at night-time, when I sometimes woke to her phantom-presence on the other side of the hanging sheets as she crept in and, in due course, out again.

It was a surprise, then, when I was just finishing up the business of dealing to Harry one morning in the front room, to find she'd broken cover. I turned away from him with flannel towels soap and bowl—and there she was, standing behind me.

I was so surprised that I addressed her formally, as Miss Frame.

She peered at me. Any news? she said.

Well, you can see, he's lost a fair bit of weight. I turned back to Harry. Haven't you—? But he's in good care—

She moved one hand as if rubbing steam from a mirror in front of her. No, no, she said. I mean the publisher—

We stood gaping at each other.

I thought you might have brought the letters in, she said.

It took me a moment or two to gather myself.

No—no—well, I have, I said, I've brought them in and—there's nothing there for you, I'm afraid—

The poor woman looked so dashed I felt sorry for her, a little, even though I must say her obliviousness to Harry's state of health took me quite aback. He was right there in front of her, for God's sake, and apart from anything else the jaundice was still sufficiently in him, I'd have thought, to catch her eye if she'd taken the trouble to catch his. But getting her eye caught was the one thing she seemed determined to ensure did not happen, by either Harry's gaze or mine. In fact without a word more she was making for the door and her escape, and there was something in the absoluteness of this silent, abrupt departure that found me pursuing her out through my makeshift passage and to the back door:

He's really quite ill, I called after her. Harry. He's really quite sick—

She stopped on the path and turned back to me. I stepped down to her level.

Something wrong with his blood, apparently—anyway, he needs constant care. His hip's a mess but there's no broken bone, apparently—

I waited. I was aware I'd said *apparently* twice. This exchange was awkward, odd.

He's an old man, I said.

I know, she said suddenly. I'm certainly aware of that—

And she turned away, and stepped into the hut.

To say I wasn't sure what to make of this gets somewhere near what I felt. There was shock, of course—almost as if she'd slapped my face, to tell the truth—and then complete amazement at what seemed to be her utter lack of feeling. Was it possible that she really didn't care about what Harry was going through—she who'd had so much from me herself these last eight or nine months as they added up to now? Was that it, did she resent his presence as much as I'd thought he resented hers, did she resent the attention I was lavishing on him just as he'd seemed jealous of any time I spent with her: was it all as silly as that? It was thoughts like this I carried out that day or the next maybe, in my ritual checking of the letterbox—

And here was the publisher's letter, lying inside, addressed to Janet.

I picked it up and looked around. She'd put a stamped and self-addressed envelope in with the manuscript as I'd instructed her, but the publishers hadn't used it in writing back: instead, a smaller envelope of their own with letterhead and the address typed, to Miss J. Frame c/-, and so on. What did this convey?

I thought back to my own early experiences, the long haul of waiting and then the letters received back, always the self-addressed envelope I'd sent with my name hand-written in my own fist and hard-earned postage attached, and inside, the standard slips of rejection. Then, as my writing expertise became more evident to others than simply to myself, the slips began to be replaced by letters from the publishers themselves, sugared with evidence at least that they'd read the manuscript that was coming back my way by surface means. Better luck next time, in short: well, this was clearly what they'd sent to Janet—when I held the envelope up to the sun I could see the shape of a letter inside. She'd done well first off, and it was far better a thing to receive than a rejection slip: but on the other hand, was she in a state to see it yet?

I looked around again. The anger from her words was still with me enough to consider for a moment depositing it in her blessed hedge along with her other bits and pieces if indeed that is what they were, to languish with them in her wretched fourth dimension. But I'm glad to say I didn't, and looking back now I can truly state that my motivations at this moment were entirely protective: though when once I'd taken the envelope inside and slipped it between the pages of a book on my desk I'd no real idea what next to do with it. And no time to think it through, either, since all this was swept aside when the one thing now cropped up that most I feared might come about—

*

As you might imagine, my ministrations to Harry at this time had much of the nature of a one-man band, and as I was pressed more and more by them I lost my health. What took me down was no more than some kind of the usual common-or-garden stomach bug, and its duration was no more than the prescribed twenty-four hours that these afflictions take to go from north to south, so to speak: though a disastrous twenty-four hours they certainly turned out to be. But the difficulties of preparing three meals a day and cleaning up the various consequences of them as I struggled through the illness were as nothing up against the chaos that then took over when, inevitably, my bug found its way to Harry too, and he declined even further than had already been the case and well before I'd even begun to claw my way back to any sort of health of my own. Whatever that doctor might have thought of our lifestyle on his first visit to 14 Esmonde Road would have faded in his thoughts had a second such call been made: but what with one thing and another (not the least of which were considerations of a monetary nature) I tried to deal with the matter myself.

And, not unnaturally, with expectation of help from Janet. To give her proper due, she did her bit, too, though generally speaking a bit is what it was and little more if she could help it: a meal or two each day, the attendant mopping-up involved and a trip to the shops two times a week or occasionally three, following which she always bolted to the safety of her hut. Given the readiness with which the bug had leapt to Harry's vitals from whatever part of me had passed it on, I can hardly blame her for keeping to herself. But the crisis came as I say, when it had made that leap and I all unprepared for it, my legs like jelly and my gut still clutched by whatever it was that now was gripping his. It was at this point I finally found myself caught out one evening and my one-man band ran out of puff and lost its tune as well, so to speak, with the question of which of us first to tidy up, Harry or me, being answered by the helpless fact that neither of us was much capable to move a limb at all.

Inevitably came the moment late one evening when my frantic crawl across to him came too late, and the little room was filled with the stench of things so far precariously kept at bay. I heard the poor man's desperate, humiliated groan.

It was at this point that I asked her for her help.

I walked or crawled to the back door and called her name. It took a while but eventually there she was, peering back at me from the dark, with a strange, guarded sort of terror on her face—

Give us a hand, Janet, I said.

What do you want? I heard her call.

I just need you to hold him—

No, she said, quite clearly. No, I'm not doing that—

I stood there flummoxed. I couldn't believe it!

I'm not touching him, she said. I'm not touching him—

Janet, I can hardly *move*—

At that, to give her some small measure of credit, she did come in for a moment. There was the smell of his wretchedness. When he saw her he turned his head to the wall.

I just need you to hold him, I said.

And she told me no again—!

For all my weakness I could feel my anger rise in me— what's wrong with a bit of crap, I wanted to call out to her departing back, what's so fine about you? But it was no good, and what's more, it was beside the point—

So of course I had to clean him up myself. And I managed somehow, though it was a business that took its toll on me as you might imagine for yourselves, and by the time I was done I was as well and truly drained as at any stage of my life I can readily bring to mind. But here's the curious thing (and I suppose that in a back-to-front sort of way I ought to be grateful to Janet for allowing it to come about): cleaning

276

the old fellow up from his helpless state and his filth turned out to be one of the most wondrous things I've ever done, and realising that this would be the case was what gave me the strength to get through to the end of it.

First, I brought the Tilley lamp around and sat it close to him as he lay there on the bed: and the awful magic of this was that it seemed to take his life away from him at last. The strange fall of its light turned him as if into a dead man—not Harry though, but as if a man I'd never known. As I stripped his sweaty, rancid shirt away and pulled and lifted at his body to peel his fouled underclothing from him, he lay there so loose and uncomplaining that he played his own part in this transformation. By the time his shreds were soaking in the wash-house tub and I had the nakedness of him at last he was everyman, any one of us laid out at the end of our journey, just an old fellow stripped back to a skull and ribs and cramped grey limbs, wrists stiff and the limp sad rag of his manhood and loose exhausted sack exposed. One of the old men at the soldiers' home, perhaps, laid out at last—

Then, with the unforgiving darkness coming through the windows and my shadow crouched and bobbing on the wall behind me, I began the business of cleaning him up again. And here was the real magic, for it was as if every movement I made with my heavy sponge restored him to me bit by bit, to the man I'd known whom so many things had taken from me, the illness but also the long absences as well and the doubts that had crept in with them these last few weeks. I wiped those thoughts away as I always had and must if he is to be believed in, for twenty minutes I scraped and dabbed at him until the moment when the washing was complete and the old fellow lay there bare and cleansed once more. I looked down at him, and found I'd found again the pity of him that I'd known, which was the centre of him of course, and as far as I was concerned the centre of me as well, the centre of all the things we had together. He was Harry once again, which meant of course that I once more was Frank—

And when I'd finished with the brush and comb and he was put right or nearly, I agreed with him that the whole wretched business had been the very bugger.

It was the rough poetry of this long moment that I kept in mind when I confronted Janet a week or so later, when once I was certain Harry was picking up at last. I was still full of its feeling, and remembering the ordeal of it was what pushed me on. I got her cornered in the hut a few days after, and there I brought up the whole business of her strange behaviour these last many weeks when I'd been hard against it and not managing so very well, and in particular the business of the cleaning up of Harry—

You left me to do the job myself, I told her. Can you imagine what that was like, the state I was in myself? I could hardly move—and on I went like this, with a fair degree of self-pity I have to admit but also with the serious intent of telling her where it was she'd let me down—and herself as well, I tried to make that clear, herself as well.

But instead of the Janet I'd thought to find in front of me I got a Janet I'd barely known existed. I'd expected tears, the usual refuge, and the usual vanishing trick thereafter. But maybe it was the fact I had her cornered in the hut already that turned things and resolved her to the bolder mood I found myself confronting:

I know what you want, she said when once I'd got it off my chest, the start of things at least. You want a happy ending—

No I don't, I told her. I just wanted you to give me a hand, for God's sake—

You didn't, she said, and as I say, I'd never seen her quite like this before, I mean standing up to me, or to anyone. I

278

could see the fear in her as she spoke this, but I could also see what it took, the courage in her too.

You want to show me life, she said. That's what you told me out on the road after we'd been to the post office, you want to give me a lesson in life—and I don't *want* one, I don't *need* one—

All right, I said, I did. I told you that. Because that's how you learn things, you can't learn things locked up here inside my garden shed! How d'you expect to learn about people stuck in here—?

She stared up at me. Why should I want to learn about people? she asked.

This took me by surprise, I have to admit, but I pressed on:

Because you want to be a writer, I said.

And here of course I thought of the letter from the publisher, inside the house and all unknown to her, and found myself a little thrown off track by doing so—

You *are* a writer, I said. You've written a book, a manuscript, and if you want to go on writing then you need to get more experience—

What I was telling her had always seemed to me a hard rule, and I thought of the value of the time I'd spent in Europe in my youth, watching listening and (insofar as I was able) talking. Of this experience I'd spoken to her before, and part of my motive in trying to bring her close to Harry had been to let her see the kind of things she might expect to meet out there in the world when once she fully entered it. But she was having none of this, it seemed, and though I don't wish to give the false impression that she said a very great deal on this occasion, what she did say seemed clear enough to me: it was Harry I'd served her up as a slice of life, and it was Harry she sent back to the kitchen untasted, as you might say, Harry and everything he stood for. I couldn't believe the directness of what she said—it was my whole philosophy of life she was rejecting, the very thing I'd been trying to impart to her along the way! She didn't need people like that, she told me. I've already had enough of men like that, she said.

Which was when I decided there was nothing for it but for me to tell her of the experience I'd had with Harry, his exhaustion, his surrender to me, the beauty of it. Of course as soon as I'd begun I wished I hadn't, because the more I gave in detail the more I felt myself betraying him, especially when I saw the look she had when I described the state he'd been in. Besides, the words just didn't come the way I'd hoped they would, and I probably should never have thought they might. In short I made a botch of it, and turned what was (in effect) a defence of a tradition a good four hundred years of age into the death, alas, of Little Nell—

It left her staring at me.

Human beauty? she repeated.

That's what you missed—

But I can't understand that, I can't comprehend it. Isn't it *things* that are beautiful, once you learn how to see them— isn't that all?

And then she said the words that so much shocked me—

Human beauty? she said. Harry Doyle—?

And so I found myself spitting it out at last:

That's precisely what's missing from what you write so far, I said back to her. I snapped it rather, I was pointing a finger at her. Harry Doyle—

I'd been leaning on her doorpost in all of this. I pushed away from it.

She looked up at me.

Don't try to change me, she said. I won't be changed—

Well, if that's the case, Miss Frame, I said, I hold grave fears for your writing future—

And then once more I thought of the letter, back inside. It was time she faced up to it. It'd teach her a lesson at least, for turning her back on me like this and on everything I stood for—

I've got something for you, I said.

I went inside and brought it out to her: and I can tell you, she went bright red when she saw it, her usual trick. She stared at it in my hand as if I were offering a live tarantula.

It arrived a few days ago, I said. I didn't want you to open it on your own, I didn't think you were ready for it yet. I wanted to make sure I was here when you got the news—

But it's *their* envelope, she said. It's not the self-addressed one I sent—

Doesn't mean a thing, it's par for the course. It just means they liked it well enough to send an individual letter first off. It's a good sign, you've made a good start—

She took it with her very fingertips. I pulled back and away—

Don't worry, I told her. It's not a bad start—remember, I got turned down flat my first time, second too, but the third time around it wasn't a pink slip, it was a letter, a proper letter—

I waggled my hand at the envelope—

Just like that one. If they think you might cut the mustard next time around they send you a letter saying so—what've they got to lose? Why shouldn't they do that? *We can't publish what you've sent us but we'd like to read your next attempt*—something like that—

She sat there, looking disbelieving.

Open it, I told her.

She sat there.

Go on, open it—

She sat there.

I felt my face screw up. I leaned forward to her.

Janet—you need to face up to this—

And so she opened it.

281

CHAPTER 12

Now Margaret has finished putting things to rights and has left me to compose myself for tonight's entertainment. She'll be back in an hour or two with our friends, and then the assembled company will replay that evening not long after Janet arrived when the pumpkin wine flowed all too freely and as a result there was some cleaning up to do. Tonight, however, I hope we'll fare better and that even though Janet will not be present (being detained, I presume, in the taxing business of getting up and addressing the horrors of a new day in her Hounslow boarding house twelve thousand miles away) we will restore something of the dignity we all lost together that night—

That this might have been the case was a notion put in my head by Janet herself. Not long before she left, when the two of us were finally clearing up the business of where she'd actually been that May evening of the party fifteen months ago (the answer to which, by the way, I'm confident you'll have worked out for yourselves by now), she confessed to me that at one point she'd watched some of our sad display from outside. Now, to say that she'd been taken aback by what she saw that night would be to say the very least of it: but it is not untrue to say that she was less taken aback in any judgmental sense than in the sense of being unable to know what to make of our antics—*brightest and best of the sons of the morning*, as the old hymn has it, definitely did not *dawn on our darkness* or *lend us their aid*. Or, to put it more simply, after years in hospital sustained by the most idealistic thoughts possible concerning both Art and the Artist, she'd been somewhat nonplussed by this her first contact with the local variety of the latter. No more so, as it happens, than I had been at the time, although I at least had a clearer awareness of the sometimes primitive nature of the cultural life of this part of the brave new world: if we are indeed a local cultivar, then we are, alas, but early in our very first spring.

Janet knows this, I think, though she is less aware of her own special qualities as I now understand them to be, her capacity (in other words, and in a manner of speaking) to offer some hot-house growth to the local crop—not to mention a spot or two of compost, of course. On the larger matter of whether she is able to meet that capacity in full, we shall see: meanwhile, on the slightly smaller matter of *how* she might get there I have a contribution to make tonight if of no more than a figurative nature—I mean as between the hot-house and the compost-box, so to speak, though to change the figure a second time around, I'll make it plain that I refer to a compromise between her cuisine and mine. As to the former, it's true that Margaret offered to provide the home-made cooking for my party, and she was very piqued indeed when I insisted that this role was mine alone: and then in turn she became intrigued when once I'd done and my house began to fill with those familiar chocolate cooking smells of Janet's (not to mention the floor with a crisp layer of sugar for my footsteps nostalgically to crunch on).

You've never shown the slightest interest in this kind of cooking before, she said. It's a metaphor, I told her as I drew from my oven a tray of biffs or were they bangs and set them on the windowsill to cool as I'd seen Janet do. They're not as neat as hers, Margaret said, peering at them as she shrugged

283

into her outdoors coat. Well, in that as in all things Janet is my master, I replied—

And if my home-made biffs and bangs represent what might be called the hot-house aspect of the nurturing of the growth of things, the earthy compost role was reserved, so to speak, for my scones and for my wine. With the former you are at least familiar, and possibly with the accretions of their meaning, too: but if the thought of pumpkin wine concerns you after that early May disaster last year when quite apart from anything else too much of it was drunk too soon, all I can say is that this time around and following Lawrence's long subsequent attentions and mine, our wine presents a prospect less forbidding when confronted in the bottle: not so cloudy, with less sediment and generally speaking with a look of more tranquillity about it. After all his tweaks quarter-turns and subtler Masonic attentions this last year and more, not to mention his shrewd and mysterious application of sugar to the wine, it promises to be plausible, and in home-grown natural products that is all one requires. For the modest earthly purposes that we share, in other words, there need only be wine. And thus both my loaf and wine, you might say, are spread upon my table, and ready for my guests: another image worthy of my late hut-dweller.

Along the way I taught Margaret to solve Janet's puzzles. Oh, they're just crossword clues! she said when she saw me solve one for her. I can never do those, how d'you do them? So I showed her, the way Janet had shown me. A kind of fish, she said. Plaice, that's a kind of fish. No it doesn't work like that, I said. The answer's not out there in the world, it's in the words, it's in the language. Stick with fish, I said. *In* and *fish*. Oh, she said, staring at the word. Oh, hold on, hold on, don't tell me—and she did it in the end, after a minute or two, and didn't it make her happy. *Finish*! she said. *In* inside *fish* equals *finish*! Very well, try this, I said, and gave her the note I'd found in Janet's desk drawer amongst a scatter of paper clips and nothing else. *Trout dose ordered*, she said aloud, and she got that in the end too, once I'd told her what to look for. But the final phrase that Janet left me, the one I found on her bed after she'd caught the train, continued to baffle us both as it has baffled me since. *Please arrange a suitable reception for the acrobat*—maybe she's the acrobat? Margaret suggested. Janet?—no, no, it's in the words, I said, try to remember that. I think it's *a suitable reception* that's the clue, I told her, though really I was no more than guessing and as I say I'm nowhere closer to it now than then. Like so much of Janet's language, it shimmers on the edge of meaning.

With *Kind hawk kills*, though, Margaret seemed to have the better of me, once I'd told her what Janet had said about how the first two words were meant to work. Harrier, she said. That's a kind of hawk. She must mean Harry. Does she mean Harry harries her? Harry kills? She can't mean that. No she can't, I said firmly, and she doesn't. You can put that thought out of your mind. I'd no desire whatever to travel in such a direction, but that was no difficulty since Margaret was little enough interested in Harry anyway, and was too pleased with her riddle-solving prowess to pursue it further. Aren't I clever! she said. And she was, I told her that, though she did say it was just a game. Isn't it? she said. Just a pastime—? And of course I put her right on that. A pastime? I said. It's more than a game. It's a window on the world, it *is* the world. It's the only one there is—well, Janet thinks so anyway—

Did I believe that, though—I mean, had Janet really won the battle? Well, to tell the truth I've no idea. No, no, that's not true: she hadn't won, because it had never really been a battle in the first place. Of the truth of her way of thinking I now have not the slightest doubt, something of which you'll soon have all the proof you need. As it's turned out, the fact of Harry's return and second departure had almost no effect compared with the impact of Janet's duplication of those visitations. She gave me a good old shaking-up, although of course who knows, it might have been coming my way in any case without requiring Janet's presence to set it off after all. My strange story about a woman, that had seemed to come straight out of her side as if I was writing one of her creations (or as if it were writing me), took its time but to my great joy has been finished, the first in many months and even years to come to a conclusion that has the ring of truth (or indeed come to any conclusion at all). I will never publish it: instead it will be a surprise in a suitcase beneath my bed waiting for some scholar beyond my death. This little shack of mine may become a shrine—who knows?—in which the typescript trembles in that scholar's hands as evidence there really was a turning in my work as I passed through the crisis of my middle years before the sumptuous but idiosyncratic triumph of my golden age. And if that age proves indeed to be a golden one by whatever measures operate when I am living it, someone might even have the gumption to see the link between Janet's imagination and my own senilia, my own brave new world of words—

These days my letterbox is where the three of us meet, Janet and Harry and I. At first her pale blue aerogrammes arrived from London so often that I was relieved when in due course the frequency of their appearances began to fall away, both because I was unable to keep up with their need for response and because their eventually more measured arrivals suggested she'd begun to find other things to do with her life. As indeed it seems she has: the Irish landlord continues to irritate in a satisfactory manner, human nature is proving as baffling on the far side of the world as it is here, and even in what passes for summer London is as chilly, it appears, as I remember it all those years ago. Her occasional dropping of local names—Notting Hill, Hammersmith, White City Stadium—shakes free some distant memories and thoughts, but as of another life. The picture of her walking in places where I once walked when I was a not dissimilar age has had the curious effect of making her recent time with me seem out of sequence, as if it is in the wrong place in history. Which of course is quite untrue, since it is her history too, her life—

With Harry, of course, stemming frequency of correspondence has never been an especial problem requiring address. Naturally he has gone again, departing pretty much as soon as I'd helped to put him back together through my fussing and my nourishments. When my friends protest at yet another such departure and suggest he's been using me once again, I ask them the purpose of putting a man to rights if not to free him to come and go? A gift is a gift, after all, and once given no longer owned by the giver. Harry had no difficulty with that concept, at least: true to form, when the moment came he simply melted away once more, and once more I was left grasping thin air, or at best, air thickened by no more than another of his notes on torn-off paper—*Well old dear, time to soldier on, will let you know my details when I know them*: the usual kind of thing, and for an hour or two the usual kind of response from me, if not tears outright then much parping of my nose against my handkerchief as I wandered around the abandoned house and garden, and the overall sense that he'd been wrenched from my very physical existence, almost from my body (and realisation too that I had at last the freedom I'd been yearning for, and needed now to find some things to do in it).

And that was fine with me. I've long been aware of the shape of Harry's stays, the arc they make from the ecstasy of reunion long-anticipated through the slow business of my steady re-acquaintance with his familiar doggy ways to this recurring moment that I describe, when once again I dive into the exquisite pain of his absence and the anxiety over his welfare that consume me whenever he and I part company and the letterbox stays bare. But so far, on his part not so bad: a couple of postcards from further south and what may or may not have been a stamped beer coaster graced with no more than a single word in his perfect script: *Foxton!* And as I have said, in a way quite *embodied* and as if he's still inside me somewhere, each postcard pricks that very considerable part of me where we meet, he and I, giving a depth and intensity to each daily moment, rinsing it with the pleasure of his loss. To those who claim it to be not wholly untrue that as far as I'm concerned the sweetest part of Harry Doyle is in his absence, I am not always in total disagreement.

Janet's decision to follow my footsteps overseas thirty years after I myself had left them there filled me with relief and fear in equal quantities. I'd been gently suggesting such a move for some time, and then not so gently when she seemed vague and that blue-black ink reappeared. Following no small amount of behind-the-scenes activity a travelling scholarship of sorts was cobbled up with all the appearances of a modern-day miracle, and when once she'd accepted this she was more or less obliged to take the plunge into international waters that it implied. Something of the tremulous moments that followed the booking and the buying of her ticket and the facing of the practicalities of departure I have already outlined. Throughout that time (although I scrupled to conceal this from her) I was on the rack with worry for her welfare outside the reach of my protection. How would someone still in so many ways so young manage herself in the wide world? How would she manage her money? What if it fell into the wrong hands—what if *she* fell into the wrong hands, and ended up in the white slave trade of which my mother had so sternly warned me?

Then, one afternoon three or four weeks before her departure date, I made one of those occasional visits to the local shops to which poorly planned housekeeping usually condemned me several times a week. There was the library to make the trip worthwhile of course, and the sad obliged decline to commerce after that, and then the usual pleasurable condescension I made to the greengrocer and fruiterer for no better purpose than to confirm the inferiority of their produce to whatever it was that grew in my garden at the time. And naturally I thought of Janet when I did that, and the business of the peppers and the walnuts and what they'd come to represent to her a full year earlier and more. How strange she'd seemed to me then, a mysterious shape that fate had thrown into my lap to be licked, and what a growing sense I had of her now, the depths and the complexities that nevertheless did not yet quite add up to a single thing that might be understood. I'd not yet seen her whole. We'd made our peace though, she and I, following Harry's departure, and her last months with me had in them some of the best of our earliest together, when she was all excitement and discovery.

At some point of the shopping excursion I'm describing I found myself on the corner of the Strand and Hurstmere Road, with the library left behind and more moderate delight waiting ahead. It was one of the spots at which I often used to take the sun with Harry, though of course on this middle-of-the-year occasion the sun was as little in evidence as he himself now was, and there was a not-so-subtle hint of rain about, which as I have said is not infrequently the case with isthmus living. So the ladies had their umbrellas ready here and there, and the gents of course their hats—and there quite suddenly was Janet in amongst them, noticeable in her fawn coat and her headscarf as she walked past Inghams on the farther corner and (as I watched) turned left into the inner reaches of the Strand. She had her string bag with her and walked with the distinctive slight trudge to her step she always had, not heavily but as if the business of moving through the world was just that, a business: and as always her head was down. I watched her move away, towards Woolies perhaps, or McKenzie's across the road from it. During her time with me she'd found both these emporia to provide excellent slices of life for her (though it was what people bought and said that interested her most, she insisted to me) and I assumed that it was to one or the other of them that she was now headed—

Without much purpose I followed her, not busily but at a quickened stroll as a light wash of rain set in. Having surprised myself not a little over the last several months by becoming slightly sentimental with thoughts of her departure as I've hinted, I had in mind a meeting in Oliver's perhaps and a cup of tea together till the rain passed. I still had the sense, which stands more clearly to me now as I look back across these last few months to that day, that there was yet something that she might tell me, though at the time I put it to myself the other way around, and told myself there were final hints and tips I needed yet to give. And so I loitered after her, confident that in the small crowd she'd easily be spotted, and tried for a start the plastic flummery of the American store I've just mentioned before moving to the local version that stood across the road. And in her usual Janet sort of way she turned out to be in neither, or in Lane's or any other shop nearby (as I moved back up the Strand again) but standing across the road at the corner, in the exact spot from which I'd first observed her!—she was looking back at me, but with no hint of recognition even when I called her name and waved.

Now all this was a bit too much like that wild goose chase I'd had the year before amid the foolishness of my fancies concerning her and Lyall Neary, and I turned away from that as much as any other part of it. Instead, I gave myself the pleasure of the greengrocery, and the disparagement of the proprietor's collection of sad and speckled winter vegetables as they seemed to me when once I got there: in fact the state of his cabbages and cauliflowers was such that I seriously considered having a word with him and asking what he had in mind to be offering vegetables to the world in such a state? But in place of that I tried him with a departing irony I expect he found as baffling as those queries regarding the secret life of peppers that Janet had put to him the year before. Too good for me, your vegies, I said to him as I backed out of his shop, after he had questioned whether I was of a mind to buy something or doing nothing better than simply sheltering from the rain. How I wished Harry had been about, though, to rib and cheek him better than I was able!

Perhaps it was this childishness that distracted me, for when I turned away and stepped outdoors I found I had to move suddenly aside from a young woman who was almost upon me. Head down and beneath a large black umbrella obviously new and held against rain that now was setting in, she didn't see me: she moved past and briskly on without looking back—for several seconds I watched her and the bobbing movement of the umbrella and the light slick fall of the rain on it as she walked away along Lake Road. Simply a young woman busy on her business: and then I realised it was Janet, and made to move after her, and stopped, and went on watching as she receded because I'd realised that *that* was what I needed to do, *this* was what I needed to see: that what I'd glimpsed in that moment under her umbrella was what I'd been waiting for, a glimpse of Janet in the world, Janet without me—Janet twelve thousand miles away, even, and alone in London's rain.

And as I watched this strange, imaginary picture that was at the same time absolutely real before me, I knew at last that all my fears for her had no meaning at all beyond the statements they made about my own everyday human terror that the sky was falling in. I remembered that glimpse I'd had in my argument with her the year before concerning Harry's state of health, when she'd shown not so much strength as a completely unexpected hardness, a real sense of where she ended and the rest of the world began and a clear sense of who she was and wasn't as a writer. *Don't try to change me*, she'd said, and that was how I'd begun to understand her from that point. Now as I watched she was fifty yards away perhaps, and receding from me as if forever, but of course if you took me out of it (as her steadily splashing tread seemed determined to do), she was walking towards something for herself and herself alone. I'd worried about how she would handle what was so obviously ahead of her now—the first reviews when they came, the critics, the public life she'd wished on herself without ever wanting it. But watching her bobbing away in the rain under the shining black mushroom of the umbrella and into her own life (by now she was half a furlong distant) I realised at last that in her own peculiar way she would manage it, she would pull it off, she would survive and far better. For she was rock solid inside.

And now, the last thing before I end: and, as I think you'll see, the only note on which the fact of making an end to this story of myself and Janet might properly be ventured.

The thought of Solomon still weighed on me, for his sake of course but in truth far more for mine. It nagged at me that he could disappear as he had seemed to do, and as you've seen, the possibility that he'd actually done so became larger than itself the more I dwelt on it. Janet's words had done their trick, in short, and became a matter of great gravity, as I'd learned to find her words very nearly always turned out to do. By the time of the events I shall now relate (which took place some several months before she left), it had become quite plain to me that there was nothing for it but to make one more trip north to find my old fisherman at his shack and thus by means of a latter-day rearguard action mount some kind of defence against the assault she'd made on my belief in a foursquare concrete world. The answer, it was clear to me then, lay in Pukapuka—

I mentioned this to young Ben one day when he was helping me with the business of cutting back the front hedge, a matter long overdue. And I'd hardly finished speaking when the solution was at hand—why, it seemed that there was nothing for it but that he must drive me there the following day, all forty miles up and forty back down again! And when we'd come to some kind of agreement over petrol costs and I'd overcome my unease that my debt to him was mounting, I found myself sitting in his shuddering little coracle of a sidecar and holding onto my hat for the seventy-five or eighty breezy minutes his contraption took to complete the quickest journey I could ever remember making from Esmonde Road to the little tidal creek where Solomon had his house: or back in the other direction, either, come to that. Fortunately I was wearing beneath my jacket that homespun jersey Janet had been making—which turned out to have been mine from the very first, to my great astonishment! Who else do you think I meant it for? she said when I protested it must be for someone else, I tried to give you a clue when I was knitting it. But it'll be too big! I told her, remembering my earlier fitting session: and there was another of life's everyday miracles when I put it on, for as it turned out it was a perfect fit after all! You've grown into it, she said. That's what's happened.

So I reached Pukapuka unfrozen: but the problem, when once I'd stumbled down the long-familiar track from the end of the secondary road, was not that Solomon was still gone, which was something I'd more than half expected. The problem was that his solemn little shack was gone as well, which is something I had no reason to expect at all!

I'd been so keen to find both hut and owner that I'd outstripped young Ben on the track down to the tidal creek— so eager was I to settle what was in effect the ongoing nature of the world, its physicality, its independence from us: its *aloofness*, even, as against this other business that I'd got myself half-believing with Janet's words and sentences left about in strange and unexpected places. I needed so much for the old bloke to be there as he'd so long been, to see again his shy look up at me from under his hat as he heard me on the track, and the slyly artful business of being with him after that, and then the eventual coming home at night with a fish or two to seal the bargain—how good it would've been to saunter in the door at Esmonde Road at six or seven that evening, I thought, and throw a snapper on Janet's plate!— that'd show her, that'd scotch this ridiculous business of just how real or not the real world might happen to be—

But the problem was as I have said, that Solomon wasn't there: and the fact that the house he'd lived in was gone into the bargain provided a considerable further difficulty too. That was the shock of it. It was as if he'd been erased, it was as if everything I remembered of him and his life had never existed in the first place.

Ben caught up with me, looking about. Where is it, he asked, the hut? Gone, I said, and rubbed my chin. It took a minute or two for him to understand. The thing was, though, I was sure I could still see where the hut had been, the boxy shape of it on the ground and so on, all of it looking as if it'd taken up a lot less space than you'd have thought, which is always the case when you see just bare foundations and wonder at how little space we need, all of us, to live our lives (a thought that has of course been many times before expressed).

Of such foundations here, though, there was barely a sign: there were places where there must have been totara piling or maybe kauri but that was all gone, and there were other places at the back where the hut had obviously sat right on the ground over many years for better or for worse, and there you could see no more than a line at most, if anything at all. But this was all there was of it, with not so much as a

294

matchstick of debris left behind and the general effect instead as of a sort of negative imprint, the hard *stamp* in the ground of something gone rather than any evidence of a remaining presence—any evidence that a building had ever been there in the first place, that is, along with the human being who'd lived in it and all his history with him. I thought of my parents' hovel back at Esmonde Road and how I'd torched it several years ago, and that moment before it collapsed into the past, taking all its history with it, the history of an entire century you might say: and the way its final burning frame had hung before me, no longer than for a couple of seconds but enough to burn into the night an image of itself like a photographic negative. And with thinking this I didn't know whether to be angry first or sad—

To make matters worse, young Ben swore blind there could never have been a shack there in the first place! Are you *sure*—? he said when I insisted, and after I'd pointed out to him the holes and indentations I could see the little place had left behind itself, footprints as it were. I can't see a thing, Frank, he said after looking around. You sure it's not further down the creek somewhere? Of *course* I'm sure, I told him, Lord knows I've been coming here since before you were born. And the Lord *did* know, because what I said was true, the hut had always been there and Solomon had always been in it and I'd known him living there for twenty years and so on, and the part of me that knew *that* also knew Solomon existed somewhere still, in a hospital or a home somewhere or just plain lying in the ground as far as I could tell. I knew as we all do that you don't stop existing even if inurned, albeit in that particular case in handy powdered form.

But the thing was, given the knock my confidence had taken these last many months, Ben's scepticism fell on fertile ground. There was another part of me that had begun to wonder not so much whether my time with Solomon had been a very real illusion after all (which it couldn't possibly have been, of course) but just how much Janet was right when she said that words made it possible for things to happen. Ideas come before things, she means, and if you don't *think* the ideas and the words they come in, you can't expect to have the *things*. The same applied to people, and the fact was that I hadn't thought of Solomon very much at all for far too long or written to him either, and then (as far as I was concerned at least) he'd vanished from in front of me as Janet had pointed out. This might well sound like a precious conceit, but on the other hand, where *was* he? And his shack as well?—whose absence of course had more than a little effect in reinforcing such disconcerting thoughts in me. On the other hand, the explanation could have been quite straightforward: its occupant was gone, the building was unsafe—perhaps the complaints about hygiene had come to a head (in a manner of speaking) and as a consequence demolition had at last occurred—?

None of which explained, however, the complete and utter erasure I now began to concede had happened.

Of his own explanation young Ben seemed certain, and as he gave it I found myself drawn away with him towards the mangroves and the river mouth, as if we might somehow happen on the old fellow and his dwelling after all, happily getting on with life but somehow in a completely different place. I couldn't see a thing back there, Ben said, and he seemed in what followed to be leaning towards the thought that I'd got the creek misplaced, in other words that I'd got the entire location wrong outright! Plenty places around here look the same, he said, all these little bays and whatnot—

And I began to wonder if he might not have the right of it. I stood on the very mud on which, I remembered, the two of us, Solomon and I, had used to drag his boat when the tide was out and the creek was down, and of course it looked like any mud in any place, the same as in the next bay and the next. I looked back where we'd just been, Ben and I, and where I'd looked for his little cottage a minute earlier: and saw nothing, no sign that anything had ever been there at any stage. The bay could have been just another bay. Yes, that's it, that must be it, I heard myself telling him. I've cocked it up, we'll look elsewhere another time. I didn't fully believe it, and yet in another way I was beginning to: but as I heard these words come out of me I felt the old man slip off, the last of him, I felt him loose his moorings, so to speak, and float away almost as if I'd finally let him down. A fancy, I know, and yet also true: for even as I write these words, a full year after the events which I'm describing, I can tell you I have still to hear a word from him or a sentence concerning his fate or whereabouts. And I've never been back to Pukapuka, either, because I know now that at Pukapuka there is nothing, and never has been.

And thereby hangs, it seems, no tale at all—

Up at the road and back at the motorbike, and really just to excuse my own strange thoughts to myself, I tried to give my young companion some sense of how this way of thinking worked: I mean the way that Janet pointed out to me. He listened very carefully as I explained about the riddles, and how they worked for Janet in helping her to understand the world—about the loquats, and that extraordinary moment when the word had seemed almost to *make* the object in my hand, as if it had created something out of nothing. I tried to tell him how, if you learned to think and see like this, according to Janet the world became a book itself, a world that you could read.

But although he was polite as ever, you could tell that as far as he was concerned what I was saying to him was really just a lot of stuff and nonsense. She's a very clever lady, is what he came up with when once I'd done. And a shit hot knitter too—

And so there was nothing for it but to surrender to the sidecar once more, and the bumpity journey home to Esmonde

Road and the defeat it seemed to represent. I can't recall my thoughts as we started off on it, whether I knew that I was leaving behind a part of my life for the last time and Solomon as well, or thought I'd had just a single round in the long battle to reassert his ontological status, so to speak, and was preparing myself for more. I've no idea because of the shock and then the very considerable strangeness of what happened next, not a hundred yards on the way back up Pukapuka Road and towards the main road south and home. The thing was happening before I knew what it was about, as we rounded a corner and with a shout from Ben the sidecar came up beneath and my body was thrown to the right and then back again and the scenery readjusted itself at a rapid rate around me—I heard Ben yell something out, and then the bike stopped slurring across the shingle to the left and he straightened it and slowed, and a couple of seconds later he stopped and we were all right again:

Help! he said. He looked at me. You okay—?

Now he was looking over his shoulder. There was something on the road back there. I watched him walk down to it. A possum, he'd swerved for a possum or maybe it was a rabbit. My heart was still pumping. I could smell dust as I sat there, and the creamy honey-scent of broom. It was still early in the day, between ten and eleven, and the grasshoppers had started up their fizzing chatter.

I watched him strolling back.

A hawk, he called out to me.

And it turned out that's what he'd been trying to avoid, as we came around the corner and caught it feeding in the road. It'd risen at the last moment from its carrion, he said, and all but hit him in the face—

A harrier hawk, he said. He pointed up into the sky. It got away, he said—

And there it was, hung in the air above us, against a spring-and-summer sky just turning bronze from blue in the early haze and heat: its blunt head, the cruel short curve of its beak, the light speckle of its breast almost white, the dark green-brown of the wings outspread. Released from Janet's words it hung above us in truth and fact, watching us, being watched, looking out for things, ready to take over and in turn be overtaken. The meeting-point, it seemed in that small moment, of everything that might be said of the world, and everything that might become of the saying of it—

AUTHOR'S NOTE

Nothing is written for the first time. As a novel about writers and writing, to some extent *Gifted* has been written out of the work of other writers. Here I acknowledge those of whose influence I am aware. Michael King's biographies *Frank Sargeson: A Life* (Penguin NZ, 1995) and *Wrestling With the Angel: A life of Janet Frame* (Penguin NZ, 2000) have been crucial sources of narrative information and vivid detail in the creation of fictional versions of two people with whom I corresponded at various stages of our lives but whom I never actually met in person. Frame's *An Autobiography* (Random Century NZ, 1989) and Sargeson's *Sargeson* (Penguin NZ, 1977) have been influential on me, and I here acknowledge my occasional use in *Gifted* of certain phrases, cadences and episodes from *Sargeson*, the latter usually in connection with the figure of Harry Doyle; of the title of Sargeson's play *A Time for Sowing*; and the use, from time to time, of cadences and words from his earlier short fiction. While my familiarity with all works by both writers may be evident from time to time, my greatest debt by far is to Sargeson's autobiography, which I re-read before writing and consulted frequently while doing so, experiences that confirmed my belief that the work ranks with Frame's autobiography as a masterpiece of twentieth-century literature in English.

No one who has read C.K. Stead's nostalgic fictional evocation of the mid-century literary North Shore *All Visitors Ashore* (Collins, 1984) will easily forget its depictions of Melior Farbro and Cecelia Skyways. When I read the novel again after completing *Gifted* I was struck by how some things seemed to have stayed in my mind after twenty-five years (for example, the two cats he gives Melior seem to reappear in my version, although eventually with different names); at the same time I was struck by the differences between his imaginary versions of Sargeson and Frame and the ones that evolved out of my own writing process. The rather darker version of Sargeson that seems to be behind Graeme Lay's character James Surrey Paterson in *The Mentor* (Cape Catley, 1978) also lingers in the mind of anyone who has read the novel. His and Stephen Stratford's *An Affair of the Heart* (Cape Catley, 2003) was invaluable in recreating the mood of the period and something of the man himself. More specifically, one of my fictional Sargeson's comments is a reworking of a comment recorded by G.R. Gilbert in volume two of his unpublished autobiography 'A Reading Writing Man'. Elsewhere, references to James Joyce and *Ulysses* will be obvious enough to most readers, who may also pick up an echo from Samuel Beckett's novel *Murphy* at one point and others from Wordsworth, Montaigne, Allen Curnow and (obviously) Shakespeare. Kevin Ireland's mention of Janet's knitting, in a public address in Auckland a few years ago, is behind my use of it in this novel. Rainer Maria Rilke's poem 'Washing the Corpse' hovers in the background of the scene in which Frank washes the sick Harry, and my interpretation of Frame's use of Rilke's theory of language, and particularly of naming, is at the core of the novel. A phrase from Walker Percy's novel *The Moviegoer* (1963) helps me describe something of the relationship of Harry and Frank at one point. Readers of Irving Massey's remarkable study *The Uncreating Word* (1970) will spot my use of his title phrase, itself originally from Pope's *Dunciad* IV, and one or two of his sentences. All the references I name here are deliberately made.

I was told about Janet's trick of giving people enigmatic verbal riddles to solve some years ago by Dr Craigie McFie, who observed it at the Maudsley Institute fifty years ago, when Dr R.H. Cawley, a psychiatrist there, gained her confidence in part with his ability to solve overnight various word-puzzles she gave him; in *Gifted*, I have transferred his role to Frank.

I am grateful to Ian Armstrong for providing me with many details remembered from life in Takapuna in the 1950s and for verifying other information for me, for example about shops of the time (although the beauty parlour I have given Takapuna is invented); he was particularly eloquent on the effects of any first draught of Lemora, the citrus wine that seemed to be favoured *faute de mieux* among North Shore literati in the 1950s. Philip Armstrong also gave me valuable and detailed information, and was authoritative on both mangroves and the Mon Desir Hotel, the latter now, sadly, defunct. I thank Peter Simpson for arranging a memorable visit to the Sargeson cottage in August 2008, and Kirsty Webb of the Takapuna Library for taking us through it so knowledgeably. Subsequently, Kirsty supplied valuable information about the property and surrounding area, and evocative photographs from the period I have tried to reconstruct in words, as well as answering questions that must have seemed baffling to her at the time, for example about the nature of Sargeson's front hedge.

Especially I thank John Newton, who encouragingly and sensitively read the first and second drafts of this novel chapter by chapter as they were written; Simon Garrett, first reader of the whole and an ongoing encourager; Kate De Goldi, who read the second draft and provided crucial professional advice; and Paul Millar, who was instrumental in finding the right publisher. I am very grateful to Nicholas Wright, Julia Allen, Reg Berry and Christina Stachurski for dropping everything and reading the second draft, and especially for their encouragement and blunt advice once they had done so. Fergus Barrowman has been the ideal publisher, encouraging, informative and incredibly efficient, and Jane Parkin a sensitive and perceptive editor with a Wildean ability to spot commas that need removing. No novelist in history can have had his manuscript accepted, prepared and published more quickly or with as little fuss.

I thank Simon Garrett for the cover design, and my son Nathan Evans for the painting that realises it. I also thank Professor Ken Strongman who, as Pro-Vice Chancellor (Arts) at the University of Canterbury, granted me the leave and funding that enabled the writing of this project during 2009–10.

Gifted is not a *roman à clef*, and apart from its two protagonists its characters are fully fictional. Had I intended to refer to real people past or present, I should have named the characters to indicate this, as I have done with Sargeson and Frame. People who think they see themselves in its pages can be assured they are mistaken.